SIBLING RIVALRY

It was a nice, warm spring day with nary a cloud in the sky. Underneath the blue skies lay a sprawling suburb that looked as though it had come out of a box, premade and perfect. It stretched for miles without a single road out of place and if you could see it from the sky, the geometrically perfect living zone might in fact be hypnotic.

Within the confines of this suburban empire stood one particular home. It was nothing special, every bit as copied and pasted as the other homes that surrounded it but today, in the backyard of this home, was a child's birthday celebration.

The backyard was filled to the brim with some mixture of adults and children, some were friends, and some were strangers, but they were all there for the same reason - free food and drink. The normal ebb and flow of such social gatherings were properly in place. Some people were having safe, superficial conversations while others hid away from the crowd of people, counting down the time to make their perfect exit.

As the children ran around playing and eating delectable treats and the grownups did their social dance, there was only one pin out of place in the harmony of the big birthday soiree. The source came from a table where incessant pounding and laughing disrupted the peace of the day.

The disruptor of peace was a loud, animated lady who was busy regaling the other adults at the table with a tale from the past.

"So, I'm at this kid party, my early twenties, and I'm bored off my ass. I'm trying to down as many beers as possible to make little Billy's fifth birthday more exciting but it's just not working for me AT ALL. At some point between everyone talking about their careers, their golf swing, whatever, the kids

LESTER
BY SHAUN MARCOCCIA

all gather around and sit down to watch some clown make balloon animals and shit.

Now, remember here, I'm fucking bored out of my mind, but I'm obligated to be here because this is the boss' kid, right? So! As I'm watching him, bouncing around with that big stupid smile on his face, I get an idea. I am going to fuck that clown!" said the lady, who sounded tipsy herself as she took a large swig from her own bottle of beer.

"Later on, after the kids all went apeshit for cake, that's when I made my move. I said some bullshit about how I had a clown fetish and wanted to see his balloon and blah blah blah, right? So, the next thing I know I'm in the closet of my boss' bedroom or, hey at least I hope it wasn't little Billy's" –she laughed uncontrollably– "and I'm going at it with the fucking clown," the lady could barely contain her laughter.

"Anyways, after getting pounded by Mr. Chuckles, I decided to finish the guy off and the whole time he's still got the big red ball on his nose," she laughed furiously, almost unable to speak.

"And his little clown wig is furiously wriggling around all over the place," she paused for another laugh, pounding the table while doing so.

"When I kept cranking him, I almost wondered if he was going to shoot Silly String out of his dick oh my god!" the lady continued hitting the table once more, making it shake hard enough to knock her beer over. Without missing a beat, she quickly salvaged the beverage before getting back into her story.

"Well, anyways, apparently in my slightly tipsy state I didn't really go for discretion and the clown ended up exploding everywhere. I mean, it was like someone filled one of those super soaker squirty gun things with yogurt, he practically took my head off. So, before I can do anything, well, the clown made a shit ton of noise and, yeah, you guessed it - my goddamn boss walks in," she let out another huge laugh.

SIBLING RIVALRY

In between tears she continued, "I mean, there I am covered in half a gallon of clown sperm, some of it is dripping off of her clothing she's got hung up in the closet around us, and she just walks right in. The look on her face was soooo priceless. Oh my god, I wish I could've framed it and put it on my wall, oh my god!"

The lady took another drink before getting back into her story.

"Oh goddamn. Yeah, yeah, I got my ass fired for it, but it was well worth it," she paused, wiping some tears from the sides of her eyes.

"Basically, the moral of the story is that, if this party doesn't pick up, I'll probably fuck that magician guy over there. We'll get into some freaky shit, like, he can pull a rabbit out of my vag or something," she burst out in laughter again, slapping the table once again.

She was so engrossed in her own story, made funnier to her by the copious amount of alcohol running through her body, that she failed to notice that no one had been laughing. In fact, the small group of people sitting around her at the seating area of the patio looked either uncomfortable or offended.

"Oh, Jesus H Christ, did they sit me with the soccer moms over here? Lighten up, people!" She took another sip of her beer, more agitated by their lack of amusement.

"Guys, c'mon if your women weren't here, you'd be laughing your asses off. Story about a college girl doinking a clown in a closet, getting blasted in the face," she laughed, looking for a partner in crime. None emerged however as some of the people got up to walk away.

To the ones that remained, she figured she would make her own leave and beat them to it.

LESTER

"Fucking prudes. I guess only the kids know how to have a good time around here. Sheesh," she said as she drunkenly walked away from the table.

She walked through the crowd, seeking more refreshments as she was running low herself. She needed it badly. Here she was on a Sunday, with better things to do but, out of family obligation, she was here for the birthday of her nephew, Chris. Early on, she started drinking away to make things more bearable but by this point she was full-on drunk, generally making the company around her uncomfortable, to say the least.

Her husband and two sons were there but her husband, Anthony, was off watching baseball with some people inside and the kids were doing kids things with other kids. The guests at this point were moving about, seemingly trying to avoid the obnoxious party guest.

To add to her annoyance, it was a fancy backyard, touched by a fading sunlight, smack dab in the middle of "Perfectville, USA". The house was nice, the patio furniture was nice, the company was nice, everything was just so very nice but not to Paula. To Paula, the house was overpriced, the patio furniture was excessive, and the company was as fake as they come. Suburban living was her idea of hell. Just the thought of being here set her on edge but she was able to control her inner thoughts, that was until about her fourth beer, and then it was all downhill from there.

Finding a spot, she was able to sit down by herself and enjoy her beer and eat some of the frilly yuppie food. All of the good food was in the kids' section unfortunately and even she was not willing to cross that line - the danger zone.

"Aw Christ, kids I'd kill someone around here for your food. Well, I'd kill any of these people for pocket lint but that's besides the point. I mean, what in the hell is this anyways?" she said to herself, trying to figure out what food she was staring at.

"The caterers labeled it but, I have no idea what the fuck Tuh.. za.. ziki… sauce is," she said to herself aloud, musing over her choice in food. As she did, she could hear a group of guys talking to one another at a nearby table.

"Yeah so, I've been working on my swing, you know. Really trying to lay down the leather, know what I mean."

Paula knew baseball. She loved it as a kid. Played it quite a bit as an adult during various work softball leagues. Could not stand watching it, unlike her husband, but definitely loved playing it. For just a moment she had considered going over to talk to the gentlemen.

"Oh, working on that golf swing, eh? Well, I'll tell you what, Tom, I can show you in about two weeks - give you some pointers."

Golf.

If there was one annoyance in life, it was golf. At least in Paula's life. She hated watching it, she hated playing it, and she hated hearing about it. Golf represented a stupid hobby paraded by rich guys and other guys that wanted to act rich, who lacked the talent to do any kind of real sport. As the men continued the conversation, Paula felt the urge to say something. Normally this would not be an issue but, many beers in, it was nearly impossible to keep it in.

"Oh man, that would be really helpful if we could get together. Two weeks you say? Yeah, I think I can make the time to–"

"Golf's for fags!" Paula yelled, cutting the man off from his conversation with his new golf buddy, Tom.

The entire table looked down, nervously eyeballing each other. None of them really knew what to say. There was a mixture of some men holding in their anger but, being at a child's birthday party and all, they did not wish to cause a scene. The other men were a little more laid back or timid just hoping the moment would pass and they could continue their conversation.

"Oh, now you don't wanna talk about golf? Oh, or is it because I said the F-word? C'mon, guys you know you still say it when no one's looking. Shhh, I won't tell," she laughed, while still holding her shushing finger to her lips.

Paula could see the look of nervousness from some and the discomfort of some of the others as she peered over at the table.

"Oh c'mon, relax fellas. All I'm saying is that golf is just a hobby. I mean, you guys are older, right? But it's just funny to me that people really get into it, like it's some kind of sport. Like, if it's such a 'sport' then why is it that real athletes like Jordan, A-Rod, or Manning start doing after they've retired?" Paula asked to the still silent table.

"The reason is because it's just a hobby, a game, like Skee-Ball or air hockey. No one is ever going to call them athletes, right? I mean, what kind of sport has golf boys picking up the ball, grabbing your golf stick, carrying your bag, your equipment? And seriously, the only time you end up on a cart in a real sport is when they are carrying you off because you are so injured by the ACTUAL sport that you're playing, you have no choice but to be carted off. In golf, they cart you over to the next hole because walking is just too athletic a feat to pull off."

The table was still quiet but a few of the seemingly more timid ones looked vaguely in her direction, giving off friendly smiles, chuckling a bit clearly hoping to humor her so that she might move off somewhere else. These clear signals though went right over Paula's head and, instead, she took it as an invitation to come make more friends.

"See, you guys get what I'm saying, right? I mean, I know you like it, and that's cool. I mean, it's not but, you know, live and let live, right? But all I'm saying is that we need to make it a thing where we stop calling it a sport. It's just a little hobby rich white guys do to get away from their wives, Tiger Woods aside. I mean, as far as being a white guy, but not about the whole wife thing."

One of the more confident men finally spoke up.

"Miss, who are you with?"

"Well, I'm with my husband so no funny stuff, mister!" she laughed.

"But I'm here because of my sister, Denise. It's my nephew's birthday and I'm here to help wish him a happy birthday because that's what awesome Auntie Paula does. Even brought him a real kickass present. Some video game with lots of street fighting, I hear you can tear peoples' heads on n shit like that."

The man's eyes lit up.

"Denise? Oh, you're Denise's sister? Yeah, we love Denise! Most of us here know her from work actually. She's in the office just across from me. One hell of a go-getter that one!"

Paula looked slightly put off by the praise of her sister.

"Oh yeah, don't I know it. Real go-getter indeed," she took a big swig of beer, sighing in annoyance.

Sensing that she was not happy with the flattery of her sister, the man looked to switch gears.

"Well, that's why we're here. Moral support, networking, oh, and free drinks of course!" the man said, raising his glass of wine.

"Oh God, another fucking wine drinker!" she thought to herself.

It was yet another annoyance in dealing with these white-collar phonies. The only thing worse than golf hobbyists were wine drinkers. She had no idea why anyone liked the overrated beverage. The way Paula saw it, all wine tasted the same, no matter how much people swished it around in their glasses. Also, what in the fuck could anyone really detect with their nose when they sniffed it? The whole thing was just rich, pretentious garbage. If he had raised a beer, she may have given him the benefit of the doubt but instead, it had to be bullshit wine which now killed his cool points with Paula.

"Well, ladies, enjoy the grape juice. I'm off to raid my sister's fridge and see if I can find anything edible," Paula said, departing the group of men.

"Nice meeting you, Paula," said the man as she left.

She did not respond back, growing increasingly irritated because, in a matter of moments, she had to hear more praise about her do well sister and be reminded that wine worship still existed. She knew that they were all a bunch of stuck-up assholes, silently judging her anyways. Pricks. The one guy did talk to her, but he was a part of that group of yuppies, so fuck him too. Paula was marching to the house to make good on the promise of raiding her sister's fridge in the hopes of finding something edible.

"Paula!" someone yelled at her.

It was her sister, Denise, and she was storming her way over.

"Did you seriously tell a bunch of my friends and co-workers your clown fucking story?" she whispered angrily at Paula.

"Yeah, I did. Just trying to break the ice, you know. Your friends seriously have the biggest stick up their asses. Sounds like they need to fuck clowns more than I do," Paula said back to her sister, cocking her head back and taking a decent swig of her beer.

"Goddamnit, Paula. You know, I invited you out here because I thought you could behave. I really wanted to see the kids, and my Karl's missed Anthony but less than a day and you are already pulling your shit!" she continued to whisper angrily at Paula.

SIBLING RIVALRY

"You didn't tell me how goddamn boring it would be here."

"It is a KID'S party! What did you expect? You watch them run around, break shit, eat pizza, eat cake, and you smile the whole goddamn time even though you know you have to go to work tomorrow after spending all night cleaning up Super... Mega... Ninja... decorations or whatever the hell this is," she said impatiently to Paula, pointing at the decorations of cartoonish ninja figures in their fighting poses.

"So. If you are going to stay here then get your shit together, sis. I'm not asking for much here. Just for you to be a functioning adult," Denise whispered once again in irritation.

Looking distracted, Denise turned away to go tend to something else and walked away to take care of whatever was bugging her nearby.

"Probably a napkin out of place," Paula thought, rolling her eyes.

It was a moment where Paula could have let things go. She had the opportunity to lay off the beer, drink some water and sober up a bit. For just the briefest moment Paula agreed with Denise and had considered her sisterly advice. Her talons dug in, and inebriated; Paula decided to take the other route.

"Well, what do you expect me to do, Denise? Honestly, these friends of yours are fucking prudes. The husband is watching baseball, the kids are doing their thing. I'm just sitting here with my thumb up my ass," Paula said to Denise, raising her voice a bit.

Denise marched back to Paula with an even more irritated look on her face.

"First thing. Lay off the alcohol! You know, I brought enough here for all the other adults but, to no one's surprise, you have put your mitts on about 75% of the shit I bought. I should have never supplied alcohol knowing you were coming over. It's like Jekyll and Hyde with you," Denise said, still trying to whisper and keep the conversation away from guests.

"What are you trying to say?" Paula asked Denise with a cold stare.

"We do not have time for this, Paula."

"Oh, I've got PLENTY of time today, DENISE."

"You do. I DO NOT!" Denise's whisper got louder, still trying to walk away to tend to another issue.

"No, no, if you have something to say then just get it out, Denise. What, you think I need this shit?" she pointed at her drink.

"I only need so much because I have to come here and deal with you and your phony ass friends, well, shit, let's be honest here: Your props. That's all these people are," Paula said in a louder tone, enough to be audible to anyone close by.

"KEEP your voice down!" Denise aggressively whispered to Paula.

"No. Why don't you say what you mean." Paula said much louder, loud enough for most of the nearby party to hear her.

"Fine, you want to know what I mean?" She got face to face with Paula.

"You are a goddamn drunk. A lousy one. Have been for years and everyone - Me, Anthony, the kids, the people at this fucking party, has been putting up with your shit, carrying you around like a pallet. For years!" yelled Denise, forgetting her guests, losing her composure completely. She looked ready to fight.

"Really? Well, you know what I have to say to that?"

Paula paused as if she was pondering her own question for a moment.

"This is what I think about your bullshit speech!" and without warning, threw the beer bottle she was holding at the side of Denise's house without looking.

SIBLING RIVALRY

It did not hit any of the guests, but a window could be heard breaking. Paula did not look in the direction of the noise, instead, she glared at Denise in a mixture of hurt and anger, tearing up as she did but standing steadfast and defiant.

Denise looked in disbelief and horror as the bottle smashed into her bedroom window. She approached it, observing the damage, making sure to stay clear of any glass that might be on the grass. As she observed the shattered window she started to speak.

"You. I want you to get Anthony, the kids, and I want you to get the hell out of here. Get the hell outta here and get out of my life. Do not come back to this house, you selfish wreck."

"Selfish?! You call ME selfish?!" Paula yelled.

Before Paula could start up a sentence, Denise cut her off.

"Either you round everyone up and leave or I'm calling the cops to do it for you. I mean it! Get. The hell. Out of here! NOW!" Denise yelled as she stood still with a furious look on her face that showed admirable restraint. It was obvious that, if jail time were not an issue, she would kill her sister where she stood.

"The cops huh?" Paula stood fuming.

"Well then! I will round up MY family and we will be leaving. Do not worry about us ever coming back. We don't need this bullshit Ken and Barbie mansion anyways. I'm getting sick just looking at it." said Paula as she walked off to get her two children, Robert and Rodney. As she did, her husband Anthony came walking slowly out of the house.

"Paula, what in the hell is going on out here?" he asked, looking confused, looking at Denise who was standing near a broken window, figuratively killing Paula with the daggers from her eyes. He glanced back at Paula who had their two children hand in hand.

LESTER

"We're leaving. That's what in the hell is going on here," Paula said as her two kids looked at each other and then put their heads down in embarrassment.

"Go round up our shit and let's get outta here. I'll be at the car. I've got the keys," she said as she walked off with her sons, not even looking in the direction of Denise who was still staring at Paula, seething.

As she walked off to the car, Paula could hear Anthony talking to Denise.

"Denise, I'm so sorry about this, we'll pay for it. I insist."

"Don't you dare cough up any money to that bitch, Anthony. You hear me?" Paula said, continuing to walk to the car.

She was confident in her last parting shot to her sister, knowing she was with company and there was not a thing she could do about it. A smile arose on her face at just about the time she felt something hard hit her on the side of the face. Whatever it was, it hit her so hard that Paula fell down to the ground.

"Bitch? I'll show you a bitch, bitch!" said the attacker, Denise, who had landed a swinging punch on the side of Paula's head just a moment ago.

Robert and Rodney both stood still in shock, watching their mother slowly get up from the ground, eyeballing Denise.

"There she is everyone. The REAL Denise. All these people around and you can't hide what you really are? Here's you aunt, kids - a big goddamn phony. Here's your real aunt."

Paula gazed at Denise with a crooked smile.

"Oh, don't you dare drag these two wonderful kids into your bullshit, you psychopath. Let me guess. You think you're "Mom of The Year", don't you?" Denise stood her ground.

"I bet you go all around talking about what a great mom you are while you get sauced all day long and have Anthony doing all of the work. Tell me, is it that hard acting like that much of a martyr without the cross to hang on?" Denise shot at Paula.

Paula started to come at Denise before Anthony got in between the two of them.

"Paula that is enough, sweetie," blocking her path, looking frustrated and shocked. He attempted to hug her, but she resisted.

"Get the fuck off me. She's the one that punched me and you're over there, taking her side, wanting to pay for her precious little window. Trust me, this one can afford it!" Paula sniped at Denise.

"Oh, because I get off my ass and work for it. Yeah, what a concept," Denise sniped back.

Paula attempted again to get by Anthony to go after Denise. In her attempt to wiggle around Anthony she had tripped which incensed her even more.

"Jesus, Paula, could you be making any more of a scene?" Denise stood now with her arms crossed, looking down at Paula who was trying badly to get back to her feet.

"Anthony, get her out of here. I'm serious. I'll call the cops on her," Denise warned.

"You bitch! You assaulted me!" Paula now found the will to get back to her feet and Anthony stood in front of her once again.

This time, instead of trying to deal with her or argue, Denise simply walked away. This really pissed Paula off, feeling that her sister got one up on her by taking the high road away from their argument.

"Say goodbye, kids. This is the last time you'll ever see your crazy aunt," Paula said to her sons, who both looked at her timidly with their eyebrows raised, confused by everything that had happened in these last few minutes.

LESTER

"I'm going inside to find my husband and if, by the time I get in there, I don't see you pulling out of here, I'm calling the cops. Have a nice life, Paula."

Denise walked slowly back to the party without turning her head.

"Fuck you, too. Hope you die in a fire, bitch," Paula said as one last parting shot, flipping Denise off.

The parting shot must have had some sort of impact because it made Denise stand still for just a moment. It was hard to say if it was anger or hurt, maybe both, but Paula got the satisfaction she was looking for - the parting shot. She always had to have the last say.

After standing still for a moment, Denise said nothing, and then she continued walking forward back to the house without acknowledging Paula. This made Paula smirk a bit, feeling as though she had "won" this fight.

"Honey, we really need to get out of here," Anthony said to Paula, trying to get her focused back on him and the kids.

"Yeah. Don't want the piggy patrol coming for us working-class folk, do we?" Paula responded, looking down at her kids, who looked sad and confused. In all of the commotion, even Anthony had nearly forgotten about them while trying to tame Paula.

"Oh God, kids, I'm so sorry you had to see that. You see, your mom and your aunt don't always get along," Paula said to the two boys.

"I am what you call a normal, functioning person and your aunt is what we call a psycho," Paula said in a very calm, motherly voice to the kids.

"Um kids, what your mom means to say is that they're... just like you two. You know how, you don't both always get along and you fight sometimes. Well, they're sisters, and right now they're fighting, saying some mean things about one another that they don't really mean," said Anthony, shooting a

14

glare at Paula, trying to hint to her to knock off talking ill of Denise.

Picking up on the visual cue, Paula begrudgingly smiled.

"Yeah kids, it's like that. Just like dad said."

"Will we see Auntie Denise and Uncle Karl again?" Rodney asked.

"I'm sure we will, guys. It might be a while but I'm sure you'll see them all again, plus your cousins," Anthony tried comforting the boys.

"Not to rush but we'd better hightail it outta here before their auntie decides to make good on the promise to call her friends if you know what I mean," said Paula, looking at Anthony, motioning with her head towards the car.

"Hey, yeah, good idea. Guys, to make up for leaving so early, what do you think of pizza and ice cream?" Anthony said to the kids who gave him a resounding cheer in response. It seemed to perk them up a bit by at least putting a smile on their faces.

"Pizza definitely works for me because I am starving and I am not making a damn thing tonight," Paula nodded her head as she got into the driver's side of the car.

"Paula, what are you doing?" asked Anthony

"Getting in the car. Why are YOU not getting into the car?"

"Well, you're drunk, sweetie–"

"And so are you but I've sobered up quite a bit since my blood got boiling. Obviously, I'm in better condition. I feel like a million bucks. Get in."

Paula stared in bold confidence, she truly felt as if she were okay to drive. It showed on her face.

"You know, I've really gotta protest here. I'm not in the best of shape but I think I drank less, and you'll be driving angry. You should never do that. Well, not either one of those things but definitely not both."

"I am fine!" she fumed at him.

"Honey, seriously–"

Paula got out of the car and into Anthony's face.

"Oh what? You now, too? Is this 'Come After Paula Day'? I told you that I'm goddamn fine! I trust my driving a lot more than yours so I sure as hell ain't gonna trust you driving now that you're sauced. I'm practically sober at this point."

"Let's just be safe here. I think I had far less to drink than you. You're pretty hammered, sweetie. This isn't the first time we've had this argument," Anthony continued to protest.

"Well, if that ain't a fine how'd ya do. Now I got you calling me an alchie, in front of the kids no less. You wanna call the cops on me, too?" said Paula as she got even closer to Anthony.

"Now, we gotta go before my wonderful sister makes good on her promise. I'm getting back in that car and driving outta here with or without you in that passenger seat."

Paula went back to the driver's seat and started the car.

"Kids, get in the back seat. Now!"

"Paula this is–"

Paula started the car up.

"Ten! Nine! Eight!"

"Shit!" Anthony said out loud as he scrambled to the passenger seat trying to avoid being left behind by his stubborn wife.

Looking around he seemed to also be in a rush to get to the car to avoid any further embarrassment as he realized people from the party were chit-chatting, looking at him and his family. As he got in and buckled up, he nervously waved at some of the onlookers and whispered to Paula, "If you even look like you're having problems, we're switching seats. Understand?"

She shot a look at him, "Just sit there and shut up. Jesus. Don't you get on my bad side, too."

The car reversed out of the driveway, and they were finally on the road, clear of her sister's threats to call the cops.

Paula had lied to Anthony of course. She was not even close to being sober and did her best to conceal it by using her words carefully and, on the road, she was being much more cautious than usual. Either way, it did not matter because she wanted to be in control of something at the moment between her sister and husband getting on her case. Being at the wheel would help calm her down some for the long ride home. Sitting in that passenger seat would just make her stew even more, and besides, she was not going to relinquish the keys to her husband, treating her like some unfit drunk.

"Who the hell did he think he was?" she still thought to herself, getting on the freeway.

As night descended, Paula knew she still had a long drive ahead to clear her mind but the more she thought about things, the more agitated she got. Her children must have felt her mood and they sat in the back, quiet as dormice. It had only been about fifteen minutes since she left the house but between everyone's silence and the lull of the car, Paula could see in her rearview mirror that Robert had fallen asleep, and Rodney was nearly out himself.

"Kids, you awake?" Paula whispered to her boys. There was no reply at all, they were officially out for the count.

"I envy them," Anthony said, looking straight out to the road in front of him.

"You can go to sleep too, you know"

"No, I don't feel tired right now. I'm still on edge."

"What are you so on edge about? You're not the one that got sucker punched by your nazi sister."

"Well, it certainly takes two to tango, Paula."

LESTER

Paula took her eyes off the road and stared at Anthony.

"What the fuck is that supposed to mean?" she whispered angrily.

"It means that this has been coming for a long time, and you know it. You can't be blind to it, Paula"

"Blind to what exactly?"

"This. Your drinking, your general attitude you've had ever since" –he pondered his words– "ever since your mother died."

The car was silent, there was no immediate response, but the tension could be felt.

"It's been years since it happened, and you've only been getting worse. I don't say it to be mean, I say it because I care about you. I don't want you to lose the only family member you have left," Anthony said to Paula in a tone that was sincere and genuine.

There was silence once again in the car on the heels of Anthony's words. It looked as though Paula might be considering the concern that Anthony had shown. Looking straight ahead with an intent, Paula finally spoke.

"Thank you sooo much for your concern, Anthony," she said in a sarcastic tone.

"My sister said something at the party that she was done putting up with my shit. She also mentioned that you were done putting up with my shit. Comparing notes?" Paula asked Anthony, looking out at the road.

Anthony could feel the tension getting higher, but he attempted to respond anyway.

"No. Do you know how crazy that sounds? That I'm comparing notes with your sister. I'm simply saying that you're getting worse, you're pushing everyone away. Hell, the kids barely smile anymore when we're at home. They walk on eggshells around you."

SIBLING RIVALRY

"That so?" Looking hurt, Paula gripped the steering wheel even tighter.

"Yeah, it is, Paula."

"Guess you just needed a little liquid courage because you haven't got the balls to say anything otherwise. That it?"

"Yeah, maybe it did give me courage. God knows I have to walk on eggshells around you more than anyone. The slightest bit of criticism and it's World War Three. I end up sleeping on the couch. Also, if it escaped your notice, I'm the one taking care of the kids after work, feeding them, having to explain your behavior. I'm sick of it, Paula."

"Sick of it?" she looked even more hurt than before with tears welling up in her eyes.

"Why don't you just divorce me if life's that tough? It's pretty goddamn obvious that's what you wanna do."

"That is not what I want to do but something's gotta change. If not for me, at least for the kids, you know. I'm your friend, I've always had your back, but it's getting harder and harder to defend you. It's been hard for a long time. I know you're still grieving but you've gotta find another way to deal with this, Paula."

"Yeah. It's all about what Paula's done to everyone, right? You're all so innocent, right? Just blame it all on Paula. That's what all of you do. You ain't no saints either. I've done a lot for this family but when I'm hurting and it's my time of need, you all forget."

"I'm just saying that you might need some help at this point. More help than any one of us can give you. I just want to see you get better."

Paula looked long and hard at Anthony, paying no attention to the road.

"Oh, what? I'm crazy? That's rich. You like to make me feel that way. That's for sure. Well guess what? It ain't workin'."

LESTER

Anthony didn't say anything this time. He just looked out the window and stayed silent for just a moment.

"You know, we'll just talk about this later. We'll get louder and the kids will wake up. It's not the time to talk about it."

"Fine by me. Best idea you've had all day," she quipped back.

The arguing had stopped. The talking gave way to an overwhelming silence in the car with Paula continuing to stew on the events of the last few hours. Between feeling nothing but rage towards her sister and total annoyance at her husband for coming after her instead of backing her up with her sister, Paula felt as though the world was against her. She could not think straight, driving angrily, speeding up whenever her thoughts swirled back to her sister.

After a while she finally looked over to see her husband asleep.

"Well, God, that must be nice," Paula sarcastically whispered aloud to herself.

She was the lone soldier still awake, behind the wheel. With the time to think about things and calm down, Paula started to come down from everything that had happened and everyone around her was so quiet, as if they were not even there.

Sleep. It looked enticing. At first, she had barely thought anything of the kids. It was not until she looked over at Anthony that it started to be a desirable thing. The lull of the engine, the breeze of the window just within earshot, the dark of the night made the idea of sleep even more hypnotic.

Paula knew of course that this was not an option and she had to stay awake because she still had a decent drive ahead of her and it was the expectation they were to stay at Denise's place. Instead, they were driving home, both in no real shape to be doing so.

SIBLING RIVALRY

"Perhaps I should've let Anthony drive," is what she pondered as her eyelids briefly closed before snapping them open again.

"Shit. I really need to get it together," she said to herself out loud, wondering what she could do to keep herself awake.

There was only one thing that could be done at this point and that was to roll down the window, let the cool air in to wake her up. It was her best bet anyways. As she did so she was trying to focus on things to keep her alert.

This task was not necessarily working, and neither was having the window rolled down. It just made things colder in the car, forcing her to roll the window back up again. Her eyelids heavier and heavier, Paula fought to prevent them from closing, purposely making her eyes as wide as they could be, like a cartoon.

Too proud to give the wheel and too strapped for time, she counted down time, "Okay. Only forty more minutes or so. You can do this"

It worked, at least for a few minutes. Before she knew it, she was back to fighting off the temptations of slumber. It could not be controlled. In Paula's mind though, it was all fine because her eyes were not letting her down, snapping her eyes open each time they closed.

There was one last resort, and she wanted to make sure that no one was looking. Before enacting her new plan, she checked on Anthony, Robert, and Rodney. They were all still very much asleep. In desperation, she took her right hand and gave herself a wallop across the check. It was a really good slap considering it was her own hand destined for her own face. The courage of the alcohol must have given her the extra oomph that she needed. She was awake again. In fact, she felt refreshed.

It was just her and the road. Yes, indeed. Now fully awake.

LESTER

Looking up she caught a glimpse of a billboard. It was a brightly colored ad for some type of neon colored treat, she was desperately trying to see the company mascot for some reason. She could not quite make it out and she found herself oddly compelled to keep looking at it. The more she looked the more she felt the strain on her eyes again.

As she zoomed in, trying to fixate on the billboard, her eyes started to slowly close up once again. Paula fought desperately, as if she were being pulled down into quicksand. With no fight left in her, made tired by the alcohol and the ambience that surrounded her; Paula would close her eyes this one last time.

PUDDING AND NIGHTMARES

The room was dark and quiet, with the exception of the repetition of beeping that echoed throughout the room. Paula's eyes weakly began to slowly open up. As they did, Paula attempted to piece together just how she got into this room. The last thing she remembered was driving her car with her family in tow, then dozing off. The time between that moment and her waking up, from what felt like a deep slumber, felt like seconds. She could tell from how groggy she felt that it must have been much longer.

These first thoughts that ran through her head had obscured the bigger question about where she was. She had established that she was not dead. She felt sore, and there was a serious lapse in time but just where was she?

As her eyes fully opened and she regained lucidity, her reality hit her that she was now in a hospital room. Her eyes jutting around frantically, she began to slowly feel around her body, checking to see if things were still in place. She was aware that nothing on her body was amiss, and this pleased her for a brief moment until, slowly, it dawned on her that her family had been in the same car as her, and they were nowhere to be seen.

Barely able to even move, Paula was considering what she could possibly do. She was unsure how any of this worked since she had barely ever been in a hospital and had no idea what buttons could be pushed or how a nurse or doctor could even be paged. Paula was so tired that she doubted she could even call for help and, if she did, if anyone would hear her. She looked around for anything familiar so that she could contact anyone outside of the walls of this room, but she saw nothing of familiarity.

LESTER

Finally, she tried her hardest to scream but luckily, before she could attempt to let out a yell, two nurses came bolting through the door. The two nurses scrambled over, one to check her vitals and the other one to start engaging Paula in conversation. Paula had a million questions but not enough time to get them out as the nurse attempted to calm her down and explain to Paula what had happened.

Before she could say anything though, the other nurse asked, "Should I call the husband?" to the nurse that was checking on Paula.

This automatically made Paula start to cry in relief because she knew one thing - her husband was alive. What condition he was in, she had no idea but for now it was enough for her.

"Calm down. Calm down, Mrs. Bowline," said the nurse as she placed her hands on the side of Paula's bed

"I am nurse Henderson, Paula," the nurse said in a soothing manner

"You've been asleep for a while and you are just waking up from it, but I can assure you that you are okay and your family, luckily, is okay too."

This was an even bigger relief which made Paula start to cry tears of joy. The whole family was okay. She was unaware if they had been hurt and how bad it was, but they were alive and that was enough for right now. It was everything she needed to hear.

"Nurse Henderson? Where is my family? I'm so confused," Paula said with her eyes wide open, visibly frightened.

"I understand, Paula. We're getting the doctor in here and also one of the other nurses is calling your husband. The doctor is going to have to explain a few things to you, but rest assured, you're good for now. Let's get your blood pressure down, nice and steady, all right."

Paula felt much better, much more relieved and started to take in the room around her as the shock of waking up in this foreign place began to wear off. She still had a lot of questions but figured that those questions could wait for the doctor, and her husband, who she was dying to see.

After a few minutes the doctor had arrived in the room.

"So, there's our patient!" said the doctor as he came in through the door, holding his clipboard.

"I am Doctor Svenhold. I've had you under my observation and care for a while now," he said

"A while? umm… How long is a while?" asked Paula, looking even more confused than before.

"Honestly, it feels like it's been a day, doc."

"Well, first of all. Everyone is safe. Miraculously, they all left the first day without any injuries outside of your husband, who had a concussion. Given what I know about the crash, you're all extremely lucky!" said Svenhold as he checked her eyes in a clinical manner.

"Second. And this may be a bit of a shock to you; you have been out for about three weeks now."

"THREE WEEKS? JESUS CHRIST!" yelled Paula, much to her own surprise.

Staring in disbelief, Paula assumed it was a bad joke. There was no way that she could have been out that long. Falling asleep in the car felt like minutes ago.

"Yes, Paula. I know it probably feels like you just fell asleep, and it can all be a little shocking, but we've taken great care of you," he said with a reassuring smile.

"Oh hell, I can't wait to see the bill. Probably want to slip into another coma when I see the receipt on that puppy," she joked.

"Paula, to be frank, you were in a coma and, as with most cases, we didn't know when, or if you would come out of it, so everyone is very happy that you're awake. I'm especially certain your husband will be happy as he has spent many a night at your side"

"My husband was here? By my side? Whole time?" She interrogated the doctor.

"Whole time. Well, with the occasional bathroom break, eating, and having to go to work getting in the way of course."

"And I thought he loved me," she joked again to Doctor Svenhold.

Paula had started to think of her husband, and it was a mix of happiness and guilt. This wonderful man had loved her so much and she had let him down at every turn, to the point that she nearly got him and her children killed. Even after that, when he should hate her, despise her, he sat there on his time off from work to be by her bed, probably while also juggling the kids between all of this.

"He's a really good man. You can't possibly know this, Doc, but I don't deserve the guy," Paula said as she smiled at Doctor Svenhold.

"Well, not to reinforce that, but you've had some nice flowers come and go in this room during your nap, thanks to him."

The doctor pointed to flowers placed at the foot of her bed and a few by the window. Amidst all of the chaos, Paula had not even noticed them before he pointed them out.

"Oh! And not to be left out, I think the kids did something for you."

He turned towards the nurse and gestured to her.

PUDDING AND NIGHTMARES

"Oh, that's right. Let me grab that!"

Nurse Henderson went out the door in a hurry.

Paula was not sure what all of the commotion was about, but she assumed it was something good which she needed right now. She had just hoped it was not a "Thanks for almost killing us" card. The chance was highly unlikely, so she awaited good tidings instead.

Coming back into the room, Nurse Henderson had a folder in her hand and gave it over to Paula who feebly grabbed the folder.

"What's this?" asked Paula, looking at both of them.

"Well, open it on up and see," gestured nurse Henderson with a smile.

Upon opening the folder, it appeared to be a big, colorful piece of paper with a smattering of drawings on it, childlike in design. The images were random, a dog here, two kids over there, what appeared to be a mom and dad, everyone smiling, and all done in markers. At the very bottom was a message that simply said, "WAKE UP!".

After glancing over the picture, she began to cry. The whole experience was so overwhelming that Paula thought about how close her children came to never making another drawing ever again all because of her stupidity and selfishness. The colors, the smiles, the love she could feel from there was all imprinted on this page. It reminded her of everything she stood to lose, and how extremely lucky she was.

"Are you okay, Paula?" asked nurse Henderson

"Yeah. I'm so sorry, it's just that, you know, I love my kids," she said, crying even more.

"Those little turds can be a real pain in my ass, I mean, I literally got hemorrhoids because of them but, they're my little turds."

She thought about what she said for just a moment.

LESTER

"Sorry about the whole 'roids thing. TMI."

"Don't worry. We're professionals," said Doctor Svenhold, chuckling.

"Oh God, Doc. That makes one of us," replied Paula, shaking her head with tears still in her eyes.

"I'm so sorry, Paula. I didn't mean to upset you with that folder" Nurse Henderson said, handing Paula some tissue.

Paula painfully smiled as she continued to cry, "No. It's okay. I mean, I'm very happy but, you know, things could've been worse, and I'm just so glad they're not"

Doctor Svenhold smiled, "We understand, Paula. It was a traumatic event. You must have had some angels watching over you that night to be so lucky."

Paula smiled back, appreciating the doctor's kind words, put the picture back into the folder and handed it back to nurse Henderson.

"I'll make sure to keep it safe for you, where I had it before, okay? I'll be right back," Nurse Henderson told Paula, as she left the room to go put the folder away

"All right, I have to go, too, Paula, as I do have another patient I need to go check on. Your husband should be here soon enough, and you are in the most capable of hands with Nurse Henderson of course. I will see you a little later to check up on your progress now that you're awake though," said Doctor Svenhold

"Okay. Thanks, doc."

She gave him a thumbs up and a smile as he left the room.

Paula had felt much better now that she had talked to both the nurse and doctor. She was ignorant to all of the finer details, but she figured that her husband could help her fill in the blanks once he arrived. After three weeks in a coma, she felt surprisingly good outside of feeling stiff, which was to be expected after such a long stay in bed.

She went from being scared to being excited, thinking about seeing her husband and children again. In some ways, Paula felt renewed by what she saw as another chance at life. The doctor was right; she was extremely lucky to be alive and, even more so, she was lucky that no one else had died or been seriously injured. The more she had considered this, the more she felt a pain in her chest as she replayed the thought in her head of an alternate timeline where her car is wrapped around a tree with two dead children, two dead parents all ending up as nothing more than a news blurb to be ignored.

Though Paula tried not to dwell on the imagery in her head of the several million ways this could have ended much worse, was she unable to shake it. How could she be renewed when she had almost cost her family so much? Her drinking had nearly cost her everything and she was downright sick with herself. She had never hated someone so much as she did now, pondering how things got this out of control.

While lying there, deep within her own pain, Paula knew she did get a second lease and would never let her family down again. She knew that it would be tough to beat her addiction, and that there would be several steps she would need to take, but she knew that when she left the hospital it would be her only priority. She wanted her family safe again and, despite the damage done, she wanted her family whole again. She just had to prepare herself for the anger that her family may have in store for her. She had to be realistic. Baby steps.

About an hour went by and Paula was allowed to do the one thing she had been waiting for since she woke up - eat!

"Oh, Jesus Christ, this is amazing. You're sure this is just regular ol' pudding?" Paula asked Nurse Henderson who stood by to monitor that Paula could eat, having just come out of a coma.

"I can assure you, Mrs. Bowline, that it's just regular ol' pudding. We don't have any kind of premium stash hiding around here. At least any stash I know of," Nurse Henderson thought aloud.

"Look, I don't know where you get this stuff, but I swear it's magical, like it was kissed by unicorns," she continued digging into her pudding.

"Oh, geez. Are you going to need more pudding, Mrs. Bowline?"

"Oh God yes! Unless you have tacos back there. Then I definitely want the taco," Paula joked.

"We don't have any tacos. I'll go get you more unicorn kisses instead."

Nurse Henderson left the room to go get more pudding snacks for the very hungry patient.

"Just bring the whole pallet, please!" Paula yelled at the nurse as she went around the corner.

"And tacos. I really want some goddamn tacos," she assuredly told herself.

As quick as she had begun contemplating tacos, to her shock and surprise, Anthony stood in the doorway. With tears in his eyes, he stared at Paula, taking in the fact that she was awake. It was the look of a man who had asked for one single wish that had been granted but was uncertain if he was dreaming or not.

"You're awake," said Anthony, still tearing up.

"I am. I really am!" said Paula as her eyes filled with tears that streamed down her face.

"Oh my god, I'm leaking, too. Get over here, husband," she extended her arms as best she could. Paula was surprised by the tears that fell so freely. The emotion hit her so hard, seeing her husband before her. It felt like she was in a prison, and he was there to free her.

The warm embrace that she felt down to her bones truly made her feel safe. It seemed like a lifetime ago that she last felt Anthony's arms around her. It felt like being at the bottom of a well and abruptly being pulled back up to the surface, with a warm blanket waiting for her to be wrapped in. She never wanted to let go.

In the embrace, her thoughts went from comfort to shame and guilt. Her mind wandered back to the terrible events that led to her being in the hospital bed.

"I'm sorry, Anthony," cried Paula.

Anthony embraced her even tighter.

"Shhh, sweetie, it's okay. Don't you worry about it all right? Everyone is just fine, not a scratch on them. Honestly, I think the tree got the worst of it."

Anthony soothingly rubbed her shoulder, attempting to calm her down.

"We're only okay by sheer luck. We shouldn't even be alive. I ran our goddamn car into a tree. That's not okay, baby."

Paula wept as she pulled away slowly to look into Anthony's eyes.

"I want to do better, baby. I don't want to live this way anymore. You were right. I'm a mess. I don't want to be a burden on the family, I don't want to endanger anyone. I mean, I got the ultimate second chance here. I can't screw this up. I gotta change, like yesterday."

She looked legitimately concerned and willing, having reached rock bottom. Paula could not remember the last time she took anything this seriously or asked for help.

"Hey, I'm with you, Sweetie. We'll figure all of that out but, for now, we just need to take some baby steps here, okay?" he smiled.

"With you in this hospital bed, it should make things a bit easier since you're starting from scratch, with a clean slate. If you think about it, that's a good start already, right?" he said reassuringly.

This actually did make Paula feel much better. For now, the only thing she craved was more pudding, and tacos of course.

"Yeah, it is a good start. Surprisingly, I don't have even a remote hankering for any alcohol. In fact, I'm actually kinda put off by it. I want water. No, I want cucumber water. I mean, I don't eat cucumbers, but I want it in my water for some reason. Is that weird?"

"Umm… only coming from you I think," Anthony responded, looking at her in confusion. Paula agreed with Anthony's observation, nodding her head.

Joking around aside, she felt renewed. The slate was clean. At least for now. Paula knew that once life went back to normal again, the normal stresses that faced her before would become more than she could bear, and the quickest way to resolve these issues would be through self-medication. She had to be very careful about every step moving forward and she would need all of the help in the world to make it happen.

These thoughts brought her back to something even more important than probably her husband - her children.

"Honey. Where are the kids? How are they?" she said hurriedly as if it had just dawned on her that she had children.

"Don't worry, don't worry, they're at home being watched by kid sitter, Tracy. She's been hanging out over there, watching the kids while I've been at work. She did it for free, knowing what was going on with us. I've tried giving her money, but she wouldn't take it," Anthony said with a big smile.

"Tracy? Oh, how nice of her. I'll have to pay her back by cooking for her, a nice meal or something, you can't pass that up, right?" she said, smiling at Anthony before getting a confused look on her face.

"Oh crap. I forgot. I can't cook worth the shit. Poor girl really isn't getting anything, is she?" Paula said with her hands on her mouth looking a little ashamed.

"No, honey. Not likely. If we give her any of the food we cook, I'm pretty sure she's never coming back."

"You're right, sweetie. In fact, I'm not sure why the kids keep returning home. Not a lot of survivor instincts in those two," Paula said smiling.

"Seriously though, how are my little turdlings?" Paula asked Anthony, tugging on his sleeve, looking sad.

"You know, they're totally fine to be honest. If it hadn't of been for the seatbelts, they would've gone flying through the windshield for sure. We hit that tree pretty hard. I'm just glad you had them put their seatbelts on."

"Oh God, and I heard you had a concussion?"

Anthony took his hat off to unveil a visible bruise that was healing.

"I'd like to say, 'you should see the other guy' but it's more like 'I fought the car and the car won' if ya know what I mean."

Paula reached over to grab his head, she gently pulled his head down to her face and she kissed him on his bruise.

"I am SO sorry about that, sweetie. So, so damn sorry. I keep forgetting it, you know. I'm just so happy and grateful to be up and about but then I remember. I remember that I almost got all of us killed. It really just kinda hits me that you're all alive, that I'm alive, and how close we all came to some real tragedy. You know what I mean?" Paula asked, trying to fight back more tears, giving Anthony his head back.

"Yeah, I do get it. It sucks. But you know, it could've been much worse and it's not. This bruise will heal, the kids will have something cool or interesting to tell the other kids at school, and though it was harsh, it may have given you the wakeup call you needed. That was life's way, perhaps, of ringing your bell," he said, looking into her eyes as she nodded her head up and down in agreement.

"Well, I guess you're in here for a little bit longer for observation. Did you want me to bring the kids here tonight?"

"No, it's okay. Why don't you bring them by tomorrow. It's just so late right now–"

Suddenly the phone rang out of nowhere causing both Paula and Anthony to jump.

"Oh Jesus!" Paula said as they both chuckled at the inadvertent jump scare produced by the phone.

"Must be a wrong number," Paula stated as Anthony reached over to pick up the phone.

"Hello? Hello? Anyone there?" he looked over at Paula, shrugging his shoulders.

"No one there. Guess you were right." He hung up the phone and stood up.

"Did you need more of that pudding?"

"Oh god! I thought you would never ask. Bring mama the good stuff."

"Which one is the good stuff?"

"Whichever one you put in my hand," she smiled and nodded happily.

"All righty, well I'm gonna go ask the nurse about getting more. I'll be right back."

PUDDING AND NIGHTMARES

"Okay. Come back with pudding or don't come back at all. No pressure," she said as he left the room to go on his pudding quest.

"Ugh. God, I can't wait to get outta here. I miss you, home," she said aloud to herself, missing the comfort of her bed and the familiarity it brought.

Once again alone, the peace of the silence was comforting, and she could feel herself slightly nodding off. Paula knew Anthony would be back soon, but she did not resist the temptation of a micro nap. Her eyes closed as she felt nestled into the warm sheets, and she had drifted off but was suddenly jolted awake.

The phone had rung again.

Being the only person in the room, Paula was desperate to get the phone to shut up, so she had no choice but to try and reach it. Though it was nearby on the table next to her, she was still fatigued and sore from having been out for a few weeks.

"Oh, Christ, why do I have to keep getting the wrong number?" she said, laboring her way up to finally reach the phone.

"Hello?" She heard nothing. For just a moment she waited for a reply before repeating herself.

"Hello? Anyone there? I think you might have the wrong number," said Paula as she shrugged her shoulders. As she attempted to hang up the phone, she heard a voice on the other end.

"And you said to me 'I don't care if you're older, I'm younger and prettier and that means I get the last cookie, not you. Old, ugly girls don't get cookies," said the voice in a soft, compassionate voice.

Paula recognized the voice, but it confused her because it was her sister's voice. It sounded as though Denise had been reciting a memory from their childhood.

"Well, sis, that's a weird how d'you do," Paula said, confused, waiting for her sister to respond to the statement. Things only became more confusing as Denise went on, as if having a separate conversation.

"Well, I may have been 'old' and 'ugly', but I got that last cookie and, even though you said that, I still split it with you. I did that because that's what older sisters do, right?"

Denise's voice was going in and out between bouts of static, but Paula made out what she was saying.

"Denise, can you hear me? I feel like the phone is maybe messed up. Helloooo?" Paula asked, looking visibly confused at this point. There was another brief moment of silence on the phone, but after another bout of static on the phone, Paula could hear crying on the other end.

"I just wish I could have saved you. That's what older sisters are supposed to do. I honestly wish I was dead," Denise's voice stated as Paula could hear her sniffling on the other side of the phone.

"Anthony!" Paula yelled out as loud as she could for her husband.

The whole hospital could probably hear it. Being confused and a bit panicked by the peculiarity of the situation, she screamed again. The phone call was setting her on edge, it made her feel beyond uneasy. Everything about it struck her as eerie.

Within a few seconds Anthony came flying around the corner, looking at Paula.   "What's wrong, sweetie, are you okay? You hurt?"

"No, no, no, I'm fine. It's this phone call. It's Denise but I can't communicate with her and she's just incoherently babbling, wishing she was dead. Did something happen to her?" she asked in a worried tone as Anthony grabbed the phone from her to see for himself what was going on.

PUDDING AND NIGHTMARES

"Hello, Denise? You there?" He looked over at Paula, confused, with his brows furrowed.

"I'm sorry, sweetie, but there's nothing there, just a dial tone."

She grabbed the phone from his hand and, just as he had stated, it was nothing but a dial tone. It made absolutely no sense.

"It was her I'm telling you. She was babbling on, talking about some stuff when we were kids, saying she wanted to die. It really freaked me out."

"Well, I'm not sure if it would've been Denise. I mean, after the accident she was supportive of me and the kids, checking in on us by phone and all, even sent a card but–"

"But what?" Paula demanded.

"She's still really pissed at you, especially after the accident. Obviously, I didn't wanna bring it up but, yeah, it seems doubtful she would've called you right now. She doesn't even know you're awake."

He tried laying it on Paula easily, but his way of telling the news did not make it any less hard.

"I know I messed up but, did she even ask about me?" Paula had her arms crossed looking both hurt and angry about her sister's reaction.

"Yeah, she did. In fact, it was one of the phone calls I was gonna have to make tonight because she told me to call her as soon as you woke up."

He came over to Paula and brushed her face.

"She'll get over it. Over everything. You both do. Always."

"Well, she's got a point this time. What I pulled at the house, almost getting everyone killed."

Looking off, away from Anthony, Paula considered her thoughts.

"I don't fault her at all. This was my fault. In my mind I want to pin this on her somehow, that she was being a bitch and kicked me outta her home, but we both know the truth."

Paula took another moment to collect her thoughts. She looked back at Anthony, "Hey. I'll figure all of that out later but, still, I don't know what happened with that phone call. When you call her later, find out what that was about."

"You sure you didn't just dream it? I'm not calling you crazy, I'm just saying that you're tired, groggy, I don't even know what, if any, kinds of drugs are in you."

Only being slightly offended Paula rolled her eyes, "Look, that phone rang. At the very least it rang and there was something on the other end of the phone, and I know what my sister sounds like."

"I know, I know. For now, let's just chalk it up to being… all of this," he waved his hands at the entirety of the hospital room.

"Yeah maybe. It really freaked me out though. If you're leaving, can you do two things? One, get me that pudding that I really wanted, and two, please stay with me until I fall asleep. I honestly won't be able to fall asleep otherwise. That really creeped my ass out."

"All right, well, one, here is your magical pudding I retrieved from my magical pudding quest, and two, of course I will stay while you fall asleep."

This made Paula smile at Anthony.

"And then I'm getting the hell out of here once the snoring starts," Anthony joked.

"What? I don't snore," she laughed.

"No. You're right, snoring is an understatement. You give concerts with that honker of yours."

Paula was laughing even more now, and she started playfully hitting him.

PUDDING AND NIGHTMARES

"Just gimme my goddamn pudding, WHICH I am not sharing with you by the way."

"Oh, I don't want that garbage. Once you get your tastebuds back, you're going to look back on this pudding binge in shame."

Paula started laughing at the comment, "Oh God, you're probably right. We thought the car crash was the low point but, here I am, binging on hospital pudding. Well, screw it, it tastes good right now and I'm sticking to it!"   Paula thrust her spoon in and consumed her magic hospital pudding, smiling the whole time, making "mmm" noises at Anthony.

As Anthony had promised, he stayed with Paula watching over her as she closed her eyes to go to sleep. For Paula it was a warm, soothing feeling, hugging onto Anthony's hand as it laid there in bed. She knew she would go to sleep and be able to make it home, but she just had to make it another night and then she had the kids, the bed, the refrigerator all to look forward to, "maybe even tacos" she thought as she drifted away.

RING!

She woke up. She did not remember falling asleep. It must have been hours since Anthony left the hospital, the hospital room was dark. The phone had abruptly awakened her from her peaceful sleep, and she slowly gathered her bearings. Paula was apprehensive about answering the phone, looking around the room as if someone else might do it for her. Realizing how late it was and how quite alone she was, Paula went to pick up the phone.

"...hello?" she timidly answered the phone.

This time there was no one on the other end of the phone at all.

"Hello? Is anyone there? Anthony?" she asked into the silence.

LESTER

The line cut out as if the phone were hung up on the other end. It had made Paula extremely uneasy earlier in the night when Anthony had been there but between the darkness, the silence, and the isolation, Paula was feeling ten times more uneasy than before. She slowly attempted to hang the phone back up. As she finally did - RING! The phone instantly rang again.

Once again, she slowly went to pick up the phone. She grabbed the handset and placed it to her ear.

"Hello? Is someone there? You might have a wrong number," she said nervously.

Again, there was no response. She did not try to confirm if there was someone on the other side of the phone, instead she listened intently hoping she might hear background noise, something other than silence. As she listened, she could hear a droning noise. The noise was silent at first but slowly it got louder. The sound was almost hypnotic, and confused Paula. She could not make sense of what the noise was. Before she could begin to make a guess, the noise stopped.

"Pssst," a low distorted otherworldly voice said on the other end. Paula sat still, not moving a muscle, waiting for the horrible voice to continue.

"Look behind you."

Paula froze. Instantly chills went up and down her spine. Filled with an overwhelming sense of dread, she slowly turned to see what awaited her. As she turned her head, she gasped as her eyes were met by a dark figure standing towards the window of her room.

In these types of situations, it is said that people have a fight or flight response, but no one ever talks about the other option, the most common one - freeze. Paula herself did just that and, more so, she was so stunned that she could not hold her gaze on the figure, could not bring herself to look at it. She feared that, if she did, somehow it would make it more real.

Normally never short of words, her voice box felt tight, and she was unable to scream, held in place completely terrorized.

RING!

Paula jumped, screaming, as the phone rang once again. In that moment, even being terrified, Paula realized that she still had the phone in her hand, and it would have been impossible for the phone to ring.

"What do you want?" she cried aloud to the phone.

"Don't forget about your friend," the distorted voice on the phone said.

Paula swung around quickly in a panic to see the figure but, to her surprise, no one was standing there at all.

This did not bring her any comfort because it meant that the figure could be anywhere now, or that she was hallucinating. Either way, her heart was beating so heavy that she could feel it in her throat.

"Pssst," the voice on the phone continued.

Paula turned around again to speak into the phone, but when she did, she was face to face with the figure. She felt the sheets getting warm and wet as she pissed the bed in sheer terror. As she shivered, frozen in paralysis, she observed the thing in front of her.

It was humanoid in nature. but nothing one would call human with long, exaggerated limbs. The pupils were missing, and it had a grin that was distorted and disturbingly cartoonish with pale skin that only added to its horrific presence. As she sat motionless, it slowly raised its hand to touch her face, smiling more and more, but Paula broke away from being silent and closed her eyes and began screaming at the top of her lungs.

"Paula!" she heard a familiar voice yell out to her.

That's when she opened her eyes.

It was Anthony. But there was no hospital room or nurses. Instead, she was inside of Anthony's truck in the passenger seat, and there was daylight. This made no sense. She was just in the hospital with that thing in front of her face.

"Sweetie, are you okay? You were yelling out loud," asked Anthony.

Still disoriented, Paula tried to form a sentence amidst her confusion.

"I… I don't know," she continued to search her thoughts.

"I was literally just in the hospital, but it was dark and there was a thing, some, I dunno, monster there with me and it was trying to touch my face."

"No. That's not possible. See, I'm driving you home right now," he said, gesturing to her surroundings.

"You were really groggy, but we got you into the car, but I guess you must've been way more out of it than I thought since you don't even remember that," he continued.

"I'm… so confused. The last thing I remember is you being by my side, and I fell asleep, then I woke up in the middle of the night and saw that thing," she pondered aloud as Anthony stared at her, concerned.

"Yeah, you fell asleep and then I took off, but I came back in the morning and rounded you up. We're almost home actually. See?"

Anthony pointed down a long road where a lone home stood out in the middle of nowhere, surrounded by bushes and occasional trees. The morning sun hit the property in such a way that it looked like a beacon, ushering her home.

The only problem was that she did not recognize it.

"That's our home?" she asked with a look on her face that told Anthony she was not joking, as her eyes looked around as if she had never been here before.

"Well, yeah, sweetie. Do you not recognize it?"

"No. I don't."

PUDDING AND NIGHTMARES

The confusion was too much, and she looked at Anthony for answers. As she looked at him, she could see the obvious concern on his face.

"Well, the doc did say there could be some lingering effects from the coma. Maybe this is one of them? We'll just take it one step at a time. You feeling okay otherwise?"

"I think so. Between the loss of time, the nightmare, and this, I'm feeling" –she searched for the words– "overwhelmed I guess."

"Did you want to get some rest when you get home?" Anthony said, coming up with the only solution he could think of with his amateur medical expertise.

"No. Please no. I'd really just like to see the kids. I think that could help. Maybe it will recalibrate my brain."

As they pulled into their long driveway, Paula noticed a dog, a beagle, sitting in their driveway. She had never seen the dog before and it made her smile, thinking that perhaps it was a nice little homecoming present for her after being in the hospital so long.

"Oh, so I see you got a little something for me when I was holed up in the hospital eh? Something for the kids or myself? A little snoopy dog," she said as she smiled and blinked her eyes in a cute manner at her husband.

He laughed.

"Snoopy? I think you mean Samantha?"

"Oh, is that what you all decided to name her? What a cute name," she said back with an even bigger smile, looking at the dog.

Anthony stared at her for a moment, once again with a look of concern.

"No, sweetie. You came up with that name for her a few years ago. That's Samantha, our dog. Do you not recognize her at all?" he asked with worried eyes.

LESTER

She stared intently at the dog, and it looked just as intently at her as if it were a contest. The more she thought about it and tried to dig up memories of this canine, none came to light. The dog was even more shrouded in her mind than her home had been.

"No. I don't."

HOWDY!

Weeks had passed and life was, in fact, much better than Paula could have expected, even with the occasional lapse in memory. Of course, there were the physical aspects to work out, but she improved each day, getting stronger, becoming more fit, fitter than she had been in years. At one point she found herself outside doing a bit of running; though her running was more a series of spirited sprints than what one might consider an actual run. Several times she has cursed her legs for not being more productive.

"Goddamnit! I was the one in the coma, not you two. AHHH! I hate legs!" she would cry out to her non-cooperative legs.

Still, it was progress. Before the coma she never would have considered running but instead sat around the house, doing nothing. Her schedule usually consisted of waking up to send the kids off, and then going back to bed until probably lunchtime. Often, she would watch TV, think about the day she wasted away, then start her daily drinking routine in the face of guilt, promising that tomorrow would be the day she did a little better. She made promises of getting up earlier, cleaning the house, doing projects, getting some exercise, and none of it ever came to fruition.

This time around Paula actually managed to get up with the kids and stay up. She would exercise after the kids left, do the chores, then sit down to enjoy a well-earned brunch. Later in the day she would maybe dive into some sort of project that ranged from home repair to any variation of arts and crafts. She found herself extremely happy because she was moving in a routine and the routine meant results. For the first time in ages, productivity was an actual thing in her life, and she forgot just how she had slipped away into the dysfunction that landed her into a hospital bed.

At times she would reflect on it, the various stages that led her to that dark cycle. She did not reflect on it too long, not wanting to invite even an echo of that despair into the carefully crafted home she was working so hard to build. In her mind, it was not wise to dwell on such things. They were now in the past and it was dwelling on the past that had pulled her into her prior bad habits.

Instead, she quietly enjoyed a bowl of corn flakes, basking in the sun that shone through the windows, just touching the oak table at which she sat. Outside she could hear the light billow of wind gently ruffling nearby foliage just beyond the window. In her solitude, she wished she could take that moment and save it forever, feel it all over some day when maybe life is not quite as harmonious. This was her life now, and she was ever so present to appreciate it.

As she cleaned out her bowl, Paula's attention gravitated towards the candy bowl Anthony and her kept for the kids as a small reward system. Just something fun for the kids whenever Anthony might spring a random question on the kids.

"Who was the first man on the moon?"

"Who has the record for most home runs in a season?"

These were just some of the questions Anthony might ask of the kids and, in turn, they would receive little mini-sized bars of candy. They were allowed to bounce ideas off one another, working together to promote cooperation with one another, not competition.

The only problem was that the inventory of candy bowl was substantially smaller than usual. In fact, this had been going on for a few days now and Paula thought she was only imagining it, until this morning. It was only a tiny bit noticeable before but now, the candy bowl was missing half of the candy from the day before.

HOWDY!

"Well, I highly doubt that husband has suddenly gained a sweet tooth but, on the other hand, the little turdlings are no thieves hmmmm," she thought to herself, stroking her chin as if she had a beard.

"Guess it's time to put on my detective hat!"

It was the sort of thing to break up the monotony of her day, allowing her to play the role of detective mom, and find out just where the missing candy may have gone off to. She was on the case and decided to pay a visit to the rooms of her children to do some snooping.

Robert's room was in decent enough shape with various papers everywhere from his multitude of drawings he had scattered through different parts of the room. She looked in any potential hiding place: drawers, closet, under the bed, but came up empty.

"Well, Jesus H Christ. Are they keeping the candy up their asses?" Paula said aloud, moving onto Rodney's room.

Inside of Rodney's room, it was a different story. The room looked as though a bomb had gone off.

"Well, apparently I need to come into this room more often," she stared in awe at the absolute mess.

"Jesus, Rodney you might end up owing US candy for this mess."

It was the same result as Robert's room though. Try as she might, somehow managing to get through the mountain of mess, there was no candy to be found in any part of the disaster area of a room. Nothing.

"Meh, you know what; I can wait 'til they get home and interrogate them. If I threaten to make one of them clean up Rodney's room, they'll sing like a canary with an ice cube up its ass."

LESTER

Paula made a crucifix with her fingers at Rodney's room and then hissed at it before closing the door.

Giving up on her search, she went back to her new routine. With chores and working out behind her, Paula could focus on the remains of the day until everyone came home. She took in the view from outside once again just before diving into her kitchen backsplash project she was excited about completing.

Just outside of the window stood Samantha. Samantha the dog that she could not remember. Even now, as things were coming back, she still found it hard to remember the dog at all. Perhaps the dog had not remembered her either because every time she went to pet Samantha, the poor beagle winced up or whined. According to Anthony this was a new, unusual behavior.

The two of them had another brief staring contest, which was becoming a regular thing. It was after breaking eye contact that Paula noticed that their empty barn, just across the way, had one of its doors open, swinging in the breeze.

"Huh, that's strange. I remember closing that door. It sure as hell shouldn't be open," she observed.

As Paula went outside to meet the warm summer afternoon, she looked suspiciously at the opened barn door, watching it slowly sway back and forth. She tried to look within but could see nothing and decided to walk closer to further examine the barn. The door itself could not have opened on its own accord. Only a person could have opened the door, which made Paula very uneasy. It could be nothing; it could be something, either way, in this dilemma, she was all alone. The thought made the hairs on the back of her neck stand up at full attention.

Proceeding with caution and trying to catch glimpses into the barn, Paula slowly walked to the door. When she got to the door, she stood at the entrance, eyeballing the contents within, looking for the slightest clue for anything out of place. It would be hard for her to judge the contents though since she, like the rest of her family, had not seen the inside of the barn in ages and she remembered nothing about this place prior to her accident.

Left abandoned for years, merely being a place to store long forgotten items, the archaic structure looked like something out of a horror film, or something staged for Halloween nights, massive cobwebs included. It smelled as old as it looked, forcing Paula to cough. One thing was certain - she wanted no part of anything beyond the doorway, not without someone else at her side. Instead, she figured she might coax the potential inhabitant to show themselves.

"Hello! Is anyone in here?" she said nervously, and with a false sense of bravado, feeling her heart rate jump up.

"If anyone is in here, I've got a gun and I definitely know how to use it!" which was partly true.

Paula did know how to use a gun. Unfortunately, she did not currently have a gun in her possession. A mistake that had her rolling her eyes as she uttered the sentence and knew she should have gone outside with the gun. The thought had not occurred to her that something could be in the barn until she met the doorway and became truly aware of the possibility.

"I'm not screwing around here. The cops are on their way as well, so you'd better get out of here." she said aloud.

Paula rolled her eyes once again as she realized if an intruder were to present themselves, Paula would be both unarmed and at the mercy of the intruder since there were no authorities actually on their way to help save the day. Paula had actually screwed herself badly. She stood still, nervous, hoping that she would receive no response from the seemingly lifeless barn.

As she stared and waited in the doorway, she got ready to run just in case anyone did suddenly show themselves. She knew she could make it to the door in time to lock it behind her and get to the gun in their bedroom safe. This she was confident in, so long as there was enough distance between her and the unknown potential inhabitant.

Then, without warning, it happened. From a small pile of hay inside the far end of the barn, something started to shuffle around. Wildly at first it shook, and before anything could happen, Paula made a furious run to the door of her home, not looking behind her, running as fast as she could. She leapt through the doorway of her home and locked her door as fast as she possibly could. Now shaking with adrenaline, and itching with curiosity, she looked outside of the window to see if she had been chased.

She looked all around but could see nothing. She thought to herself that maybe she had made it up, that her imagination got the best of her. Still, she fought off the urge to relax. The intruder could still be in the barn, biding their next move, which could be a possibility since they were informed by a potentially gun wielding woman that police were on their way. With that thought in her head, Paula took it upon herself to run to the bedroom and get the gun out of the safe.

She got the rifle out the safe and made it back to the front door. Now, still on edge, Paula did another look around the property. She knew she would have to go back out there to confront a very real threat or a completely harmless specter of her imagination. She drew a deep breath and readied herself to open the door.

"Okay Annie Oakley, on 3… 2..."

It was just then that she could hear the door rumbling as if something was fighting with the door. Looking through the peephole, Paula could see nothing which only served to make her even more uneasy. Now panicked, she started to yell.

"I've got a rifle in my hands. I am not afraid to use this thing!" as she continued to look out the side windows looking for a person and finding none, not even a voice.

Suddenly, as quickly as the rumbling came, it went. It was oddly quiet now which gave Paula just the slightest moment of calm before realizing that someone was likely still out there. The silence only amplified her confusion as she started to formulate the possibilities of the situation. It even dawned on her that maybe it is a person, and they were hurt or injured. She was not about to take any chances though. Perhaps that's what the individual in question was banking on, that Paula might drop her defenses.

"Enough is enough!" she thought, as she readied her gun.

Not wanting to tip off the phantom in question, she silently counted down to open the door and pull her gun on whatever was standing in front of her. She closed her eyes and began to count to three.

"One…"

"Two…"

"Three!"

She quickly opened the door and slung the gun out in front of her, ready to confront the mystery guest. In front of her she saw no one, nothing but empty space. Before she could make sense of the situation, she heard a high-pitched squeal coming from below her, and then, something short lunged at her. Instinctually, she kicked at whatever it was and landed her shoe into something solid and heavy. After making contact with it, she felt a small sense of relief as she watched a wild pig, that she just freshly kicked in the head, run away from the door.

Paula laughed at herself as the pig looked behind at her, grunting, before running off into the brush just beyond the barn, obnoxiously squealing the whole way. There was no phantom, no specter, just an angry pork chop who had been awoken from its beauty sleep.

With that, Paula went back outside, still laughing off the incident, to the barn to finally shut the door. The wild pig did not totally explain how the door got open to begin with, but it stood to reason that someone would likely not be hanging out with a wild pig in a random barn. Still, Paula took no chances and, with her gun in tow, waltzed over and closed the barn door.

She jokingly thought, "Maybe the pig stole the candy?" before retreating inside to enjoy the rest of her day.

The day had come and gone and, before Paula knew it, the family was back home. The kids had come back from school and Anthony was home after a long day's work. The kids and Paula began to settle in for dinner when Paula was ready to ask the kids a random quiz question which prompted her memory about the stolen candy. It was a perfect opportunity to solve the great mystery.

"Hey, my little goblins, quick question," said Paula with a smile.

"You see that candy jar?"

She pointed to the candy jar.

"It's been getting significantly lower over the last few days, and WAY more went missing since yesterday."

She looked at both of them with a moment of silence.

"You know anything about the missing candy, guys?" she said with her hands folded over one another on the table.

The children both looked at each other confused and then looked at Paula with equal confusion. The confusion on their faces seemed genuine. There was no look of shock or guilt, and the two children were not particularly good actors either.

"Mom, honestly, we thought you and dad were eating the candy. I mean, we didn't know why but we'd talked about it

HOWDY!

on the bus and just thought you were bored and eating a bunch of the candy," said Rodney, shrugging his shoulders.

"Yeah, I was really just hoping you wouldn't eat all our candy. It worried me," said Robert with his sweet yet slightly sad, confused face.

"Oh, you guys really have no idea, do you?" she thought aloud, tilting her head off to the side in puzzlement.

"Hey, let's find out if your dad is the big culprit eh!" she said with a mischievous smile.

This in turn made the children smile; for they too were now part of the great candy caper and wanted to help their mother solve the case.

"It sure wasn't the dog," Paula said to the kids.

"This leaves only one person in the house that craftily has been concealing their sweet tooth for ages it would seem. Perhaps it was a candy conspiracy all along!" Paula threw her finger up in the air as if she were onto something big.

"A nibble here, a nibble there, laying low enough not to be seen. This time though, perhaps he had been too greedy and finally showed his hand," Paula's eyes squinted.

"Turdlings! We are going to crack this case!" she confidently proclaimed to the cheer of the children as they made their way to the garage.

"Gotcha!" said Paula to Anthony as she surprised Anthony from behind at his workbench in the garage.

"Jesus Christ, Paula. You scared the crap outta me. You trying to kill me?" said Anthony with a half-smile, trying to be a good sport.

"Kill you? I dunno, is candy stealing a capital crime in this state, kids?" she asked her two half-pint detectives that stood behind her giggling.

"YES!" they both excitedly stated out loud.

LESTER

Paula smiled at the kids and then turned herself to meet Anthony's gaze who was smiling but slightly confused.

"Stealing candy? I think you're barking up the wrong tree, woman. If there's candy missing you might wanna shake down one of these little knuckleheads here," still smiling as he was wiping off his work bench.

"C'mon, confess. I have witnesses down here, you know. Confess and we'll go easy on ya. Well, maybe not Robert because you ate all the mints, and he is way pissed off," said Paula

"Got my eyes on you boooi!" chimed in Robert, with his eyes squinting at his dad, using his fingers to indicate he's watching his father.

"Guys, seriously, you're really barking up the wrong tree here. I don't even really care for candy. You know that. Why would I steal the stuff?" Anthony asked with a smile still on his face.

All joking aside, Paula had hoped that Anthony would have an answer to the big candy mystery, but he seemed as much in the black as everyone else. She could interrogate her children even further, but she knew them so well, and their reactions did not line up with past offenses made in the house. No wide eyes or stuttering, trying to make up an elaborate story. She wanted to ask one more time but without being outright accusatory.

"Rodney. Come clean, was it you? You selling candy to your classmates to earn some money on the side? You are a bit of a hustler," she smiled.

"Okay. First of all, I'm not a thief and I'd never steal from the holy candy bowl. Second, that's a great idea. Thank you in advance," Rodney said with a fox-in-the-hedges-like smile.

This gave everyone a slight chuckle but did not help clear up the mystery. Upon considering Robert, she knew that he definitely would never steal anything, and the jar was out of his reach anyway. Rodney was both very inventive and driven when he set his mind to something, but Robert was the complete opposite. Stealing would have been too hard, too much work. The jar would have to grow legs and jump into his lap, even on his most ambitious of days, for him to steal something from that candy jar.

"Well, okay. I guess since no one is going to confess I'm going to have to put a little hiatus on the candy jar for now," said Paula.

"No way, that's totally not fair!" Rodney raised his voice.

"Yeah, we didn't take nuthin at all. We told you," Robert protested as well.

"Hey, someone is stealing candy in this place and it sure as hell ain't me or this one," pointing towards Anthony.

"The crime cannot go unpunished, so I've decided that everyone gets punished equally and we can revisit the candy jar down the line."

Paula did believe her kids, but she wanted to hide the jar and see what happened when it was not in an obvious place any longer. The entire dilemma intrigued her a lot, more than it should have.

"Oh my god, this has become the center of my life now," she thought to herself as she left the room to hide the controversial item.

Paula could hear Rodney half-jokingly yelling, "Boo, you suck!" from the kitchen as she entered her bedroom with the jar.

Despite the protests from the kids, Paula hid the candy away in the closet, in the top shelf, making it far more difficult than before. She had considered hiding it in the gun safe but figured the safe was specific to guns and did not want any of the desperate candy addicts to discover the code and, in turn, now have access to something far more dangerous than candy.

With the treats hidden, the children fed, and the nightly routine of watching some TV together behind them, it was time for bed. The first order of the night was tucking in Robert, who had to have his night light. Robert had an overactive imagination and the darker the room was, the more he saw things that were not actually there.

"Mom, can you read me a bedtime story?" Robert asked his mom.

"Oh, sweetie, I thought you'd never ask," Paula said in a sugary sweet voice. "I have two fabulous choices tonight. I have your brother's math book as one option. OR I have the second option, which is a book called IT, about a killer clown that goes around trying to eat children."

Robert looked genuinely offended, "I don't want either of those."

"Then sleep it is," she said, still using the sugary sweet voice.

"I mean, how come we don't have fairy tales and mother goosey books like normal people?" Robert curiously asked.

"Well, that's simple, Robbie boy," she said, as Robert looked at her waiting for an answer.

"We are definitely not a normal people in this house. If I find one though, I'll let you know. Maybe they'll have one of those books on them, eh?"

This caused Robert to laugh heartily, kicking his little feet.

"All righty, you get to bed now. If the bedbugs bite then be sure to bite them back okay," she said, kissing him on the forehead before getting up to turn off the light and close the door.

"Love you, my little goblin," she said, closing the door.

"Love you back, mama," Robert's muffled voice responded through the door.

The house was dark, and everything was silent which always made Paula a little nervous, so she always made an attempt to keep a few things lowly lit throughout the house, not only for her but for Robert as well. Paula hated the darkness and the endless silence. She always anticipated the sound of a sudden noise and the danger it suggests when, typically, it was nothing to worry about at all. Imaginations run wild though, and, at night, it could be hard to sleep through it, even with the safety of her husband by her side.

As expected, the earlier events of the day and the mystery of the missing candy danced around in her head. Looking over at the clock, Paula realized it had been about three hours since she laid her head down on the pillow. She tossed and turned, looking for every possible angle that might be the magical sweet spot so that she might finally fall asleep.

"Shit. It's gonna be one of them nights, huh?" she thought to herself, eyes wide open.

"Probably fall asleep about 15 minutes before the alarm goes off, just in time to get up to pack lunches, do breakfast. Oh, fuck, kill me," Paula continued on her thought.

She decided she would just have to get up and find something else to do so that her mind might think about other things and, if she was lucky, might physically exhaust herself enough to get at least some sleep before morning came along. Miserably, she walked down the hallway towards the main living room. TV would certainly be a good place to aid her in her quest to be lulled to sleep.

"Maybe I can find one of those boring old timey British shows on PBS or something. That should definitely help put my ass to sleep," she thought aloud, as she continued her walk to the couch.

LESTER

As the thought rushed over her, she suddenly heard the quick pitter-patter of feet just ahead of her. It gave her pause. Though most of the house was dimly lit she could not see anyone, but she had heard the noise moving away from her as she stood still in the dark. The noise came from the extra family room which was not lit at all. As she stood still, she continued to hear the footsteps escape her as they went further away and then outside.

It finally dawned on her that the front door had been opened. She could just hear the sound of the night air shifting, crickets chirping, and all other manner of nighttime noises entering her home, which gave her an overwhelming sense of anxiety. Without another second to spare she ran back to her bedroom to go wake Anthony up.

"Anthony, wake up!" she said, shaking Anthony but remaining quiet enough not to wake up the children who were asleep in their rooms.

"What's wrong, sweetie?" replied Anthony who woke up slightly dazed and confused.

"There's someone in the house. Or at least there was someone in the house. I think they ran out the front door."

"Are you shittin me?!" replied Anthony now wide eyed and raising himself out of bed.

Immediately he went to the gun safe to retrieve the same rifle that Paula herself had used earlier. He put some pants on quickly before grabbing his rifle.

"Babe. Grab the 45 and go wake up the kids, bring them in here and call the cops," Anthony quietly said to Paula.

"What are you gonna do?" she asked Anthony.

"I'm gonna go out there and check things out myself. I don't need to check outside but I need to secure the front door until some cops get out here."

HOWDY!

Anthony put himself in front of both kids' rooms while Paula went and rounded them up.

"What's going on?" a tight eyed Rodney asked before seeing his half naked father standing in the doorway with a rifle pointed at the ceiling.

"C'mon kids I'll fill ya in in just a moment okay, get over to the room," Paula said as she ushered the kids to her bedroom.

Paula wasted no time heading over to the phone to call the police. She was surprisingly calm for how amped up she felt by the events of the night, not knowing if an intruder was lurking around the property. The kids seemed more confused than scared with the both of them hanging out on the bed, whispering to each other as she finished her phone call.

"Mom. Let me go down and help dad. I'm sure he could use the help."

"Rodney, you are staying here. Your dad does not need your help, so sit down," Paula impatiently replied.

"But mom—"

"Not another word, Rodney. Sit there and don't move a muscle. We're waiting on your dad. Now pipe down so I can listen for him."

Paula put her ear at the closed door waiting to hear anything from her husband. It was dead quiet out there which briefly gave her a small sense of unease.

"Paula! Come down here, bring the kids, it's okay," Anthony yelled from the family room.

This instantly made the unease in Paula's chest go away.

As she walked down the now well-lit hallway, she could see the kitchen just off from the family room was a total mess, like a raccoon had been in there. It only further confused her.

"That couldn't have been an animal," she pondered out loud as she walked past the kitchen and into the family room.

LESTER

"Well, the door was definitely open," said Anthony who was looking outside into the front yard.

"I don't get it, sweetie. Nobody even lives out here," she said aloud, looking outside as well.

"I told you about the whole pig thing earlier and I swore that's what was in that barn. Do you suppose there's someone in there after all?" Paula said with a look of concern on her face.

"Hell, I dunno. Could be. Wild pigs don't open doors and obviously it wasn't these two" gesturing at the kids.

"No, look at 'em', they were dead asleep when I got them up," she replied.

Both Paula and Anthony eyeballed the barn and, sure enough, the door was swinging around, open again. Opened front doors, opened barn doors, the hard thumping of human-like feet. It was disconcerting to Paula to know she had been wrong about the whole thing. Perhaps it had been some person in the barn the whole time. She sat in her house, watching TV for hours unaware that someone had taken up residence in the barn.

"How long had they been there? Why were they there?" she thought in a panic.

"I'm gonna go out there," said Anthony with a determined look on his face.

"Christ, are you crazy!?" Paula blurted to Anthony in a concerned, hushed voice.

"We have no idea who's in there, and it could be more than just one!" she added.

Even Rodney chimed in, "Yeah, dad, you shouldn't go in there. Right Robert?" Robert nodded his head up and down rapidly, indicating his full support for his brother.

"I'm sure it's nothing," Rodney added to his statement.

"This ain't 'nothing', Rodney," Anthony pointed towards the evidence of the crime scene.

Anthony then focused his attention on Paula.

HOWDY!

"Cops'll show up and probably arrest whoever's in there or they might run off when they see the cops. They might come back, unless they know that we aren't the kind of people you want to mess with" replied Anthony, looking even more serious and determined to prove a point.

This was all for show of course since the Bowline family were some of the nicest people you could ever meet, but Anthony clearly wanted no one to think they could just roll up into his barn and take up residence. He had a family to defend and did not want anyone coming back or, worse yet; word getting out that their barn was a good safehouse. It may not have been the best decision, but he was doing it regardless of what anyone else thought.

Paula hung back at the front door with the kids still inside, who had their faces attached to the windows like sucker fish. Still not one hundred percent sure what was going on around them, they wanted to make sure they could duck back into the house at any sight of trouble. They all watched Anthony slowly make his way to the open barn door.

Once he got there, he stood at the same barn doorway that Paula had stood at earlier, peeking into the dark barn. This was bad enough in broad daylight but at this time of night with almost no light, it was impractical and dangerous. Paula extra didn't like this now that the thought had just occurred to her.

Anthony suddenly went back to the house to go grab his keys for his truck.

"Gonna go make some light for that damn barn," he said, walking out the door with his keys.

He got inside, started it up, and moved the truck close to the barn. Now there was plenty of light shining on the inside of the barn. There would be nothing that could hide from the bright lights of Anthony's truck. With the lights set, he figured he would play it safe and even embellish the truth a little about his current ambitions.

"All right. Whoever is in there. I've got myself a rifle and I will do whatever I need in order to defend my family. I can tell you that the police are on their way. If you give yourself up right now, I'll let them know how much you cooperated with me," said Anthony with a very assertive cadence.

"However, if you don't come out then I'm probably coming in, and you don't want that. I'll burn this barn down if I have to make my point," he said as he doubled down on his threats to the intruder.

Paula was watching the events with anxiety, knowing that Anthony was in a dangerous situation. She watched him make his threats and then he stood there silent for just a few moments with his gun ready to go. Suddenly Anthony spoke aloud.

"This first one is a warning," Anthony shouted as he pointed his gun in the air and gave off a gunshot.

This made Paula much more uneasy, and as she turned her head to her left, she could see the kids with their faces both strongly pressed against the glass. You could see the look of worry on both of their faces.

"It's okay, kids. Dad's got this. He's just letting 'em know who's boss is all," she said to the kids.

Anthony lowered his gun.

"Now, that first one was a warning. The next one is for you!" said Anthony with a very serious tone. The tone was so serious that even Paula wondered how committed Anthony was to potentially shooting the intruder.

It was quiet for just a moment, like a standoff with an invisible foe. It was so quiet, Paula wondered if this was all just in their heads. Just as she was trying to piece the puzzle together of something more innocent, or a misunderstanding of events, suddenly Anthony yelled.

HOWDY!

"Hold it there!" Anthony hollered as he pointed his gun.

Before him stood a shadowy figure into the far part of the barn.

"What is it, honey?! What's going on over there?!" yelled Paula to Anthony

"We got someone in here!" he replied loudly to Paula

"Shit! Rodney I'm going out there with your dad, you lock this door behind me, understand?" Rodney's eyes got big as if he were both frightened and excited at the prospect of his new responsibility.

Paula was tired of missing all of the action and, with two guns on their side, she felt more than confident. She ran up behind her husband to see what was going on.

"What the hell Paula?! You left the kids by themselves?!" Anthony angrily shouted at Paula.

"The kids are fine. They're inside and the door's locked. Besides, the cops are gonna be here soon enough," she replied.

"So, what do we have in here?" as she looked around into the light, looking for the mystery guest.

"I could swear I just saw it!" said Anthony as he nervously dotted his eyes back into the barn, aiming the rifle into the barn.

Before they could say anything else they were interrupted at the sounds of their kids running towards them screaming.

"No, don't do it. Don't hurt him. It wasn't his fault!" both of the boys screamed as they came running down towards the barn. They placed themselves between their parents and the barn.

LESTER

Anthony quickly lowered his rifle.   "Kids, what in the hell are you doing? Get over here! Now!" Anthony angrily ordered the two kids.

"No dad, you can't shoot him, he didn't mean any harm. He's just hungry is all," Rodney said with Robert nodding in agreement as usual.

"Okay, guys. Who are you talking about?" Paula worriedly asked the children.

"Promise you won't hurt him, okay?" Rodney asked with a worried look on his face.

"I ain't hurting nobody, but you two gotta get over here now and tell us just what's going on, and I mean pronto, guys," Anthony waved them over hurriedly.

The kids walked over to their parents both with their heads down and a worried look on their faces. Paula had no idea what was going on. She could not begin to imagine just what this was all about. If this was an imaginary friend, then it was certainly the most complex one she knew of.

As the kids approached, Anthony was the first to question them.

"Kids? What's this all about? You tell me right now!"

"We didn't mean for it to get so crazy. Lester moved into the barn a few weeks ago, around the time mom went to the hospital," Rodney said with his head still down.

"It was mostly me giving him the candy. Robbie just kept quiet is all."

"Did he touch you?" Paula angrily asked.

"No, no. It's not like that at all," Rodney responded with his eyes furrowed, almost looking offended at the accusation.

"You telling me there's some guy living in our barn living off our candy, stealing our food?" Anthony confusedly asked Rodney.

HOWDY!

"Well… umm… that's the thing," Rodney looked at Robert as if to find the right words to come up with to finish his sentence.

"Lester is… not from around here," Rodney continued.

"Not from around here?" Paula said.

Paula and Anthony looked at each other, both confused.

"Well, I don't care where he's from," Anthony shouted.

"He's got 'til the count of five to show his face!"

Robbie ran off from the group to the barn door much to everyone's surprise and shock.

"No. You can't hurt him. I won't let you!" Robbie screamed, as he stretched his arms out making himself like a shield.

Just then, Rodney went running off to the barn door entrance too.

"Oh goddamnit! Get back over there you two. Now!" Anthony demanded.

"Only if you promise not to shoot him," Robbie demanded.

Anthony and Paula looked at each other, worried and angry about their current situation but they knew at this point they would have to play along in order to get the intruder to show themselves.

"All right. Fine. I'll keep the gun lowered but I wanna see someone coming outta there with their hands up," Anthony demanded back.

The two brothers talked back and forth in secrecy, clearly negotiating their next move. They both appeared to agree on their next course of action.

"Okay. We both agreed that'd be fine," Rodney said in his most diplomatic voice.

LESTER

After Anthony and Paula both walked forward to meet them at the barn door, the kids both looked at them nervously.

"So, we have to warn you about something before Lester comes out," Rodney said, looking at both of them with caution in his eyes.

"You know how I said that Lester wasn't from around here?"

"Yeaaaah, I remember," Paula said in a confused tone.

"Well, he's, like, really REALLY not from around here," Rodney said, shrugging his shoulders, looking for words that escaped him.

"What, like from Russia or something? You hiding a commie in there or something?" Paula asked, her face contorted in puzzlement.

"Uhhh, I don't know if he's a commie or not, but he's definitely not from Russia," Rodney replied, pondering his answer.

"All I can say is, just don't be scared, okay? He's different looking," Rodney said, looking at both Paula and Anthony.

"I'm sure we can handle it if he's disfigured or whatever, sweetie. Seriously though, let's stop with all the theatrics. Just rip the band-aid off and get your friend out here already," Paula impatiently pleaded with Rodney.

"Ummmm okay," Rodney said with his face winced up.

He quickly walked into the barn. Paula and Anthony watched as Rodney talked to someone in the barn over stacks of boxes, but they could not make out what was being said.

"Okay, you can all come in," Rodney shouted to his parents.

Paula and Anthony moved in slowly, they looked at each other both very aware of how weird the whole thing was.

HOWDY!

Robert moved up close to Rodney, waiting for his parents with a big smile on his face.

"Lester. You can come out now. You can meet my parents," Rodney told the mystery guest that hid behind the boxes.

There were a few moments of silence. The trill of insects took over the silence as everyone seemed to await the response of the mystery guest that hid behind the boxes in front of them. Paula just started to form a thought that perhaps the whole thing was an elaborate game from the kids, impossible as it may seem. Then out of nowhere a voice emerged. It was high in pitch, innocent, pleasant.

"Don't hurt me," the voice yelped out in a worried fashion.

Paula was taken back and confused by the tone of the voice.

"Is this a child?" she thought.

"I don't mean nobody no harm. Surely didn't mean to frighten anyone at all," apologized the stranger.

"You say you didn't mean to hurt anyone. Well, first, why don't you come out from behind those boxes, and show us your face?" asked Paula

"Shucks, Ma'am, I want to come out but at the same time I'm worried my appearance might… give y'all the ol' heebie jeebies," the voice worriedly replied.

"Are you disfigured or something? That's honestly the least of our concerns. I'd like to know who I'm dealing with here. I wanna know who's been living in our barn," Anthony said in a fairly calm manner.

"Okay. I'll come out, but don't be scared now," stated the voice from behind the boxes

LESTER

Slowly, the unknown intruder started to sidestep out from behind the boxes. At first it looked like a tall, lanky man, from what they could see. The hands were up to show that it posed no threat, which made everyone temporarily feel more at ease. Unfortunately, as the mystery guest stepped out further, Paula and Anthony were horrified as they saw a bright yellow, exaggerated, round, lemon colored head come out from behind the boxes.

From the neck down, everything about him was so plain, so normal. Black shoes, brown slacks, suspenders, and an open cardigan that gave way to a button-down shirt beneath. Even the bright red bowtie did not appear out of place. Everything outside of Lester's clothing was completely mutant.

The bright neon yellow head was almost leather looking. It almost looked like a mask, but it had bright sky blue eyes that moved, and animated facial gestures. There was a tuft of brown hair that sat upon the humanoid looking head which made the sight even more perverse. It almost looked like a cartoonish nightmare. The image shocked Paula. She was unable to scream, instead she froze in terror of what she was seeing.

Everyone stared as the man with the rifle, the family patriarch, went cold and made no noise at all. Instead, he rocked forward a bit and then fell backward with a hard thud onto the ground. To the disbelief of Paula and the kids, Anthony had passed out in shock.

"Holy shit!" Paula yelled out loud, shocked.

"Oh shucks, I done gone and made everyone scared again," sighed Lester.

PIGSKIN BLUES

Paula looked down at her husband, trying to grasp the entire situation. In all of her life, she had never seen anything like Lester, and the sight of him gave her a shot of adrenaline. Paula knelt down to check on her husband to see if he was all right while negotiating in her brain if this was real or perhaps a nightmare.

"You know what, I done enough to you kind folks. I can just move along and find somewhere else to shack up. Lemme just git my little hobo stick and move on out. I'll be outta yer hair in no time-a-roo," said Lester with a very sad, disappointed look on his face as he started to reach down to gather up his meager belongings

Paula was still trying to grasp the situation and what she was seeing. Frozen, with her entire body a statue at this point, she tried to muster up the words to communicate with the harrowing enigma that stood before her.

"Wa– wait!" she yelled out.

Lester stopped dead in his tracks, hands back up to continue to show it was no threat.

"Don't shoot!" he blurted out.

"Don't worry, I won't shoot you, Lester," replied Paula in a calm tone.

"I also don't want no one crammin' my own underwear up my butt, thank you very much," Lester said which greatly confused Paula.

"Umm underwear up your butt?" Paula quickly asked.

"Yeah, mom, that's my fault. I told him about wedgies, and he's been kinda paranoid about them ever since," Rodney told Paula with a guilty look on his face.

LESTER

"No one's getting my undies," Lester said, suspiciously looking around.

Paula stared at the thing in front of her, perplexed. She had a million questions but, even at the idea of being rude, she asked the most obvious thing.

"What are you?"

"Well. Hmmm. That's actually a good question, ma'am," Lester replied, looking down at the ground.

"All I can remember is ending up in this here barn. I don't remember how I got here, what my name is, what I'm doing here. Nothing," shrugged Lester.

"Wait. How do you know your name is Lester?" Paula inquired.

"Well, the name Lester was written down on the back of my collar. The little buckaroos found. Figured that was my name," he answered with a shrug.

"The only thing I knew was that I wasn't supposed to be here. I knew that much. So, I hid here and, well shucks, that's when I done met these two little horny toads. They kept givin' me all them tasty nibblins. Sorry about tonight though, that wasn't rightfully neighborly of me, breaking in. I know it was wrong, but I had a hankerin' for some sweets," he said with a huge smile that spread across his wide, exaggerated face

Paula was trying to figure out what to do, but before she could do anything else, Lester spoke again.

"Aw shucks, where's my manners?"

Suddenly she saw Lester move towards her.

"I can take care of that," said Lester.

Then as if he were picking up a kitten, he now held the unconscious Anthony in his arms.

"Where do ya want him?" Lester queried with a smile.

"Oh!" exclaimed Paula, taken by surprise, "Ummm you can bring him inside to the couch," she said, pointing at the house.

"Oh wow, y'all inviting me into your humble abode?" asked Lester happily.

This made Paula chuckle nervously a bit.

"Sure, why the hell not? Let's just keep the weird train a goin' I guess," throwing her hands in the air.

When they got into the house, Lester gently laid Anthony on the couch. Paula came and checked on him to make sure Anthony was okay. She was fanning him, having no idea how to care for anyone that has passed out. Her kids have never done it either, so she was in the blue.

"Ummm, even though you already raided us, were you still hungry?" she asked.

"I'm hungrier than an ant-eater on an ant hill," he said back with a big smile.

"Ummm, Rodney, Robert, can you go get something from the kitchen to eat? Also, a glass of water for when your dad comes to?"

"Ma'am, are you sure you don't want me to leave? I've already been a bull in the ol' China shop here. On top of eating your food, y'all seem a little put off by yours truly," Lester pointed to himself.

"No, no, your appearance is" –she searched for words– "different," said Paula.

"If you take off, I think something bad might happen to you. You know, people might not understand, they might be–" she searched for the right word again.

"Afraid?" asked Lester.

"Well, yeah," she conceded with a pained face.

"I'm gonna have to talk to my husband about what to do here. In the meantime, just make sure you stay put," she said to Lester.

Paula could not believe the words had left her mouth. She went from being angry and frightened to sympathetic for this unexpected guest. In her gut, she knew she could just call up the authorities and this issue could be solved but then she considered what that might mean for him. Instantly thoughts of imprisonment, experimentation, and autopsies flooded her mind. This being seemed so innocent that she found herself wishing it no harm.

It was just then that Anthony appeared to be coming around. As he slowly panned around, looking for the abomination that stood before him, Paula got his attention to see if he was all right.

"Was… was I dreaming?" Anthony asked, looking confused and scared.

"Ummm. No, sweetie. You weren't," she responded with some apprehension.

"What I saw… That's not of this world, honey. I am nothing if not open minded but just what in the hell was that?!" he said, still looking around.

A commotion could be heard in the kitchen with cabinets, pots, and pans all being knocked around.

"Kids? Everything okay in there?" Paula yelled out to the kitchen.

"Don't mind me, I'm just looking around at all this cool stuff that's not candy," Lester yelled back.

"It's okay mom, Lester's just looking at… stuff," Rodney said.

Paula turned her focus back to Anthony.

"SO. Basically, I have no idea who or what Lester is. He seems to be lost, he has no memory other than waking up in our barn and he's been ducking in there ever since. I think the kids found him and treated him like a stray. That's about all I know at the moment. I mean, he seems really nice just kinda… weird and a little spirited," she said to Anthony, stroking his hair as he laid on the couch.

PIGSKIN BLUES

Anthony was looking off to the side, still listening, but you could tell he was listening from afar, wrapped up in a million different thoughts. Amidst his thoughts, he was able to pull out a question.

"How did I end up on this couch, by the way?"

"Oh, well, Lester brought you in here" she responded.

"It was able to pick me up and bring me over here by itself?" he said with a surprise look on his face

Anthony was not exactly a bear of a man. Though only average height and average weight, Lester's feat of strength was worth noting to Paula, who had not considered this fact until just now. Lester was able to pick him up like a kitten and easily carry him to the couch. Truth be told, she had no idea what Lester was capable of. Exciting as this new experience was, she was going to have to be cautious. She did still have her manners, especially for a new guest.

"Its name is Lester and yeah, he's quite strong. He could've easily arm curled you" she said.

"Is that supposed to make me feel better, Paula? Some weird yellow alien that has superhuman strength? Why have you not called the cops? Authorities? Whoever in the hell deals with this kinda thing," he said with his eyes wide open.

Looking freaked out, Anthony pulled Paula closer.

"Paula, I have objections here. You know?"

Paula could understand, especially after having an adverse reaction to Lester's appearance. She figured maybe Anthony just needed some time. She would likely have to approach this later but before she could say anything else, Anthony slowly got up.

"Shit. Can you bring him over here?" Anthony asked Paula, arranging himself to sit upright on the couch.

"Hey, guys. Can you bring Lester over here?" Paula asked, still sitting next to Anthony.

LESTER

The kids came out of the kitchen; behind them, with chocolate smeared all over his face, Lester slowly walked into the living room nervously.

Anthony looked at the two kids as if to say, "Could you give us some privacy?" and with that look, Rodney took his dad's cue.

"Uh hey, Robbie, let's go close up the barn door outside," Rodney said as he grabbed his younger brother's hand and went out the front door.

After they left, the room was quiet - way too quiet. Lester stood still for a moment while Anthony silently continued to stare ahead, rubbing his chin, thinking. This made Lester feel awkward, so he started to look around the house, checking things out for the first time, not in the dark on a candy raid. Things remained quiet.

"Heckuva home ya got here," blurted out Lester nervously.

It was obvious he was trying to make small talk. He was not particularly good at it, but it did the trick.

"So, Lester, my family has informed me that you are in our barn without memory, trying to lay low?" said Anthony, now making eye contact with Lester.

"Yes sir. I'm just a little ol' tumbleweed in the wind I am," Lester said, now meeting Anthony's gaze.

"Well, I'm not fond of strangers, and you are the ultimate in what I'd call a stranger. My number one priority is to protect my family, you see. I'm sure you understand."

Paula was not comfortable with where this was going. She found Lester to be oddly intriguing and also felt sorry for him, but the look on Anthony's face said it all - Lester was probably going to end up a true tumbleweed. Anthony did not want Lester to be their problem. At least her husband would give him the decency of leaving on his own accord.

PIGSKIN BLUES

"So, what I'm trying to say is–" Suddenly Anthony was cut off.

Just outside they could hear the kids screaming. Jumping up to look outside, Paula could see her kids being chased by something, but it was too dark to make it out. Anthony, Paula, and Lester all dashed outside where they were met by an angry wild pig who was about to run down Rodney who stood between it and Robert.

The kids were too far away, and no one had time to react, even yelling at the pig would be useless given its concentration on running the boy over. Suddenly, faster than the eye could see; Lester appeared right in front of the children wearing a football helmet emblazoned with a big shiny "L".

"Hiya li'l porkchop!" Lester exclaimed in his high-pitched voice.

And as the pig approached, Lester ran a few steps forward and, to everyone's shock, kicked the wild pig. The wild pig went airborne, sailing over the ground and then over the trees, eventually landing far away from mesmerized eyes.

"It's gooood!" yelled Lester, who was now holding his hands to make the upright Field Goal gesture from American Football.

Everyone looked in pure amazement. Not a single word escaped their mouths, not a muscle moved on their faces or bodies. Within seconds, this strange being transported through thin air right in front of the kids and kicked an animal, weighing at least one hundred pounds, further than some people can kick a soccer ball.

"This couldn't possibly be real," they all collectively thought, jaws wide open.

"Pigs can't fly? Well, they sure can with a little ol' encouragement," said Lester with a giant smile on his bright yellow face.

LESTER

Paula and Anthony ran right up to the kids to check on them. The kids assured them that they were okay and there was no need to worry. They were more entranced by the house guest that just punted a wild pig to the opposite end of, what seemed like the state, maybe the world. Just moments ago, it seemed as though Anthony was ready to send Lester packing but as he stood there with his children unharmed, you could see a change of heart on his face.

"Lester. I still don't know much about you but, ummm maybe, given that you just defended my sons–" Anthony pondered, looking around at the kids and then Paula.

"Well, I have no idea what I'm doing and, hell, I may regret this but, would you like to stay here with us for now, 'til we can get things all figured out?" he asked Lester.

"Wait. Are you asking me, Lester, to stay at your swanky little ranch?" asked Lester quietly.

"That's exactly what I'm saying. I owe ya! I mean, it's just for now, but yeah, you can stay here a bit," replied Anthony.

"Excuse me. I'm gonna totally freak out now," Lester said calmly.

And then Lester lit up like a Christmas tree, glowing bright lights all around him.

"Y'all better stand back some. It's about to really jolly up in here," Lester continued, shaking violently like he had an Earthquake going off inside of him. The whole time there was a massive smile on his yellow face.

The moment the family backed up; Lester fired off like a rocket into the sky. Little fireworks seemed to come off of him. Some of the fireworks made images: Lester smiling, Lester laughing, the Bowlines in stick figure form, and a pig with a cape.

The Bowlines were both amazed and concerned at the same time. People from all over would be able to see the fireworks, even at this late hour. They would likely get a visit from the local cops, maybe even the fire department.

"Lester, get down from there!" Anthony yelled up into the sky.

"Yeah, c'mon, you're going to attract a shit ton of attention!" Paula also yelled into the sky.

Rodney and Robbie stood still, beaming up at the massive amounts of lights and explosions filling the sky.

"Cooool!" they both said with giant grins.

The explosions stopped as abruptly as they had started but there was no sign of Lester in the night sky. Suddenly they heard something falling.

"Ow! Ow! Ow! Ow! Ow!" a voice said, getting gradually closer to the ground. Before everyone knew it, Lester hit the ground with a massive thud that sent dirt flying up into the air. The entire family went running to where the impact had taken place.

"Lester! Lester! Are you okay!?" yelled Rodney as he made his way first to the impact, which was a human sized hole in the ground.

As everyone else came up to the crash site, Lester popped his head up out of the ground. His face was completely flattened like it had been ironed clothing.

"You know" –he looked around– "For some reason I thought the ground would be a lot softer," Lester continued.

He put his thumb to his flattened lips and blew on the thumb, reinflating his head back up to its normal shape.

"It ain't," he finished this thought, now spitting out a fist sized rock.

Before Lester could do much, he was ushered into the barn by the Bowline family. When they got into the barn Paula started laughing at the absurdity of the whole event while

Anthony gave her a concerned look. The kids in particular were oohing and awing at the feat Lester had just accomplished, thinking it was the coolest thing they had ever seen in their short lives.

"Do it again!" yelled Robbie to Lester.

"Yeah, that was awesome. Best fireworks ever. I agree with Robbie," Rodney said, pumping his fists, smiling.

"Yeah, let's not," Anthony protested.

"Lester, what the hell was that?!" Paula asked excitedly with her eyes wide open.

"Oh–" he paused.

"I don't reckon I know to be honest. I just kinda got a little excited and then I was off to the stars," he said.

Paula knew she was going to have to set some ground rules, namely ones that ensured Lester would not be seen and make sure he would not draw any attention to their home. She felt though, if she simply asked, he would oblige.

One thing was certain. Life was about to get interesting around the Bowline household.

MY HERO

After the excitement of the previous night, there was no way that Paula could send the kids to school. She needed some time to really sit down and tell the kids the importance of keeping this a secret. Though she did not wish to scare her children, they had to know that for Lester, this could be the difference between life and death.

First thing in the morning they had a special family state of the union address as Anthony was getting ready for another long day at work. The kids sat on the couch directly in front of Paula who paced back and forth rapidly, attempting to think of what to say to the kids. Rodney and Robbie sat still, watching as their mom shifted her eyes around in contemplation.

"All right, guys. Here's the deal," she said, putting her clasped hands up to her lips, giving herself a moment to speak.

"So, Lester, as we know, is not from around here," the kids nodded their heads in agreement, saying nothing.

"Now, if we let this little secret out to anyone and I mean absolutely anyone outside of this house, well, just about anything could happen to poor Lester," she continued.

"Ummm if you've ever seen E.T. it would kinda be like that–"

"Oh, so we would be chased off by guys with walkie talkies and fly off to the moon?" asked Robbie, interrupting his mom.

"Wellll, not exactly," Paula said, trying to find more polite, delicate words for Robbie's sake.

"Dude, what mom's trying to say is that if we say anything a bunch of government guys are gonna come get Lester and cut him up like a turkey," Rodney said, pulling the band-aid off.

LESTER

Robbie stared at his brother, and then he stared at his mom with his mouth ajar.

"What?! People are going to come to our house and eat Lester?!" he said with a genuine look of horror on his face.

"No, no, no, sweetie they're not going to eat him," Paula said, trying to reassure Robbie.

"They're going to… ummm–"

"They're not gonna eat him," Rodney said to Robbie which got a welcomed nod and smile from Paula, who was grateful that Rodney attempted a little damage control.

"They're going to kill him and then slice him up to see what his insides look like," Rodney continued. This made Paula reverse the smile she gave Rodney that turned into a deadpan scowl.

"Oh my god, that's worse!" yelled Robbie, who looked even more horrified.

"Eating people?! Cutting them open and looking at their insides!? Oh my god, are they gonna do that to us too?!" Robbie asked, looking more concerned than ever.

"Okay!" Paula looked at Rodney in frustration.

"Thanks, older brother. Tons of help. Really appreciate it," she said sarcastically as Rodney sat beside his brother with a mischievous grin on his face.

"No one is eating anyone, and no one is cutting anyone open, all righty," she said with authority, staring at Rodney with her eyes wide open conveying she meant business.

"But!" she followed her previous sentence, "I must stress the seriousness of what COULD happen if someone found out about Lester."

Robbie stopped freaking out long enough to let his mom gather her thoughts, and Rodney wiped the smile off his face realizing the brevity of this incoming advice.

MY HERO

"Basically, what I am trying to say is that if anyone were to find out about Lester, well, we honestly don't know what would happen to Lester," she said patiently to the kids.

"Government goons might come to the house to bring him to some place where we would never see him again or the media could show up at our door, making life really unpleasant for him."

The kids nodded their heads and looked at each other, making an unspoken agreement among each other.

"And all it takes is one person. Just one. Before you know it, they tell someone, and that person is telling someone else. We know how Lester has felt about scaring people. For his safety and his privacy, you guys cannot tell one single soul," Paula said now at eye level with her sons.

"Can you guys promise me that this will stay a secret?" she asked with her hands clasped.

The two brothers looked at each other again.

"For Lester?" Rodney said to Robbie.

Feeling a sense of pride that his brother was letting him in on this oath, Robbie sat up straight with a smile on his face, "For Lester!" he exuberantly agreed.

Paula herself was extremely pleased to hear her kids were so onboard with the idea of concealing Lester. She had initially thought there might be some pushback which is why she decided to keep the kids home.

"Now that you both agree, I can let you in on the good news," she said smiling at the two kids who also had big smiles on their own faces anticipating the mystery news from mom.

"I hope you two are ready because summer starts early. I decided given the situation we are in now, I can't really risk anything, so I'm pulling you both out from school early."

"YEEEAAHHH!!", both of the kids shouted at each other, fist bumping one another.

LESTER

"Oh mom, normally I would be insulted that you don't trust us enough to keep a secret but right now I totally don't give a crap," a wide eyed, extremely excited Rodney said.

"Rodney, don't say that word!" Paula quickly responded to Rodney with her brows furrowed.

"Crap? You say shit all of the time," Rodney casually said back to his mom.

"Did you just say 'shit'? Seriously, what is wrong with you? Don't say that word. Jesus, kid!" Paula looked at Rodney in disbelief. He was such a smartass, but the interaction still caught her off guard.

"See, mom. Crap doesn't seem like such a bad word in comparison," Rodney chuckled.

"Oh! My! God! You little heathen, go do– something. Something that doesn't involve breaking anything or swearing and DO NOT teach that garbage to Lester," she said, half annoyed at Rodney and half amused.

"No sweat, ma. You can teach him that crap," Rodney said as he bolted out of the living room.

"I can still bring you down for adoption," she yelled out to Rodney who was no longer in the vicinity.

She looked at her other son, "Well, at least I have you my sweet little Robbie. Rob. Goblin. My little Roblin."

"Don't worry mama, I won't say crap or shit," he responded innocently.

She stared at Robbie for just a moment then got a little closer, just within earshot, "You just did, son. You just did."

"Oh!", he caught himself.

"Sorry," he whispered back to his mom, clutching his blanket to his face in embarrassment.

One of the biggest marks on Paula's agenda was figuring out more about Lester. He had already shown that he had superhuman strength and, out of nowhere, shocked everyone by flying into the night sky, shooting off pyrotechnics at will like some crazed cartoon. The more she thought about what he did, the more she wondered about the sheer impossibility of it all. It defied physics. The feats of strength were acceptable but, even for an alien, the fireworks event was an eyebrow raiser. Though not afraid of Lester, she was a bit concerned and wanted to establish some boundaries, especially with the children.

Paula found Anthony out by his truck. He was still packing everything up, getting ready for work even though he had a sleepless night, still reeling from a most unusual night. He did not have much of a choice in the matter as the bills were not going to pay themselves. Paula was sure he was going to be at half-speed at work, distracted that a bright yellow superhuman cartoon alien was hanging out with his family miles away.

"Hey, you," Paula said, coming in to plant a kiss on his lips.

It was quick and robotic in nature, as he was distracted by his task at hand. She was a little offended by his lack of enthusiasm but went on.

"So, it looks like everyone has a big day ahead of them today huh?" she said, trying to make some kind of conversation.

"Yeah. About that," he stopped what he was doing.

"Last night I said Lester could stay until we figure stuff out," he said, looking directly at Paula.

"You did. You change your mind on that?" Paula said, looking disappointed and concerned.

"I'll keep my word but, for now, just be real careful, all right? We honestly know nothing about Lester," he said.

"I'm sure it will be okay, sweetie. I mean, you saw him last night, he's a real sweetheart, the kids love him, and he did protect–"

"I know, Paula. Just be careful because, it's like being around a wild animal that's all friendly-like. You don't know how sharp its claws are until it's too late. Know what I mean?"

The words hit Paula with a bit of heft, and she thought on it for a moment as Anthony wrapped up.

"I'm sure it will be fine, sweetie. He's just another kid, right?" she reassured Anthony, half trying to convince herself.

"Yeah, a kid who can pick up grown men like a sack of potatoes and fly hundreds of feet into the sky," he quickly said back to her.

The more Anthony pressed his case, the more Paula felt the need to be contradictory and protect Lester, even if she had her own concerns.

"So then just say it, you want to get rid of him," Paula huffed, now with her arms crossed, wearing an agitated look across her face.

Anthony let out a sigh and looked at Paula again.

"That is not what I'm saying. Just please, tell me while I'm at work you'll think of something we can do about this because he can't stay here. This is not our problem. He's not our pet, and definitely not one of our kids. Can you do that for me, please?"

Still feeling obstinate, Paula stubbornly pondered on the question and begrudgingly conceded.

"Fine. I'll try to figure something out while you're out. This doesn't happen every day, so you have to give me a little bit of time, okay," she told Anthony.

"That's fair. Also, try to keep your distance if you can," he said, getting into his truck.

"We can't be rude, Anthony. Jesus," she replied, sounding a little agitated again.

"You'll figure something out. I gotta get on. I'll see you tonight, okay? Remember what I said," Anthony said to Paula just before driving off in his truck, kicking dust up into the sunny morning sky.

"Love you, too," she quietly replied in an annoyed delivery, watching his truck drive off down the road. She stood still, arms folded, wondering why he couldn't be bothered to say that one simple phrase to her. It used to come so easily but, for a while now, it was rare and always on her to say it. It came back for a brief time after the accident but faded away just as quickly.

Paula did not have time to dwell on it though. She had another task to attend to: She had to go have a talk with Lester. The kids had their talk and now it was his turn to receive some ground rules of staying at the Bowline residence.

As she approached the barn, Paula could hear Lester's high-pitched voice and a mix of laughter. The kids obviously made their way over to hang out with their new friend. Paula was not worried about Lester, even if Anthony had tried to instill the fear of God into her. She could not explain it, but she had a good feeling about him.

The only thing on the property as scared of Lester as Anthony was Samantha, who did not dare go within a mile of the barn. She spent the past few weeks growling, whimpering, and barking at the barn. It was a mystery to Paula before, what was upsetting Samantha, but now the mystery was revealed. Samantha did not care for the new barn inhabitant. That was a problem for another day though.

Paula moved over to the barn. The voices got louder as she got closer and without even knocking on the barn door, it somehow opened on its own.

"Well, howdy dowdy. Look what the sun done dragged in!" yelled an enthusiastic Lester.

"Good morning, Lester," responded Paula, "And how did you sleep last night?"

Lester cocked his head off to the side, pondering the question.

LESTER

"Sleep? What's that?" he asked

This caused Paula and the kids to laugh, assuming he was joking. When she looked back at Lester though, his face was serious, inquisitive, looking for an answer to the question. He legitimately was not sure what she had meant.

"Sleep? Do you not do that?" she inquired.

"Well, it's when you close your eyes and you rest. It gives your body a chance to recharge. You'd kinda die without it. At least we would," she answered him, still looking puzzled.

"Oh, I don't do that at all. Never even heard of it before. Is that sumthin' new?" he asked with his hands on his hips, nodding his head like he just heard a silly joke.

"No. It's what we– people and, well, just about every single creature on this planet does," she said, both explaining sleep and visibly being confused by his lack of understanding it.

"Ol' Lester's gonna have to take your word on that one. I was up all night just trying to rack my noodle over who I am 'n' such. Also, I may or may not be out of the candy you gave me last night," he said while shaking an empty bag upside down.

This got a smile out of everyone.

"Don't worry Lester, we'll refill your bag with some more candy. Maybe that's what's keepin' you alive," she joked.

As she gathered Lester and the children around for the big talk, Paula made sure to close the barn door. She could not risk even a bird peeping in. They all sat down inside, and she wanted to let everyone know their role moving forward.

Lester looked around nervously.

"Ooooh boy. I think we're about to have 'the talk'," he looked at the boys.

"The talk? What's 'the talk'?" Rodney said aloud looking back and forth at his mom and Lester.

"I wanna know what 'the talk' is. Is it bad?" asked Robbie, looking a little nervous.

"It's like when people start yappin' a whole bunch about important-like things. You have to listen to stuff. I'm not a fan. It cuts into my thinking-about-other-stuff time," Lester said with a panicked look on his face.

"Well yeah, there will be some yappin', Lester, but it is really important. What I have to say could make sure that nothing bad happens to you," Paula tried to explain.

"Something bad? Like what?" Lester asked, looking really panicked.

"People from the government are going to cut you up," Robbie said with a sad look on his face, remembering the conversation from earlier.

"Cut me up?!" Lester yelled, looking even more panicked.

"No, Robbie's confused. No one is going to cut you up," Paula said in a very stern, matter of fact manner in an attempt to regain control of the conversation.

"BUT! You do have to be quiet and not make a lot of noise out here, Lester. I'll be square with you. If anyone found out about you, I don't know what they would do to you. People would come here, take you away, and we'd never know what happened to you," Paul calmly explained to Lester.

"So, what you're saying" –Lester calmly started– "Is that if I don't behave, people will show up here and take me away?" he nervously asked.

"Yeah, something like that," Paula replied.

"And cut me up?!" Lester panicked again.

"No, I didn't say—"

"And eat my brains?!" Lester said with his eyes wide open, fully panicked.

"They're gonna eat your brains?!" Robbie yelled, also in shock.

LESTER

"Oh man, I am totally freaking out!" Lester also yelled, now running behind a stack of boxes.

"No, Lester, Robbie, everyone. No one is being cut up and no one is eating anyone's brains. Okay!" Paula attempted to once again regain control of the room.

Lester poked his head out from behind the boxes, "You promise?"

"I can't promise anything, but I can say with ninety-nine-point nine percent certainty you won't be cut up or have your brains eaten."

"It is also dependent upon you two keeping YOUR mouths shut. We went over this already, but I will repeat myself: Do NOT tell anyoooone. Comprende?" she told the kids.

"What about my best friend Vinnie? He would love Lester," asked Robbie.

"Yeah, I wanna meet ol' Vinnie. Sounds like a swell fella," Lester chimed in.

"No one is meeting anyone. Robbie. Remember that if the secret gets out, we may never see Lester again. Can you swear you won't tell a soul?"

Robbie thought on it for a minute and nodded his head up and down in agreement. Paula could see a visible sense of pride wash over his face, as if he was almost proud of being the holder of this amazing secret. He imitated a key being turned on his lips to indicate the secret was locked.

"Lester. YOU have to keep a low profile. No fireworks. No nothing that will attract outside attention. This doesn't just affect you. Who knows what will happen to us. You got it?"

"Yes ma'am," Lester came out from behind the boxes to the rest of the group with his shoulders slumped.

Now that the rules were cleared up, Paula had to ask Lester if he remembered anything else. Unfortunately, he was none the wiser than the previous day. This led to her other question, which was about his powers.

"Lester. Question. How do your powers work?" she asked.

"Well, shucks, I guess if I think about something hard enough I just kinda make it happen" he replied.

Lester looked over Rodney.

"I tell ya boy, you look ready to cut down a whole forest with that thing," said Lester

Robert and Paula looked over just as Rodney himself looked down at his chin where a grizzly beard now sat on his face. It was real. Rodney tried to tug on some of it to figure out if it was real and was astonished by the mountain of hair on his face.

"SWEET! Mom, can I keep it?!" said Rodney, excitedly.

"No!" she said laughing.

"Oh my god, get that thing off his face, Lester!" Paula demanded, while continuing to laugh.

"What thing?" replied Lester, quickly.

The beard was gone from Rodney's face as quickly as it appeared. Paula was just wrapping her brain around the appearing-disappearing beard act when suddenly she heard snickering from the kids. Lester started in on the repressed laughing as well. It made her wonder just what was so funny. Then it struck her. She felt her own face. Now she had the beard.

"Oh my god, Lester, get that off my face!" she yelled while laughing.

"Get what off yer face? Your mom's a very handsome woman, am I right fellas?" Lester said to the kids, which only made them laugh ten times harder.

After a few more seconds of laughs, Lester removed the mischievous beard from her face. It went into thin air, just like magic. Paula still had no clue how he was doing it but, to be fair, neither did Lester. It was a part of him, just like breathing or tapping your fingers. He was something special and this made Paula smile. It was a happy thought that they were the only ones in the world in his odd, unique presence.

"So, what do you all wanna do with your ol' pal Lester today?" he suddenly asked.

Everyone was a little indecisive about the question. No one had planned anything, especially with a brand new visitor around.

"We should totally show Lester around, mom!" Rodney excitedly said.

Paula thought this was a good idea actually. Lester could get to know the places of the house that he had previously not seen while invading their kitchen.

"Yeah, we should do that. Would you like a guided tour of Bowline Manor, Lester?" Paula asked the yellow oddity.

"Would I? Oh, you betcha! The place sounds even nicer when ya got them big fancy-like words behind them n' all."

"First stop: Robbie's room," said Paula.

As they entered, Paula and the kids could visibly see that Lester was blown away by Robbie's little room. The posters, the dolls, the action figures, the bright colors on the walls. Paula figured this would be his favorite part of the house since Lester had a real child-like nature about him.

"Whooooa! This place is paradise!" Lester said with eyes so big they threatened to pop out of his face. His mouth was just as open with a smile that stretched from ear to ear.

"This is my friend, Wilbur," Robbie said to Lester, holding up a little stuffed stegosaurus.

"Pleasure to meet you, Wilbur," Lester said, shaking Wilbur's paw.

"And this is Trok the Destroyer, he's a mutant lizard man that knows kung-fu," Robbie brought another toy.

"Well, I've never met kung-fu but it's nice to meet you all the same, Trok," Lester shook his mutant lizard paw.

MY HERO

"And this is Cedric, he keeps me safe at night," Robbie said, showing off a little brown plushy monkey.

"How d'ya do, Cedric?" Lester paused.

"Protect you at night? Protect you from what?" Lester timidly asked Robbie.

"Oh, the monster in my closet," he said casually going on to the next stuffed animal.

"And this is Cedric's best friend, Timmy," Robbie continued.

"Ummm, can we get back to his whole monster in the closet business?" Lester asked, now side eyeing the closet, looking nervous.

Robbie just kept going down the list of action figures and plushies.

"Oh, I can't forget about Commander Jack!" Robbie showed off a very buff soldier, armed to the teeth with weapons.

"Seriously, no one's gonna talk about the monster thing?" Lester said, looking around the room, eyes wide.

"Commander Jack fights against this guy right here. This is General Gravesword. He's the bad guy. Him and Jack are clones, but they don't like each other because Jack was given a good life and lots of love and taught how to be a ninja and–"

As Robbie continued to babble on, Lester kept motioning to the closet door.

"Lester, there's no monster in that closet," said Paula as she swung the door open.

"See," she reiterated by putting her hand in and waving it around in the emptiness.

"I've seen it though," said Robbie, looking offended at his mom's insistence that the monster was not real.

"It comes out at night. It wants to eat me," Robbie continued, looking sad.

LESTER

"What!? And y'all still live here?!" Lester said, looking shocked as he tiptoed out the door.

"Y'all should come live in my barn. No monsters in there. Well, none that I know of." Lester had an unsure look on his face with equal parts confusion and newfound fear.

"Lester. I love my son, but Robbie suffers from an overactive imagination. You're fine," Paula confidently said.

"Besides, no monster would wanna come visit your room anyways," Rodney chimed in.

"Sorry, bro, but that would suggest something interesting happens here and, no offense, but ain't nothing interesting happening to you. Well, except Lester of course."

"Appreciate that," Lester said, holding Robbie's wiffle bat for protection, looking around the room.

Paula had wondered how long it would take the kids to show off their favorite thing in the room - their video game console. Sure enough, the boys saved the best for last.

"Enough of the toys and stupid monsters in closets," said Rodney.

"He's sorry about that!" yelled Lester into the closet.

"Bro. Let's show him the bad boy," Rodney smiled at his brother.

"Yeaah!" Robbie smiled back, agreeing with his brother.

"What kinda bad boy we talkin' about here?" asked Lester.

"The Evolution!" they both said to Lester in unison with squinted eyes and mischievous smiles. This was some serious business.

As he watched all the lights flash on the screen, Lester was completely enthralled. The kids were playing a military first-person shooter called *Blood storm*, and Lester was making little jumps and squeals every time one of the kids died. It was obvious he wanted in, but the poor guy was going to have to learn how to play first.

The boys let him have his turn so that he could learn the ins and outs of shooting "terrorist scum", starting him on the tutorial level of the game. He fidgeted around with the controls but just could not get a grasp of the game. He kept dying over and over again and started to get a little upset.

"Why I oughta!" he said with his brow furrowed and shaking his fist.

"I shot that guy, like, a million times but he didn't die! He even looks in my direction and I die. This game is CHEATIN!" Lester said, shaking the controller in his hand angrily.

Lester was a natural. At least, at losing his temper at video game consoles.

"Aww shucks, ya little tumbleweeds. I'm just no good at this little doohickey," Lester said disappointedly. Suddenly though, Lester had a look of inspiration across his face.

"You know, fellas, I always say 'if you can't beat em, join em'!"

This caused the kids to look at one another in confusion.

"Whaddaya mean?" Rodney cocked his head, squinting at Lester in bewilderment.

Before the kids could do anything else - POOF! They disappeared into thin air. Lester and the kids were completely gone.

Paula was dumbfounded.

"Kids? Lester?" She looked around the room.

Her confusion changed to panic. It was not every day you saw people disappear into thin air.

"Kids!?" she started to yell, looking around even more.

Just as she was getting ready to head out to the barn to

see if Lester had teleported all of them to the barn, she heard a voice.

"Mom! Mom!" said the small voice.

As she turned, she looked in total puzzlement. She saw video game-like avatars of her two children and Lester staring back at her from within the TV.

"Lester. Did you– bring the kids into the game?" she asked with concern.

"Sure did! We're gonna go ahead and put these nubs–"

Lester was corrected by Rodney, "Noobs."

"Oh, I mean noobs, in their place," said Lester finishing his sentence.

"Hey, you wanna join in? I'm sure we got more room for ya," Lester asked Paula.

"No, I'm okay. I'd much rather be out here not being shot at, supervising my children that are being shot at."

"That sounds swell!" Lester yelled back enthusiastically.

Before Paula could say much more, Lester and the kids were already off yelling; shooting anything that moved, having the time of their lives.

They ran around erratically with no real plan other than impromptu chaos. Eventually they came up to a wall of opposing soldiers that pinned the kids and Lester down in a spot. The kids laid out a strategy to attempt to outflank and destroy the opposing soldiers, but before they could do so, Lester came up to them with a question.

"Uh hey fellas, why's this thing beepin'?" he said holding up what looked like a countdown timer connected to a big brick of a C4 explosive.

The kids looked in horror and yelled as the numbers counted down, "2... 1..."

"Someone fart?" Lester asked nervously.

The C4 went off and a giant explosion occurred, sending their avatars flying all over the place. As Paula gasped, all three of them came flying out of the TV, as if the game had tried to toss them out on their ears. After the initial shock of landing, the three of them looked at each other and started laughing.

"Oh boy! Who wants to respawn?" asked Lester.

"Me! Me!" exuberantly exclaimed both children, never having known such fun in their entire lives. It showed on their faces, and Paula's concern dissipated as soon as her kids got back up and dusted themselves off.

"Lester, kids, c'mon, I don't want you going back in there," Paula said kindly but firmly.

"But moooom, c'mon!" protested Rodney.

"Let's do what your mother says, fellas. We can go zappity zap some other time," Lester said, patting both kids on their shoulders.

Paula was just happy to see her kids back. In a sense, though she was not scared, it troubled her how easily Lester could just disappear with the kids on a whim.

"Now, Lester, I'm not mad at you, and I know you were excited but if you're going to do something like that again, ask for permission first, okay?" Paula said to Lester who now looked a little like a chided kid.

"Yes, ma'am," he replied with slumped shoulders.

"Hey, chin up, yeller feller. The day is still young, and the sun is still out. Let the kids show you the rest of the place. Don't worry about it, okay. Just learn from your mistakes," she said to Lester, reassuring him with a smile.

"Well, you know what, I think you're right. I feel better already. Ol' listening Lester heard you loud and clear. Learn from my mistakes. Now I'm off to see the rest of Bowling Alley."

"Did you mean Bowline Manor?" Paula asked Lester.

"Yes. Yes, I did," he said deadpan, walking off with Rodney and Robbie to go finish up his tour.

LESTER

As the day went on, Paula decided to knock out a bunch of her chores. She was cleaning up the living room which had a smattering of things everywhere. Kids toys, dishes, random clothes. The house never stayed clean for too long. After a bout with the dishes, she was anything but thrilled to have to clean this up, too.

"Paula. Whatcha doin'?" Lester asked Paula, making her jump.

"Oh shi– oot. Hey, Lester. I'm just trying to put everything back where it belongs. The place is kind of a mess but duty calls, you know."

Lester looked around at everything with big, inquisitive eyes, and said "All righty, everyone. Y'all know where ya belong?"

Paula cocked her head and stared at Lester, perplexed.

Suddenly, all the various items that were strewn about sprouted up on their feet and started walking around the house. Yes, they had legs and they casually walked back to every little place that they were missing. One of them, a toy sheriff, was even nice enough to tip their hat at Paula. She thought it was quite neighborly of him and tipped her imaginary hat right back. The whole time, even with everything Lester had already done, she was amazed. The whole thing left her with a sense of wonder. She almost felt like a kid.

And, just like that, the majority of her chores were off the list.

"Things returning themselves back where they belong? Oh my god, yes!" she thought.

Paula could certainly get used to this.

With the chores done in record time, Paula was able to hang out with the group one more time. It was obvious that

Lester wanted her around, and the kids seemed just as happy to have her presence.

In the mix of the day's events, Paula had forgotten about Samantha. When she went to go look for Samantha, she found her at the opposite side of the house, alone and whining. This was getting worse. Paula was unsure what to do with Samantha but wondered if ripping off the band-aid would be best.

She grabbed Samantha by her collar and led her down the hallway. As she did, Samantha's whining got louder.

"My God, Samantha. What is with you?" Paula said to her in annoyance.

"It's not like he's gonna bite you or anything, ya scaredy dog."

When she got to Robbie's room, where the kids were playing with Lester, Samantha was furiously trying to get away, barking non-stop. This was not an act of aggression; it was an act of pure terror. Samantha practically dragged Paula the opposite direction of where Lester was. It was an astonishing feat, and, for Samantha's sake, she let go.

The whole time Lester looked around in confusion, not sure of what he had done.

"Ummm, I don't wanna point out the obvious, but I think the ol' pooch-a-roo don't like me too much," said Lester a bit sad.

"I'm not sure what it is, Lester, but I'm sure she'll come around. Hey, we did, right?" asked Paula with a smile on her face, hoping to change the mood of the situation.

Lester shot a smile back to her and Paula went back to go check on Samantha. When she finally made it to the other side of the house where Samantha was, she found the family dog hiding behind a couch, shaking. She was absolutely terrified. In fact, poor Samantha had soiled herself. Paula was not angry though; she actually felt bad for Samantha. She felt, even with

LESTER

Lester's presence being a source of agitation, that she ought to bring her in and have her looked at once and for all. Perhaps there was a chance that Lester's presence had nothing to do with it. She had to be sure.

The following day, Paula did just that.

Anthony had to use his lunch time to go pick up Paula and Samantha, to bring the two to the vet, since Paula's license was still suspended. Paula was extremely lucky to have only been fined, but it cost her at least a year of driving, and she hated having to rely on anyone to help her do basic chores. This was no different, but she understood, as did Anthony, that it was Samantha's sake. The poor pooch was not doing well, and it seemed to be more than just the presence of their unexpected visitor.

For the first time in days, Samantha was seemingly happy and playful. The fuzzy girl was extremely happy to see the vet and responded well to all his commands. The Bowlines were a little perplexed. As the veterinarian examined her, he looked quite perplexed himself. With a thorough exam, nothing could be found to be wrong with Samantha.

"I'm telling ya doc, this dog has been depressed, like, someone died. She just sits around whimpering all day long," said Paula, waving her hands around, baffled.

"We had a visitor recently and the dog was so terrified of them that she literally pissed herself and was shivering," added Paula, shaking her head.

"Well, I can't speak to the dog's psychology, but I'll say that, physically speaking, Samantha is in tip top shape. I can certainly recommend someone to you who lives a bit out of town but as far as I can tell, this is one happy dog," said the vet assuredly.

The doctor continued to examine Samantha.

"I'm sure this new visitor would be the main culprit. I've never heard of a dog reacting like that, unless it's been abused. Perhaps she's worried that you'll be giving her away to this new person? Hard to say, not knowing anything, and I'm not totally qualified in that department. I'll go ahead and get the information for the pet therapist."

The vet left the office to get the information and Samantha tried to tag along with him which everyone thought was pretty cute. Once back inside the room, alone with the Bowlines, Samantha got quiet again. She started to look worried and when Paula went to comfort her, Samantha just sat there still, almost emotionless, a stark contrast to what she had done with the doctor. The puzzle just kept getting more pieces by the minute.

Later, on the way home, Samantha became more and more upset. She was getting more withdrawn and began to whimper again.

"God, Paula, I hate to say it, but do we reevaluate things with Lester? I mean, Samantha seems to be really messed up by his presence," Anthony said with a worried look on his face.

"Well, I dunno, sweetie. It doesn't seem entirely linked to him. When the doc left the room she reacted badly to us, you know. Also, Samantha was like this before we introduced Lester to everyone. She'd been kinda a little off for about a week or two before Lester came around," she reasoned.

"Well, I dunno, honey. We'll see how things go, whenever we can see the dog shrink but, we'll have to start experimenting ourselves, see what works for her because something's off," said Anthony who shook his head in frustration.

LESTER

"I'll try to take her out on the weekends, get some fresh air, away from the house, see if that helps at all. Lester is just temporary, don't forget that," he continued as he looked off down the road in deep thought.

When they got home, Anthony had little time to do anything other than drop Paula and Samantha off. The only problem: Samantha refused to get out. She sat in the back seat, planted, as if she had no intention of going anywhere. When Anthony and Paula tried to call her out of the seat, she looked uncomfortable, like a child negotiating not going to school or the dentist. The whimpering was immense, and when they tried to reach in to grab her, she would slink back and whine even more.

Not wanting to use physical force, as she was already traumatized and scared, they had to figure out some way of getting her from the back seat. Before they could do anything the dog suddenly disappeared into thin air.

"She's in the barn now. Sorry about scaring anyone, but it looked like y'all need a little help getting that ol' poochy outta there," said Lester as he blew smoke off of his finger as if it were an old six-shooter in a cowboy movie.

Anthony was still not used to Lester's powers. This one was certainly new to him. Though it took him aback for a moment, he was happy with the result since he needed to get back to work as soon as possible. He hopped into his truck with nothing to say and was off to work. Surely, he would be home late due to the vet and Samantha's antics.

As he drove off, Paula could hear the whining and barking coming from within the barn. She went over to open the barn doors. At this point, Paula was losing her patience with Samantha. She wanted to be kind and compassionate, but she just wanted her to be normal again, and for the whimpering to stop. It seemed to go on more and more with each minute of each day. Walking up to the door, she was loading up her happy face to not frighten the poor dog.

When she finally opened the door, Samantha came slowly walking out, when she froze up at the sight of something.

"Hi there, li'l friend. I sure hope we can be friends. I brought a little chew toy to bury the ol' hatchet," said Lester as he tossed the chew toy towards Samantha. As it landed, Samantha examined it slowly and, after closely inspecting it, was freaked out by something, perhaps the toy itself, and ran away towards the backyard.

"Oh, Lester, I think you're going to have to keep your distance from Samantha. She's got some problems, and I don't think it's because of you, but at the same time, your presence here is adding some stress" –she paused– "If you could just give her a little bit of room."

"Say no more, m'lady! Lester will make sure to give the little fuzzy beast a whole ocean of space. If'n I see her, I'll shuffle my yellow patootie back to the barn. Yesiree!" he said, seeming to understand what Samantha was going through.

"I appreciate that, Lester," she said with a smile, pondering something.

"Hey, for being such a good sport let's go get you a treat. Ever heard of ice cream?" she said with a bigger smile.

"No," said Lester abruptly. "But I think I'm gonna like it," Lester winked with a smirk.

True to form, Lester did in fact love the ice cream.

"Well slap my pappy! That's some good eatin'!" Lester yelled out loud as he did what he called his new ice cream happy dance.

"You look like a possum having a seizure," Rodney said, laughing at Lester's dance.

"Oh thanks! I'll give you some tips later," Lester said, taking Rodney's words as a compliment.

LESTER

"We need to show you some other dance moves. Here!" Rodney grabbed his football and started to emulate a touchdown dance, including spiking the football.

Lester shrugged his shoulders.

"WOOHOO! YEAH! ICE CREEEAAMMM!" he yelled loudly as he copied Rodney's football dance. Also copying Rodney, he spiked the ice cream into the ground.

"Oh no!" shouted Paula.

"Lester, you're not supposed to spike the damn ice cream, you're supposed to eat it," she continued, staring at the mess on the floor.

"Oops. Lemme handle that bad boy," Lester exclaimed as he shot his index finger up.

Suddenly from the kitchen, one of Paula's mops came walking out on its own. It looked over at the mess on the floor.

"All right, all right, who made dis mess over here, eh?" it asked in a tough New Yorker accent.

Lester looked around for a little help, but he knew he was guilty and had to cop to it.

He shyly raised his hand.

"Oh yeah, dis guy thinks it's funny to go messin' up my floor, eh?" The mop stared at Lester.

"Well, I didn't mean—"

The mop cut Lester off.

"Didn't mean to," he mocked Lester.

Everyone sat quietly.

"I'm gonna clean up dis here floor. When I do it'd better stay clean. Am I makin' myself one hundred percent clear over here?" the mop said to Lester, now standing right in front of him.

Everyone nodded yes.

"It won't happen again, sir," Lester said, looking worried.

"Ya darn right it won't!"

The mop cleaned up the ice cream on the floor, muttering the whole time. With the floor finally shining again, the mop started to walk back to its closet.

"Kids these days, no respect. Am I right?" he asked Paula.

"Oh. Oh yeah, big time. I hear ya, Mr. Mop," she stumbled along in agreement with the mop.

"Da name's Tony, not Mr. Mop. But hey, you call me whateva ya want, toots."

"Wait, what?" Paula looked around in confusion.

"Lateh!" Tony the Mop said, as he went back into the cleaning closet.

"You know what, I'm not even gonna ask," she said to herself.

"Seriously, what kinda mops you letting into this place?" Lester asked Paula as he shook his head disapprovingly.

The kids laughed.

"You're the one that sent me that jerk," she said to Lester slightly chuckling.

"I think we can all agree we don't go near the cleaning closet," Lester said looking around at everyone as they continued laughing.

"No. Seriously. I'm pretty scared of Tony the Mop," Lester deadpanned.

Though they were all having a good time, Paula had something on her mind. She had to ask Lester if there was anything at all he could remember about his past.

"Tony aside, I have to ask if you can remember anything about yourself, Lester. Do you remember anything at all?"

"Honestly, it's all a blank space up in the ol' noggin," said Lester, resting his face on his hands, looking a bit put out.

"Seeing Samantha was like something I'd seen before. Like something was happenin' all over again."

"You mean like Deja vu?" Paula responded

"Oh! Gesundheit," said Lester

"No, Lester. Deja vu. It means that you've experienced something before, or at least it feels like you've done that thing before which, of course, is impossible. Still, sometimes you can get hit by that feeling."

"Oh boy, well I don't know if I like the hoogie boogie or whatever fancy dance word you used to describe it. Made me feel really… weird."

"In what way?" asked Paula

"I felt unhappy. It was just for a moment, but I done felt like a frog under a log. You know what I mean?"

She did know what he meant. Though she was unsure why the Deja vu necessarily brought the sadness upon him, she at least recognized that he must have felt hurt or dejected by the way Samantha had been reacting to him. Anyone could be sympathetic.

"All righty, well I think I'll be shoving off to the barn, let you fine folks git on back down to your little pow wow," said Lester

"Lester, did you want to stick around and watch some TV with us before Anthony gets home?" she asked Lester

"Now what in tarnation is a TV?" he inquired.

"Oh. Well, it's what we used before, you know, for the video games but instead of games it has people acting out stories and things like that," said Paula, doing her best to describe the art of TV watching.

"Well, hotdog! That sure does sound swanky," he replied, jetting up from his chair.

Lester and the kids gathered on the couch as Paula turned on the giant TV. It completely blew Lester's mind away.

They switched around the various channels to Lester's continued amazement.

"Whoa! Now how you fittin' all them people in that fancy doohickey?" Lester asked. Before anyone could reply, he got up and looked around the TV, examining every inch of it, trying to wrap his head around what he was seeing.

"Real people just hanging out in that little box. I thought you said what I did was magic, but this right here is magic," Lester pointed at the TV set, completely enthralled.

They set about watching some classic TV shows. They watched *Addams Family*, *Donna Reed*, *Lost in Space*, and *I Dream of Jeannie*. Lester was still trying to figure out the science of TV and his brain was thrown through another loop with the black and white shows. He had only ever known color.

"They didn't have the technology back in the day for color, that's why everything was in black and white on these older shows," Paula told Lester.

"Oh, good, that makes sense. I thought old people were gonna be in black and white or something," Lester replied while still in his TV trance.

They continued to remote surf for a little longer, settling on some *Bewitched*, much to Lester's increased amusement. After the show was over, Lester stood up and slowly looked around the room with a big smile spread across his face.

"You know, y'all. I think it's about time we had ourselves a little hoedown of our own."

Then, suddenly, the color from the real world started to drain out of existence, replaced by blacks, whites, and grays. The clothing started to morph as well. Everyone in the room started to see their old clothes transform into something from the 1950s. The furniture had changed as well. The appliances were the same, but they became specific to the time period of the 50s, just like the clothing. As Paula and the kids started to look around their settings, they could not help but laugh at everything that was going on. Even Robert, who normally was scared of everything, was sincerely giggling, having a good time.

Paula noticed that the outside looked a little different too. Right outside of the screen door, she noticed that the trees looked slightly off, less natural and more plastic, more artificial. As she opened the door, she started to walk forward towards the trees when suddenly she bumped into a wall. The wall teetered a bit.

"Careful now, you don't wanna knock down the set," Lester said.

Paula looked at the wall. There were dark painted trees, just like the trees outside of her home, the moon included in the giant painting. She realized it was actually a set piece like one might see on a TV show. She looked behind it and there was a sound stage with a door that read EXIT. Paula was completely baffled.

"Paula. We're about to start. Git on in here," said Lester, waving her over.

Still confused, Paula walked back to the living room area of the house. Her confusion led to anxiety. She wondered if this was a permanent thing, if they had been transported somewhere.

"We're about to start recording, Paula," she heard from off in the distance. Though Lester was standing right next to her, the other voice sounded just like his but from behind the wall of the living room.

"I'm sorry?" she responded.

"Oh, you wacky actress types holding up the show. If you don't get into your spot, we're gonna have to cancel your contract," said the voice.

As she looked at the wall to figure out what she was hearing, the wall pulled away to the side to reveal an old, bulky

TV camera. Behind it was what appeared to be a director with a big bulky headset on. It was Lester, or at least his spitting image, also in black and white, holding a script.

"Oh, you better do what this ol' hamdog says, Paula. This guy's a real pickle," Lester whispered to Paula.

Paula stood still, shocked between seeing her entire wall disappear like a set piece and now a second, perfect copy of Lester. She figured it was best to go along with the madness, even though she was quite anxious.

"Ummm... what do I do? What do the kids do? I don't understand what's going on, Lester."

The director poked his head out from the camera.

"Paula, your motivation is that you're a robot space witch who is trying to conceal your identity from everyone, except your husband, of course. He's just come home from a long day at work and you're trying to make him dinner but you're having serious problems on account of you being a robot space witch," instructed Director Lester.

This version of Lester had a more brusque delivery than the normal Lester. In fact, he gave a bit of a grumpy, matter-of-fact aura.

"Oh, and the kids?" she asked.

"The kiddos will be trying to eat your food, but they hate it because they're human and you're not," replied Director Lester.

"Wait, my character has kids? Isn't that impossible, being a robot space witch and all?" she asked, confused.

"Ma'am, do you know anything about robot space witches?" asked Director Lester with an agitated sigh.

"No."

"Then what's with all the questions? Let's roll people. Got a show to make," Director Lester yelled loudly to everyone on set.

LESTER

"Paula, you go stand at the stove. Actor Lester, I need you outside of the door. Kids you sit at that table over there and pretend to be eatin' whatever junk your mom has served up," ordered Director Lester.

Everyone scrambled to their places upon command. The kids seemed to be having the most fun, sitting at the table playing around with the fake food, smiling the whole time. Paula was still nervous, but gradually came to the idea that, much like the video game situation, this was one of Lester's powers and it reminded her of being a kid, pretending to play house. She felt as though she was transported back in time, waiting to make fake food at her fake stove and oven with her play kitchen set.

"And we are rolling in 3! 2! 1!" said Director Lester as he pointed at Paula.

"Oh uhhh. I sure can't wait for– my husband to be home–" said Paula nervously as she had no script and was purely improvising. She had remembered that, much like being a kid, you make things up as you go along.

Suddenly, the door swung open. Where once there was silence, the entire set now filled up with laughter and applause but there was no audience or speakers. The sound scared Paula and the kids to death. They all jumped. It was surreal standing in a room with five people and hearing the sounds of over one hundred people clapping away, including some whistling. The whole time, Lester was standing at the door, soaking in all the attention and applause, nodding his head in appreciation.

"Well, I'll tell ya, sweetie. It's been a humdinger of a day," said Lester.

Realizing she had lines, Paula broke from staring off, trying to find the invisible audience.

"Oh uhhh, what happened... dear?"

"I didn't get the darn promotion and on top of it, Charlie mistook my presentation as a donut and ate the whole thing. I had to redo my whole entire presentation with only five minutes to spare, and all kindsa wacky shenanigans ensued."

Paula paused at this.

"How– how did you do a presentation with only five minutes to spare?" she asked, baffled.

"No idea. It wasn't really in the script and–" Lester could see Director Lester angrily shaking his fist at him furiously.

"Soooo how's that dinner comin' along?" Lester asked, moving on from his previous gaffe.

"Oh, it's going swell. I think," she said, nervously smiling, still trying to improvise as best she could.

"Mmmm mmm that smells… wonderful," said Lester, clearly lying.

"Heck, it smells so good we probably shouldn't eat it," Lester excitedly said to a wall of laughs from the imaginary audience.

The kids were laughing as well.

"Oh, well, Lester. I spent all day long cooking this dinner. It would be a shame not to eat it," replied Paula.

"What is it?" asked Lester.

"Ummm… oh!" –she examined the pile of fake meat– "It's pork loin. I think."

"Well, now that we've established I'm vegetarian, how are my boys doing over here?" said Lester to another round of big laughs.

Out of the blue, music started playing. It was clearly the theme song to the show with a classic band style score, reminiscent of the old black and white TV shows. Without warning, an announcer's voice came on over the music.

"Iiiiiit's The Lester Shoooooow!" said the booming voice.

"Starring Lester as Lester!"

LESTER

Lester flashed a big smile and waved, with a huge roar of applause from the audience.

"Also starring Paula Facehaver as Paula Lesterrrrrr."

The zoomed in camera showed Paula looking around, confused for the mystery announcer as the applause continued.

"And Robert Facehaver as Kid Lesterrrrr."

Robbie sat at the table, smiling, looking around as sounds of adoration from the crowd poured in.

"And Rodney Facehaver as Ferret Lesterrrrrr."

The camera quickly cut to Rodney who was looking around with his brows furrowed, mouthing in confusion "Ferret?" which garnered a few laughs among the applause.

Big letters slowly lowered from above in front of the set that spelled L E S T E R. Huge shouts of joy and clapping from the audience followed up the big letters and, shortly after, the letters were drawn back up to a thunderous applause.

Paula could see that the SILENCE sign was now on to quiet the crowd, and the quiet of the invisible crowd was eerily instant.

"Well, my little pookie pie obviously I can't eat those hockey pucks you got goin' on over there, so I'll just have to check in the cabinet," said Lester, fussing around in the cabinet.

"Oh, and what is this that I see?!" said Lester excitedly.

"It's Lester-o's! My favorite!"

The camera zoomed in on the box which had Lester's face on the front, smiling like he just won the lottery. Behind the smiling face on the box was a bowl full of miniature Lester faces.

"Oh man, this cereal right here is packed with all kindsa things n stuff. It's got vitamins, minerals… rocks. Everything a body needs to grow big and strong."

Lester flipped over the package to reveal a big bulky muscular version of himself.

MY HERO

"You'll be kicking sand into people's faces, push-upping, start randomly bench pressing people you don't even know!"

He turned to Paula.

"Go ahead and try some, sweetykins,"

Lester offered the box to Paula as he held his giant car salesman smile.

Paula willingly stuck her hand out, waiting for Lester to pour the cereal out. She popped the cereal into her mouth and, almost involuntarily, started spitting the cereal out. It tasted like sawdust, one of the worst things she had ever put in her mouth. This drew the ire of Director Lester which led to Lester making an attempt to fix things.

"Oh yeah? Well, you're just some roboty witchy space person that no one in the audience needs to pay no mind to," said Lester, attempting to sway the imaginary audience.

"In fact, I'll show you!" Lester then attempted to eat the Lester-O's himself.

"Oh boy. That's–", he looked for the right words.

"Edible," Lester said, as he kept his smile going while his eyes contradicted that smile with their own grimace.

This of course drew more fist shaking from Director Lester who was grumbling, red in the face with anger.

"So just remember everybody. Lester-O's. Edible!" Lester said as he threw the cereal box out the window.

"Well anyways, now that I'm done snacking on– that stuff. I never had a chance to ask you about your day," Lester said to Paula.

Before they all knew it, a door opened and every bit of black and white had been replaced with color, all the furniture updated back to their current versions, and all their clothes back to normal.

Reality was back.

It was all due to Anthony, who walked through the door after a long day of work. He was none the wiser to what had been going on, as everything had transformed almost instantly, back to the way it was.

Everyone had stopped dead in their tracks from the confusion of their world turning from 1950's sitcom to modern times. Everyone's mouth was ajar, which led to Anthony giving everyone a blank look.

"Uhhhh, everything okay around here?" he asked.

Paula, the kids, and Lester all looked at each other for a moment.

"Yeah, everything is… fine," said Paula, thinking about her answer.

She was between the idea of telling her husband, hoping he might get a kick out of what just happened, but also siding on caution, assuming that he might not like what happened at all.

Anthony still did not know that Lester had transported their children into a video game much less that he had transported them all decades back in time into black and white TV land. It might be a bit too much. She decided to take things slow with Anthony. He was already itching to get Lester out of their barn and their life.

"We were just in the middle of playing around. We'd been sitting on the couch, showing Lester the wonders of television," Paula said, trying to cover up their little adventure. It was at least half true, she figured.

This was a good enough answer for Anthony. Times were odd, considering there was a magic humanoid lemon-colored alien hanging out in their house these days, so seeing everyone with a look of shock on their face as he walked in the door was now the most normal part of his home life. Judging from his demeanor, Anthony was not irritated by Lester. It was more like a member of the family getting a dog that was their responsibility. They were peacefully cohabitating.

Lester did not seem to mind at all. He appeared to be grateful that Anthony let him stay, despite his otherworldly presence. Almost anyone else would have freaked out and called the authorities, even if that being had saved their offspring from a murderous pig.

Anthony came in between the kitchen and living room to see how the kids were doing.

"Kiddos, what's the word, eh?"

"Oh, we had a lot of fun with Lester today," Robbie yelled out with a big smile on his face.

"Is that right?" Anthony looked at Paula with his eyebrows raised. Paula knew it was an unhappy look, but the kids and Lester were none the wiser.

"Robbie continued on, "Yeah, dad. We played video games, gave him a tour, played–"

"House!" Rodney interrupted his brother.

"Is that true, Lester? Did you have a lot of fun with the kids today?" Anthony asked Lester, still eyeballing Paula.

"Yes, sir! Totally did not go to a 1950's black and white alternate universe," Lester blurted out nervously.

"Wait, what?" Anthony looked at Lester confused by the statement.

"Inside joke!" Paula blurted out.

"Hey. Dinner. How about dinner eh?" Paula was trying to distract Anthony from Lester's statement and it seemed to work.

Anthony had a long day and Paula knew that food was the best way to lure him from further conversation, especially if his mouth was full. As Anthony wandered into the kitchen, Lester piped up again.

LESTER

"Why not give him some tasty, healthy Lester-Ooooo's!" said Lester with a big smile on his face.

This made Paula and the kids burst out laughing. Lester started belly laughing in response to his own little inside joke.

"Lester-O's? I don't think I get it," said Anthony, looking around confused, smirking.

In between his laughter, Lester replied, "Oh, trust me, you don't wanna get it!" This made Lester, Paula, and the kids laugh even harder.

They were all practically in tears which only further baffled Anthony as his smirk got bigger. He wanted to get it, but eating was a bigger concern.

"Well, no one is dead, or on fire, so I'm not even gonna ask," Anthony said, slightly chuckling.

"Can we eat already?" Anthony continued, still smiling, looking around at everyone as they were winding down from their laughter.

After dinner, the family settled into their nightly routine of watching TV. Every so often the family would take turns to go visit Samantha in the master bedroom. This was the one place in the house she appeared somewhat comfortable. This was the one place where she whined the least, even if she was still anxious. Lester seemed to be on his best behavior, sitting in the corner, soaking up all the TV he could with his eyes wide open, just staring at the screen, continually asking questions.

The evening ended with Lester going back to the barn with his own little bag of candy. Paula had talked about fixing up the barn for Lester so they could make it more comfortable for him which made Lester extremely happy. Touchdown dance included. Everyone was in bed and ready to get some shut eye.

Later that night, as the house lay silent and peaceful, Paula had a terrible nightmare.

She dreamt that the house was empty. She spent what seemed like hours looking for anyone, and it was pitch black.

MY HERO

Paula was confused and crying, looking for her loved ones where none could be found. The house phone rang out in the dark silent house, making Paula jump. Part of her was relieved to hear something alive in the house. The other part of her was apprehensive. She found herself slowly creeping over to the phone, as if it might bite her if she answered it.

"Hello?" she said as she picked up the phone.

There was silence on the other end of the phone. As she listened for anything on the other end of the phone, she could hear a faint noise. The noise grew louder, but it sounded muddled, as if someone were talking underwater.

"Hello? If someone is there, I can't hear you on my end."

Paula held the phone tighter against her ear to hear anything. The phone became suddenly louder, causing her to jerk her head away from the phone.

"The funeral was as good as a funeral could be," the voice on the other end of the phone said.

The voice was very familiar to Paula, she had heard it her whole life. It was her sister, Denise.

"Denise? Hello? Denise, it's me!" Paula frantically said into the phone. There was no reaction to her words though, just the caller still rambling on.

"Robbie. Rodney. Anthony. They're in heaven now. I'm hoping you don't have to go there too. I'm not ready to see you leave me," Denise said in a numb delivery.

This made Paula start to shake her head furiously.

"No! No! You're lying!" yelled Paula.

She slammed the phone, ending the call, and stood in her cold, empty house, looking around for signs of life that would never be seen again. Paula could do nothing but cry her eyes out, heaved over like something was burrowing its way into her stomach. It was the knot of anguish twisting in her stomach, and she had never felt anything like it before.

LESTER

Paula was startled by the ringing of the phone. Assuming it was her sister, Paula picked up the phone as fast as she could. In the time since she had hung up the phone, she was looking for a voice, any voice of comfort to relieve her pain. The news was so sudden, she thought she was already crazy or might go crazy from the sudden shock.

"Hello, Denise?" she asked, crying into the phone she clutched in her hand.

"Mom? Is that you?" asked a small voice over the phone. It was a bad reception, the voice was distorted, moving in and out of clarity.

"Rodney? Robert? What… who is this?!" she hysterically asked.

The voices continued on the other end of the phone, but it was slowly drowning away, becoming more muddled by the moment, making the voices incoherent. She pleaded into the phone to give her one more sound of her children, but the voices were finally gone.

Alone, in a dark house, she sat on the floor with the phone in her hand, wishing she could just see or hear her children one last time. It seemed as though she had just been playing with them but somehow this was her reality, completely unaware that she was in a nightmare. It felt so real. She truly wished, in that moment, that she could die.

Then, the phone rang again.

Paula scrambled around to pick up the phone and ended up dropping it. Finally able to get a grasp on it, she picked it up and yelled into the phone.

"Kids?! Is that you?!"

Instead, she heard another voice on the other end.

"Whoa, whoa. Calm yourself down li'l missy," said a high-pitched voice on the other end of the phone.

"Lester? Is that you? I'm– I'm confused…"

"Well shucks you don't need to be confused. You're stuck in a jam of strawberry proportions. A dang dirty dream. A nightmare!" said Lester.

It suddenly dawned on her that it was very dreamlike. She started to piece together the fabric of her reality, finally realizing that it was in fact, all a terrible nightmare. As she started to realize this, Lester started to crawl out of the phone.

"Just a moment. Dang diggity candy got me packin' on the pounds and now I can't even fit through a telephone anymore," Lester said as he struggled and wriggled out of the telephone's mouthpiece.

Now promptly on his feet, he looked at Paula with a smile on his face.

"Why don't you let me help you up ma'am?" said Lester with his arm stretched out.

She accepted his hand, and she was back up on her feet. She noticed that the sun outside was coming up, but it was more majestic than it had ever been, like something out of a movie.

"What do ya say? Wanna go for a little flyover?" he asked Paula.

"That's impossible, Lester," said Paula.

She looked back at Lester and noticed he was suddenly wearing what looked like a Superman outfit but instead of a big *S* in the middle, it was a big *L*. *L* for Lester, of course.
This made her start to smile, and her heart filled with joy. Her heart felt as radiant as the oversaturated sun that lit up the dreamy sky.

Even in her sleep, this new being was there, helping her get through things, even this pain, this guilt she had hidden from those around her. The bad dreams would never stay that way for long apparently. Not when Super Lester was around, that is.

LESTER

As they flew over the world, looking down at the gorgeous landscape, Paula took in all of the ethereal beauty around her. Flying felt so liberating, like nothing she had ever experienced before, even in her best dreams. This was different. Controlled.

They finally set foot at a picturesque orchard with fruit hanging off every branch and bush. The sun, still breathtaking, laid upon their skin, saturating them with warmth. Still in his Super Lester suit, he went to grab the shiniest berry that Paula had ever seen but was met with resistance by a squirrel who also wanted the berry.

"Listen li'l fella that's my strawberry and I saw it first," said Lester to the little ornery squirrel.

Unexpectedly, the squirrel furiously spun in a circle, faster than the eye could blink. The squirrel was now wearing a Superman-like outfit as well, now decked out with huge muscles, bulging out of the suit. The squirrel flew up, eye level to Lester with its arms crossed, and an angry look on its face.

"Whoa, squirrely. It's not a big deal," Lester said, backing away.

"Why don't you go on and take that berry?" he continued, making a gulping noise in obvious fear of the super powered squirrel.

Lester reached into his own super pockets, "And my wallet, my keys, oh and my shoes," he said nervously as he started to take his super boots off.

The super squirrel was happy with just the berry though. He plucked it off, blew a raspberry at Lester, and then flew off into the distance with loud, heroic music parading behind it.

"Well, I guess we're not the only ones dreaming tonight," laughed Paula.

MY HERO

"Well hotdog on a stick, what a little stinker," said Lester scowling in the direction of the long gone super squirrel.

"I tell ya I could've given him the ol' how d'you do if I wasn't feeling so darn generous!"

Lester looked around nervously for a moment.

"You think it heard me?" he said, looking scared, now ducking behind a tree.

"No, I think you're safe, Super Lester."

"Good for its own sake, cuz I would've messed it up some," he said, now emerging heroically from behind the tree.

"Lester, how do I get out of the dream? I know I'm in it, but I want to wake up," asked Paula.

"Oh! Well, you just have a password, a codeword, some kinda word thingy that you use as your li'l anchor," responded Lester.

"Geez. I dunno. Maybe gobbledygook," she said.

"Oh boy! I love gobbledygook!" laughed Lester.

"Why don't you go ahead and try it out now, see if you don't wake up," Lester said to Paula, encouraging her.

Paula stood back, brought her arms in, and with a loud yell she shouted "GOBBLEDYGOOK!!"

Her eyes opened. She was in her bed, awake now.

"The trick worked," She excitedly whispered to herself.

With a grin on her face, Paula realized she now had a way to awaken from any bad dream. Still, she had no idea if Lester was actually in her dream or if she had merely dreamt of Lester. Either way, she was happy with what she had learned. Paula could not describe it, but she felt invincible. She wished everyone could feel the way she did.

With a few hours left to sleep, Paula went back to bed with peaceful, happy thoughts swirling around in her head. She felt safe and renewed.

LESTER

"Everything's gonna be all right," she thought as she fell asleep.

In fact, "It's going to be great!"

SIR CHARLIE CHEESEBURGER

The weeks passed. Lester had become closer to Paula and the kids. They played around with Lester and taught him all sorts of things. In turn, he had brought them on many an adventure within the confines of their land. Not many people made their way out to the property but, when anyone did, Lester was good at hiding away. Occasionally though, Lester would pull little pranks on any salespeople that happened to stop by.

One day in particular a pushy vacuum salesman would not accept no for an answer from Paula.

The salesman was a short, portly man with glasses, a fedora, and a burly mustache. The man was exactly what Paula had pictured a stereotypical door-to-door salesman to look like. From the onset, she was met with a lot of artificial, pitchy banter.

"Well, how do you do, ma'am, on this here fine day?" attempting to sound far more charming than his appearance let on.

Gauging that the pitch was right around the corner, she apprehensively replied, "Oh I'm doing okay, and judging by your enthusiasm, I imagine you are, too,"

The salesman laughed in an exaggerated fashion, putting his body into it. Nothing was that funny, especially what Paula had just said. It annoyed her.

"So, how can I help you today, buddy? You lost?" Paula asked.

"The name's Clyde and I am certainly not lost because I've come to your house today with a very special offer. The offer of a lifetime honestly," he said, looking around at the property, rubbing his hands together.

"I highly doubt it," Paula said, still listening to Clyde the cologne-heavy salesman out of pure curiosity.

"I have noticed that this particular property is very far away from town."

Clyde looked around at the vastness of nature, spread his arms out to indicate the emptiness of the surroundings.

"Enthusiastic and observant!" Paula said with a smile, trying to hide her irritation through veiled humor.

"Guilty on all counts," Clyde laughed again.

"But let me be serious for just a moment, ma'am, if I may," he continued.

"I can't imagine that you make it into town very often. I cannot even begin to imagine that you have time to maintain your vacuum, assuming that you have one," he said with a very serious face.

Paula did not need a vacuum. In fact, she already had one she paid too much for some years ago, and if she did need an upgrade in her carpet cleaning, it was not going to be from this guy.

"Clyde, is it? I am really sorry but I'm just not in the market for a new vacuum cleaner. Really appreciate you stopping by though."

It was the nicest, most diplomatic way Paula could think of getting him off her doorstep.

Clyde laughed again.

"Oh, ma'am, I can tell you are really going to make my life difficult," he said with a big rosy smile, still aiming to make the big sale.

"Now, I can't totally do this because I could get into really big trouble. Bosses, right?" he winked at her, "But I am willing to give you a full ten percent discount on what I've got sitting inside of my trusty station wagon right now."

Continuing to get more annoyed, Paula attempted to end the conversation again, "No honestly, I'm good since I–"

Clyde cut her off before she could speak.

"Now, if you could just see it, I think maybe that'd change your mind, ma'am. Hold on just a second."

Before Paula could protest any further, Clyde the salesman fumbled around in the back of his station wagon. His mode of transportation was a beat up, tacky, old, car; much like Clyde himself.

"TADAAAA! There she is in all of her glory. Bet you don't have anything like this in that house of yours."

It was a very shiny vacuum. Silver, steel, rigid, like something that was modern back in the 1970's. It was nowhere nearly as functional looking as her jet black vacuum that turned on a dime with cyclone technology included. This thing still had a bag on it. Paula's eyes could not roll any further into the back of her head.

"You can't be serious?" Paula asked with an eyebrow raised.

"Oh, she doesn't look like much, but if you let me come inside and demonstrate what this baby can do, I just know you'll be convinced."

Clyde put the vacuum down and stood proudly beside it, awaiting permission to enter into the home and 'wow' her with this zenith of house cleaning technology.

"Listen, I've been very nice to this point but I'm going to have to insist on no. I'm seriously not interested, okay," Paula said in a stern but still polite voice, attempting to get her point across before she tossed diplomacy out the window.

"Ma'am, what do I have to do to get this fine vacuum inside your home?" he obnoxiously retorted back.

This made Paula's eyes visibly roll this time and she attempted to maintain her composure, "For the very last time–"

LESTER

"That's it. You are a terrible salesman," said a third mystery voice.

The salesman looked around confused. This had gained the attention of Paula as well.

"Did you hear that?" asked Paula.

"I did. No idea what it was but I definitely heard something. Hey, maybe it's some divine intervention perhaps?" Clyde laughed.

"It's definitely a sign if there ever was one," he continued, snorting as he spoke.

Paula wished for something, anything to stop the guy from talking because apparently using manners was not getting it done. She hated the man now, his rosy fat face, and the mustache that sat upon it. She wanted to rip the mustache right off.

"Hey, bozo! I said quit while you're ahead. Perhaps you should sell hearing aids instead," said the mystery voice again.

"Seriously, what is that?" asked the salesman to Paula.

"Sounded like it came from your end," said Paula as they both looked around, confused.

They both looked at the vacuum. Their ears had both mutually focused on this one item. There was no way they could both possibly be hallucinating so they inspected further, and they both leaned in to examine it.

"MEEP! MEEP!" yelled the vacuum, and it quickly scooted off.

It moved around much faster than anyone might anticipate for a vacuum. Though the situation was odd and defied reality, the salesman instinctually ran after the vacuum.

"Pardon me ma'am, they don't normally do this. I apologize," Clyde yelled running down the driveway after the rogue vacuum.

Paula stood in her doorway, and watched the portly middle aged man run down an empty road after his now sentient vacuum. She could not stop laughing at the sight which was only made funnier by his yelling, "Come back here!" at it frantically.

"How does a vacuum suddenly come alive and run away all on its own?" she thought to herself. The answer was fairly easy.

"Leeeeester!" she said, still half-laughing.

"What? What? That could've been any ol' person who made a house vacuum suddenly come alive and run off and chase its dreams!" insisted Lester, who came slinking out from the kitchen.

"Nice touch with the roadrunner bit," she said, still smiling.

Lester chuckled.

"Yeah, I think that guy's gonna have about as much luck as that coyote does trying to catch that thing," said Lester, making them both laugh.

This was only a small example of the kinds of things going on at the Bowline residence over the course of weeks since Lester had started living in the barn which was now fully decorated. Lester had some of his own furniture, a mishmash of things brought over from the house and garage that just took up space. Now cozy, Lester truly felt at home in his little house.

The barn often became a popular hangout for everyone when Anthony was at work. Sometimes at night, Paula and the kids would go to the barn for a slumber party where scary stories could be exchanged.

One night in Particular, Paula told her scary story a little too well and it saw Lester and the kids running off into the night screaming.

Paula told the story in the darkness of the night armed with only a flashlight. As she began to tell the story she placed her lone source of light under her chin to up the scare factor.

LESTER

"What I have to tell you all needs to be kept a secret. I've never told it to anyone before, but I am telling you now for your own safety. Tonight, I am glad we are out here in numbers because alone you wouldn't stand a chance."

Paula paused and quietly looked around the barn as if she were scared.

"You see, I grew up here. You kids probably didn't know that."

The kids shook their heads in unison indicating they had no idea. Lester just looked at the two children shaking their heads and then back at Paula with his eyes wide open, already with a look of worry.

"Yes. We left this farm a long time ago after the incidents that occurred long ago on a night not unlike the one we're having tonight. It was myself, Denise, and our young brother, Johnny."

"You had a brother?!" blurted out Rodney with his eyes bulging out of his face.

"Yeah. Did. 'Did' being the key word."

Paula stood up and started to slowly walk around telling her story.

"You see, one night when we were out in this here barn, doing something very similar to what we're doing right now, we heard noises. Initially, we just blew the noises off. Must be the wind making the tree branches move, perhaps a loose door. No one was volunteering to go take a look, to see what the noise was. So, we stayed in the barn, pretending not to hear it, pretending to be safe."

Paula kept walking around, feeling various parts of the farm's pillars as if she were reminiscing.

"Finally, the noises became too much, too loud. It had to be investigated."

Paula turned her back to everyone.

"Denise and I both decided that we would go outside and see what the noises were. We insisted that Johnny stay inside where it was safe," Paula continued, doing a great job of acting by sounding sadder and more somber as she continued her story.

"We went outside, and it wasn't windy at all, not a gust, not a breeze, just still air. The trees did not sway, and no door was out of place. It was perfect. This, of course, only made things worse because it meant that there was in fact an intruder among us."

The kids and Lester all huddled together, getting shoulder to shoulder, looking around in the darkness with terror written all over their faces.

"Denise and I knew we had to get back into the barn, not only for our own safety but we also needed to get to Johnny because he too was in danger. As we opened the barn doors we saw Johnny, but he was shaking violently, as if he were freezing."

She took a long pause, inhaling and exhaling slowly.

"Denise wanted to know why he was so cold, but he said that he wasn't. Johnny said the reason he was shaking was because of the man that was behind him. He told us that behind him stood the Behind-The-Back Man and he was waiting this whole time to get him into the darkness, so he could take him away forever."

Paula still had her back to the trio and was pretending to sniffle, trying not to laugh.

"Denise and I both knew if we could just shine our flashlights on him, the Behind-The-Back Man wouldn't have the darkness he needed, and Johnny would be safe. We raised our flashlights up, confident we could save our little brother but, just as we did, the lights died out. They were fully charged but for some reason, the lights flickered and died."

Lester and the kids were beyond terrified now. In Lester's case, his body was shaking like he just stepped out of a freezer, the kids clutched him so tight they risked cutting off circulation to his arms.

"Without warning, my brother was sucked backwards into the darkness. He couldn't even scream. He was there one minute and gone the next, like he never existed. Just gone," Paula said with a trembling voice.

"We stepped backwards, into the moonlight so that we would be safe. We couldn't yell or protest, we were just frozen in fear, unable to move. Finally, a voice came out of the darkness and said to us 'You can never escape your fate, for behind you I will always wait'."

Paula was silent again. The kids and Lester waited in anticipation, frozen in fear just like the sisters in the story. As if things could not get worse, Paula's flashlight appeared to flicker.

This was no accident as, unknown to them, she toggled the power switch.

"We ran out of the barn as fast as we could!"

Paula slowly turned around with her face down.

"Every day since then, my sister and I have known that every day, every night, he's behind us waiting for his chance to–" she looked up at the kids and Lester.

Suddenly her eyes got wide with a look of sheer panic. She was looking past the three of them, as if she saw something behind them and yelled.

"NO! NOT AGAIN!"

Without warning, the flashlight died.

Lester, Rodney, and Robert all yelled at the top of their lungs. They all gave Paula quite the show as she could hear the kids and Lester furiously scrambling away from their spot, charging past her, heading to the barn door in panic. As they did, Paula could not help but laugh, which did not register with the scared bunch, and they all went bursting through the barn doors to reach the safety of the moonlight.

As they made their way out, Rodney and Robbie stuck together, standing in the most well-lit spot they could immediately find. Lester on the other hand did not handle things so well, running through the barn doors and then down the driveway with seemingly no intention of ever stopping.

"Monsters in closets! Behind-The-Back men! I am gettin' outta this madhouse," he yelled. As he ran with his hands outstretched, he could be heard screaming in the darkness as he now bolted down the main road.

It took a while, but eventually Paula, Rodney, and Robbie were able to retrieve Lester. She was able to calm everyone down and let them know that there was no Johnny and there was certainly no Behind-The-Back Man. This was enough for Rodney; Robbie was only half convinced but Lester was another story altogether.

Lester had to have everyone stay over for about two nights after that. He kept looking around all the time for the "Behind-The-Back Man", turning around every so often to try and find the creepy specter he believed was now behind him at all times. He looked somewhat like a dog chasing his own tail. Every so often Paula could hear Lester complaining "You won't get me nappin' boy," to the imaginary Behind-The-Back Man, he could swear was creeping up on him.

Still, even with these little hiccups, it was always fun around the house. Paula felt young again, like a child. There were sleepovers, the eating of bad food, games, things like hide n' go seek, they had tents, and she had become closer to her kids in the process. They could not remember seeing her this laid back and carefree probably ever. For Anthony, you could see he appreciated the change which crept into their lives in every facet; mentally, emotionally, physically.

The one question that kept popping up each day, and never left the minds of everyone around.

"Where was Lester from?"

Lester certainly had no idea. If you asked him, he would just blankly look off in wonderment, still frustrated that he had no recollection of his own life before ending up with the Bowlines. He even felt like there was something important he was supposed to do, which made it that much more frustrating. For now, at least, he had accepted the only thing he could do was enjoy the time he had with his new family.

The only family member that still did not cozy up to Lester at all was Samantha. She still whined constantly and, if Lester was near, she would act as if someone were trying to murder her. When she went to the behavioral therapist, they were hard pressed to find anything wrong with Samantha. The only idea that came up was the introduction of a new "person". Even if that person was brand new, perhaps unresolved issues from before were made only stronger by his presence.

This left one too many question marks, so Lester staying in the barn was something that worked out for everyone involved, especially Samantha. They all loved the family dog, so they wanted her to be as happy as possible. Lester understood his role and stayed away from her at all costs, never going in the house, unless invited inside.

Everything was seemingly perfect. Even Anthony had backed off a bit about having Lester leave. Perhaps it was because of Paula's stretch of happiness since Lester's arrival or simply Anthony being too tired to fight. Either way, it took the pressure off Paula for the time being.

Unfortunately, harmony was about to be tossed on its ear when the family received a knock on the door one day. When Paula answered it, she could not believe her eyes.

SIR CHARLIE CHEESEBURGER

"SURPRISE!" yelled the person on her doorstep.

Paula was equal parts happy and horrified to see her sister standing before her with a big smile on her face. Behind her stood her entire family, most of them looking not quite as enthused as Denise.

"Hi there, sis. What uh– what's going on here?" Paula asked, looking around at everyone. She noticed Karl waving at her from outside of the family RV.

"Well, life is too damn short. You know, after what happened with you. I thought it would be great to stop by and spend some time with my little sister before hitting the open road with the family for a grand tour of the country in about a week or two, or at least most of it," Denise smiled.

"Oh, you know, as excited as I am to see everyone; this may not be the best time," she said to Denise.

Paula noticed the smile on Denise start to dwindle. Denise had clearly gone through a lot of trouble to come out and it was obvious she was trying to reconnect with Paula. Truth be told, Paula probably wanted that more than Denise even did. Lester was the main concern, but she could not pass this opportunity up because Denise was right, "Life's too short."

"But we'll make it work!" Paula continued much to the elation of Denise who regained her smile.

"Oh, get over here, you," Denise moved toward Paula and wrapped her up in a tight embrace.

Paula did not even think twice, hugging Denise just as hard. It was a genuinely beautiful moment between the sisters. Even Denise's kids were smiling at the completion of the sisterly reunion.

Overnight, the house had become stuffed full of people. Denise's husband, Karl, and their three children, Gina, Dani, and Chris now filled out every little nook and cranny of the Bowline residence. Ill prepared for the sudden addition to their home, the

LESTER

Bowlines had to discover a way to make things work. The other issue, the biggest one, was figuring out how to keep everyone away from the barn.

If Paula made the barn an issue, she felt as though she might draw extra attention to it, giving Denise's kids something forbidden to desire during their stay. The kids would naturally want to know what is in said barn and exploring they would go. Denise and Karl might ask a few too many questions as well.

On the other hand, Paula could not just say nothing about the barn. It was off limits even before Lester arrived and now, with him having his own residence within the barn, it was imperative to keep everyone away, so Paula had no choice but to mention it. She did so almost in passing.

"Oh, by the way, everyone, the barn: I have to warn you in advance that you'd better stay away from it. We rent it out every so often and work really hard to keep it clean for any visitors. You know, a little extra income here and there."

That was the way Paula explained it, and it seemed to work well as no one asked much about it afterwards. Surprisingly, and to Paula's relief, they appeared to have no interest.

Perhaps Lester thought that the family might get ahead of themselves and accidentally discover him. Even if the kids showed little interest, he wanted to leave nothing to chance. So, Lester took it upon himself to get ahead of everyone else and introduce himself to the relatives.

Enter Sir Charlie Cheeseburger.

One night while the Bowlines and the relatives were at the dinner table, there was a knock on the door. No one was expecting company, so this drew some confused looks. Paula got up from the table as everyone chatted amongst themselves. Upon answering the door, to her amazement, she was greeted by a man dressed in a traditional tuxedo with a bowler hat. His face was fairly round, his hair was white, and he had a big white mustache. Paula had never met the man before in her life. Taken aback, all she could do was stare at the man.

"I'm sorry, are you lost?" Paula asked him.

"No ma'am, to the contrary. It appears that I have been found," he said in an accent that, to most Americans, could be passed off as British.

"I was just passing through and was wondering if you might have some shelter and food for an ol' chap such as I, on my adventuring through this great country of yours?" asked the man with a jolly demeanor.

Paula could only stare. She had no idea what the man was talking about. Was he homeless? Was he an adventurer? Why would he be randomly walking down her long, winding road at this hour? Before she could answer, he would continue.

"Oh yes, how terribly rude of me. Allow me to introduce myself. I am Sir Charlie Cheeseburger the third. I come here from the land of England, exploring your great United States of America for my own personal leisure you see. Tally ho, bangers and mash, wouldn't you know it that I lost my way and ended here at your very doorstep," he said to Paula with his perpetual jolly grin.

Paula took a moment, still puzzled.

"I'm a little confused. Did you need to borrow a phone? Ask for some help?" Paula asked.

"Oh, heavens no, not at this hour, my good woman. I knock upon your door at this most inconvenient of hours to ask if I may stay inside your barn, pending that there are no other occupants that I might offend."

"Oh uhhh. You see it is occupied–" said Paula who, before finishing her sentence, was cut off.

"Gotcha!" said Sir Cheeseburger in a very high-pitched voice. He winked at Paula, and then she knew - it was Lester!

LESTER

"Oh my god, Lester! What are you doing?!" she nervously asked.

"Don't worry, ol' chaparoo, Lester's got this. Well, ol' Charlie Cheeseburger does anyhoo," he proclaimed, winking at her.

With that, he waltzed into the house.

"What a lovely home, and thank you so much for inviting me in," he said, looking around the house as if it were his first time.

"Paula, who is this?" asked Denise, still sitting at the dinner table with everyone else.

"Oh, pardon me, my good lady. I am Sir Charlie Cheeseburger the Third, and would you believe it? This kind lady here has offered me room and board in her delightful barn just within view of this fine domicile," he said, still looking around at the rather fine homestead.

"Oh my god, that is so nice of you Paula! Did you need something to eat, Mr. Cheeseburger?" asked Denise.

"My good lady, it is Sir, and, if it is not too much trouble, I shall join you for what looks like an exquisite assortment of most tasteful delights."

"Sir! Sir Cheeseburger, it is no trouble at all. You pull up a seat, there is enough room and food for everyone!" responded Denise, clearing off a chair for him.

"Ma'am. I am truly honored," said Sir Cheeseburger, bowing his head in appreciation.

As he walked to the table to go sit in the chair that Denise had readied for him, he looked back and winked at Paula, as if to say, "We got this!".

Paula was still a nervous wreck. As good as his intentions may be, Lester may have landed them in a worse situation. Over the weeks, Paula had discovered that while Lester's magic was powerful, it only lasted so long. If his magic gave out at any point, he could be compromised, and Paula was going to have to give her relatives one hell of a story, if they did not all die of heart attacks that is.

Sitting down at the dinner table, Denise and Karl had a lot of questions for the newcomer. They had never met anyone from England before. Even their kids seemed genuinely interested in everything he had to say. At one point questions arose as to who he was, where he came from.

"Oh, I must say that this is not quite proper table etiquette I'm afraid but, in the name of being a good guest, I shall tell you what your inquiring minds wish to know," said Sir Cheeseburger, twirling his mustache.

"You see, and I am so very ashamed to admit this, but I am a lesser known member of the royal family who has decided to take a trip, away from it all you see." Sir Cheeseburger really caught the attention of the room with this remark.

"Royal family? You mean, like the 'Queen of England' royal family? Kate? Princess Di?" asked Denise excitedly.

"The very same family! Yes, indeed, my good lady," responded Sir Cheeseburger.

"You see, for many years I have served as the Archbishop Duke of Blimeychunder. Day in and day out, all I do is count all of my money, and have tea and crumpets, occasionally watching the football match on the telly– sorry, 'soccer' on the 'TV', as you Americans call it."

His audience was captivated.

Paula was standing behind everyone else in the kitchen, doing some dishes, trying as hard as possible not to laugh as tears streamed down her face. The best part, she thought, was that Anthony, Rodney, and Robbie all had no idea who Sir Charlie Cheeseburger really was. She was the only one in on the joke. She listened on, chuckling as he continued his story.

LESTER

"Bored with my simple life, I knew that I had to escape the confines of my luxurious prison in Blimeychunder. I had to take life by the teabag and squeeze it until it bore no more juice. Yes, I had to set sail and discover the world!"

He thrust from his chair in dramatic fashion, pointing his finger at the sky. He looked around at his audience, who sat quietly, entranced by his tale.

His face then turned solemn.

"Alas, I did not know the consequence of my transgression. For you see, the royal family put out a hunt for me. Alive or dead, I do not know how they are to bring me back to Buckingham Palace, but I can assure you, either way is most displeasing you see."

Everyone sat in stunned silence, eyebrows cocked everywhere, confused faces. As Sir Cheeseburger gazed upon his stunned audience, he smiled warmly.

"For you see, this is why I am taking the byways of this lovely country, ending up in places like this, laying low from, how do you say here? 'The fuzz' I believe", he paused.

"If my intrusion brings any concern I can simply go about my business and leave you fine folks alone. You took me in, not knowing my story and I would hate to bring any worry upon you," he said, continuing to smile.

Instantly, Denise and Karl spoke up.

"No, no!" using their hands to wave him down, implying for him to stay put.

"Don't you worry at all. Right, Paula?" Denise asked her sister.

"Oh, of course. We are honored to be in the presence of Lord Sir Charlie Cheeseburger the fourth," replied Paula with a big smile on her face, still trying to hold back her laughter.

"The third, ma'am," Sir Cheeseburger interjected, correcting Paula on her error.

"The third!" she continued, unphased.

SIR CHARLIE CHEESEBURGER

"In fact, if those tallywackers come a knockin' here, I will punch them right in their Queen loving faces. Oh yeah. Take a bullet if I have to!" Paula stated with her fists raised.

"DEEELIGHTFUL! I shall take you up on your kind offer," Sir Cheeseburger said, clapping in Paula's direction.

Everyone laughed as Paula made fake punches at the air. It was settled, everyone thought. Sir Charlie Cheeseburger the third was going to stay there for an indefinite amount of time, inside the barn, where hopefully he would remain undisturbed.

Later that night the whole family practically had a party. The young kids were amped up on soda and treats while the adults had been imbibing on their adult beverages. Music was playing in the background as people talked loudly, and Sir Cheeseburger the Third showed the children some of his dance moves, which was mostly some poor variation of the Charleston because that's apparently how the royals danced, according to Sir Cheeseburger.

Unfortunately, things went awry when at one point Sir Cheeseburger went over to ask for some candy. As he spoke, his regal British accent started to disappear, and in its place was Lester's high-pitched delivery, alarming everyone. He tried to brush it off as the air being dry and affecting his voice.

Quickly, he rushed off to the bathroom. Once inside, his whole face started to morph into a yellowish color, his eyes got bigger, as did his head. He was changing back!

Paula excused herself to go check on their guest. Once she got into the bathroom, she was horrified to see that Sir Cheeseburger was now Lester once again. Lester tried morphing back into Sir Cheeseburger, but it was no use. They sat in the bathroom for what seemed like an eternity trying to find a solution. He had made his presence known to everyone, and his disappearance would certainly raise some suspicions.

LESTER

In the meantime, while they pondered their lack of options, Lester took it upon himself to eat the candy that he had grabbed before taking off into the bathroom. It was about a minute in when Lester was chewing, and he started to transform again. The bowler hat, the mustache, it was all coming back.

"No wonder he loved it so much! The candy was giving Lester his power, it was his fuel. Like Popeye eating his spinach," Paula thought to herself.

Lester was strong enough once again to keep up his ruse as Sir Cheeseburger. He roared in excitement and went back out to go meet his adoring public. Paula stayed back for a moment to get her nerves back in check.

"Crisis averted!"

Later in the night, shortly before bed, Paula took Anthony and the kids outside for a small talk, away from the relatives.

"So, kids, what do you think of Sir Cheeseburger?" Paula asked with a big smile on her face.

"I like him, he's funny!" blurted out Robbie without even batting an eyelash.

"Robbie's right, he's hilarious, even if I have no idea what he's talking about half the time," Rodney added to Robbie's take on Sir Cheeseburger.

"I'm going to let you both in on a secret, but you can tell NO ONE. I'm only telling you two because I trust you can keep your mouths shut and also, so you won't be confused over the next few days, weeks, years, however long my sister is staying here."

The kids both looked at Paula, intrigued.

She whispered, "Charlie Cheeseburger is really Lester."

Both of the kids started hysterically laughing out loud.

"That's awesome!" said Rodney with tears in his eyes, still laughing, holding his gut.

SIR CHARLIE CHEESEBURGER

Paula's biggest worry was how Anthony would take the news but, to her shock, Anthony was laughing as well. He got a real kick out of it. For Paula, it was good to get it out of her system with some insiders, after having held back laughter for what seemed like an eternity.

After a few minutes of uncontrollable laughter, the kids wiped away their tears and calmed down.

"I soooo can't wait to watch the rest of this," Rodney said to Robbie.

Robbie giggled, "Yeah, I'm not saying anything, I wanna see what he does next."

"We will ALL keep our little secret," Anthony added.

"Let's make sure we keep it cool like Fonzie, guys. It's one thing to keep a secret but you can't make it look like we're hiding something either," he told the kids.

"Act natural?" asked Rodney.

"These two dweebs are pretty weird so they should be okay," Paula said, sticking her tongue out at her sons.

Paula knew everyone was capable enough to keep the secret, and besides, she did not have much of a choice. They would all start to wonder where Lester ran off to. Might as well get it out of the way. Plus, it would have sucked for Paula not having any co-conspirators to share the joke with.

Before bed, Denise had insisted that Sir Cheeseburger stay inside. The barn was no place for a man of such great status she protested, but Sir Charlie Cheeseburger told her that he wanted the American experience of staying in roadside barns.

He even made up some elaborate story about barns not existing in England, at least not in Blimeychunder, where, according to him, electricity was a new thing. Paula laughed at the politeness Denise and Karl showed even in the face of the most ridiculous statements from Sir Cheeseburger.

LESTER

Her sister was certainly no dummy, so Paula wondered how much was Denise being overly polite and how much was Denise being fooled by Lester and his elaborate tales. He could be quite charming.

The weekend was a smash and, thankfully, all the relatives avoided the barn area. Everyone had respected Charlie Cheeseburger's living quarters enough, allowing him to revert back to his Lester self for at least a few hours.

Every day, usually around ten in the morning, Sir Cheeseburger would be out and about with everyone. It typically consisted of grand tales about his previous adventures leading up to his being at the Bowline residence. His favorite thing was to talk about his land of Blimeychunder.

"Yes, yes. You see, in Blimeychunder we have the world's biggest ball of ear wax, located at the Earwax Museum, right next to Dapper Danny's pub. All may contribute to the great ball. It is perhaps our biggest source of income in all of Blimeychunder."

These were the type of far-fetched, impromptu stories that Sir Cheeseburger regaled his company with on a day-to-day basis. The visitors found them immensely entertaining of course, and it made Paula nervous, hoping Lester's elaborate ruse would not be discovered.

Of course, Lester knew nothing at all about England, other than what he had seen on TV. He figured the relatives had no idea either so he could say whatever he wanted. If they asked any questions or challenged him, well, he was from England so what would they know? He's the Lord Archbishop Duke of Blimeychunder!

Unfortunately, at one point Paula and Anthony were approached by Denise, who finally started having suspicions. Denise was a smart, educated woman and her politeness could only go so far. When they relayed this to Lester, he came up with a plan to throw off little miss smarty pants, Denise.

"Oh, Denise, I am so glad that I caught you."

Denise had been sitting outside just relaxing when she heard the voice. It was the familiar voice of Sir Charlie Cheeseburger that called out to her. When she turned around to greet him, he was holding something in his hand, what looked like a brochure.

"My good lady I do hope the morning has treated you well, I do say," Sir Cheeseburger greeted her.

"Oh yes, very much so. What do you have in your hand?"

"Wouldn't you know it? With all of this talk of my home of Blimeychunder, I just happened to have a brochure on hand in case you ever wanted to visit my charming little area."

He handed the brochure to Denise and, sure enough, there it was, a full color brochure of the mythical Blimeychunder. There were random photos of people with little to no teeth smiling, sheep wearing human clothes and hats, something looking like the great ball of earwax that Sir Cheeseburger had mentioned before. It looked even more disgusting than she had imagined.

Inside the brochure, on the inside sleeve, there was what was supposed to be a few lines of text promoting Blimeychunder:

Tally ho and salutations!

Do you envision yourself being on top of a tall hill overlooking a quaint British countryside? Well, here at Blimeychunder we have tall hills, but all of the views are obscured by an endless, dense fog. It is a fog lover's paradise with a fog so thick you will need your very best cheese knife to cut through it I dare say.

LESTER

Denise looked confused to say the least.

"Thank you?" she said, still looking at the brochure, clearly baffled by what she had read.

Attempting to dissuade Denise from any potential visits, Lester pointed to one particular highlight in the brochure.

"Oh, you must simply read this part. I do so find it descriptive about our charming locals."

According to the brochure, in Blimeychunder it is law that any disputes be solved by drunken fighting and that no one was safe from this policy. The record for longest fight belonged to two elderly ladies who took more than an hour to thrash each other. Given the description of the fight it was like something from a professional wrestling match with walkers being thrown around, headlocks, and denture marks all over each of their bodies.

Denise was utterly terrified by this.

"Yes, yes. I remember this battle quite fondly as, you see, I was given front row tickets to this squabble. It only ended when Margaret grabbed Doris and gave her, what her son referenced as, a "German Suplex". I'm not terribly privy on such barbarisms but, my word, it looked quite painful, and Doris did not get back up. Well, not until it was time to go to the pub of course. Everyone gets up for the pub," said Sir Cheeseburger so cheerfully.

"Oh– that sounds like a lot of– fun," Denise responded with a slight look of horror on her face.

"Also, one important term to know is the term 'chum chicken', which refers to anyone that is afraid of the local lake sharks that infest Great Blimeychunder Lake."

This further horrified Denise who had a look on her face that yelled "What in the hell kind of place is this?!"

He told all manner of outlandish things to the relatives during their visit. This had all members of the Bowline family running off into various places of privacy, so that they could laugh to their hearts content. The Chum Chicken story in particular saw Paula curled up in a ball in her bed, laughing in tears after overhearing him outside with Denise. Lester must have had some serious powers because somehow, he never once broke his straight face.

Unfortunately, the brochure had not been quite enough. Denise still made more inquiries about Blimeychunder, complaining to Sir Cheeseburger that she could not find it on the internet. It was particularly annoying to Paula who wished her sister would stop playing detective. Lester apparently found it as an opportunity for further fun.

"It is a shame that you can't see the majestic land on the magical world wide web," he said sadly.

"Unfortunately, you will never be able to find my land on any internet as the people of Blimeychunder are EXTREMELY anti-technology!" he said with his eyes wide open.

He then drew himself closer to Denise and her family, as if to speak in secret.

LESTER

"Truth be told, if they ever caught wind that the internet had posted any information about them, well, they would sue," he said quietly.

"Who would they sue?" asked Karl, looking puzzled.

Lester looked surprised.

"My good man - The entire internet!" he loudly said.

"These are serious people, I dare say!" Lester got up from his chair and paced around the room.

"Up until the twentieth century the townsfolk still considered roads to be a tool of the devil and they would furiously round up any cobblestone and have it burned at the stake!"

Denise, Karl, and all of their children could only stare in fascination.

"Now this is true that the cobblestone did not feel pain as such, but it was, I assume, the principle of the whole thing," Sir Cheeseburger told everyone.

"Plus, truth be told, I think it was just an excuse to get together and drink. Did I mention how popular the pub is?"

Drunken old ladies fighting over petty grievances, lake sharks, inanimate objects being burned at the stake, the disturbing amount of drinking. The relatives were equal parts confused and horrified by each tale. They seemed to be convinced that this could be a real thing given Sir Cheeseburger's unwavering delivery of each absurd tale. It was either all a bit exaggerated or Sir Cheeseburger was crazy. They had no way to dispute all of the information though, as much of it was documented in the very fancy brochure that Sir Cheeseburger had given them.

Even with that, everyone did really enjoy the company of Sir Cheeseburger as he was extremely pleasant and well-spoken which had a calming effect on everyone. He was the life of the party, often getting everyone involved, elevating the mundane to magic all within the blink of an eye. The kids loved him, especially with his amazing magic tricks which seemed oddly impossible, even for an illusion. Denise and Karl recommended he be a magician; give up the life of a Lord Archbishop Duke for his real passion. Sir Cheeseburger claimed that his passion was traveling, and that magic would only pin him down.

There was only one bad apple in the bunch of the relatives and that was Cousin Gina, the bratty thirteen-year-old who had been bullying the younger Rodney and Robert. No one could do much to curb this because, unfortunately, the two boys had not told anyone they had been bullied, not wanting to be tattletales.

Lester, however, had somehow caught wind of this and decided to take charge over the situation.

One night while everyone was asleep. Gina had been awoken by sounds coming from outside of the bedroom in which she and her brothers had been sleeping. Careful not to wake anyone, she wanted to investigate the noise that had been keeping her up through the night. Gina walked out down the hall and towards the mystery sound.

"Hello?" she whispered to the dark empty hallway with no response.

"Hello? Really? What, like, a frickin' ghost is gonna holler back at you?" she muttered to herself.

Upon inspecting the sound, it got louder and louder, leading her into the kitchen. She had determined the noise was coming from the refrigerator. To her, it was quite deafening, she was surprised no one else woke up.

"The fridge huh? Well, I could use a little snack since I'm out here. So long as it's not something made by Aunt Paula," she said, reaching for the handle.

LESTER

When she opened the door, she heard someone talking. Her eyes got small as she clinched her brows in confusion.

"Pssst! Down here," whispered the voice.

As Gina looked down, she wondered if she was losing her mind. She looked around for a voice that should not exist, especially inside of a refrigerator. Gina shook her head, attempting to shake the cobwebs out. She had been tired but now, she was awake and sharp. The noise in the fridge had stopped and she stood still, looking around, wondering where the noise had gone. With the room dead silent and no one around, she heard the voice again.

"Hey, woman! I said git on down here!" the voice called out.

Gina jumped as she looked down, shocked to see a sandwich talking to her, flapping its pieces of bread like human lips at her.

"If you mess with them kids again, this salami sammich is gonna flip da script and eat YOU!" it yelled out at her with all the sandwich cadence it could muster up.

Gina screamed, slammed the refrigerator door, running off, and ran back to her room as fast as possible. As she ran, she could hear the voice behind her.

"I know where y'all live! Don't make me come after dem feet!" threatened the sandwich that ran behind her, after her feet.

Screaming and running through the house, Gina woke everyone up. She finally made it back into the bedroom, slamming the door behind her. The entire family had come out to see what all the fuss was about. Her parents knocked on the door.

"Gina, open the door! What the hell is going on in there?" demanded Denise.

Gina flung the door open.

"It was the sandwich. It wants my feet!" said Gina, visibly shaking.

SIR CHARLIE CHEESEBURGER

She looked down and noticed the sandwich was on the floor just at the threshold. The sight of the sandwich made her hysterical and she jumped onto her bed instinctually.

"You can't have my feeeeet!" she yelled at the sandwich, prompting concerned looks from everyone, especially her parents.

"Girl! Are you on drugs!? It is a sandwich," said Denise. She went over and picked the sandwich off the floor.

"See, look, it is bread and some salami," Denise said as she walked towards Gina with it to show Gina there was nothing malicious about the sandwich.

This only made things worse as Gina crept back against the wall.

"Get it away from me!" she yelled, kicking the sandwich out of Denise's hand, which landed on Karl. He looked none-too-pleased with his new salami hat.

Gina did not manage to sleep much for the rest of her trip, but she did not bug the brothers for the rest of the time she was there. The brothers could not figure out their new fortune until one day when Gina bumped into them.

"Oh my god, I'm soooo sorry. Really sorry. Okay. I didn't mean to," Gina said erratically, looking around in a paranoid fashion before quickly walking off.

Rodney and Robert looked at one another. They said nothing but gave each other a bewildered look.

Hearing someone clearing their throat, they looked over and saw Sir Cheeseburger, who looked back at them and winked. It was just then that the siblings understood exactly why Gina had such a drastic change of heart. She had been motivated by a friend. Or at least by a sandwich.

The weeks passed and, soon enough, the relatives were on their way out. They said their goodbyes

"Sir Cheeseburger. It has been… something," Denise said, trying to find the words to describe her interactions with the eccentric yet charming Lord Archbishop.

"If we are ever in England and I see Blimeychunder… Well, we are going to keep driving right through, she said as everyone laughed.

"Driving through? But I've got money on you to win your new visitor meet and fight," Sir Cheeseburger responded, looking a little let down.

"Yeah, we will just have to do lunch," –she paused– "In another city,"

"Well, I'll be sure to bring some of our finest culinary delights, m'lady."

"Maybe put them in an Email attachment from the sounds of it," Denise joked.

"All righty, well, no Haggis and tree bark tacos for you," Lester said back with a slight smirk.

"I can honestly not tell if you are joking," said Denise as she stared in legitimate confusion, nervously smiling.

"Well, either way, I will certainly never forget you, Sir Cheeseburger. You are most certainly" –she paused again– "one of a kind."

This made Sir Cheeseburger smile as he said nothing and simply bowed at the waist to her.

"Kids, you make sure to watch after your mother, here. She is doing an amazing job," said Denise with a genuine smile on her face, looking directly at her sister.

"She's doing awesome. We're really super proud of her," Rodney surprisingly chimed in.

It caught Paula off guard. Tears threatened to swell up in her eyes from the small comment.

"Yes, she is, Rodney. I'm proud of her, too," Denise said, agreeing with her nephew, continuing to smile.

She leaned in and gave Paula a big hug.

As Denise embraced her sister, she whispered into Paula's ear.

"Never forget this moment, okay?"

Still fighting back tears, Paula shook her head up and down.

"I won't. Not ever," she said quietly back to Denise.

Having had their moment, Denise and Paula recalibrated themselves.

"And I am going to miss the rest of you as well," Denise said to Rodney and Robbie, which made them both smile.

Both of the kids ran in to get their hugs from Aunt Denise and their Uncle Karl. There would be no hugs for the cousins though, so they settled for a series of waves and head nods. Gina, still traumatized by the sandwich incident, politely put her hand up and nervously smiled at them. She was trying her best to behave and give a proper goodbye.

"We will see you soon. I promise," Denise said one last time before getting her family into their family RV.

Everyone waived and said their goodbyes as they drove off down the road with the rising sun accentuating their path.

Paula knew that it was all a bit much to take in, being crammed in with everyone over the past few weeks but she missed her sister and her family. She could not remember the last time she felt that way about her sister. Now with everyone gone, their place would become quieter again, and would probably feel almost empty with all the additional space back.

One thing was certain though, Sir Cheeseburger could now retire, and Lester could come back to his normal form. Once he did, he felt out of sorts with his old body, and he had to do some stretches to fit back into his bones. He seemed to have enjoyed the past few weeks, and the company.

LESTER

"Well, I'll tell you what. Those were some good ol' fashioned down to earth homecookin' folks right there. I'm sure gonna miss 'em," said Lester with a big smile.

"Oh, and they'll definitely miss Sir Cheeseburger," Paula said back with a smile of her own.

With that, Lester grew a little mustache and looked at her.

"Well, well, madame, we shall all undoubtedly miss his royal cheeseburgerness m'yes"
He slightly bowed his head.

"Cheerio I say. Pip! Pip!" he continued, walking away to his barn with his nose in the air.

Lester liked people, and Paula knew it was almost criminal that he had to stay hidden, but it was for his own good. It was impossible to live on candy forever and no one would understand him. His appearance alone would cause terror. She had pondered if Lester could at least go out into the world, disguised by magic, even if just for a tiny bit.

For the most part, it seemed that Lester was perfectly content hanging out at the property. He seemed aware of the dangers that lie beyond the confines of his home. Paula had been worried that her sister and her family's presence would have made him long for more, but it did little to disparage him. He still walked around with his big smile and happy-go-lucky attitude.

As the weeks went along, Lester found ways to entertain himself and everyone else. Samantha, the family dog, still had zero fanfare for Lester. She continued to whine anywhere near Lester's presence. Lester tried making peace with Samantha from time to time by offering treats or pets, but only experienced barking or whining that always ended up with her running away from him.

Gradually, she became more aggressive towards not only Lester, but everyone else around the house. She seemed extremely agitated all the time. This was never more evident than one day when Paula could hear Lester yelling from another room.

"Ow! You bit me!" Lester yelled out.

When Paula arrived, Lester was holding his finger, looking somewhat scared with his big eyes looking at Paula as if he were in trouble. Samantha remained some feet away growly loudly.

"What the hell happened?" Paula inquired.

"I was coming through the hall, and I noticed the doggy had dropped her biscuit. Well, I tried to be all neighborly-like and hand it to her, and that's when she went for my biscuits instead."

Lester was still holding his hand, massaging it.

"You're hurt? I didn't think you could get hurt."

"Oh," Lester giggled.

"Guess it's just a reaction. My fingers are feelin' fine, swanky in fact. I think my feelings are hurt a lot more than anything. This dog really hates me," Lester stated matter-of-factly.

"Well, I still don't know why but I'll go ahead and get her to safety, poor little thing," Paula remarked as she walked over to grab Samantha's collar.

Suddenly, Samantha bit her too.

"Shit! WHAT THE FUCK, SAMANTHA?! Now you don't like me either?" Paula held her hand like Lester did just a few moments ago. In her case, she actually was holding it and rubbing it to comfort herself. Samantha had nipped her good.

Samantha continued to growl and snarl.

The kids had come out from their bedrooms to see what all the fuss was about. As soon as they did, Samantha turned her attention on them and started growling at them. Her hair almost appeared to be raised, like an angry cat.

"Kids. Don't move a muscle. Lester, you go ahead and go out to the barn."

The kids did as Paula said, and Lester, without replying, sneaked off as quickly and quietly as he could. Samantha barked even though the conditions were more fitting for her.

With her attention still focused on the boys, Paula snuck up behind Samantha, grabbed her collar and dragged her off to the master bedroom. She tried being as gentle as she could with the dog, but Samantha thrashed around violently, trying to get away from Paula's grip.

As Paula closed the door, she could hear Samantha continue to whine.

"All right, guys. I don't know what's going on, but do not go in that room. Also, say nothing to your dad when he gets home, okay? I'll talk to him about this."

The children just nodded their heads up and down. They looked at each other, worried.

"Mom is Samantha gonna be okay?" asked Robbie.

"Sweetie. Yeah, I think she'll be fine. She's still adjusting to Lester and maybe the vets were wrong. We're all gonna find out as a family what's wrong with her and get her back on track. Together."

Paula was lying, of course, as she had no idea what had been going on with Samantha but the last thing she wanted was for Robbie to worry about his little buddy. Rodney knew. She could see it on his face, but he, too, hid the lie to spare Robbie his feelings.

"Yeah, Robbie, it'll be fine. She just needs some rest is all," Rodney said as gave his brother a soft, friendly pat on the shoulder.

SIR CHARLIE CHEESEBURGER

Rodney's body language did not match his words at all, which made Paula that much more appreciative. It was admirable that he sucked up his own confusion and feelings, for that of his younger brother, putting on a brave face.

As Lester's stay continued to be extended, Anthony started to question Paula more about what the plan was for this magical stranger that they still truly knew nothing about. One night in particular, it came to a head before they were going to bed when they got onto the subject of Lester.

"So, Paula, what is the endgame here with Lester?"

"You know, I'm not really sure. I haven't looked that far out into the future and whatever I come up with stinks. There's no good answer," Paula said, looking off in thought.

"Well, we have to come up with something, and soon, because he's a nice enough guy… thing… but staying here just isn't a permanent solution," Anthony shot back at Paula, looking slightly agitated.

"I mean, we got really lucky when your sister came by weeks ago that no one found him out, especially after his Charlie Cheeseburger stunt, but we can't keep this up forever. This is way beyond us," he continued, looking frustrated.

"Anthony. What do you suggest we do, just kick him out? He's got nowhere to go, and we can't hand him over to the authorities. You'd be sending him to his funeral," Paula said, becoming agitated herself.

"Yes, but we haven't explored any next steps. This can't be our sole problem. I mean, he loves the world, he can disguise himself, right? So why not send him out there, he can be his own problem, ya know?" Anthony looked at Paula, hoping for some compromise.   Becoming increasingly angry, Paula pursed her lips.

"Okay. First of all, Lester is not a 'problem', as you call him and, two, we're not going to just ship him out into the world unprepared. At the very least, if he wants to, we need to train him or coach on doing that. He's like a kid, he's still not ready."

Paula was pleading to Anthony in a sense, hoping he could see things her way.

"Then get him ready, Paula. You guys are here all day long. You should be able to whip him into enough shape where he can get out into the world and leave us in peace. You say he is not a problem but we're the ones that are having to keep everyone and everything at bay for this enormous secret sitting out in our barn," his voice raising.

"He will leave when he is damn well ready, if at all. We didn't put him in that barn and keep him a secret just to kick him out now or down the road. He's a part of this family now. What's that say about us? I mean, his first act around here was to save the damn kids from that pig. You forget that?" Paula slightly raised her voice as well.

"No, I didn't forget nuthin', but whatever we owed him, the debt is now paid goddamnit."

Anthony got out of bed looking ready for a fight, his face red with impatience.

"He's a swell thing but we're not just putting up a friend or even a transient, Paula. We have something that isn't human and probably not even of this world hanging out in the barn. This is big. Bigger than we are!" Anthony shouted, his face getting redder by the moment.

"You know what. This is the end of this discussion. He is staying whether you like it or not. He earned his spot in this family. We will figure things out but, for now, it's up to us to protect him from whatever's out there."

Paula was going to stick to her guns no matter what Anthony thought or how angry he got. She knew she was right in the matter and had to stand up for her dear friend, Lester.

"Oh yeah, and what about Samantha? She's not been herself since Lester came into our lives. Now she's gone from the endless whining to growling at people, biting at people now; she's losing her goddamn hair from all of the stress, she barely eats. That's certainly not normal at all. Not for her," Anthony yelled.

"That dog was sick before Lester and she's going to continue to be sick, Lester's got nothing to do with it. Stop trying to find all of the different ways to badmouth Lester. He's a good, holy being. He's pure. If you're jealous of him or spiteful of his good nature, well, that's your problem but stop trying to press your issues on him. Lester stays! You're just going to have to learn to make peace with that!" she yelled back at him, her face defiant.

Anthony looked at Paula for a moment, silently. He said nothing as he grabbed his pillow and went into the closet to grab a spare blanket. He headed towards the bedroom door.

"If you need me, I'll be on the couch. This is bullshit, Paula. I have a say here too, you know."

To his credit he did not slam the door, attempting not to wake the kids up, even though they likely heard the arguing from their parents' bedroom.

The next day, Lester was none the wiser about the argument or Anthony wanting an exit plan for him. He met the day in his usual way and even saw Anthony off at his truck.

"Well, hidey ho, Anthoroni," said Lester with a big grin, waving at him.

Lester was met with indifference as Anthony said nothing, ignoring him as he shuffled around his equipment before slamming the door and taking off.

"Well, I'll be a cold cup of coffee. Get a load of Mr. Big-bad-grumpy-sad-pants," Lester said, as he watched the truck take off in a puff of dirt. He understood that something bad had happened between Paula and Anthony, which left him looking at the morning sky with his eyes shifting around in thought.

Paula, alone in her own thoughts, knew that they might have to consider a next step for Lester because, even though she was carried away in the moment, Anthony was not wrong that they could not care for Lester forever. Life happens and, in the case where no one is around to protect Lester, he would be left to the wolves anyways. It was, however, something Paula thought she could save for down the road. Things were good right now and she could not recall a time in her life when she was this happy.

Every single day was like being surrounded by magic. There was laughter, playing, creativity, endless amounts of fun. She had not had a single drop of alcohol since her accident, and she attributed some of that to the presence of Lester that helped her reconnect to her inner child. She was closer to her children, even if she seemed to be growing distant from her husband. Paula would find her way back to Anthony, she just had to guide him. She just needed to convince him of the magic and light that is Lester.

Her plan was to reconnect with Anthony by getting away for a weekend. Just a few days away from everyone and everything. Perhaps she had spent so much time around Lester and the kids that Anthony did feel a little jealous and his plans to push Lester out were more propelled by emotion than actual logic. She thought it might not be a cure, but it could certainly be a band-aid, giving Lester more time at their residence so she could formulate some kind of a plan down the road.

She called her sister Denise up, knowing she had been back for some time from the big family trip.

"Oh, so just the weekend?" Denise asked Paula on the other end of the phone.

"Yeah, Anthony and I just need to get out for a bit, the place is getting a bit crowded around here with the kids and Sir Charlie Cheeseburger."

"Is he still there?" Denise was surprised.

"Oh, no. He actually left for a bit, but he came back because" –she thought of a quick lie– "the Blimeychunder special forces or, whatever they are, were hot on his trail, so he came back to lie low for just a tiny bit."

"There is something weird about that guy. I like him but his stories just do not add up to me," Denise said in a questioning voice, still suspicious of the gallivanting Brit.

"Oh, he is definitely weird but he does mean well and he's awful nice so I wouldn't go looking too much into things," Paula told Denise, hoping to dissuade her from further Lester inspecting.

"Well, I guess you are right, but I have never ever heard of a Blimey–"

"Can you do this or not, Denise?" she interrupted Denise.

"I'm sorry?" Denise inquired, sounding a little upset.

Paula paused and closed her eyes to refocus herself before choosing her next words. She did not know what to say without unveiling her true ambitions, but she also did not want to bullshit her sister any longer.

"Truth is, I need for us to get away for a bit, like, really bad, you know," Paula pleaded with her sister, channeling her desperation through her voice.

"Is everything okay over there? I mean, with you two?"

Paula paused again, thinking of maybe a lie to candy coat her marital issues. She still had time to reel it in. In this moment though, Paula was feeling emotionally raw and did not care.

LESTER

"I don't know to be honest. I've been so focused on… the kids and Samantha that I don't think I've noticed that my marriage is in the total shitter," Paula said to Denise, starting to cry a bit.

It was completely unexpected, and it caused her to sniffle, loud enough for Denise to hear, whom she was trying very hard to conceal her woes from.

"Oh God, I am so sorry, sis. I thought things were going great when we came over, but I guess there is always more than meets the eye."

"Yeah. Yep. Been going on for a while and I never really cared to see it. He hasn't touched me in months, I mean even a kiss or anything, it's like he's angry at me. Not just whatever is going on now but maybe it was this way before the accident, and I never gave enough of a shit to notice."

Paula started crying even harder, trying to muffle her cries so no one else in the house would hear her. It was bad enough that Denise was hearing her. She felt pathetic and ashamed to be letting any of this out. She wished she could hang up the phone and rewind time to put it all back in the bottle.

"Jesus, Paula. Do you want to talk about it? I can always call you back tomorrow when I am not inundated with all of this work. I can make the time," she asked Paula with genuine care. Paula could feel her sister's sincerity as she grasped the phone.

Paula thought on the question and realized that she had disclosed too much. Though she could not put everything back into that proverbial bottle, she could prevent more from spilling out. It was a moment of weakness.

"No. I appreciate it. The only thing I can do is go on this trip and, I dunno, have some us-time and just restart–something."

"Sure. I get it. I will go ahead and take care of the kids and your barn guest over the weekend," Denise calmly said to Paula.

"Thank you, sis. This means the world to me," Paula responded back.

"Paula. If you change your mind and want to have that talk about that, or anything else… I'm here for you. Could have that conversation tomorrow if you are up to it."

Denise left the invitation open in the air for Paula to grab. Though she thought about it for a moment, Paula chose to close the bottle up for good.

"I really appreciate it, sis. I do have to go, but I appreciate that and the offer to chat."

"Well, okay. I will be there first thing in the morning on Saturday. I will get all of your tidbits then?"

"Yeah, sis. I'll talk to you then. Okay. Bye."

After hanging up the phone, Paula sat on the bed wondering about the trip, Lester, the complexities between her and her sister. She could have opened up and they could have had a conversation about a lot of things, not just her marriage. They had started to patch up the old wounds and reconnect but, why could she not be honest? She sat on the thought for some time but could not find an answer.

Her thoughts shifted over to this big trip. It was supposed to be a romantic getaway or at least a way for Paula and Anthony to get away from everything and perhaps elicit old emotions from a better time. It would be a trip in a cabin in the woods, by the lake. Pure heaven to the both of them.

The only problem is that the trip never happened.

The day before they were supposed to leave, Paula and Anthony loaded everything up into the truck. The truck would not start up at all. This struck Anthony as odd considering it had been running just fine the previous days. As he inspected the truck, he realized everything was fine, nothing was wrong, there was no reason for it to be acting up at all. However, he had an idea on why the car magically had issues all the sudden.

"It's him, Paula," Anthony angrily grunted at Paula.

"Who? What are you talking about?"

"Goddamnit, Paula, it's Lester. There is not one damn thing wrong with this truck. I've looked all around this thing for two hours now and there's no reason it shouldn't be starting."

Anthony tossed his toolbox into the back of the truck.

"I'm no mechanic, but I know my way around a truck well enough."

"You just said it yourself that you're no mechanic. Perhaps it's something you don't know about without getting into the car like the carburetor, alternator, pistons, whatever the hell else I don't know anything about. I mean, we should have it looked at instead of just going off about Lester. He's not even here, he's in the barn as Charlie Cheeseburger," Paula attempted to rationalize with Anthony.

"Jesus, Paula. Are you blind?" he angrily asked.

"His magic is probably stronger by the day, who's to say he can't multitask. He can do whatever he wants just thinking it!" Anthony said in an angry, hushed tone, careful that no one could hear him.

Paula was speechless. She wanted to believe her husband but, at the same time, she knew Lester well enough. There was nothing sinister about him. He even wished them a great trip and said he would make sure everyone was taken care of while they were gone, or at least Sir Charlie Cheeseburger would.

Paula's lack of speaking gave way to Anthony closing his utility box and walking away without saying a single word. He was visibly frustrated and angry. He showed no intent of kicking Lester out but, to Paula, it appeared that the situation was headed towards an impasse. She feared there would be an ultimatum to choose between the two and she would be the bad guy that kicks Lester out. She hated the idea.

Later that night, after having called Denise to let her know her babysitting would not be needed; Paula sat in her room, wondering what might happen next. She mostly wondered about the strained relationship she had with her husband.

Lester was just another wedge in their relationship that had started back when she was drinking heavily. Paula had known that he started using work to get away from being around her so much. She knew he never cheated on her, as that was in contrast to Anthony's character. The biggest reason was to nurse his own sanity. Whatever sanity he may have had with an out of control, unhinged Paula.

The way she figured it, he had dived into his work and even as Paula had gotten better, it was likely that he had fallen out of love with her through all the struggles, likely staying around for the benefit of the kids. They seldom spoke, rarely were they intimate, and she knew the seeds of this indifference were planted firmly during her drinking days.

She still loved him and wanted things to be like they were, but that was years ago. They had practically become nothing more than roommates up until the crash. Once she had gone through her rehab and gotten better, the scare of her mortality had worn off and things went back on autopilot.

The scary thing to her is that she had never even noticed it, it had eroded so slowly. On her end, she had wondered if Anthony maybe even hated her, even though he acted like he at least tolerated her. He was never mean to her but perhaps Lester was the last straw. He had tolerated so much and got his peace back and in comes this stranger who becomes the star of the show. The stranger has to be looked after, cared for, lies have to be made up, elaborate plans constructed. Paula, sitting by herself, came to see things as Anthony might.

She just wondered if, armed with this knowledge, she could reverse course and how she could do it. She had been fooling herself by imagining some weekend getaway could fix things. It was going to take more, and maybe there would be an ultimatum up ahead and, ultimately, she would have to choose her husband. As good as Lester had been, she would have to start the process of seeing him off at some point. She had no choice.

Just as Paula was contemplating just what she was going to do, she heard a tapping on her door.

"Come in," she replied.

It was her sons who entered the room both with their eyes bright.

"Mom. Lester wants to talk to you. He said he's got a plan for you and dad," Rodney said, jumping on the bed with Robbie at his side.

"A plan? Oh, I don't think he can fix this, kiddos. Your dad and I are… okay" –she paused– "we're just having a bad spell; you know like when you two argue. Same thing," Paula smiled, lying to her kids, knowing that it was much worse, but she put on a happy face for their sake.

"But I will go see what Lesteroni wants," she said as she got up to leave the room.

Once outside, she was met by Lester. Her yellow friend held aloft a kind smile and bright, innocent eyes. Paula smiled back and wondered what crazy idea Lester might have cooked up, and how she might humor it.

"Paula. I think Lester might have a great idea for the two of you. I know you were both hoping to get away, but that darn chicken bone of a truck done thwarted your plans," said Lester, pacing around as if he were giving a presentation.

"If you can, I want you and ol' Anthony to meet me out here, first thing in the morning with your nicest clothes on. I won't lie. What I got planned will take a little faith, but I think it can be just the Hail Mary you both might need."

Paula was still smiling, listening to what he had said. She was skeptical that Lester could do much in the way of help. She assumed it would involve some of his magic and humor to try and cheer them up, lighten the mood, not something long term. Without much to lose, she figured she might as well give it a shot. Nothing was getting better between the two, even if Lester were to leave tomorrow. She needed that Hail Mary.

"You know, Lester, I'm not sure if Anthony will go for it but I'll try to convince him as best I can," said Paula with her head pointed at the dirty ground, still smiling, still the brave face.

"Things are a little complicated with adults, you know. You'll just have to accept that this might not go the way you hope, you wonderful creature, you."

She looked back up and smiled at Lester.

"Well Adults are just big kids," he said.

She mulled over what he said to her and then looked into the night sky.

"You want to hear something honest, Lester?"

Lester's face perked up as he listened to her.

"Time is a motherfucker," she said, not wavering or blinking as she looked at the stars.

"Time has a way of wiping the smile off of your face," Paula added, feeling the tears attempting to push their way out of the ducts. She held them back though, angry at their insistence.

Lester put his hand on her shoulder as she continued to stare up, almost defiantly.

LESTER

"Goodnight, friend," Lester said as he gave her shoulder a small, reassuring squeeze and walked to the barn, leaving Paula alone with her thoughts.

As he did so, Paula wondered what he had planned. He had no way of understanding the complexities of any relationship, especially an adult one. The worst part is that she would have to get Anthony onboard, who was already combative and not particularly fond of Lester. If Paula had to put her faith in Lester, then Anthony was going to have to put his faith into Paula. She was taking a massive leap of faith off a cliff, she felt.

"Adults are like children. We really never do grow up, do we?" She sadly thought to herself, looking into the stars of the summer night still wondering what crazy idea Lester had concocted.

COOTIES

The morning came and it took seemingly forever to get there. Paula fell in and out of sleep the entire night. Anthony was lying beside her, but he may as well have been in another room with the aura he gave off; one that was icy and distant. Before they were at least being good roommates. Now there was an emotion not felt before between the two of them - anger.

"You don't truly realize how much you care about someone or love them until they've shunned you. Even if you don't truly care for someone, it can be a feeling that stings like no other, but especially when it is someone you care about, someone who once truly loved you."

"How do you go from being the most precious thing in someone's world to the thing they can't wait to discard?"

These were some of the thoughts that had rolled around in her head. Paula almost wondered if she would have been better off dying in the car accident. She did not truly believe that, but she felt it in the moment as her heart was hurting as never before. Feeling as though she had sleepwalked through a portion of their marriage, waking up to the realization that it might not last was far more sobering than not drinking. Before now, she had not seen it coming. To her, his not saying anything at all was the writing on the wall. It was just a matter of time.

Paula knew that whatever Lester had planned, it was not going to work. She would have to convince Anthony to go along with a plan he wanted no part of with a woman he no longer wanted at his side. As the sun crept through the blinds, she could feel him behind her shuffling around on his side of the bed. It was the worst part, what she was dreading - having to break the silence.

LESTER

Nothing is more uncomfortable than being the first to speak after such a long pause, after the feeling is anger or sadness, enabling yourself to be the first to be shot down. She knew also that what she was to ask could make things worse. Still, she had to ask. These were desperate times.

"Hey, sweetie," Paula said as she turned over to see Anthony, whom she knew to be awake.

Anthony's eyes were half open. He was not sleeping but he was still at least resting. Paula had trouble getting a read of his emotions and she hoped for the best.

"Hey," said Anthony, looking tired and agitated.

"How'd you sleep?"

"Fine," he replied, emotionless.

The lack of conversation made Paula even more nervous. Things did not appear to be off to a good start.

"This will sound weird but, can you do something for me?"

She spat out the words nervously, hoping she would not look foolish in her next question. She had no pull or power over him anymore. Anthony would have to be agreeable to anything she asked next.

Anthony pondered what the question might be, perhaps assuming it would be a monumental task she might request.

"What is it?" tersely he replied.

"Don't ask too many questions but, after you eat, can you get dressed in something nice and meet out front?" Paula timidly asked.

Anthony squinted his eyes and looked at her in confusion.

"I know it sounds crazy, and I don't really know what to expect, but we're going on an adventure. No idea what kind of an adventure. But it's going to just be the two of us," said Paula with big, pleading eyes.

COOTIES

She was not making a demand, she was begging. It was beyond a wife and husband dynamic. The desperation in her plea was beyond titles or names, it was from the heart and every memory she had created with the person she stared at from across the bed. All she wanted was to see that he had any place left in his heart to even try.

"I'm a little confused but, we've got the weekend. So– yeah, I'll do whatever," Anthony said as he got out of bed to get his clothes on.

"I'll eat and then get dressed. Shouldn't take too long," he continued with a look on his face that lacked enthusiasm.

Paula got herself ready. She was also lacking in excitement. The day before had at least felt like a trip, a possibility of the two possibly rekindling a flame that had flickered out when she was not looking. Today felt more like a death march to her. Just another step towards the inevitable. There was so much hanging in the balance between Lester being pushed out and her husband pushing himself out. She did not want to choose anyone or anything, she just wanted things to be harmonious.

Anthony slowly picked at his food. Paula could feel that the original trip was more work than pleasure for him, and he was only going at her behest. One could take that as a good sign, that he wanted to rekindle things, but it was more out of keeping the peace, out of obligation. Quietly, he sat in the chair, not even acknowledging her presence. It was not out of spite, but more out of a lack of interest.

This did nothing for Paula's concerns, and she could feel the dread rise up from her gut, into her heart, and then into the final ascension of her eyes that threatened tears. To be something akin of a ghost. The thought had her rushing out of the room just in case she was unable to fight the urge to cry.

LESTER

As Anthony finished up his breakfast, Paula came back around to the kitchen to finish off the small amount of food she had put aside for herself. She wanted to say something just to fix whatever tension may be there. She felt as if she took one step forward in the bedroom but perhaps two steps back, and now found herself completely speechless. For the first time ever, she almost felt awkward in her husband's presence.

"I see Lester out there," Anthony said, looking out the kitchen window. Still looking apathetic, emotionless.

"When you're done, we'll head out there, get this over with," Anthony said, still uninterested.

Like the failed trip, Anthony was still there out of obligation and nothing more. Paula wondered if this was all pointless.

As she finished up her last few scraps of food and drank her juice, she stared off wondering what Lester could possibly be up to. Lester was not qualified to play psychologist and wondered if he would be setting them up for a game of tag or hide 'n go seek. While fun, these were not solutions for intricate adult problems.

She took on Anthony's demeanor as the minutes wore on. Her apathy nearly exceeded his own because there was not much else to do since feeling was only giving way to pain. It was time to face disappointment, it was time to face the truth. She had no idea why she had consented to this plan. It was doomed to fail.

As Paula got up to walk out the door, she wondered if they were above counseling, at least for the sake of the children. If she was desperate enough to seek marriage assistance from a yellow-skinned, reality-bending, space alien then perhaps considering someone with a college degree and years of training in the field might at least be a possibility. More expensive than a session with Lester, but probably more fruitful.

COOTIES

Anthony and Paula walked slowly outside to Lester, who had his back to them, looking out at the still rising sun. The air had a slight chill to it, the feeling that summer air has when you know the cooler weather is about to lift and make way for the day's warmth. It felt nice and comforting for Paula, but the feeling died when she looked over at Anthony who sat stone faced, briefly watching Lester as he gazed off into the distance.

"Your ol' pal Lester can see far off into outer space you know," Lester said with his back still to Paula and Anthony, breaking the silence.

"Your little peepers can only see so far. It's not fair that you can only peek so far, that all you can see are squiggly blurbs and bits of light when something is too far off," he continued, now turning to face them.

"I feel like that's probably true with your little lives here."

Lester looked up at the sky.

"You float out there in space, drifting further and further away, looking back at where ya came from and now all you see are the little squigglies and fuzzy lights. Ain't nothing clear anymore."

Lester reached out his hands. One hand extended to Paula and one extended to Anthony.

"You just need someone to bring you home."

Paula and Anthony looked at each other confusedly, both asking one another with their eyes, "Bring you home?" It made little sense but the less sense it made, the more they wanted to explore the statement. They both put out their hands and placed them in Lester's, compelled by curiosity.

"All righty. I need you both to close your eyes. This might feel a little funny, like you're being warmed up from the inside," he said reassuringly.

LESTER

"Don't worry though, I'm not gonna turn y'all into a Salisbury steak dinner," he joked.

"Oh boy, I need to get one of them bad boys later," said Lester now with his attention on the possibilities of Salisbury steak decadence.

"Anyways!" he blurted out before getting back onto his train of thought.

"Eyes closed. Good thoughts 'n stuff. All that happy mumbo jumbo with treeeees and rivers, ocean waves, a roasting fire, Salisbury steak–" he was drifting off, staring off in an almost trance-like state.

"Lester!" snapped Paula at him.

"Oh! Hey! What are y'all doin' in Lester's dream?" excitedly asked Lester.

"This isn't a dream. You were off in La-la land," stated Paula.

"Right!"

Lester centered himself.

"So, eyes closed. Except me," Lester said looking around, passing off that he had spaced out.

Paula and Anthony closed their eyes. Paula felt a little ridiculous, so she knew that Anthony definitely felt ridiculous. This sort of thing was not for him - held hands, closed eyes, thinking of ambient places, tapping into your inner being. This was the kind of stuff he would normally call "new age hocus pocus". This would usually be the point where he would chuckle about this sort of thing, but he was still clearly miffed.

As Paula closed her eyes, she felt nothing but silence and the cool morning air dancing around her. She stayed focused in her darkness, concentrating, waiting for the next commands from Lester.

"Just let yourself go and concentrate, empty all of the thoughts in your head, let nothing in. Lester's gonna go ahead and be quiet so you can get your noggin further into the void. Keep moving on towards empty thoughts," Lester said before going silent and allowing Anthony and Paula to venture towards the aforementioned void.

Paula was still focusing on the black that slowly gave way to intrusive colors that swirled around in the darkness on the black of her eyelids. The colors held no shape and produced no image, fading into nothingness the longer her eyes were closed. Mesmerized by the phosphene state, Paula began to feel as though she was entering a state of meditation. And then it happened - the warm glow that Lester had spoken of previously.

That warmth and the glow surrounded her head at first and then it worked its way down the rest of her body, down to her toes. In an indescribable fashion, Paula could feel the warmth penetrate her very being, her mind. Tempted as she was, she dared not open her eyes as Lester had warned. Though she felt safe, it was a new sensation, and she was slightly scared of just where this trip might be heading but she held steadfast.

In very little time, she felt as though she was wrapped up in a blanket. Paula felt at peace. The process seemed to happen quickly, and just when she thought she might be reaching the end of Lester's inner journey, she was flooded with memories. They overtook the faint lights that previously swam before her eyes, flashing images of everything her mind could possibly recall. Still frightened, she was too intrigued to turn away now. She wanted to see all of the memories that reeled like a film.

The moments all fell before her, as if she was reliving her life in bits and pieces at a far faster rate. The good memories, and the bad, all came streaming so quickly yet at the same time she could feel every single one, as if time had impossibly slowed down. Paula wanted to grab ahold of each memory, but they faded out, making room for new ones. How or why Lester was doing this was beyond her comprehension, but she could not pull herself away. The only indication that Anthony was also reluctant not to pull away was that she could still hear the real world around her, silent and still, ignorant of the personal wormhole she sailed through.

With a feeling that either she was being downloaded or uploaded, Paula could see her adventure down memory lane was coming to a close as the memories of her children emerged and eventually, she could see her first meeting with Lester. The oddest part of this experience came at the end when she could see herself just briefly through Lester's eyes in that moment, standing still, holding his hand as well as Anthony's. She had no idea if it was real or if she was just imagining it. Still, her eyes remained shut.

"Okay, you crazy little chicken tenders, go ahead 'n' open up your eyes," Paula heard from Lester, still seeing herself through what she assumed were his eyes.

She was glad to finally be able to open her eyes. The whole experience was overwhelming, emotional, and at times a bit scary with the last part of seeing herself through someone else's eyes being quite unnerving. To her surprise, she could feel that her face was wet. As she felt her face, she could feel the streams that had been tears. She was surprised and shocked; she had not felt them the whole time she was in her state.

"Lester, how long were we out for? It felt like years but… not… all at the same time," Paula asked, still looking at her hands examining her wet fingertips, feeling discombobulated.

"Oh, you two spelunkers were out for maybe a few seconds. Ol' Lester got a little worried when y'all started leaking on your faces."

"Both faces!" Paula thought, prompting her to look over at Anthony who was wiping his face, embarrassed by the tears that had inhabited it moments before. While he was not the most stone cold macho man on the planet, Anthony rarely cried. It was not as if he had felt it collided with his masculinity, but it was not his natural state to do so. In fact, Paula could not remember the last time that he did cry. All she could do was stare.

"Anthony are you okay?" she asked instinctually.

"I'm fine. I have no idea what in the hell happened. I felt like I was in there for an eternity. It was… overwhelming," stated Anthony who was attempting to hide his face, wiping away the last of his tears.

Sparing her husband his dignity, she attempted to turn her attention over to Lester.

"Lester, what in the hell was that? I don't get what just happened. At all."

Paula was still extremely confused, trying to make sense of the chaos of their inner journeys.

"Sorry y'all had to go through that little noggin scramble there, but it was necessary for the next step of our big bad super-duper space adventure!" laughed Lester.

"Jesus Christ, Lester, that was pretty scary. I don't know if we can do anymore," said Paula with her eyes big and wide, a look of worry on her face.

"Don't worry! The next part of this will be even funner than that little ol' park with the giant rodent guy everyone loves. You'll never wanna come back. And that's my guarantee or else I'll give you this free pair of snazzy shoes!" he said as he held up a pair of familiar looking shoes.

"Hey, those are mine!" Paula looked down at her feet, noticing that her shoes were missing, and she was barefoot, standing in the dirt.

"No takesy backsies," Lester said, covering the shoes up with his arms.

"Leeeester. Give them back," said Paula with her arm and hand extended.

"Well fine," Lester scoffed, giving the shoes back to Paula.

"But I still guarantee you're gonna have a blast at ol' Lestertopia!" he continued.

The both of them, Paula and Anthony, looked slightly nervous.

"Is this going to be like an amusement park? Should we be worried?" asked Anthony.

Lester got a big smile on his face.

"You'll have to trust ol' Lester. It's gonna be a place that you'll never forget, a place only you two could ever visit. It's not even a place, it's an experience!"

Though still apprehensive, Paula and Anthony both nodded their heads as if to say "okay." Lester spoke no further and started to walk over to the barn. Following his lead, the couple followed shortly behind Lester to the barn door. Confused, they said nothing, awaiting his next commands.

"Inside of that door is something you both lost. All you have to do is open them doors up, walk in, and go retrieve it. Though Lester prefers games, this isn't ain't one of 'em," said Lester as he now moved away from the doors, making way for Paula and Anthony.

"Don't worry, ya rapscallions, you won't be away too long, and I'll be on out here waiting for you. There's no reason to be scared. Everything is gonna be all right," he continued calmly with a smile on his face.

Paula felt reassured by Lester's demeanor, and she now approached the door with a little less fear than before. Her timid feelings were replaced with curiosity and an eagerness. She was now surprisingly curious to see what lay behind the doors.

As she placed her hands upon the door, she looked over at Anthony who stared back. It was a quiet agreement, but he nodded his head as if to say, "Let's do this!" and placed his hand upon the door as well.

Together, they pulled the doors open and were met by a shiny bright light. At first, they could see nothing but a sheer brightness, but they mutually continued moving forward, feeling their way around in the glow, holding hands, protecting their eyes with their free hand. As they continued moving forward the light dimmed and they were enveloped in a fog. Looking back, they could still see the door but no aspect of the barn. Still, they moved forward.

As they continued, still holding hands, the fog started to lift up around them. Shapes started to come into focus, sounds started to emerge as if their heads were coming out from water, smells began to appear. Finally, the fog had cleared away and they found themselves in a familiar place. Instantly, they had goosebumps and Paula, taken aback by what she saw, was immobilized.

It was the very place that they first met and had started dating. A place called Bullseye's Bar and Grill where everyone of drinking age hung out. This was the spot she hung out at in her early twenties with all of her friends almost every night while going to community college. This old haunt was hundreds of miles from where they lived and, to her knowledge, Paula believed it to have been torn down long ago.

The feeling of nostalgia overwhelmed her, and she could not make sense of it all. She knew Lester had magic but, "Could he have really transported us across the country?" she thought. The more she thought about it, she tried to reason that even Lester's magic must have its boundaries.

Paula continued to be moved by her surroundings, so much so that she failed to notice her old friends sitting at "their table". This was a special table they referred to as the "Bitch Bunker" that they lovingly created during their reign of Bullseye's back in the day.

LESTER

The girls were at the table letting loose. They were yelling, hooting, drinking, being typical loud, young girls looking for a good, rowdy night out. Paula was frozen in place. It was not a dream. Everything was too perfect and physical. She knew this by touching the bar area she stood next to that had a glossy wood grain with small imperfections, chunks of wood that had gone missing over time, the wet circles from the bottom of glasses that had accumulated water at their bottom.

This place was very real. For just a moment, she had wondered if she had just dreamt her life from this moment forward, that Anthony, the kids, Lester, had all been the product of an overactive imagination, too much beer, and other substances taken before entering the bar.

Standing in place, and considering her sanity, she looked over to her right and she saw her husband, but it was not exactly him. He was younger, more clean-shaven, and was wearing the very same clothes he wore that night, including his baseball cap which was adorned with a fighting Irishman logo, his old Notre Dame cap which she hadn't seen in ages.

Looking back at her, Anthony had a bewildered look in his eyes too. He looked incredibly confused about what was happening. Though he looked younger, this clearly was not the same Anthony she met that night so many years ago. He was staring at Paula, trying to figure her out, almost afraid to speak or move.

Finally staring at one another, Paula figured she would break the ice.

"Anthony is that you? You know, you? Future…. you?" she timidly asked, hoping she was right and that she was not dreaming all of this. Otherwise, she was going to look like a crazy person, which she did not need in a time where she had wondered if she was amidst one of the all-time epic mental breakdowns.

"Yeah. I think so. You're from... further down the road, too, right? Like, we're married?" He looked at Paula, with his eyes big and intense, clearly freaking out as much as Paula at this point.

This calmed Paula down a little bit. She knew one thing for sure: That was her Anthony and wherever they were, they were there together. No drug or amount of alcohol could have caused such mass mutual hallucinations amongst two individuals.

"Yes," she said, "I am your wife and" –she looked around wide eyed– "I have no idea what the hell is going on!"

Suddenly, it dawned on her. If Anthony was looking a good fifteen years younger, then she probably was too.

Immediately she ran over to a nearby mirror to take a look at herself. What she saw in the mirror, she was awestruck. There, before her, stood a much younger and much thinner Paula, about twenty to twenty-five pounds lighter as a matter of fact. She was wearing clothes she would never dream of wearing in her thirties as a mother. She did not want to brag to herself, but she was looking pretty damn good.

As impressed as Paula was, it hit her like a ton of bricks.

"Holy shit! Lester didn't just send us across the country. He sent us across time!" she exclaimed to herself. The thought hurt her brain a little, it defied all natural law and exceeded all expectations of Lester's powers.

She turned to Anthony. When their gaze locked, it was obvious that he was having the same revelation. As his eyes drifted from hers and observed the room around him, he focused on something behind Paula that rearranged his face into a look of total perplexity.

"WHAT. IN THE ACTUAL. FUCK?" Anthony slowly said aloud, causing Paula's own face to scrunch up in puzzlement.

LESTER

Before she could turn to see what the surprise was, she heard a familiar voice from another time and place yell out.

"Jesus fucking Christ! Will you get over yourself, betch!"

When Paula turned towards the voice, it was her old friend Rhonda, who had her arm around another girl at the table who was also laughing, her other friend Katie. Paula froze up once again. She had not seen any of them in years, losing gradual touch with them over time as she became closer to Anthony, and they eventually moved. Over time, communication with her friends all but died out. She had started to find her friends one by one again, but their interactions were never the same.

The moment was certainly bittersweet but, at the same time everything good swelled up within her, filling her with a warmth, as if she were bathing in it. Everything about that moment, those days, her feelings about meeting Anthony that night, her youth, all accumulated into a feeling that was beyond description.

"Holy shit, are you just going to sit there staring at us all night like a retard? Get your ass back over here. God, you must be fuckin' trippin'," laughed Rhonda, as well as the other girls at the Bitch Bunker table.

Anthony was still dotting his eyes around everywhere. Paula could see he was extra confused because he would eventually, in time, know the girls at the table but clearly, at this point in time, he was still a stranger. All he could do was stand there, wondering what he was supposed to do next, as if he were supposed to stick to a script.

Paula walked up to Anthony, and whispered, "Honey. Come with me and I'll introduce you as the guy I just met, who I did actually meet tonight many, many years ago…" she paused for a moment.

COOTIES

"You know what? this just gets way fucking weirder the more I say it, so just follow my lead. Okay?" to which Anthony nodded with his confused eyes bugging out of his skull.

"What up skankasaurus?!" yelled Paula at Rhonda as she approached the table with Anthony shortly behind her.

"If it isn't my sister from another mister. Goddamn I missed you. All of you," she accidentally let out with a big, nostalgic grin.

All the girls at the table stared at her in confusion. First, they all started looking at each other and then they turned to Paula, staring at her for just a moment.

"This bitch done gone to outer space!" said Rhonda, which set the entire table off in laughter.

"Seriously whatever you dropped; I want in on that shit!" Rhonda said, laughing even harder. Now the whole table was beside themselves with laughter. Paula stood there, chuckling, taking in the old days, feeling the instant nostalgia of her surroundings.

"So, who's the he-puppet standing next to you?" Katie asked.

Paula had nearly forgotten Anthony was standing behind her. It confused her as to why Anthony seemed to refuse to chime in at all since he would eventually get to know these girls, most of all Rhonda who had been Paula's best friend at that time. She assumed that Anthony was still trying to get his bearings. They were only there a few minutes but the jetlag of whatever trip they took seemed to weigh on them. It's not every day you travel back in time, if that's what this, in fact, was.

"This he-puppet? Oh, this is Anthony. I saw him over at the bar and we were just chatting it up. Well, that is before I was interrupted by you skanky ass bitches."

This caused another round of laughs from the table. It felt so good for Paula to say that. It was like old times, and it was a time she could regularly call a group of people "skanky ass bitches". The term is none too common in adulthood but especially rare in the case of motherhood. Paula was ready to let loose on the night.

"Paula?" Anthony chimed in.

"Aren't you gonna introduce me to these skanky ass bitches?" he asked with a deadpan face.

The women at the table all looked a little taken aback by what they had just heard, and then they looked at each other before bursting into laughter once again, as did Paula.

"Oh, I like him!" Rhonda chuckled.

"He can sit his ass on down with the Bitch Battalion for sure!" she slapped the table, still smiling and giggling.

In their original timeline, Paula and Anthony did hang out with the girls at the Bitch Bunker, having the time of their life. Reimagining it was one thing, but the idea of reliving it gave Paula a jolt of electricity. It had already worked so well that Anthony was being his pre-children self. His sense of humor and all-around zest had faded over the years. He already seemed like himself, and they had been at the bar no longer than ten minutes.

As Anthony went off to grab his own chair to sit at the Bitch Bunker, Paula sat in her normal spot. It was pure instinct, like nothing had changed over the years, like it was yesterday.

"Okay. So, I admit. I'm a little fucked up. Why don't you ladies kindly remind me what the fuck the plan is tonight?" said Paula trying to play the role, looking around at the girls.

"Well, WE were going to be hanging out here tonight, drinking our asses off but maybe YOU should be hanging with the new man-puppet. He is kinda cute. I mean, I'll take him if you don't want him," Rhonda said, winking at Anthony, causing the girls around the table to jokingly call out "Woooooo!" in unison.

"Bitch, that is my man-puppet," replied Paula with a big smile on her face.

"Honestly, I dunno, girl. There's nothing on the calendar tonight. I'm all ears if you've got something to do tonight," Rhonda back said to Paula.

As soon as she finished, Anthony shot his hand in the air like he was a student in class. The girls turned their attention to him.

"I've got something we can all do," he said with a smirk on his face.

"Oh no, we ain't into none of that Caligula shit, man," joked Rhonda.

"No, no. Tempting, but no. I've got something I need a little help with," he said, leaning in.

"I'm listening," Rhonda leaned over, looking very interested in what this man-puppet had to say.

"So, about two months ago, I get fired from my job. My old asshole boss, Jim, rode my ass for months, giving me impossible tasks, knowing I would fail. The lazy piece of shit would sit up in his office all day long, asking me to do some of the most unsafe BS and, again, with impossible time frames. The guy clearly didn't like me," he said, with the women now even more focused on what he had to say.

"So, he works me to the bone until I can't possibly do all the stuff he's asking of me which leads to me being fired. I come to find out the reason he does this is because he's trying to find a 'legal' way to can me so that he can give my job to some relative of his, who he's going to pay less."

All of the girls at the table were extremely irritated at this with a chorus of sighs, opened mouths, eyerolls, and commentary.

"Man, fuck that asshole!"

"Who does that fucker think he is?"

"You got hosed!"

The angry sentiments floated around the table as Anthony relived his injustice, seemingly remembering everything like it was yesterday. Paula was impressed by his ability to jump into his old role and to remember it all. The girls quieted down just long enough for Anthony to continue.

"So! I wanted to get a little revenge, but I wanted to do it when the timing was right. Too soon and obviously they'll know it was me, so I bided my time, hoping it might even wear off and I might forget but, I've had a lot of beer, and I know trouble when I see it. I'm looking right at it," he said as he panned around at all of the girls at the table which caused all of the girls at the table to flash a devious smile.

"The kinda trouble that wouldn't mind slashing some tires and egging a house, let's say," Anthony continued with a grin. Those devious smiles from the girls got even larger.

"Eggs? Man, I'll throw my own shit at that motherfucker's house!" yelled Rhonda.

"What are we all waiting around for? This sounds like my kinda night, man-puppet!" she declared.

"Hey, what was your name again?" Rhonda asked Anthony.

"Fucker. Mother Fucker." said Anthony in deadpan delivery which caused everyone, especially Paula to just about die of laughter.

"Now let's go avenge me losing my shitty ass job," he yelled.

All of the women at the table pumped their fists in the air and yelled out. The girls were extremely amped up and ready to go. They had no plan and not a single care in the world. They were drunk and ready to pelt eggs at anything that moved, and Anthony had provided them with a target. Onward they marched.

They rolled up quietly in three separate vehicles to the lonely house down the old country road. The owner of the property was of course Anthony's old boss, Jim; a fat, angry old man who spent more time on his ass than any human being should legally be allowed to. He had a gravely, hoarse voice and often walked around chomping on cigars whether they were lit or not. Jim always smelled like some combination of mayonnaise and old, dank shoes, and he knew it. He would often purposely get close to people to let them in on some of his own misery, punishing the poor person's nostrils.

His house was just as old and broken down as himself. Unkempt, dilapidated, even had Jim's smell. The house looked like it also ate one too many bacon sandwiches in its time. The scenery outside was much prettier. Tall grass lit up with the spotlight of a bright moon, unguarded by any clouds with a lush wind tickling every blade of greenery around them.

Paula remembered this distinctly because the night had reminded her of youth, and how the world felt when the sun went down. As she got older, the night just became another cycle in time. Just like the days, months or years; the majesty of night lost its magic. When she was younger, she felt freedom in it. The entire world was asleep, no people to bug you except the company you kept in these late hours. It was quiet, the trees felt alive and wise, the sounds of nature spoke louder in the silence of the darkness, moments seemed more captivating.

She had no word or name for it, but she remembered this being one of the last times she would ever feel this way. Looking over the landscape as everyone quietly emerged out of their vehicles, she felt the nostalgia wash over and, looking at Anthony, who was staring off at the moon with a smile on his face, it felt that much more powerful. A memory she had kept throughout the years but could not feel anymore, like it had been someone else's. Now, in this moment, she was feeling all of it, and it overwhelmed her senses in all of the best ways possible.

"Sweetie, can you believe this? We're back at Slim Jim's place about to egg the crap out of it again," Anthony said, breaking the silence Paula was entranced in.

"This time we won't get caught though. We stuck around a little too long last time to admire the handy work but this time we'll make sure to get the hell out of here before they show up," Paula said, referring to the first time they attempted to egg Jim's property.

They originally assumed since his car was there that Jim was upstairs sleeping. Just imagine their surprise when his wife's car pulled up with Jim in the passenger seat, yelling and chasing everyone off of his property. They were glad to get out before he got his hands on his gun. He was stupid and reckless enough to point it at someone and shoot.

Paula and Anthony were armed with the knowledge that they had at least thirty minutes to get the job done. Another fortunate bit of knowledge was that this time they knew Jim hated animals as much as he seemingly hated people and there was no dog, no measure of security to prevent them from giving Jim a parting gift from Anthony.

"Ladies, if I might have your attention!" yelled Anthony.

"Yes, Captain Mother Fucker!" yelled Rhonda.

"Hey, do we gotta line up and salute or some shit?" she half asked the other girls that were huddled around, looking at Anthony for his commands.

"We have about thirty minutes max here. I trust you have all of the provisions we acquired at the store?" Anthony asked with a stern face.

All of the girls nodded.

"I trust you have your guts in check?"

They nodded once again.

"There is no dog, no one coming for a good half-hour, nothing to stop you in that time, short of your imagination. Ladies, make Captain Mother Fucker proud!"

Anthony ended his speech with his arms spread and his eyes closed with a wicked smile on his face.

The drunken bunch from the Bitch Bunker yelled in excitement, charging the house with all the fury of a horde of Vikings about to take a village. Not quite as vicious as Vikings from days past and not quite as graceful, as one girl tripped and fell on her face with another girl running into a post. Luckily beer is a great anesthetic and they easily laughed off whatever pain would have normally afflicted them, allowing them to continue their charge to victory.

Eggs were being lobbed like grenades, cracking and exploding against the side of the large, ugly house. Paula and Anthony were in the fray too, chucking eggs indiscriminately with what felt like a pallet's worth of egg cartons. They had really loaded up this time.

"Hey Mother Fucker, you said something about slashing some tires, right?" asked Katie.

"Yeah, I did, that's ol' Slim Jim's truck right there," he answered, pointing at his beat up old Ford Bronco.

Katie walked over and pulled out a giant military style knife. It was sharp, bulky and had massive, serrated edges. It looked like it could have gutted a polar bear and it was almost comical being held in Katie's tiny hands. At no more than five feet, the knife was probably bigger than her.

"For the Captain!" she yelled, plunging her giant Rambo knife into the driver side front tire.

LESTER

Anthony watched as she drunkenly yelled before jamming her battle sword into each and every tire of the truck. Paula was right next to Anthony, hanging on his arm, laughing with him as they witnessed the chaos around them. The last time they had done this, on a scale of one through ten, it was probably a six. Tonight, the Bitch Bunker and Captain Mother Fucker were easily scoring an eleven. Paula had wondered if there would still be a house standing by the time they were done.

"Watch this, baby," said Anthony to Paula, as he picked up a loose stone in the garden.

Before she could register what was going on, Anthony threw the stone with maximum velocity through the front window. At first, she was shocked, her motherly instincts and age had taken over at this point. The fear of getting arrested, the idea that maybe they had gone too far had entered her mind as she heard the glass break.

"Jesus, Anthony! What in the fuck?!" she instinctively yelled, staring at Anthony with her eyes wide open while the other girls egged him on, hooting and hollering all around them.

"Hey, it's our night, right?" he said. "I mean, Lester clearly sent us back here to have a little fun and boy, I'm having more fun right now than I have in years," he laughed with the others.

"Okay. But uh, just don't go too far. We don't know what the ramifications are here."

Paula was worried about the uncertainty of this weird timeline, unsure if maybe Jim and his wife would show up sooner than they had in the past.

"Don't worry, we're not going to kill anyone. Just a little home redecorating is all," he said, picking up a brick.

"Wanna try your luck?" Anthony held out the brick to Paula, with a mischievous smile on his face.

"No, I'm not gonna throw a brick through someone's window. Eggs are one thing but what the hell?"

As soon as she responded, she could hear the clucking of chickens behind her. They did not sound quite chicken in nature, but more like drunken chickens. The imposter chickens were openly mocking Paula and her refusal to throw the brick at Jim's house which now looked like it had been hit by a hurricane.

"What's wrong, sweetie? Somebody got a big ol' case of the chickens?" said Rhonda who was clucking even louder, flapping arms included.

"No, I mean, c'mon, this is fucking crazy. It was one thing to egg the place but Katie's slashing tires and now we're throwing rocks and bricks through the guy's windows. This is some real shit, guys!"

Paula was not as brazen as she was back then and the fear of getting caught was making her more antsy by the minute.

"Oh, noes," Rhonda said mockingly.

"Not only do we got a chicken in our midst, but we also got ourselves a smelly, dank ass pussy. Ol' chickenpussy. Girls, I think we got ourselves a new nickname for Paula up in here!"

Rhonda's trash talking was supported by a chorus chant of "Chickenpussy" that filled the night air. There was a mixture of "Chickenpussy" and clucking going around, the group had gone feral and were now openly instigating Paula.

"Fine. Give me the goddamn brick," she demanded from Anthony who was in the middle of doing his own clucking.

Paula's old instincts had kicked in. Even as a mother or a wife; Paula was never going to let these uppity bitches mock her.

"You sure?" Anthony asked with a trolling smile.

"Oh, now you're the voice of reason? Just give me that goddamn thing already."

Anthony handed it over with a wink.

"I don't know girls. She's got the brick, but I don't think she's got the STONES, if you catch my drift," Rhonda mockingly egged Paula on.

"Hey, you know what, I've got this big ass brick in my hand."

"You gonna throw it at me?" Rhonda laughed.

"That black hole you call a vagina would just snatch this thing up like all the men floating around in that nasty ass thing. Now shut up. Adults is thinking here," Paula quipped back.

This retort garnered a huge laugh from everyone around, including Rhonda.

She was eyeballing a spot to throw the brick. After all the buildup she wanted a good spot to lob the lethal object at. Finally, she locked on to her target.

"Bombs away!" Paula lobbed the jagged brick with a surprising amount of force and, as she had planned, the stone went hurtling through the bedroom window on the second floor.

"Because why in the fuck should they get to sleep tonight?!" laughed Paula.

Everyone else made a collective "Dayuum!" which was followed up by more hooting and hollering. Anthony sure seemed impressed, not only by her drastic change of heart but also her ability to land her mark. The combination of power and accuracy was certainly admirable. This garnered her two thumbs up and a smile from Anthony.

"Chickenpussy is dead. Long live the Queen!" proclaimed Paula, raising her fists into the air.

"How about Ho Montana instead?" joked Katie, making everyone laugh.

"Naw. That title's already taken by this one," Paula deadpanned, pointing at Rhonda.

COOTIES

"Hey c'mon you know," –Rhonda thought about it– "Naw, yeah, it's true. It's true." Rhonda nodded her head up and down, smiling ear to ear and winking at Paula.

Paula, alongside Anthony, looked around at the destruction they had caused. The house was littered in eggs, and many windows were smashed in. The truck fared no better than the house with all of its windows also smashed in, and all of the tires slashed. Paula wondered if anyone was considering lighting the house or truck on fire.

This was far more destructive than their previous visit which was mostly a few eggs and Anthony drunkenly peeing in the fountain of the garden. Jim and his wife came home to witness, in horror, Anthony relieving himself with the happiest smile on his face. Anthony ended up in jail for his little pit stop in the fountain.

This time around though, it looked like a bomb went off. Several, in fact.

Though her older, wiser self should have been troubled by what she bore witness to, she instead had a feeling of nostalgia while also being in the time she was being nostalgic about. She looked over at Anthony and her friends and it gave her goosebumps. The night air hit her, and she closed her eyes to absorb the smell, the slight gust brought a chill to the back of her arms.

"It's really something, right?" a voice said.

Upon opening her eyes, Anthony stood beside her. He was smiling, seemingly just as giddy as Paula was.

"Here we are back when we first met. Reliving it all and then some. I mean, are we going to relive… everything?" he asked aloud.

Looking off to the side he pondered, "I mean, Lester never said anything."

Paula was so engrossed in the moment that structure or time was of no concern to her.

"I'm sure there's a method to all of this, and I don't wanna think about it really. I just" –she took a moment to articulate her thought, looking at the night sky– "want to let go and enjoy whatever this is."

"Yeah, me too. We haven't been like this in... forever," said Anthony, now holding Paula's hand.

"In fact, you know what else we did this night for the first time?" he asked in a devilish manner.

Paula smiled, holding both of his hands that were now wrapped across her chest as he stood behind, holding her.

"Oh, I remember vividly," she smiled, looking down almost bashfully.

"Hey! Hey! Save it for the wedding night!" yelled a voice.

It was Rhonda, who was smiling, and pointing at a cathedral just off in the distance. This was odd as the building had not been there before, not in their current adventure and certainly not all those years ago when this event first took place.

"What in the hell is that place?" inquired Paula.

"Bitch, you ask too many questions. This is where we get off. Get your ass on through those doors and enjoy all the free shit your dad bought you guys."

Rhonda ushered them away towards the far off cathedral.

"I love free shit, so I'll meet you in there, okay!" Rhonda continued, waving them away from the group, towards the much out of place cathedral.

Paula and Anthony both looked confused but, like with all things about this night, it was best to move when prompted to do so. Holding each other's hands, the two walked through the brisk summer night towards the cathedral that stood what seemed like a mile away.

The winds of the night continued to tickle the hairs of Paula's body and the moon was bright as ever. The further they walked away from Rhonda and the rest, the quieter the landscape became. It was peaceful and calming. Paula and Anthony did not speak, in fear of ruining the beauty of the silence they were immersed in. Instead, Paula hugged on Anthony's arm as they slowly strode across the moonlit grass. This was what Paula loved most about the nighttime, moments like these that could never be emulated in the daylight. It felt intimate and personal, like they were the only two people in the world.

It was not long before the couple got within a stone's throw of the cathedral. She could not understand why she did not recognize it before, but the cathedral was the very place her and Anthony married. Perhaps it was due to the darkness and distance before but now, standing in front of it, Paula recognized the architecture, the signs, the steps that led to the two giant wooden front doors. Judging from the look on Anthony's face, he recognized it too.

"Oh my god, sweetie. This is where we got married!" exclaimed Paula, still looking around in disbelief.

Anthony was just as dumbfounded, looking at every little detail.

"What in the literal hell? This is weird, even for… whatever this is," he said, still examining the property.

"Do you think, we maybe– walk in?" asked Paula, pointing towards the two big front doors and looking at Anthony.

"Well, I mean, it makes sense. Why else would the place we got married be sitting out here?" he said, walking towards the doors, putting his hands on the handle to test if they opened.

LESTER

He gave a slight pull, and it gave way. He only partially opened the door, waiting for Paula, making sure she was ready to go through the doors and move into the next part of their journey.

"All right, whenever you're ready, I'm ready, sweetie," Paula said, grabbing the other door handle, steadying her body, waiting for the word to open the door with Anthony.

"All right, well… on the count of three."

"One…" They looked at each other.

"Two…" Nervously, they both smiled at each other preparing for whatever mystery lay for them on the other side of the doors.

"Three!"

Both Paula and Anthony slowly swung the doors open, moving back, peeking their eyes into the cathedral entrance. It was foggy like before, when they walked through the barn at their home and into the bar, going back in time. They grabbed hands and slowly started to walk forward together through the heavy mist that surrounded them.

Whatever nighttime sounds they were hearing began to disappear, becoming more muffled, like they were heading underwater. As those sounds died, they could hear the emergence of various noises. There were a lot of voices, the sound of an instrument, "An organ perhaps?" Paula wondered. The fog started to lift, and the sounds became clearer, the sounds filling their ears with greater clarity.

Holding hands, they looked around to see the inside of a church with rows of pews all filled with people, all dressed quite nicely. They stood still, taken aback from what they were seeing. It dawned on them that they were in fact back at their own wedding. Paula had assumed this might be what she saw when they approached the cathedral, but she could not truly prepare herself for the moment. Standing next to Anthony, who was dressed in his tuxedo looking the best he ever had, she gazed around and saw friends and family lost through time, some still living and some departed.

One particular person made Paula start to weep. It was her mother, alive and well, smiling back at her. Her appearance was ghostly, and as Paula continued to watch her, she erupted into tears. They were tears of joy, accompanied by a smile on Paula's face. "Did I die and go to heaven?" she briefly thought, as she held her hands over her mouth in shock, still smiling. She wanted to run over and hug her mom, squeeze her and never let go of her but the obligation of her situation kept her firmly grounded in place. If this was a dream, she never wanted to wake up.

Anthony caught wind of this, and looked over at Paula, holding her hands.

"Are you okay?" looking lovingly into her eyes.

"Yeah, I'm okay. I just can't believe it. She's right there, Anthony."

Paula looked back at him, smiled, and gripped his hands tighter.

Before they could say anything else a voice chimed in from the front of the room.

"What are you two doing out here together? I thought your dad was supposed to walk you down the aisle?"

It was Anthony's mother, hunched forward around her seat, looking confused.

They both stared at each other and were suddenly reminded that this is not how things went that day. Paula's father, Don, had walked her down the aisle and Anthony was of course at the altar waiting for his blushing bride.

"Oh, uh, change of plans I suppose" said a voice from behind Paula and Anthony.

LESTER

Coming out from the back area of the room was Don, Paula's confused looking father. Apparently, he could sense something was amiss and was trying to cover for the soon to be married couple.

"Hey, buddy, you think I can finish walking her down?" he asked Anthony to which Anthony obliged, handing Paula off to her dad just before heading down the aisle to wait for her at the altar. Anthony smiled at her as he walked down the path.

"All right Princess, it's your big day. Are you ready for this?" Don asked his daughter with a smile.

"Pappy, I am ready," she said, still weeping from having seen her mom, and generally being overwhelmed by being back at her own wedding.

"Are you going to be okay?" he asked her, looking concerned.

"It's my big day, Pappy. Just wedding tears, ya know."

Her father just smiled at her and gave her a kiss on her forehead.

Arm in arm, they walked down the aisle together. As they did, Paula observed the crowd. She could see her mother, Liz, still smiling back at her, graceful as ever. Rhonda was in the crowd too, doing her very best to behave but, looking back at Paula, she made a sexual gesture with her right index finger going in and out through a hole she formed on her left hand with her index finger and thumb. This caused Paula to laugh out loud. She could not expect Rhonda to fully behave, right?

Paula saw her sister, Denise, sitting with Karl and they were both smiling back at her. Denise was visibly holding back tears, making Paula even more emotional, drawing an even bigger smile on the bride's face.

"You're beautiful," mouthed Denise to her as Paula strode forward.

Finally at the altar, Don handed his daughter off to his future son-in-law, giving his little Princess, Paula, one last kiss on her forehead. He looked at Anthony and ran his finger across the side of his own nose quickly to gesture "Keep your nose clean" and gave him a wink, accompanied with a smile. Anthony smiled back. The two of them got along famously so Paula knew Anthony felt her dad's affection with his antics. Paula thought it was sweet.

As they faced each other, they saw one another in a new light. At least this was how Paula felt, looking into Anthony's eyes. She could feel it in her soul. The priest came up between them with his book in hand.

"Dearly beloved, we are gathered here today to join Anthony and Paula in holy matrimony. If there is anyone here today that believes these two should not be married, speak now or forever hold your peace."

There was a pause as everyone looked around hoping that no one would speak up and ruin the wondrous occasion. Not a soul chimed in as the room stayed silent.

"Good! I would've just tossed you out on your ear anyway," chuckled the priest which got a big laugh from the entire room.

"Marriage is not all hellfire and brimstone. It is not a service or an obligation. It is the meeting between two mutually kindred spirits who, in all the trillions of stars in this universe, managed to find one another and say, 'from here to eternity, I stand by thee'."

"It is an honor to be among each other's company, traipsing through this life, often blind and unprepared, knowing that this person that stands across from you will be yours for all eternity, not in bondage, but in love."

Paula and Anthony stood so many feet apart, staring at each other, smiling. She was attempting to stop the continuous flow of tears and Anthony, surprisingly, seemed to be on the verge of tearing up. The entire experience was magical, as if it were something fictional, they were lucky enough to relive. Time had nearly removed all of the feelings and memories that encompassed this day.

"Times can be tough. No one is immune, but if you remember this day, this moment, and the people that took their precious time to share it with you, then no challenge may veer you wrong. It is in each other that you will stay straight and conquer all obstacles before you; through strength, encouragement, and love. For without these things, what is love but a word? This is a union and throughout you will lead by actions and grow closer for it, building a story that only the two of you can ever truly know."

The two continued to look at each other, remembering the details of the day, living them all over again, nearly forgetting that anyone else was in the room with them.

"Now that I am done lecturing you two, I do believe you have some vows to exchange," said the priest, looking at the young couple.

"Oh, vows?" Anthony said aloud, garnering random chuckles throughout the crowd.

They all assumed that he was joking but Anthony had no vows written down, and he had forgotten that part of the ceremony, being so many years ago. Paula, too, was thrown off by the question. She knew she was unable to remember her vows and she did not have a place she had kept them. Paula could see Anthony fumbling around in his own pockets in the hope of finding them.

"My goodness did you two rookies leave your vows behind?" laughed the priest.

"Not drama students, I take it? Couldn't memorize them, eh?" the priest said, continuing to smile and joke around.

"Well, let's go ahead and improvise this then. Luckily, I've been doing this long enough to have some vows on hand for just such an emergency."

This caused a sigh of relief for the couple, both smiling and laughing at the absurdity of the situation.

"Paula, look at your soon-to-be husband and please repeat the following words to him."

"I, Paula, do take you, Anthony, to be my loving husband and partner."

"I, Paula, do take you, Anthony, to be my loving husband and partner," Paula repeated to Anthony, with a blushing smile.

"I will trust you as you trust me."

"I will trust you as you trust me," she repeated to Anthony.

"I will love you as you love me."

"I will love you as you love me," smiling, she repeated the vow.

"I will honor you as you honor me."

"I will honor you as you honor me," again she repeated.

"I will laugh with you."

"I will laugh with you, even if the jokes are bad," Paula repeated while she and everyone else in the room chuckled.

"I will uplift you in times of sadness."

"I will uplift you in times of sadness," she warmly repeated.

"I will be there forever more."

"I will be there forever more," repeating her last vow with a giant smile on her face.

"Anthony, she did her part, so now I need you to look at your lovely bride and repeat the same vows. Please, repeat after me."

"I, Anthony, take you, Paula, to be my loving wife and partner."

"I, Anthony, take you, Paula, to be my loving wife and partner," the words came out of Anthony's mouth with a giant smile.

"I will trust you as you trust me."

"I will trust you as you trust me," he repeated back to Paula, looking sincere in his statement.

"I will love you as you love me."

"I will love you as you love me," Anthony said, staring at her, captivated.

As he repeated the line, Paula looked at him and remembered that it was just earlier in the day they were barely saying anything to one another, wondering if their marriage was about to die a slow, horrible death. Here he was though, about to recommit himself.

"I will honor you as you honor me."

"I will honor you as you honor me," he repeated to Paula, which filled her being with a warmth she had not felt since perhaps the birth of their children.

"I will laugh with you."

"I will laugh with you, because my jokes are seriously funny."

Again, everyone laughed, most of all Anthony.

"Is it too late to break out of this deal?" joked Paula which got an even bigger laugh out of everyone in attendance.

Anthony just nodded his head with a big smile on his face, as his eyes rolled.

"Clearly, she was wrong because I'm a hoot!" is what his body language was saying.

"I will uplift you in times of sadness."

"I will uplift you in times of sadness," he said, getting more serious again.

"I will be there forever more."

COOTIES

"I will be there forever more," he finished, looking deeply into her eyes.

As they held hands, she looked down at them, linked together, and for a moment she almost felt bashful. She could feel herself blushing, like a child in love again.

"Anthony, Paula, please make sure to be as open and honest with one another as you would with yourselves. Communication is the bedrock of a long, fruitful commitment such as this and, to do this you must honor and respect each other in ways you've never done before. You are each a class of your own to one another that is exclusive and bears no intrusion.

The person standing across from you is your life now and you will do everything in your power to pay them back for choosing you, out of everyone in the world, to share this sacred bond with."

The couple stood across from one another, joined in the moment, smiling. They were both older and had endured the hardships of time, the hardships of marriage and, on their faces, the look of two people given a second chance at one another.

"Rings. Hey, Best Man, do you have them on you? We definitely can't improvise rings," joked the priest once again.

Anthony's best man, Chris, came up with the rings, nearly tripping in excitement for his big moment. Having regained his balance, Chris was able to accomplish his mission and the happy couple now had their symbolic tokens of love in hand.

"Paula. Please place Anthony's ring onto his finger" he instructed her, as she placed the ring on his finger with little resistance.

"Paula, do you take Anthony to be your lawfully wedded husband?"

"I do!" said Paula a little louder than she had planned.

"Do you promise to love, cherish, and honor him so long as you may live?"

"I do," Paula said, looking lovingly into Anthony's eyes.

"And with this token, do you swear to uphold your oath before friends and family alike?"

"Yes. I do."

It was a lot to take in and Paula had to look down. The whole process felt so surreal. It was obvious Deja vu, and it nearly made her dizzy. Once she looked back up and saw Anthony, she was able to get her bearings back.

"Anthony. It is now your turn to place the ring on Paula's finger."

Paula held her breath a bit as Anthony perfectly slid the ring upon her finger.

"Anthony, do you take Paula to be your lawfully wedded wife?"

"I do."

Anthony stared at Paula with great intensity.

"Do you promise to love, cherish, and honor her so long as you may live?"

"Yes. I do."

"And with this token, do you swear to uphold your oath before friends and family alike?"

"Forever," he said, staring at Paula in a trance.

"Or… I do. Obviously," he corrected himself to the sound of a few giggles.

While Anthony's gaze was still intense, he was now smiling, looking like a man in love. On her finger sat a shiny new ring, and Paula stared at it; like all of the bad had been erased and something anew was just created.

"Every day upon your fingers, may these rings rest as a shining reminder of the very vows and promises exchanged here today between the two of you. They are your beacons in times of darkness that will always guide your hearts back to harbor when light is scarce."

There was a brief moment of silence where the two lovebirds were able to look at each other and breathe.

"Well, I've yammered on long enough. I now pronounce you husband and wife. KISS THE BRIDE ALREADY, ANTHONY!" exclaimed the priest.

Anthony needed little prompting and, for the first time in what seemed like forever, Anthony gave Paula a deep, passionate kiss. If she had to rate this particular kiss it would have been a top five kiss for sure. She closed her eyes, taking in the kiss, savoring it just in case it never came back again. Her stomach was flooded with butterflies, and she held on to Anthony, bringing him in closer.

"Whoa, whoa, save it for later, kids," joked the priest one last time.

The two released from the powerful kiss, giggling, smiling at one another, still locking eyes. Everyone around them was cheering and clapping for the newlyweds, but they barely noticed. It seemed like they were the only two people in the entire room, the world for that matter. Even now, this was a part of their quest together, coming back in time to be reborn together. They felt stronger than ever in this moment. Their bond was exclusive, this could only belong to them.

They were prompted to leave the cathedral as it was now party time since the bride and groom were official. As Paula walked back down the aisle heading out the door, she looked toward her mother in the crowd and the thought occurred to her that going through the church doors may be another unexpected jump to somewhere else. She stopped dead in her tracks.

"Mom!" she yelled, fighting back tears. Her mom smiled but looked slightly confused at the outburst.

"Come here!" Paula asked of her mother, who reacted to the command by getting up and trying to shuffle out around the crowd of people to reach Paula.

Finally standing in front of her daughter after getting around everyone, Paula wasted absolutely no time and lunged at her mother to give her a giant hug. The hug was so tight and powerful, she thought she might break her mom. She did not care however because she never got to say goodbye when her mother passed away and she wanted her mother to feel just how much she loved her.

Her mother returned her embrace as they both let out tears. For Liz, it was more of a matter of the wedding, giving away her daughter that she was so very close to. She had no way of knowing she was a ghost, giving Paula one last chance to see her alive. There was no way she could understand the magnitude of this moment.

"It's okay, Paula. Anthony will take care of you now," she said, still tightly wound in Paula's embrace.

"Don't forget from time to time to see me. This won't be the last time we ever hug, my dear," Liz said, as she looked into Paula's eyes with a kind smile on her face.

This made Paula cry even harder, and she buried herself into mother's shoulder.

"I don't ever want to let you go, mama."

Paula held Liz even tighter, if that was even possible.

"You do have to let go though, dear. You have to move on from here. This church, these people, this life, it all changes when you walk through those doors, and there is nothing wrong with that," she said, pulling back from Paula and looking into her eyes.

"Now go. Enjoy your honeymoon. Enjoy your life, sweetheart," Liz insisted, still smiling and grasping Paula's hand reassuringly.

COOTIES

She could not explain it, but it was as though, in her mother's wisdom, she was speaking beyond the themes of marriage. This was the goodbye she had always wished for, the one she never got the first time around, which led her down the dark hole she fell through when her mother had passed away.

It was here, her official farewell, that she came to peace with her mother's passing. Grasping her mother's hands, she stared one last time, still crying.

"I love you, mama," she told her mother, one final time. Paula felt it from her gut, it brought her both pain and peace at the same time. She willed herself to release her mother's grip and walk away.

"I love you too, Paula. Always, my dear," Liz said as Paula bravely made her way to the doors.

Paula did not dare look back. She knew if she saw her mother again that she would take hold of her and never leave this place, even if it meant spending eternity in this room. Hand in hand, she walked briskly with Anthony, attempting to leave the church as fast as possible, kindly smiling at the people in the crowd as they applauded their wedded bliss.

The two came upon the cathedral doors not knowing what to expect next. The doors opened up from the outside and again they were met with the similar fog they had experienced earlier. This meant they would end up somewhere brand new and Paula could not guess where it would lead and when this would end. Though happy, it was all a little exhausting being pulled into so many directions in so little time. In the case of seeing her mother it was also bittersweet, even if the interaction did leave her feeling fulfilled and complete.

As they walked through the fog once again, they could hear the sounds of applause, cheering, and laughter slowly die behind them. Once the silence hit, Paula felt her heart drop, knowing she would never see her mom again. However, she was grateful. No one gets to revisit the one they love the most, and they certainly do not get a second chance to do things right. With these thoughts swirling in her mind, she never broke stride, putting on a brave face for Anthony who was looking at her; his face asking, "Is everything all right?" Paula merely smiled back, holding his hand, marching toward the next destination.

Walking forth, there was no noise even as the fog dissipated, and the scenery became whole. They could both visibly see that they were now approaching what looked like their hotel room they stayed at during their honeymoon in Las Vegas. It was a suite in a hotel not too far off the strip. The familiar whir of the air conditioner and clean smell of the room came back to Paula's nose. The way it overwhelmed her senses was instant.

Two things were special about this room. This was not only the place where they would begin to celebrate their marriage together, having the time of their lives in the desert gambling mecca, but it was also the place where they had conceived their firstborn son, Rodney.

"Oh, my God, we're back in Vegas!" Anthony said with a huge smile on his face.

"I wonder if we can actually leave the room though, these doors are a little unforgiving," he joked.

"God, I hope we can leave the hotel room. I've wanted to come back to Vegas ever since we left it!" exclaimed Paula, looking around the room, touching familiar parts of it. It was a nice suite with a lot of amenities and features, smelled nice too. Paula noted that when they got back to their home, they really needed to book a Vegas trip again, kids or not.

"You know," Anthony looked at Paula.

"The strip was a lot of fun, but we also had a lot of fun in this room all week long too, if you remember," he said with a devilish grin.

COOTIES

"We honestly did enough in here to conceive, like, 10 babies," he joked, as Paula continued looking around the suite.

He stared at Paula, smiling, "I can't remember the last time I saw you this way. You're beautiful. I mean, you always are, but there's something different. Maybe it's me."

He had Paula's attention now.

"I guess I've neglected to notice it for a long time now - how beautiful you are, how lucky I was that you chose me, that you let me get you pregnant and carry our children, not once but twice."

Paula stared back at Anthony with the happiest smile.

"Well, we don't want to break the timeline, do we?" Paula said in a flirting fashion, now slowly taking off her shirt.

"Better get to making babies all over again."

"I couldn't agree more!" he quickly responded with a massive grin, quickly taking his own shirt off.

Every single emotion was bottled up from the events of the day and it came out in the form of Paula thrusting herself onto Anthony, kissing him. She had no care about bearings or figuring anything out. She knew exactly what room this was and what had happened here in the past so why wait for the inevitable. Paula knew she wanted nothing more than to be with Anthony, and she wanted to relive the feeling of giving herself over to Anthony whole, giving herself over to the idea of becoming a mother.

The thought actually turned her on quite a bit and Anthony was more than willing to cooperate. She knew he also was turned on by being able to have the moment all over again, being able to let go completely. It was part romanticism and also; Paula really wanted hot and heavy, toe-curling sex. It had been a long while and Paula was in primal mode, ready to tear Anthony apart.

LESTER

Paula wasted little time, foreplay being unnecessary at this point, and undid his belt, furiously trying to get at his pants. Anthony attempted to help her in this department, being just as eager as her, and tried to loosen the belt up, but she slapped his hand. He did not attempt to lend her a hand after that as she aggressively continued to get the belt off. Now successful, she threw him onto the bed and removed his pants.

Pulling off her own pants, she stared at him with pure intent.

"I want you to fuck me like you've never fucked me before!"

Rock solid and practically shaking with anticipation, Anthony was more than ready.

"Then get over here and let me fuck you," he said looking at Paula like she was prey in the wild.

MEET MR. SQUIGGLES

It was late at the Bowline residence. The moon was out, bathing the landscape with its luminous glow. Underneath the moon and its glow was the Bowline barn that stood firm with its various closed doors and windows rustling around as a light breeze from the night air sought its entrance. Within the barn it was mostly quiet, with the faint sounds of creaking wood giving ambience to the inner dwelling. On the floor, on a blanket of hay lie Paula and Anthony, intertwined in a deep, peaceful sleep.

Paula slowly awakened at first, not moving, taking in the landscape. She was greatly confused at first, half between a state of sleep she had just emerged from, and the waking world she now entered. Given the travels she recently encountered on her trip through time with Anthony, she was surprisingly not in shock at the sudden change of scenery.

Even in the darkness, she could see her husband. He was older now, and he had a beard. She knew she had changed back, too. This confirmed they were back home, in their own time. Her feelings from the events of the day were not removed though. The first encounter, the wedding, the sex in their hotel, was still there in her heart. That same heart pounded gently as she looked at her husband, the father of her two wonderful children.

"Sweetie," she whispered, to which Anthony snorted.

He looked ready to wake but then sank back to sleep, merely repositioning himself.

"Baby, wake up," Paula said a little louder, giving him a little shake.

This time he did wake. It was slow, and he started to catch his bearings a bit. Suddenly he shot up.

LESTER

"Whoa! Are we… back home?" asked Anthony, looking around in the dark barn, trying to familiarize himself with his surroundings while still waking up.

"Yeah, I think we made it back home, sweetie," Paula said happily.

She looked down, and it dawned on her that they both had their clothes on.

"Had the whole experience been in their heads? Was it all a dream?" she had wondered.

"Honey, look. We've got our clothes on. I thought we had sex?" Paula said, looking confused.

"We did," replied Anthony, looking down at his own clothes, still absorbing his surroundings.

"I know we did. We definitely went back. I mean, I could physically feel everything. It was real. I could touch, taste, smell, you name it," he continued, still looking confused.

"I mean, this is weird but, did Lester put our clothes back on?" he added with one of his eyebrows cocked upward.

"You know, I– I have no idea how any of his magic works. I just kinda go with it. Whatever it was, it felt very real. I know what I felt in there and how I felt" –she stopped herself– "what I FEEL for you."

"Same," he nodded back at her.

"Going back and retracing our steps, it's just good to see you now, as you are," Anthony said as he stared at her in the dark as best as he could with only slivers of moonlight outlining her body. He grabbed her hand.

"We're gonna be better from here on out. I promise."

He looked down at the ground and then brought his eyes up to meet hers. The statement made Paula smile ear to ear, and if he could fully see her, he would see that she had been blushing.

MEET MR. SQUIGGLES

"Let's go ahead and get on outta here though," Anthony said, smiling at Paula.

As he got up, they both stretched. Their bodies were sore, and they were still groggy.

"God, I feel like we've been out for hours, days even," still shaking out the cobwebs of their deep sleep.

Suddenly, they heard the door shuffling around. It caught the two off guard and they both stood close to each other in a surprising defensive position, ready for anything to come through the door. It flung open with a cascade of bright moonlight pouring in with a silhouette standing at the threshold of the barn.

It was Lester. They both felt a little foolish with Paula thinking "Well, who the hell else could it've been?"

"Howdy, lovebirds. Welcome back to Casa De Lester," he said with the usual smile on his yellow face.

Paula and Anthony both seemed extremely happy to see him. For Paula, it meant they were back in reality. The whole trip was amazing to her but at the same time she was exhausted and could not wait to get back and see her children. It was the one missing equation of her experience with Anthony. It was good to be home, and Lester was a good welcome home party.

"I've got some bad news though," Lester said with a serious look on his face.

Paula and Anthony were taken aback. They looked at each other with worry and confusion, mouths open.

"I'm sorry you two, but" –Lester stalled, like he was trying to gather the right words– "it's the year 2050!"

"WHAT?!" yelled Paula, looking shocked beyond all belief. Having been on the journey she just embarked and how tired they had both felt, she did not even question the news.

Anthony was completely lacking in words, he just stared at Lester and then at Paula.

"GOTCHA!" said Lester, with a mighty chuckle.

Paula and Anthony both let out a moan of frustration mixed with a massive sigh of relief.

"LESTER!" they both yelled, putting their hands over their chests in an attempt to calm their poor hearts down.

"Naw, you two've only been gone a few hours. The little kidaroos are inside eating pizza. Come on inside, pull up a chair and join us. It's pizza that came from your freezer, I spared no expense," joked Lester, walking towards the house.

"Be in in just a minute, Lester," said Paula who cocked her head back in relief that they were not in fact in the year 2050. Anthony still had his hand over his heart, sharing eye contact with Paula, silently agreeing in relief.

"I almost forgot," said Lester, coming back towards the Bowlines.

"Did y'all find what you were looking for?"

They smiled at one another, nearly blushing. Anthony brought his face to Lester's and whispered, "And then some, Lester. I think we're good," he said reassuringly.

"But how in the hell did you do that?" asked Paula of Lester.

Lester thought about it for a moment, looking at the sky, pondering his answer. He shot his face back down quickly and looked at both of them.

"Magic!" he jubilantly said, shrugging in a matter-of-fact way.

"Could it have been anything else?" Paula stated the obvious as she started to walk towards the house with everyone else following her lead.

As she entered the house, she was greeted by Rodney and Robert who both ran up to greet her and Anthony.

"Mom! Dad! You guys are back!" they said excitedly.

"Yes, my little turdlings we're here. We didn't go too far," said Paula hugging both of the kids.

They also ran up to hug their dad.

"Geez, kiddos, we weren't even gone that long. You act like you haven't seen us in years," added Anthony to the conversation.

"Oh, I know, it's just that we're not used to you not being around this late. Even with Lester, it just felt kinda weird. I mean, we didn't see you all day long and you guys were kinda mad at each other again," said Rodney who looked a little sad.

"Well, everything's good now, kids. Yeah, your dad and I had a little talk about things. Found a umm… new perspective about, you know, stuff and you won't have to worry about so much of the bad vibes around here, ya know."

This appeared to make the kids happy as their sad demeanor shifted to smiles.

"So, get back to your pizza, I know I sure want some, guys," Paula continued, looking for some pizza to eat as she was extremely hungry from the events of the day, as was Anthony who was way ahead of her, eating a pizza with no plate.

"Yoooou savage," Paula jokingly blurted out to Anthony.

"Hey, why don't we all hang out on the couch for some family time," Lester urged the family, ushering everyone over in the TV room.

Grabbing pizza slices, they all happily marched over to grab their respective spots on the couch to talk about the day, hang out with each other. Lester sat on the far end of the couch to give everyone their room. Everyone was so hungry that not much could be said, as Paula and Anthony were scarfing down their pizzas. Being the bottomless pits they were, Rodney and Robert were also quiet as they shoved the delicious food into their mouths.

LESTER

Lester then stood in front of everyone without a single slice of pizza in his hand. He looked around the room at everyone, smiling ear to ear with his hands behind his back. As the family continued to eat, one by one they all raised their heads from their plates to look at Lester, who stood still, saying nothing.

"Something going on, Lester? You look like you've got something on your mind," Paula quizzed Lester as she put her plate down.

"Aw shucks, I just thought since y'all are putin' that tasty pizza in your face holes, why doesn't ol' Lester go ahead and entertain ya a bit," he said with glee.

It sounded like a great idea. A little ambience to have while the family sat around the couch having some fun, eating frozen pizza that, for some reason, tasted particularly good tonight.

"I want you all to meet my friend Mr. Squiggles," Lester said as a giant frowny face appeared opposite of everyone close to the opposing wall.

The face looked crude, like it was drawn by a child on a blackboard. It looked innocent enough, even for a giant frowny face randomly sitting in one's living quarters. By now, the Bowlines were used to Lester's playful ways whether it was going on an adventure or having the adventure come to you. To them, this was just another visitor, one of Lester's friends. Everyone was actually intrigued to meet Lester's pal.

"Well, everyone, let's say hi to Mr. Squiggles," encouraged Paula of everyone around the couch.

"HELLO, MR. SQUIGGLES!" everyone said at once, including Lester.

MEET MR. SQUIGGLES

"Hi, everyone," Mr. Squiggles replied back to everyone in a slow, sluggish delivery still wearing his frown. He looked around, observing the room and all of its inhabitants.

"So, how are you Mr. Squiggles? To what do I owe the pleasure?" asked Paula.

Still Mr. Squiggles looked around as everyone, especially the kids, waited for his answer.

"There's no pleasure for Mr. Squiggles. I'm just here," he said in a pitiful way, making everyone instantly feel sorry for him.

"Mr. Squiggles, are you okay?" asked Robert, who seemed to genuinely want to help his new friend.

"I definitely need help," he replied.

"With what, Mr. Squiggles?" Robert cocked his head, looking worried.

"I need a help-ING of that tasty looking food in your hands."

This made everyone in the room laugh, breaking up some of the tension. He was in no need of help; it was just his demeanor. To Paula, he was just a playful little Grumpy Gus.

Robert got up and grabbed another slice of pizza to feed to Mr. Squiggles, throwing it in his waiting mouth. Everyone gave a small little cheer while Mr. Squiggles chewed the pizza. It struck everyone as odd that the pizza did not go out the back end like they had expected. Paula was ready to have to clean up the floor, but their guest was capable of eating. Saved her from having to wipe down the hardwood.

"Are you happy now, Mr. Squiggles?" asked Robert.

"It was serviceable," replied Mr. Squiggles, as frowny as ever.

"I know what will cheer him up. It always cheers me up," Robert said as he got up from the couch.

LESTER

The family thought nothing of it as he walked away. Paula figured it was some toy he loved, which Robert had many. To keep the conversation going with their new guest, Rodney decided he had questions to ask in Robert's absence.

"Mr. Squiggles, where are you from?" Rodney inquired while eating his pizza, swinging his feet that dangled from the couch.

"I'm from out of town," answered Mr. Squiggles in his slow, pitiful delivery that everyone patiently waited on.

"Lester brought me here," he said, eyeballing Lester.

"Yeah, we're good ol' friends from way, way, waaaay back, me and this guy," Lester said, holding up his hands to demonstrate an exaggerated length; his arms stretched out longer than any normal being's limbs are capable of going.

"Lester! Did you get your memory back?" asked Paula, with her eyes wide open in surprise.

"No. No I didn't. That's weird. I wonder how I know that me and the Squigglenator go way back," Lester wondered aloud, rubbing his chin.

"That's because you do know me from way back," Mr. Squiggles confidently told Lester.

This surprised everyone, most of all Lester who stared off into space completely confused. He looked as though he was searching his brain for a memory pointing to Mr. Squiggles.

"Lester, maybe Mr. Squiggles is a key to getting your memory back. Go ahead and ask him some questions and he might know some answers!" Paula said, encouraging him to ask away.

"Oh, yeah. That's… that's a swell idea!"

He jumped to his feet.

"Boy I got a million of 'em to ask. I mean, what do I ask first?" Lester said, pacing around flailing his hands around in excitement.

MEET MR. SQUIGGLES

"Ask anything Lester! I mean, where you're from, that's a good start," suggested Anthony, gesturing out to Mr. Squiggles.

Before Lester could get anything out, just from around the corner, Robert showed up with the thing that often made him happy and it was Samantha, the family dog, who had been perfectly happy in hiding.

"Oh! Oh! Ummm, Robbie, me boy, I don't think that's a swell idea," Lester said, looking worried, knowing about how Samantha had been reacting to him since his arrival.

"No. Samantha will make Mr. Squiggles happy and feel real at home," he chuckled, holding Samantha up, walking closer to Mr. Squiggles.

As he brought Samantha closer, she growled loudly.

"Robert, get Samantha out of here! NOW!" Anthony ordered him, which made Robert look sad and concerned.

He clearly only meant to be nice to Mr. Squiggles but had caused a scene, and Robert's feelings looked hurt, knowing he had messed things up by bringing the dog out.

"I'm sorry– I was just trying to make Mr. Squiggles happy."

Samantha was now barking and thrashing around, trying to get loose.

"Robert, just let go of her. Let her run back to the room. Do it now!" Paula ordered Robert, losing her patience.

As he let go of Samantha, she did the unexpected and went running towards Mr. Squiggles. Furiously, she barked at Mr. Squiggles, standing between him and the family sitting on the couch.

Lester's attention had focused inward and was concentrating on what questions to ask Mr. Squiggles. He seemed to be lost in his own world, maybe even having his own epiphany, as the chaos ensued around him. The Bowlines were now attempting to get Samantha away from their new guest, Mr. Squiggles.

Mr. Squiggles seemed to be growing agitated himself by Samantha's barking and threats, lunging at the guest every so often. His brows furrowed down and his frown became even greater when he finally spoke.

"You made me mad."

Mr. Squiggles sounded angry and pitiful at the same time. Before anyone could move a muscle, two crudely drawn hands appeared at the side of the face.

"Lester!" yelled Paula.

Lester looked over at Mr. Squiggles just as he turned his hand into a fist and sent it down on Samantha at full force. There was a giant YIP! From Samantha who now lay on the floor, twitching.

"I want a help-ING of that tasty thing," Mr. Squiggles said, now picking up Samantha with the same hand he had crushed her with.

Everyone screamed in horror as Mr. Squiggles slowly put the family dog near his face and dropped her in his mouth, the same place the pizza had gone just moments before when things were still seemingly normal, fun, and innocent. The entire Bowline family could do nothing as they watched in horror as this frowny faced monster slowly chewed their beloved dog and family member, hearing her howl in pain from within its crudely drawn face.

"NOOOOOOOO!" yelled Lester.

Whether it had been from fear or trauma, Lester had been frozen in place the whole time, unable to move, unable to stop the events from occurring. His eyes were wider than ever, looking on in sheer terror as something of his own creation had taken a life in such a cruel, merciless way. His eyes were glassy, as if tears were about to well up.

MEET MR. SQUIGGLES

Lester was not the only one traumatized by the actions of Mr. Squiggles.

Rodney was crying and yelling at Mr. Squiggles, as Paula and Anthony grabbed him to run out of the room. Robert had to be picked up by Anthony on the way out, as he was completely paralyzed by what he was witness to. He had wet himself as he stood still crying profusely, unprepared for the violence he was experiencing, instantly feeling the guilt of being the one who brought Samantha out to meet Mr. Squiggles.

Holding their children, Paula and Anthony, ran outside as quickly as they could. Still trembling in ways they never thought possible, in total shock. Paula and Anthony stared at each other, shaking. They were trying to grasp if any of it was real. One minute they were on the couch enjoying pizza with the kids and the next minute their family dog, their third child, Samantha, was being eaten alive by a figment of someone's imagination.

Lester was still inside.

They had no intentions of going back in to see if he had gotten rid of the abomination or not. Paula was unsure of what to think. Lester was her friend, he was basically part of the family, but maybe his powers were too great even for him to control and someone died tonight because of his actions.

She knew it was an accident, but Lester was now a genuine hazard. She had to think about the safety of her family first and foremost. Paula knew, looking at Anthony he had to be thinking the same thing. "What in the hell can we possibly do in this situation?" she considered as she was still trying to calm down as her kids panicked like crazy, beyond inconsolable.

"I killed Samantha! It's my fault!" yelled Robert in between tears, face red from the pain and anguish of it all. He was heaving from crying so hard, snot coming out of his nose.

LESTER

Paula was sick with empathy knowing that it was enough for him to experience the pain of losing his friend, Samantha, but also knowing he would live with the guilt. It truly had not been his fault, no one could have known but it is hard convincing such a young boy of this fact.

"Robert, sweetie. Listen. It's not your fault. No one, not a single one of us could've known that was gonna happen. You understand?" she said, holding Robert tightly as he continued to cry. She rocked with him in an attempt to calm him down as he continued to wretch in sadness.

"Why didn't Lester stop him mom?!" Rodney asked through his tears, being held by his dad.

"He can do anything in the world! He could've stopped Mr. Squiggles!" Rodney reiterated.

"That's a good point," Paula thought to herself as she looked at Anthony.

The whole time Lester had been frozen in panic. Perhaps Lester was scared of Mr. Squiggles, maybe Lester's life was in jeopardy, and he was not to blame for what happened. Without knowing much about Lester's life, there were a myriad of reasons he was there, and they had never considered any of the reasons to be dangerous ones.

Mr. Squiggles seemed to know who he was and reacted violently whereas Lester has always been kind, gentle, and innocent. Perhaps Lester was a victim. This was beside the point though because, whatever was in the house was beyond their help. They were powerless and had to look out for themselves.

"Anthony what the hell do we do?" Paula asked her husband who was just as dazed and confused as she was.

Still, shifting his eyes around for answers, he came up with the only conclusion he could.

"We need to get the hell outta here is what we need to do!"

MEET MR. SQUIGGLES

Paula concurred.

The only thing that was important was the safety of each other and the kids. They needed to get out immediately. The only problem with this plan was that the keys to the truck were inside of the house, in the kitchen, the room next to Lester and Mr. Squiggles.

Paula and Anthony had both realized this at the same time.

"Shit," huffed Anthony, putting his head down in anger and disappointment.

He knew he was the one that was going to have to get those keys, Paula could see the fear on his face.

"Fuck!" he quietly snapped, gritting his teeth.

"The keys?" asked Paula with her head cocked sideways, looking more worried than ever.

"Yep. And I'm gonna have to go get them," Anthony replied with all the worry of a person about to run into a burning building.

Anthony looked at the opened door.

"Okay. Get the kids away from here, out by the street at least, hide behind one of the closest bushes. When I get the keys, I'm gonna bring the truck around and you can hop in with the kids and we can get the hell out of here."

Paula knew this was the best plan he had at the moment because she certainly had nothing up her sleeve. This was too unusual, too ludicrous, no one could be prepared for it. At one point she had considered having Anthony get the gun but, she knew, it was either the keys or getting the gun. They probably had one shot at getting either thing.

"All right. I'm heading in. You take the kids and go hide, okay!" said Anthony.

"Mom, where's dad going?" Rodney asked, his face awash with worry.

"Daddy's gotta go get the keys, baby," she replied to Rodney, putting her hand on his face, her eyes sympathetic to his concern.

"No. He can't!" protested Rodney.

"Sweetie. If daddy doesn't get those keys, we could all be in danger. He needs us all to be strong and do what he says. We have to go wait by the road and hide. The longer we talk about this, the smaller daddy's window is gonna get. We need to hurry, baby!"

Rodney was in total opposition of his dad heading back into that house by himself, but he understood the brevity of the situation. Rodney realized that by holding things up, it could limit his father's success. So, begrudgingly, he nodded his head in approval.

Anthony patted him on the shoulder, "That's my main man. You need to be there for Robert and mom. Man of the house until I get back with those keys, all right."

Again, Rodney nodded. He was ready to do his part.

With that, Anthony jogged into the house as Paula and the kids scurried off towards the road to find a bush to hide behind and wait for the truck. Paula could not see much through the bushes and the angle she was at did not peer through the door, only a stream of light poured out through the doorway into the darkness of the night.

It hit her how just quickly things had changed when she saw the barn standing by itself. She stared at the barn, perplexed by the events of the day, from having the love with her husband renewed and reborn, to the most horrific experience of her lifetime all within hours. The moments all seemed like a lifetime apart.

MEET MR. SQUIGGLES

"Mom, look," whispered Rodney to his mother, pointing at something.

It was Lester. He was walking outside, toward the barn. He appeared to be in a catatonic state, in shock, walking with his eyes wide open, mouth ajar, walking instinctually to the barn, his home. There was no sign of Anthony anywhere. As she waited for any sign of him, Lester made his way into the barn and disappeared from her sight.

"Shit! where are you, Anthony?" she whispered aloud.

The kids were getting worried. There was no whining or crying but you could sense their panic every moment their father was not accounted for. Paula had to start thinking of what to do in case the worst happened, but she was frozen. Every idea was as bad as the last.

There was no way she could go inside to get the keys; risk dying in the process, leaving the kids to fend for themselves. The other option was to walk all the way to the nearest town. No one ever came out this way so there was no flagging anyone down and if she wanted to call anyone to help her, the phone was inside the house in the kitchen by the keys. Paula knew it. She was shit out of luck.

From out of nowhere Anthony went running into the barn after Lester. He lacked any look of panic on his face at all, Paula was unable to really assess what was going on. He stood outside of the barn doors looking in with a confused look on his face.

"Paula," he yelled into the darkness.

She came rustling through the bushes with the kids and ran up to Anthony as fast as she could.

Paula noticed Anthony had the keys in his left hand and a gun in his right hand as she approached.

LESTER

"Sweetie, that Squiggles thing is gone," he said while poking his head out of the barn doors.

"Lester is– I dunno, stunned I guess is the best word to use. He just walked right past me like I wasn't even there when I went to get the keys; scared the shit outta me."

Anthony drew a deep breath and tried to gain his bearings once again.

The kids were huddled closely against Paula, still scared, shaking, and confused.

"Dad, I don't wanna go back in there. I'm afraid Mr. Squiggles'll get me," Robert said quietly with terror in his eyes.

"What if it's still in there, just somewhere else?" asked Rodney.

"Listen kids. Mr. Squiggles ain't in there no more, so it's gonna be okay, all right," promised Anthony to the kids, looking unsure himself if that was one hundred percent true.

"Y'all gotta get inside, outta here, with your mom."

"What are you going to do, Anthony?" Paula asked, suspecting the worst, eyeballing the gun he held in his right hand.

"I'm gonna do what I have to," said Anthony with his eyes looking regretful, like he was in charge of putting down a rabid dog.

"He's part of this family, sweetie!" she gritted through her teeth.

"NO. HE'S. NOT!" Anthony sternly said to Paula, gritting his teeth as well.

Taking a moment to close his eyes and collect himself, he explained himself.

"Look, I appreciate everything he's done, including for us, but… baby, Samantha's dead. That could've easily been one of the kids. At the very least, I have to ask him to leave because this is something way beyond us. I mean, you do understand the gravity of this, right?".

With the kids huddling around her, Paula looked at Anthony for just a moment, "Kids, your mom will be right back. Stay here with your father."

She began to open the barn door.

"What in the HELL are you doing?" grabbing Paula's arm, not forcefully but in a concerned way, like a person about to walk into traffic.

"I'm going in to talk to him. Yeah, it's scary, it's terrifying, but just imagine what it's like for him. He's been good to us and was there for our times of need, so maybe it's time to be there for him. If we send him packing, who knows what happens to him or anyone else out there. This is our responsibility, Anthony. He trusts us. I'm gonna go talk to him. Get the kids inside and put that gun away," she said, staring at Anthony.

He said nothing back, just staring into her eyes, knowing there was no changing her mind about the decision she was making. Anthony looked as though he wanted to say something, like he wanted to protest but he grabbed the kids, looked towards the house, and marched the children forward.

The children could be heard protesting. They had no desire to go back into the house, not so soon after the events of Mr. Squiggles, but they were also confused about what their mom was doing. They were confused and distraught about the whole night and Anthony, walking towards the house, was doing his best to comfort them.

Paula knew she was doing the right thing, but she also knew she had a tough job ahead of her by having to go in and talk to Lester. He was part of this family in her mind, and he had made a huge mistake. She was clueless how his magic truly worked but she did not want to assume that Mr. Squiggles was of his own creation and, if it was, perhaps it was a creation gone bad. This could be a major teaching moment.

For as much as she loved Samantha, she was reminded of when she herself was a child and accidentally killed her own goldfish by flushing it down the toilet. We all make mistakes but driving off Lester might send him down a path that would not work out for anyone, and besides, how could she turn her back on him? She knew she could never live with herself. She loved the poor, misunderstood creature.

As she walked into the barn, she saw no sign of Lester.

"Lester?" she called out, hoping he might respond.

There was no response back, but she could hear a noise just behind a pile of cardboard boxes. Moving around the boxes, Paula could see that Lester was sitting behind the boxes, holding himself, staring off into space with a look of worry. Paula said nothing, she just observed Lester. Kneeling down to comfort him, he finally spoke.

"I'm a murderer."

"No Lester, you're not a murderer. Mr. Squiggles ate Samantha, not you," she stated calmly and firmly.

"Yeah but Mr. Squiggles is a part of me. He came from my doing and so he was my responsibility. I don't even know how I remembered him, honest Injun."

Lester looked ahead, contemplating the events that had gone down tonight.

"I'm a monster. It's only a matter of time before something downright awful happens again. I know Anthony was gonna ask me to leave, I could hear him outside and, well, maybe he's right-a-roo," said Lester solemnly.

"Listen, Lester. The thing about family is that you stick together. I couldn't send you out there into the world alone any more than my own kids. We all make mistakes, even huge ones and, yeah, everyone is scared, but we can get around this thing.

Together. It's what we call a teaching moment," Paula said, putting her hand on Lester's shoulder.

"How is ol' Lester ever gonna face your main squeeze and the little fellas again though? I'm so ashamed of what I done," Lester said, now looking down at the ground with great sadness in his eyes.

"Quimby," Paula said aloud much to the confusion of Lester who looked at her for further clarification.

"Quimby was a kitten we had taken in a few years back, before Robert was ever born. A cute little calico, playful and curious, loving."

Paula now looked at Lester eye to eye.

"One day, Rodney was playing around with his bow and rubber arrows. For some reason, he thought it would be funny to play hangman with the cat. It was very brief, but he put the string under Quimby's neck, lifted up, and I don't think Rodney really understood that it would harm the cat, it happened so quickly. Well, it crushed Quimby's throat, and she suffocated to death quickly. Probably dead before she hit the floor."

The revelation caused Lester's eyes to get big and he put his hands over his mouth in shock.

"We never got a cat after that because it kinda traumatized him, you know. One day he might, he's getting older, but he learned a valuable lesson even if, unfortunately, it was at the cost of that poor kitten's life. But I'll tell you what, I didn't send Rodney packing, I didn't put him down."

Lester looked away towards the ground, to consider what Paula was trying to tell him. You could see he understood the advice but, of course, still felt guilty.

LESTER

"One day, you'll feel better about this. Life is about mistakes, some huge and some small, but all important. Learn from your past, you know?"

"What about them, inside?" Lester said, looking towards the direction of the house.

"Well, none of them are perfect either. They've all done something, many things to be ashamed of, and I'll happily remind them of that. No matter how scary Mr. Squiggles was, or traumatic the loss of Samantha is, we all learn from it, and we forgive, we move on. Do your best every day, that's all anyone can ask. Everyone will come around. You know, above all, Lester: Learn to forgive yourself. Don't carry that weight with you. Life's too short," she reassuringly told Lester.

He did smile, knowing that Paula was trying to comfort him, but you could tell it still hurt. It would likely take some time but ultimately Lester would learn from his mistake and regain the trust of the household, Paula was sure of this.

"You staying out here the rest of the night?" she asked.

"Yeah. I got a lot of thinking to do. You said a whole mess a stuff and it's swimmin' around my ol' noggin' like a little puzzle. Plus, some things are starting to come back from my past because of Mr. Squiggles."

"Oh, well that's something, right? I mean, some kind of silver lining!" Paula said calmly.

She felt like they were closer to unveiling the mystery of Lester. The preference would have been to solve it without casualties, but what was done was done in regard to poor Samantha. If it helped jog his memory, then she was choosing to look on the positive side of things.

"You're right. It is something! Maybe something big, like I done found a lost treasure. Yeah. I'll be up all night, digging as fast and hard as I can to get that gold. YARRRR!" he jubilantly yelled with a small giggle behind it.

MEET MR. SQUIGGLES

Paula made a slight chuckle and smiled as she could see the light re-enter Lester's eyes. Her pep talk seemed to help Lester, who was crushed by the violence of his interaction with Mr. Squiggles. Knowing she was now going to have to pep talk and get the family back on Lester's side made her a bit nervous.

The kids were traumatized, and Anthony was at his wits' end which was an unfortunate turn of events after the adventure Lester had sent them both on to rekindle their love. It felt like she was back at square one. She had to be brave and put on her patience cap. Paula was the matriarch of this family and she was compelled to take charge of this situation.

Walking inside the house, the kids were inside of the living area by the window. They had no ambitions to be in the TV room where Mr. Squiggles had eaten their beloved Samantha what seemed like hours ago. Anthony could relate, and he sat next to the children, talking to them, still calming the two down from the horrific event.

"Hey guys," Paula calmly stated as she sat closer to the children.

"Scary night, huh?" to which both of the children nodded.

"You know, it is really scary, but we all make mistakes. When I was younger, I flushed a goldfish down the toilet. I don't know why I did it, but I was young and didn't really grasp what I was doing."

The kids sat, patiently listening with their heads down.

"We all do some things we regret that maybe we didn't have any control over."

"Like the time I hurt Quimby?" said Rodney who was now looking up at Paula. As he looked at her, Paula could see guilt in his eyes. Clearly, he remembered killing the poor kitten and he never forgave himself.

"Yes. Just like that, Rodney," she said with a tone of understanding, putting her hand on his shoulder.

"I think what we really need right now is to show some empathy toward Lester. He's like you guys, he's a big kid who is still learning in this world. He had no way of knowing what Mr. Squiggles would do, what his magic is capable of. Because of tonight's events he has to live with what he's done, and he has to learn from it, that his magic is not just a toy, that unless he can control it, he can't use it," she said looking at everyone around the house, including Anthony who was still on edge. Clearly, he had something to say but he bit his lip in front of the children.

"Did you see Lester, mom?" asked Robert.

"I did see him, yes," she smiled, looking at Robert who now had his head up.

"Is he okay?"

"He is… very sad right now, Robbie. He has a lot of thinking to do because he's sad about what Mr. Squiggles did and he's worried that people are afraid of him now because of it," said Paula, trying to be careful with her wording in regard to Lester.

"I don't think I'm scared of Lester. Just Mr. Squiggles. I don't ever want to see Mr. Squiggles again. He's bad," Robert stated now with tears in his eyes and his lip quivering.

"Yeah, mom. Lester is our friend. He can't help what Mr. Squiggles did. It wasn't him, he's always been good to us," Rodney said, backing up what Robbie had said.

"I'm glad you guys feel that way. Lester has decided to stay in the barn for the night and wants to be left alone, you know, to have that time to think, like I said before. It was just as scary for him I imagine."

Both of the kids nodded their heads up and down in agreement.

As the conversation was going on, Anthony kept looking around at everyone with a lot of concern. Clearly, he was not sold on Lester's staying. Just minutes before, he was armed and ready to storm into the barn and do what he felt was necessary.

Paula was glad she at least got him to the point where he was going to ask Lester just to leave. She felt as though his actions were not over dramatic because he was merely thinking of his family. Afterall, it's not every day that someone conjures up a stick figure monster that eats the family dog.

Later that night, after having tucked the children in, Paula knew it was time to talk to Anthony. He was not quite as combative as before the adventure that Lester had sent them on, which felt like it was a lifetime ago at this point. Most of the night he was quiet, saying very little. This had worried Paula a little since he had been so vocal in the past and typically, if he was concerned about something, he always chimes in but, this time, he conceded with little fight.

"Hey baby, I know that I talked to the kids about Lester earlier and they seem okay with everything but you– well, you seem a little off. What's going on in your head?" she asked Anthony, rubbing his shoulder from behind, understanding of whatever response might come next. She knew he was on edge still.

"I'm just tired. Exhausted. Know what I mean?" he turned to her.

"Obviously I'm not okay with everything. At all. True, we all make mistakes, but that power is" –he searched for the right words– "too much."

"He just conjured something up from thin air and just like that" –he snapped his fingers– "that thing ate up our Samantha and she's gone forever."

He looked at Paula.

"The kids are younger, and they might be able to put that out of their minds but, I just can't get that out of my head, and I know I never will. The magic he had before was so innocent and, I dunno, silly, like a game. It was harmless but this, this is dangerous, you know. Like, we have a grizzly bear in the house, and it can accidentally swipe a paw at us in good fun and next thing you know, our guts are sprawled out on the floor."

He looked into Paula's eyes with great fear and astonishment before placing the gun on the nightstand and he sat quietly for just a moment collecting his thoughts.

"It's funny to think I was going to try and shoot him. I bet you a million bucks they would've just bounced off him. I still think we could ask him to leave though, become someone else's problem. We could call someone from the government, the authorities. Paula, this whole thing is insane, and I feel like I'm the only one that understands the weight of it all," he said as Paula listened without interruption.

"You have to understand that I love you and I love the kids more than anything and I'm worried. I'm worried and I feel helpless. Going back in time with you, feeling that connection, seeing my kids after coming back from that, I feel protective of all of your lives. I almost lost you months ago, the kids almost lost their mother, and there's this thing, an alien? A lab experiment? Who knows!"

Anthony was getting more worked up.

"There's this creature just sitting in there with these powers we can't even begin to understand and you're telling us all to calm down, to be understanding and sympathetic. It's hard to be calm when we're sleeping over a nuclear warhead. That's what I saw tonight. I just wish you'd see it too."

Anthony was more agitated than before with his calm demeanor now gone. Though he was not being argumentative, he had certainly made up his mind, and it contrasted the ideas that Paula had.

The bottom line: Lester was a threat.

MEET MR. SQUIGGLES

"I just love you. I love the kids. I loved Samantha and now she's gone. Maybe I just need to sleep on things. It's been a long, draining day and it was capped off by something nasty. A good night's sleep and then we can revisit things in the morning," Anthony said while holding Paula's hand.

He said his piece, expressing himself in a way that Paula could respect. She knew exactly what he was feeling, even if she disagreed and knew in her heart that Lester was something special, that he was something kind. It would take time for Lester to gain Anthony's trust and Paula knew they could get there but, for tonight, it was best to not contradict Anthony and let him wrestle with the thoughts and emotions of tonight's events.

"I love you too, baby. You're right, a good night's sleep is what's best. We'll do this one step at a time, together," she said, looking into his eyes smiling.

In turn, Anthony half-smiled back at her. Clearly, he enjoyed her compassion, but was entirely too exhausted to coach his face muscles to muster up any more than a slight reassuring grin.

As they settled into bed, Paula nestled herself into Anthony's chest just like she had at the Vegas hotel. The darkness, the swaying of the wind outside, the feeling of the silky sheets, being held by Anthony, it was comforting. She closed her eyes and felt the peace of it all surrounding her, she embraced it whole and felt her bones settle into the bed. She was so comfortable that within seconds Paula fell asleep.

Deep in sleep and dreaming away, Paula was in her own little world revisiting the good parts of the day. She was dreaming about being back in time with Anthony, revisiting her old friends, talking to her mother again, it's like Lester himself had teleported her back.

LESTER

This time around though it was foggier, and things skipped around. Still, there was an overall feeling of tranquility to it. Every moment was as good and happy as the last, reliving some memories that were left out of her journey earlier in the day. Her life was wonderfully encompassed as she slept through the night in total splendor. Her memories being of all positive thoughts and emotions with all of the negative ones edited out. As dreams go, she could not ask for better.

Slowly, some hours into her sleep, she started to emerge from her slumber and back into reality. With the thoughts still fresh in her mind, she turned over to see Anthony, knowing he was there in real life and accessible to kiss on the head, even if he slept through it and was none the wiser. It meant something to her.

As she turned over though, she noticed that Anthony was missing. She looked at the bathroom door to see if he occupied it but quickly noticed that it was dark and empty. Confused, Paula started to look around the room to seek some clues.

As she sat up in bed, Paula looked at Anthony's nightstand. She remembered distinctly that Anthony had placed his handgun on the stand before they went to bed and now it was missing. That's when it hit her that, even though they spoke about waiting and not making rash decisions, about sleeping on it, he went and did the one thing he was not supposed to do. Paula just wished with all of her heart that she was wrong for both Anthony and Lester's sake.

Paula threw on some clothes as fast as she could to go head out to the barn. She did not dare wake the kids up. They already had a traumatic night and needed the rest, so she stealthily sneaked past their bedroom to avoid their attention. Before running out to the barn she did one sweep of the general area but there was no sign of Anthony.

MEET MR. SQUIGGLES

She was now one hundred percent sure that he was in the barn and the thought made her sick to her stomach. Lester could be dead already. When she fell asleep, she could see the desperation in Anthony's eyes. She thought it would pass and, in the morning, he might see things her way.

"Goddamnit, sweetie!" she quietly grumbled into the darkness of the house.

Diplomacy was going to be key if Lester was not dead already. A thought rushed over her that terrified her. She was so concerned about Lester; she had never considered if Lester might have defended himself and things went south. There was no firing of a gun and, even from the barn, the gun would have made enough noise to wake everyone up. Things were getting worse by the minute.

With no time to waste, Paula tossed her shoes on and made her way to the front door. As she reached for the door handle, the door flung open, knocking her back a bit.

It was Lester. In his hands he was holding Anthony who was hogtied with a gag in his mouth. Lester himself was dressed up like a cowboy; gallon hat, boots with spurs, tight jeans, like he just came out of a honky tonk.

"Pardon me, ma'am. It looks like Quickdraw Lester done found a dirty ol' rat trying to plug a few holes in his fancy li'l gitup," exclaimed Lester, still with a big smile on his face.

Paula could only assume that Lester still thought of the whole thing as a little game which may have worked out for Anthony who was kicking and thrashing around, trying to say something through his gag. This just made Lester laugh.

"Now, calm on down there ya mangy ol' yella bellied horny toad!" said Lester as he tossed Anthony on the floor like a sack of potatoes.

The landing looked rough, especially for Lester who usually played gentle, careful not to hurt anyone.

LESTER

Paula wondered if Lester was actually angry with the way that he had thrown Anthony to the ground. She could see why he might be angry, but it still surprised her. She had never seen any kind of malicious behavior from him, outside of kicking the angry pig to the moon, but that was in defense of the family.

"Ma'am, this scoundrel moseyed on up to muh sleepin' quarters. Luckily, I can't sleep at all, so I was able to get the jump on 'em and take away his ol' hand revolver. See!"

He took out Anthony's gun which was emptied of the bullets and then he threw the gun beside Anthony.

"The lowdown lily livered varmint was fixin' ta do me in with that thar thing!"

Lester was still smiling. Paula still wondered if he was actually angry, or in character as Quickdraw Lester. She hoped that Lester had believed Anthony was just playing around. Lester's demeanor was the same as always. He was hard to read right now, which made it hard for Paula to assess the situation enough to manipulate it for everyone's best outcome.

Thinking of something to say, to recover from Anthony's actions, Paula tried to come up with a lie.

"Oh, Quickdraw Lester, I see you got that ol' bandit. I've been walking around looking for Black Bart the Bandit and luckily you found him, you know, before he could rob you of your candy."

The lie was perfect. Paula was proud of how fast she came up with it. Lester would be none the wiser of Anthony's true intentions. She knew that Lester would brush it off as a little fun and then afterwards, she could be the one to kill Anthony for going behind her back and lying to her. One thing at a time though. She could always punish Anthony later.

"I do apologize, my good ma'am but that cheese ain't gonna cut," Lester said, tipping his hat.

MEET MR. SQUIGGLES

Paula was a little shocked by the statement. It was not at all what she had expected. The only good indication right now was that Lester was still smiling.

"While I can appreciate you coverin' for this here withered ol' turkey jerky, well, I do think he'll have to be dealt with."

"Dealt with? Well, surely you can let me– your deputy, take care of this rascal, right?" Paula said, trying to find a way to get the ball back in her court.

"My apologies, ma'am, but I don't believe you've been deputized," he said, tipping his hat again.

"No. This here horse muckin', two timin' pile of horse fleas is gonna have to face a jury of his peers," he said while looking down at Anthony who was still fussing and fighting the ropes.

"Lester. You can't be serious? We're just playing a game here. You understand that, right?" she asked both confused and a little worried, pleading as general worry started to set in.

"Ma'am, I ain't got no choice in the matter. This boy here, he's gotta go to trial for the attempted murder of Quickdraw Lester!"

Paula was truly shocked and frozen in place as Lester picked her husband up with one arm, turned around, and walked back to the barn with him in tow. She shot up and got in front of Lester in protest, trying to find some way to stop him from moving forward.

"Ma'am, I'm just doing my job. If I were you, I'd find some character witnesses to bring to the trial. Bring anyone you can think of to testify to his character because it's not looking good, ma'am. The prisoner could very well end up with a wedgie or even an Indian Rug Burn. The judge is a real stale piece of bread, know what I mean?"

LESTER

Lester broke no stride, continuing to carry Anthony to the barn.

The things he said did make her feel a little better even though Lester was more committed to his role than usual. He only spoke of silly things like wedgies and Indian Rug Burns, so she at least knew Lester was still treating things good natured. The whole time he had been smiling as well so that was also a plus.

Little positive signs aside, she still needed to round the kids up so that they could be star character witnesses for what was bound to be one of the oddest trials the planet has ever seen. Though she knew Anthony's life was not on the line, she also had no ambitions to see her husband have his underwear pulled over his head.

Paula knew eventually she would have to have a real talk with Anthony, try to re-center him, do all the damage control she was capable of but, for now, it was time to wake up the kids.

It was time for the trial of the century.

THE TRIAL OF WHATSHISFACE

All the children wanted to do was sleep. Sleep was so very nice ten minutes ago before Paula came barging into the room. She kept blathering on; something about Lester, dad, a trial, and them both needing to be character witnesses for their father in a trial being prosecuted by Lester. They had little time to put their clothes on but did so in a hurry, and off to the barn they went.

"So, what is this whole character witness thing again?" Rodney asked his mom.

"Well, you two will be asked by Lester to say good things about your father."

"Well, what if I say he's a dirty butthole?" Rodney laughed.

This caused Robbie to start laughing uncontrollably, which in turn made Rodney laugh even harder.

"Rodney, watch your mouth. Seriously!" she barked at him.

"Kids I need you to think of this as a game, kinda. Like, pretend that dad's life is on the line here and he'll only live through the ordeal if you say really super nice things."

Rodney stopped in his tracks.

"Wait, dad's not in actual trouble, is he?" he asked.

Paula had to think about her answer because she had no real idea how to answer that. While he would not face a firing squad, a wet willy was certainly still trouble but, it was better not to let the kids worry.

"No, no, your dad went to talk to Lester after everything that happened, but your dad had his gun on him–"

"Dad was going to shoot Lester?" Rodney cut her off.

"No, dad had it on him for his own protection. We all love Lester but, you know, your dad was still scared after everything that happened with Mr. Squiggles. Would you go walking around tonight without protection after seeing that?" she asked her children.

They both looked at each other and nodded in agreement.

"So, Lester's mad at dad now?" Rodney inquired.

"Yeah, I think his feelings are hurt about it, and this is how he's choosing to deal with it. I'll be honest with you two; I don't know what's going on exactly, but this is Lester, so I think it's a safe bet that it's going to be something different, the opposite of normal or boring, that's for sure."

The kids both smiled. It made sense to them.

"So, we're going to have fun?" Robbie chimed in.

"Yeah, you can think of it like that. Most courtrooms are real stuffy, they make you fall asleep, but I don't think that's going to be the case here," she said to the kids as she slowly walked closer to the barn.

"Mom, have you been in a courtroom before?" Rodney asked with a smile on his face.

Thinking about her wild teens and twenties, she wanted to plead the fifth.

"You ask too many questions, turd spawn. Now keep walkin'," she shot back at him, sensing his smile getting even bigger.

Approaching the barn, Paula could hear a lot of different noises coming from within. It threw her off at first since she had never heard so much as a peep coming out of the barn. For a moment she wondered if other people were inside the barn, as she got closer, she could hear high-pitched voices inside squabbling. It was obvious there were quite a few inhabitants in the barn.

THE TRIAL OF WHATSHISFACE

Before entering the doors, she wanted to go over things with the kids one more time.

"Remember, guys, just make sure you go up to the bench whenever you're called and answer questions about dad. Say REALLY good things about him, okay? Dad won't thank you for getting him a pie in the face."

She was sure that at this point, Anthony was inside and extremely angry since he was hogtied and gagged. Reality hit Paula. She knew it was going to be tough, if not impossible, to turn any of this around. The idea of diplomacy seemed to be out the window.

As entered the barn, she was floored to see an entire room of Lesters inside, which happened to look a lot bigger than she remembered.

It was a makeshift courtroom with a smattering of Lester-like jurors moving into their seats. There was also a Lester looking judge, but he was dressed up like a British magistrate with a full white wig who kept banging his gavel to no avail as the Lester jurors all kept bickering with one another.

There appeared to be Quickdraw Lester who had his own Lester lawyer. They sat at their own bench, huddled down, likely talking about the case. Paula was greeted by a nicely dressed Lester who appeared to be another lawyer.

"How ya' doin', ma'am? I've been assigned to your husband's case. I don't know if I can get him off for trying to rob that liquor store, but I will do my diddly darndest to get him off light with the judge," Defense Attorney Lester promised.

"Rob? Liquor store?" She looked confused.

"I thought he was up on charges for attempted murder? For trying to kill Quickdraw over there." she pointed at Quickdraw Lester.

"MURDER!? Ooooh man, I'm totally gonna lose this case," Defense Attorney Lester said as he turned to the nearby water carafe and drank the entire carafe furiously while shaking, obviously stressing out.

"Hear ye! Hear ye!" shouted Magistrate Lester, which everyone still ignored.

The juror Lesters were still arguing among themselves, the Lester lawyers were now arguing with each other, largely ignoring anything. Finally, Magistrate Lester picked up his gavel and flung it at some random Lester juror's head.

"I said shyuuuut uuuuup!" yelled Magistrate Lester furiously at the entire courtroom as the random Lester juror massaged their sore spot from the Magistrate's gavel plinking off his head.

"Now, I got a whole bunch of these in case any of ya pipe up again!" said Magistrate Lester, wielding a new gavel and shaking it at everyone in the courtroom.

Next to Paula, amidst the throwing of gavels and threats, the kids found it impossible not to laugh at it all. It was indeed quite hysterical, but the Magistrate did not see it that way.

"Hey, you, over there! Defense Lawyer guy. My arm isn't so good these days, think you can thwap those kids on the head for me?"

Without batting an eyelash, Defense Attorney Lester picked up his folder of random papers and swatted both kids on their head.

"Hey!" yelled Rodney.

"Sorry, just doing my job," apologized Defense Attorney Lester, shrugging his shoulders.

"Now that everyone has shut their blabber holes, this court is now in session."

Magistrate Lester banged his gavel, getting everyone's attention and full silence.

"Sooo, uhhhh… what are we doing again?" he asked, looking around the room for anyone who might know.

THE TRIAL OF WHATSHISFACE

"We're having a trial because this guy tried to kill this guy," said Defense Attorney Lester pointing from Anthony to Quickdraw Lester.

"What!? Did you really try to kill that guy?!" Magistrate Lester asked Anthony in total shock.

The only problem was that Anthony was gagged and had no way of speaking. He muffled furiously and thrashed around because he was also still hogtied.

"Good God, man. Untie the defendant so that he might defend himself!" he ordered Anthony's bumbling defense lawyer.

"Oh, lemme take care of that, sorry," he said, quickly trying to untie and ungag Anthony.

"Hurry up, fella, I don't want any gavels flyin' at my noggin," continued Defense Attorney Lester, finally getting Anthony untied.

"Okay the defendant is now untied," proclaimed Defense Attorney Lester, standing up straight to show the deed had been done.

Anthony was pulling off his gag and still getting some of the ropes undone when Magistrate Lester asked him the question once again.

"So, uhhhh, you try to kill that guy?" pointing at Quickdraw Lester.

Anthony sat still trying to collect himself.

"Lester, you need to end this. We need to talk. Now." he said, looking down at the floor, taking a deep breath.

"Lester? Who ya talkin' to son?" asked Magistrate Lester, shifting his eyes around in confusion.

Anthony pulled his head up.

"I'm talking to you, all of you, you're all Lester and this isn't fun anymore. This isn't a game."

Everyone in the courtroom sat silently.

LESTER

"Ummm anyone know what this pickled Charlie is talkin' about?" asked Magistrate Lester.

"Oh, I am soooo sorry, your honorship. My client done been bonked on the head when he was viciously roughed up by that hornswoggler over there, Quickdraw Lester," Defense Attorney Lester said, now pointing his finger over at Quickdraw Lester.

Quickdraw looked around a little bit

"Who, me? All I did was hogtie that ol' mudbather up and bring him to justice. He's lucky that's all I did to 'em!"

Without warning a gavel went plinking off of Quickdraw Lester's head.

"OW!"

"I said ORDER!" yelled out Magistrate Lester.

"You never said anything!" protested Quickdraw Lester.

"Oh, yeah. You're right," he agreed with Quickdraw Lester.

"Oh, hey, since you're over there can you give me back my gavel," he asked Quickdraw Lester, who was now massaging his head. The now staggered and wobbly Quickdraw brought the gavel back to Magistrate Lester.

"All righty, so back to the murderer guy," said Magistrate Lester who was cut off by Defense Attorney Lester.

"Objection!"

"To what?" inquired Magistrate Lester

"You can't call my client a murderer, you're the judge!" Defense Attorney Lester said as he threw his hands up in annoyance.

"Oh yeah. Ummm let's go ahead and strike that from the record," he said, looking over at a stenographer that was a female Lester.

In fact, Paula herself suddenly realized that some of the Lester jurors were female Lesters as well. Paula looked carefully at one of them, trying to figure things out but suddenly Defense Attorney Lester poked his head next to Paula's.

"Whatcha' lookin' at?"

She noticed that the entire court was quiet and all the Lesters were mystified, trying to see what she was looking at.

"Oh, nothing. Just thought I saw a fly on that– lady over there."

"All right, all right, let's git this over with everybody. Your king–" Magistrate Lester was cut off as he spoke.

One of his guards whispered in his ear.

"I mean to say your Magistrate, NOT KING!" –he corrected himself– "Would like to see this trial over with sometime today. I'm a very busy man and I don't have time for all of this tomfoolery, you understand?"

"JESUS. I DON'T WANT TO PLAY ANYMORE!!" screamed Anthony in agitation.

"Mr. Murderpants!" Magistrate Lester yelled.

"Stop saying murderrrr!" Defense Attorney Lester shouted out in frustration.

"If I get one more outburst like that, I'm holding you in contempt! Or something rather," Magistrate Lester continued.

"You got me, boi?!" Magistrate Lester asked Anthony.

"Yes… your honor. I understand," Anthony replied, looking defeated and tired.

There was obviously no way out of this lunacy. He was no match for Lester's power, and he knew it. Though he was never malicious, and Paula never had a reason to be afraid of Lester, something about the whole thing unnerved her.

It was a feeling that things were different this time. Usually, Lester would stop once he realized that not everyone was having a good time, like a hurtful joke. This time though he seemed to be out of control, as if underneath all the humor he was hurt or angry, and he had no way of stopping this train of thought. Paula knew that, for now, it was best to play along and let things ride out.

"Okay Mr. Fancy Defender guy, can you tell us who you are defending?" Magistrate Lester asked.

"This is–" Defense Attorney Lester pulled his face up to Anthony's.

"Ummm, what's your name again?" he asked Anthony.

"You know who I– ugh. My name is Anthony," he replied to Defense Attorney Lester with great annoyance.

"All right, got it!" Defense Attorney Lester confirmed.

"So today I am defending my client, Bethany."

This got a moan out of Anthony, who started to interject but then changed his mind.

"Oh, what's it matter? Yeah, Bethany. That's me," he stated with a major grimace on his face.

Prosecutor Lester stood up and took a moment before he spoke to the courtroom, pacing around.

"I will be prosecuting that thar murderin', frog liver lovin' son of a shovel for attempting to, but not successfully attempting to murder, my kind, wonderful, pillar of the community client, Mr. Quickdraw Lester. Quickdraw, you come up and take a bow. Git on up here!" Prosecutor Lester egged him on.

To that, Quickdraw came to the middle of the room as he received applause from the Lester jurors, and then the judge. Hearing nearby applause, Paula realized Defense Attorney Lester was clapping too.

"Knock that off!" she swatted at his hands.

"Oh, sorry, I forgot," Defense Attorney Lester said quickly putting his hands down.

The clapping had died down a bit and Magistrate Lester started to address Defense Attorney Lester again.

"Well, these are some seeerious charges for your client, Defense. What do you plead?" he asked.

As the judge was talking, you could see Quickdraw Lester giving out autographs to the jurors.

"Well, your holiness, we plead not guilty because the supposed victim is not dead. So, you know, no harm, no foul and stuff," Defense Attorney Lester stated.

"I am sorry, Mr. Defense, it does not work that way. I do, however, accept your plea of not guilty," Magistrate Lester said, approving the plea.

As the magistrate spoke, Paula noticed Defense Attorney Lester was now getting his documents autographed by Quickdraw Lester as well.

"Oh, Jesus Christ! Will you knock that shit off?!" yelled Paula as she knocked down the papers that had been getting autographed by Quickdraw.

"Oh, yeah, sorry about that. Professionalism and all," Defense Attorney Lester said as he scrambled back to his chair, looking like an admonished child.

"Let's go ahead and get this shindig underway then, shall we?" exclaimed Magistrate Lester.

"Defense. Do you have anyone that you would like to call to the stand?"

"Yes, I would. I would like to call up the nefarious, no good, ding dangler of a monkey's sister. I'd like to call up Brittany!" Defense Attorney Lester dramatically stated as he turned to his own client Anthony.

"Thanks for the ringing endorsement, counselor!" Anthony angrily muttered at his Defense Attorney as he got up to go to the bench.

"Oh, I mean, this real swell guy who totally didn't try to murder anyone," Defense Attorney Lester said, trying to backpedal on some of the unflattering wording he just used to introduce Anthony.

Sitting on the bench, Anthony looked worn out and ready for whatever line of questioning was about to come his way. Paula just hoped Lester would get this out of his system, possibly get bored and move on.

In the meantime, Prosecutor Lester was approaching the stand. He was pacing back and forth looking at Anthony like he was trying to conjure up a strategy, twiddling his fingers. After a long pause he finally walked up to the stand.

"Sir. Can you please point to the person in this room that you tried to kill?"

"No. I didn't try to kill anyone!" Anthony shouted.

"Oh, dang. I thought that would work." said Prosecutor Lester.

"Well, I got nuthin' then," he continued as he walked back to the bench.

The prosecutor could be heard conversing with his client, Quickdraw.

"This guy's got us on the ropes over here," Prosecutor Lester nervously said to Quickdraw as the both of them looked at each other, equally concerned.

"All right, that was a tough round of questioning" said Magistrate Lester, looking extremely impressed by what Prosecutor Lester had done at the stand.

"You're up Defense. You'd better have something good because that's a tough act to follow," the magistrate continued as the jurors all nodded their heads in agreement.

"Tough act!? He asked me, like, one question! All he asked was if I attempted to murder someone," Anthony said, looking extremely agitated again.

"Did you?" asked Prosecutor Lester from his seat.

"No, goddamnit!" Anthony yelled at him.

THE TRIAL OF WHATSHISFACE

"Just checkin'," Prosecutor Lester shrugged.

"Defense. Go on and git up here and talk to your buddy. GIT!" Magistrate Lester ordered Defense Attorney Lester.

Scrambling to get on his feet, Defense Attorney Lester approached the stand to talk to Anthony. Instead, he started pacing back and forth like Prosecutor Lester, mad dogging Anthony. Then suddenly, without warning he lunged at Anthony.

"Did you try to murder than man over there!?" pointing at Quickdraw Lester.

"No, I didn't!" Anthony replied, looking shocked.

"I said, DID YOU TRY TO MURDER THAT MAN?!" Defense Attorney Lester yelled at Anthony again even louder.

"NO! Dude! You're supposed to be MY fucking lawyer!" Anthony yelled back, balling his fists and shaking them angrily in frustration.

Calmly, Defense Attorney Lester walked away from the stand.

"Okay. So, my client says he didn't try to kill that guy over there. I have no further questions, my lord," Defense Attorney Lester said before then walking back to his seat.

"Oh, man, that guy is goooood. Maybe we should get HIS autograph!" Prosecutor Lester said out loud to Quickdraw Lester; both equally astonished, nodding in agreement.

"You— I'm not gonna lie; I forgot your name. You can leave the stand," Magistrate Lester said, pointing Anthony back to his lawyer.

"Anybody got anyone else they want to put up in this stand thingy? I'm hankerin' for a nap," said the magistrate pointing at the stand, looking sleepy.

"I do! I uhh got these kids over here that know this guy," claimed Defense Attorney Lester, now pointing at Robert and Rodney.

LESTER

"All right, then bring them up," Magistrate Lester ordered.

"Like, both of them at the same time?" asked Defense Attorney Lester.

"No, you Stromboli, one at a time. It's like you ain't never been to lawyer school or anything," Magistrate Lester responded, pounding his gavel in his palm in a threatening manner.

"Oh, right! One at a time. Gotcha!"

Defense Attorney Lester looked at the kids.

"All right, I'm gonna send you up first, smallest one. You're real tiny and cute, so I think they'll gobble up whatever you say."

This made Robert smile of course.

The whole time both children had been giggling and holding in laughter, so Robert was still thinking of this as playtime, even if he did get whapped on his head earlier by his dad's lawyer.

As he approached the bench, all the Lester jurors were oohing and awing at the sight of little Robert. He smiled back at all the Lester jurors and hopped up onto the seat with help from Defense Attorney Lester.

"Okay. So, what's this thing over here?" asked Magistrate Lester.

"So, this one belongs to that one," Defense Attorney Lester pointed to Anthony.

"He's a character witness who will tell you, the jury, of what a good man my client is."

Robert looked around at the courtroom with his big bright eyes.

"Please state your name for the jury, son," Defense Attorney Lester asked Robert.

"My name is Robert," he quietly said.

THE TRIAL OF WHATSHISFACE

"Well, Robert, what can you tell me about good ol', sweet, loveable, courageous, fine upstanding Quickdraw?"

"Ummm, I don't know him. I thought I was supposed to be talking about my dad?"

Robert looked confused; first at his dad's lawyer, and then at his dad. Robert was visibly unsure what was going on.

"Oooh, fine, if we must," Defense Attorney Lester said, looking a little upset.

"So, why don't you tell us stuff about what's-his-face over there," Defense Attorney Lester limply pointed at Anthony.

"Oh, well, my dad. My dad is really nice, he's hard working, he can be funny."

"Can he do balloon animals?" Defense Attorney Lester excitedly asked.

"Ummm, no, not that I know of."

"Oh, so he's boring? Okay, whatever. Carry on," Defense Attorney Lester said disappointedly.

"Ummm, I think that's about it," said Robert shyly looking down.

"Would you say that he's, I dunno, capable of murdering and eating people, drinking their blood, that kinda thing?"

"Objection!" yelled Prosecutor Lester.

Everyone looked at him.

"Oh, wait, that's kinda helping me probably. Umm never mind. You can keep going," he said, sitting back down in his seat.

"Well, I'm not gonna sustain that. I wanna hear about the blood drinkin' n stuff!" inquired Magistrate Lester.

Robert instantly jumped to his dad's defense.

"My dad doesn't drink anyone's blood or murder people. He would never do that. He's a good guy!"

LESTER

The courtroom let out a collective, disappointed sigh. They really seemed to be interested in hearing about a blood sucking murderer.

"So, just to recap: Not a murderer, not a blood sucker, nice guy, and all that jazz?" Defense Attorney Lester asked Robert.

"Uhhh… yeah, all that stuff," he replied.

"Well, your honor, if you can't convict him of murder, you have a good case for being the most boring person ever. I personally volunteer to prosecute on that case," said Defense Attorney Lester looking just as let down as the jury.

"Now, we are all very disappointed about there not being a story about some dude goin' round sucking people's blood, but he can't be tried for it," Magistrate Lester said much to everyone's low protesting and complaining.

"Are you done with this witness?" he asked Defense Attorney Lester.

"Oh yeah. He's all yours, dumb Prosecutor guy," Defense Attorney Lester said under his breath as he walked back to his chair.

"Why thank you very much– wait. What'd you call me?" angrily asked Prosecutor Lester.

"Who? Me?" Defense Attorney Lester looked around.

"I'm pretty sure it was that guy," he then pointed at a random juror, who looked around in confusion.

"I got my eyes on you, boi," Prosecutor Lester said to the juror, who looked both befuddled and scared at the same time.

Prosecutor Lester messed around with his folder a bit, shuffling through papers, making it look like he was doing lawyer things but was really doing nothing at all. Everyone just kind of watched as he kept shuffling around the papers, skimming through his briefcase.

"Oh boy, I'd really hate to be you right now. I'm fixin' to put the hurt on ya," he said, still looking through his papers.

"GET UP HERE!" yelled Magistrate Lester.

"Oh, certainly your honor! Sorry about that. Just going through the mountains of paperwork on this kid."

"But they're all blank," said Quickdraw, holding up all of the blank papers in Prosecutor Lester's folder and briefcase. Perhaps he thought he was helping as he also had a big dumb smile on his face.

"Objection!" yelled Prosecutor Lester, pointing at Quickdraw Lester.

"I don't even think you know how any of this works, dummy," Magistrate Lester said to Prosecutor Lester with a face that was none too pleased. He was clearly bored with everyone's stupid antics.

"Now start talkin' to the kid before I put this gavel somewhere real unpleasant-like," Magistrate Lester said, now showing the gavel to the prosecutor.

"Are you… talking about my butt?" Prosecutor Lester said, adjusting his tie nervously.

"NO! Why would I stick anything up your butt? Weirdo! Now talk to the ding-dang kid!" Magistrate Lester ordered him.

Prosecutor Lester hurried over to the stand to go talk to Robert, who looked like the most confused person in the entire courtroom. Prosecutor Lester walked up looking all business, coming down to Robert's level not too far from his face.

"So, smaller kid. Tell me. Would you say your dad is a dookie head?"

Robert started giggling.

"Nooooo," he shook his head, smiling the whole time.

"So, he's not a caca faced monkey butt or anything like that?" Prosecutor Lester followed up.

Robert laughed now.

LESTER

"Noooo," shaking his head once again.

"Well, clearly the defendant is a dookie head and a caca faced monkey butt so how can we trust this child to tell the truth in this sacred court of law?" said Prosecutor Lester raising his hands in the air.

"Objection, your holiness! Clearly my client is a dookie head and a cacafaced monkey butt, but I don't want all those dumb jurors to know that," Defense Attorney Lester said to the judge as the jurors all looked angrily at Defense Attorney Lester.

"Nothing personal," Defense Attorney Lester said as he walked back to his chair to a chorus of boos from the jury with a random crumpled piece of paper hitting him in the back of the head.

As he sat down, he gave a reassuring smile and thumbs up to Anthony. Anthony just cringed and put his head into his hands in pure frustration before gently slamming his head onto the desk.

"I'm gonna say overruled in this case. The jury is pretty ugly," Magistrate Lester said as the jury now angrily looked at the judge.

They began to now boo the judge.

"Awww, shaddup!" he said to the jurors.

"Back to your whole dookie head bit," he now said to Prosecutor Lester.

"Oh, yeah. Well anyways, you say he's none of these things but surely, he must be a murderer. Surely, he's tried to kill you, the other kid, the lady?" Prosecutor Lester asked Robert.

"No. The only thing he's ever killed is" –Robert thought for a moment– "a bug maybe."

THE TRIAL OF WHATSHISFACE

"And I bet it was in coooooold blood," replied Prosecutor Lester as the jurors looked shocked, some holding their hands to their mouths in terror.

"What? It's just a bug. You know. Not a big deal, right?" Robert said, surprised at everyone's reaction.

"Just a bug?! JUST A BUG!? Oh, my goodness gracious holy horny toads. This man is so sick and depraved that his own kin has gone sociopath," Prosecutor Lester said in dramatic fashion, getting an even bigger rise out of the jurors.

"Ladies and gentlemen, I have no more to add to this… this travesty," Prosecutor Lester said as he turned to Defense Attorney Lester and blew him a raspberry.

"Though, I guess I do have one last question before I go back to my seat. You've got one last chance to be honest, if you can, being the son of a cold blooded murderer and all. My question is, did your dad attempt to murder that man over there?" pointing at Quickdraw Lester.

"No. Not that I know of. I was sleeping when it happened," said Robert, looking a little worried.

"Can anyone confirm that?" asked Prosecutor Lester.

"My brother, Rodney can," Robert said, pointing at his brother.

"Well, your honor, I have no more use for this little tater tot. Hows about we get his brother on up here for some Q and A?" Prosecutor Lester said to Magistrate Lester, walking up to his bench.

"All right, littler kid, you can go back to your seat. Bigger kid, you can come on over. Git on over here, boy," Magistrate Lester said to Rodney, waving him up.

Rodney took to the stand, sitting down, looking around the room. He looked over to the jury, where they were all making eye contact with him.

One of them smiled.

LESTER

"What's up, kid?" the juror awkwardly said, throwing him a thumbs up.

Rodney looked at Prosecutor Lester bright eyed, ready to answer any of his questions. He genuinely looked like had been getting a kick out of the whole thing, which relieved Paula since she knew that Lester was sour at Anthony but hoped the kids would be none the wiser of the tension between the two tonight. To the kids, it was just playtime with Lester and nothing of the situation weighed on them at all.

"Older kid," Prosecutor Lester started.

"It's Rodney," Rodney interjected.

"Oh, sorry, kiddo, I meant to say Rodney. Well, Rodney, I would like to ask you the same questions that I asked the smaller one over there."

Pacing back and forth, Prosecutor Lester was using time to build up to his dramatic questioning.

"Has he, your parental unit, ever killed someone?"

"No way. Like, Robbie said, he's a good dad and he would never kill anyone," said Rodney with great confidence, crossing his arms.

"Well, what about tonight, kiddo? Your father was armed with a six-shooter when he entered the barn to try and kill that guy right over there," said the prosecutor, pointing at Quickdraw Lester.

"He ever come walking into your room to talk to you or the small one while brandishing a gun?"

"Well," -Rodney thought to himself- "no," he responded.

"He'd never use a gun on anyone," said Rodney, defending his dad.

"Could've, should've, would've. Save it for the judge," said Prosecutor Lester shaking his head.

"Hey! I am the judge," Magistrate Lester said, pointing to himself.

THE TRIAL OF WHATSHISFACE

"Oh, yeah. Talk to that guy," Prosecutor Lester said, pointing Rodney to Magistrate Lester.

"I'm gonna go take a fiver," continued Prosecutor Lester as he started to walk outside.

As Prosecutor Lester walked outside, everyone looked around in confusion, first at each other and then at the judge, as if he had an explanation.

"All righty, well– let's hope that guy's coming back," said Magistrate Lester who now turned his attention to Rodney.

"All righty kid, I got nuthin' for ya so, you can go sit back over there unless the Defense– hey, where's the defense?" Magistrate Lester asked out loud, noticing that his seat was empty. As soon as he had asked the question, Defense Attorney Lester came walking in.

"Oh, hey, everyone. What'd I miss?" asked Defense Attorney Lester, much to the irritation of the judge.

"You missed a lot. Have yourself a nice meal?" he asked Defense Attorney Lester.

"Meal? No way. I was just usin' the ol' potty room. Yeah," he said, looking around with a hint of guilt on his face.

"Is that why you've got a bib on with sauce and noodles everywhere?" Magistrate Lester said, pointing at the bib that sat on his chest covered to the point where little white was visible.

"Well, Mama Mia! Umm… I'll share some of my leftovers if you promise not to send one of them fancy gavels airborne at my noggin."

"DEAL! Go ahead and bring that bad boy on over here!" the magistrate exclaimed.

Defense Attorney Lester brought his doggy bag up to Magistrate Lester who opened the box right away and started to eat the leftover pasta.

"Oh yeah, this kid said a bunch of other stuff to the other guy. If you want him to say anything right now you can," Magistrate Lester said, continuing to eat his pasta.

"Hey, didn't we already talk?" Defense Attorney Lester asked Rodney.

"No, dude. I'm the older brother– Rodney."

"Oh, yeah, yeah, right, I totally knew that. Just doing some lawyering stuff. You know how it goes, right, jury?"

The jury just looked at Defense Attorney Lester unimpressed, one of them sleeping with their head cocked back.

"So, uh, did you say good stuff about your dad?" he asked Rodney.

"Yeah. That he's a great dad and has never killed anyone," replied Rodney, still looking confident.

"Well, that's debatable, but you can go ahead and sit on down now."

Rodney shot his dad's lawyer a surprised look.

"Also, I have to stop thinking out loud," Defense Attorney Lester said, shaking his head.

Just as Rodney was taking his seat, Prosecutor Lester came walking through the door, also wearing a bib with spaghetti stains on it and was walking around with a slightly protruded belly.

"Don't mind me. Just coming back from uhhh… taking" -he thought hard- "A massive… poop!" Prosecutor Lester said out loud, reveling in his own clever, non-suspicious answer.

"Yeah, the other dummy already tried to pull that one," Magistrate Lester said, pointing his finger at Defense Attorney Lester.

Defense Attorney Lester gave Prosecutor Lester a friendly wave.

THE TRIAL OF WHATSHISFACE

"Just hand over the doggy bag and shut your spaghetti hole," Magistrate Lester ordered Prosecutor Lester.

Prosecutor Lester begrudgingly walked over and handed him the doggy bag full of pasta.

"Oooh! More stuff," Magistrate Lester rubbed his hands together, smiling at the prospect of more spaghetti.

"Oh, yeah, we're all done with the kid. You got any other witnesses you wanna bring up to the stand?" he asked Prosecutor Lester.

"As a matter of fact, I do, boss," he said, now turning to the jury.

"I call to the stand–" he waited, building the anticipation for who the witness would be.

The entire courtroom was completely enthralled by his words, anticipating what he would say next, some of them leaned forward in their anticipation, all except the one random juror who still had his head slumped back, dead asleep. He woke up, looked around and mimicked what everyone else was doing.

Now with everyone's undivided attention he announced:

"The father of the bug that was MURDERED by that man right there," pointing to Anthony.

The entire court was in an uproar talking and whispering among themselves.

Anthony, on the other hand, just had his face buried in his hands.

"Oh, Jesus fucking Christ! You gotta be kidding me," he said, now shaking his head.

The whole courtroom watched as a little bug walked down the courtroom, making its way to the stand. This was taking some time though since the bug was relatively small. everyone sat around, trying to be as patient as they can be. As they waited, Magistrate Lester finished gobbling up his leftover spaghetti. Over the silence of the room, you could hear some people clearing their throats but mostly Magistrate Lester hastily eating the leftovers.

As the bug finally got to the stand, Prosecutor Lester gave him a boost to the top of the stand.

"Oh, hey, I shoulda done that the whole time," the prosecutor thought out loud to the head shaking of many in the room.

"Well anyways we're gonna go ahead and–"

Prosecutor Lester looked over at Magistrate Lester.

He had spaghetti sauce and noodles strewn all throughout his wig. The magistrate, still looking confident and dignified, looked at Prosecutor Lester and the bug witness, waiting for them to begin.

"Ummm, boss, you got a little something over there," Prosecutor Lester said, pointing up towards his own head where hair was supposed to be. Magistrate Lester gave himself a small brushing which knocked an entire meatball out of his hair.

"We good?" Magistrate Lester asked Prosecutor Lester.

"Ummm… yeah, sure, why not?" replied Prosecutor Lester.

"Ohhhh, man, I ate waaaay too much spaghetti," Magistrate Lester said, now starting to slink down in his chair a bit.

"Carry on," he continued, slamming his gavel down.

"Thank you, your majesty," Prosecutor Lester said, now looking at the bug on the stand.

"Ladies and gentlemen, we are here today to hear the testimony of this bug right here, the father of the bug that Stephanie over there killed in brutal, cold, icy blood."

The jurors listened intently as Prosecutor Lester made his statement.

THE TRIAL OF WHATSHISFACE

"I will go into thorough depths with this witness to give you all of the cruel, gory, grizzly details of this homicide. I will expose the sick and twisted psychology of the man sitting over there. The man pretending to be a friend, a father, a husband, but at the very heart of it, is really an unfeeling sadistic sociopath."

The jury was now lunged forward, really sucked into the mish mash of words and accusations the prosecutor cleverly uttered.

"I will prove beyond a shadow of a doubt that he is guilty beyond a measure of a doubt!"

He got even louder and more assured of himself.

"Now watch, folks, as I break this case with this testimony," he said, rubbing his hands together.

The jurors were all big-eyed and mouths ajar, waiting for what might happen next. The anticipation was gnawing at them.

"Mr. Bug, if you could, would you please tell the ladies and gentlemen of this courtroom what happened on that fateful day that this man over here killed your wonderful, beautiful son that had such a very long life ahead of him. Well, long for a bug and all. Please, bring us through the entire incident," Prosecutor Lester said in an empathetic way to the bug, now bowing down to be at eye level with the bug and wearing sympathy on his face.

The bug flailed his arms around and appeared to be explaining the events of the day but being a bug, nothing was really coming out. Everyone watched anyway, trying to figure out what the bug was trying to relay to them. Most nodded their head out of courtesy, totally unaware of anything the bug was trying to say at all. Some of the jurors awkwardly looked at each other hoping that someone else might know what was going on, but to no avail.

LESTER

Once the bug was done, it plopped down in the spot it had been standing.

"Ummm. Did anyone get that?" Prosecutor Lester asked around the courtroom.

Everyone mostly looked around at one another, heads shaking as if to say "no".

"Yeah, that's what I thought because, you know, he's a bug and all he was doing was just kinda flopping his li'l appendages around and all," Prosecutor Lester said disappointedly, realizing his folly.

Everyone continued to look around awkwardly. Some jurors cleared their throats in the dead silence of the courtroom.

"Yeah, this probably wasn't a good idea."

The prosecutor looked down at the bug.

"Uhh, awful sorry, Mr. Bug. You're free to go ahead and take off. You need any help getting– Oh you're just gonna crawl on down? Okay, that'll work."

The bug crawled down the chair and then proceeded to slowly walk out of the courtroom while everyone remained quiet, impatiently watching the little bug take forever to reach his destination.

"Well, I guess that'll be all, your honor," Prosecutor Lester said to no response.

He looked over and saw that Magistrate Lester had dozed off.

"Hey, spaghetti breath!" Prosecutor Lester yelled at Magistrate Lester.

"Oh, yep, definitely guilty. Send him to the slammer!" the magistrate incoherently muttered as he thrusted up from his slumber, hair still a mess of spaghetti art.

"I said I'm done," Prosecutor Lester grumbled to Magistrate Lester, angrily looking at the magistrate as he walked back to his seat.

THE TRIAL OF WHATSHISFACE

"Oh, all righty, everyone. This is the part of the session where you will hear closing arguments. Now, this guy over here is going to tell you why you should vote guilty and send this guy into an alligator pit. This guy over here is going to do a terrible job at explaining why you should vote not guilty and, by some miracle; you might decide to choose that option and not send this guy into an alligator pit," Magistrate Lester said to the jury, looking more bored and tired than ever.

The Magistrate was already uninterested before, but now he had a spaghetti hangover which only made matters worse.

"Prosecution, you're up first. Git em! I SAID GIT EM, BOI!" Magistrate Lester shouted, riling Prosecutor Lester up, much to the chagrin of Defense Attorney Lester.

As he approached the jury, Prosecutor Lester had what appeared to be a balloon. Without warning he started blowing the balloon up and, once he did, he started messing around with the balloon. At first, no one could tell what he was doing, as he was hunched over hiding it from the entire courtroom. Finally, he stood up straight.

"It's a li'l ol' balloon hat!"

Everyone started smiling in pure joy at the sight of the bright, shiny balloon hat.

"Aw, here you go. Enjoy the hat, li'l skipper," he continued, now placing the balloon hat on one of the random juror's heads, who was now happily clapping.

"Ladies and gentlemen of the beloved jury. I think it's safe to say we're all pretty good friends now."

Everyone nodded their heads in agreement.

"You would take advice from me, put up your hand if I needed to high five you, loan me five bucks if I asked for it."

One of the jurors was now reaching into their wallet.

LESTER

"Oh. No, sir. That's not necessary," the prosecutor stopped the juror.

The juror put their wallet away and blankly smiled back at him.

"So, being friends, I think it would be safe to say that if the prosecution says this low down, dirty, triflin', pineapple pizza farmin' tapeworm is a murderer, well, snickerdoodles! Then that means I'm relying on all my good buddies here on the jury to do the right thing and find this summer sausage guilty of attempted murder in the one kabillionth degree!"

After having paced around the courtroom, Prosecutor Lester got close to the jury again.

"We've all been through so much together."

He cozied up to one of the jurors.

"There's you with... your whole face thing."

This made the juror look to another juror, nodding their head up and down in agreement.

He went on to the next juror.

"And then who could ever forget... you... with... your opposable thumbs and all."

The juror put their thumbs up and stared at them in excitement with their mouth open.

"Yeah, exactly! You get what I'm talking about, ol' thumbs guy!"

Prosecutor Lester walked away and stood before the entire jury.

"So, why don't you do your ol' pal a big ol' favor, and make sure to convict this soulless, murder attempin' deviant to murder in the highest degree. Make sure he never ever hurts anyone ever again. Especially me."

He paused.

"Because I hope that you believe, like me, in the foundation of justice and everything it holds true. That she, lady justice, will always be there, glorious and fair, to guide us to make the hard decisions because she, in all her grace, makes no demands of herself that she does not demand of us."

All of the jurors could be seen crying and weeping at the words of Prosecutor Lester. Then, between all of the sobbing, a concussive noise could be heard. It was the sound of a clap, and then another clap.

It was Magistrate Lester, drenched in tears, beginning to rise as the pace of the clapping sped up. Finally, at full furious force, the jurors all stood up and clapped with Magistrate Lester. Prosecutor Lester humbly shook his head and waved his hands dismissively as to say, "You shouldn't have!"

Now facing a full concert of applause, Prosecutor Lester bowed to the entire judicial audience; judge, jury and all.

Of course, Anthony's Defense Attorney, too, was standing up and applauding with a few tears coming down his face.

"This guy's really good, I tell ya. Could really learn from someone like him. Wow. Bravissimo!"

"Seriously, will you knock that shit off!" Paula said as Anthony swatted Prosecutor Lester over the head with his own portfolio full of papers.

As the entire crowd of people started to sit back down, Prosecutor Lester said one last parting word.

"And don't forget, my brothers and sisters, that I am honored to be surrounded by such wonderful individuals. If I could make just one humble request, not for me, but for you; I ask you please" -he now bowed his head- "call your mother."

Now, they were all sobbing even more, and the entire courtroom filled up with frantic chit chat, some jurors hugging each other as Prosecutor Lester walked back to his seat with his head down in an ah-shucks manner with his lip curled and eyes closed, obviously taking in the poignancy of his amazing speech.

"Oh, man, he's right! I gotta go call my mom!" Defense Attorney Lester yelled out loud with tears still streaming down his face. Before he could leave, Anthony grabbed him by his necktie and pulled him back down.

"You stay put, goddamnit, or I'm gonna put that portfolio up your ass," he threatened Defense Attorney Lester, looking more impatient than ever.

"Oh, right, the whole trial thing. Forgot," Defense Attorney Lester said, looking disappointed that he still had this dumb trial thing to do. He sat down looking sad and dejected.

The courtroom eventually started to calm down as the chit chat and the hugs subsided. Having regained his composure, Magistrate Lester banged his gavel to get the court back in order. Everyone eventually settled in, and he was now ready to address the courtroom once again.

"All right ladies and gentlemen. We just heard the argument from the prosecution. A real good one, like a total doozy of an argument," he said, holding his hand against his heart.

"All good things must come to an end though. Now it's time to hear from this guy over here about why you shouldn't vote guilty," pointing to Defense Attorney Lester.

"All right, come on up here, dead meat," Magistrate Lester summoned the bumbling Defense Attorney.

"Hey, ummm, you got any advice for me?" Defense Attorney Lester asked Anthony.

Clearly flustered, Anthony stared at Defense Attorney Lester.

"Yeah, my advice is to get up there and do your damn job. Whatever the hell this is, let's get it over with. Jesus!"

He shook his head in annoyance.

"So… no advice?" Defense Attorney Lester shyly asked.

THE TRIAL OF WHATSHISFACE

"Get the hell up there!" Anthony yelled, pointing towards the jury, his face red with fury.

"Oh! Oh, yeah. Sorry. Oh, geez." Defense Attorney Lester nervously muttered, scrambling to his feet to get away from the very angry Anthony.

Defense Attorney Lester stumbled over to the jurors, straightening out his suit, looking back at Anthony to give a timid smile and thumbs up.

"Good day, everyone. Good to see you again. Been a long time," he paced around in front of the jurors.

"In front of you sits an innocent man. He is a man that has been pushed to the brink of sanity and pushed off it by the help of that man over there, Quickdraw Lester."

As Defense Attorney Lester pointed at Quickdraw Lester, Quickdraw pointed at himself, looking around in confusion as if he was saying "Who, me?"

"Yeah, I'm talking to you, buddy!" Defense Attorney Lester added.

Quickdraw got under the desk as Defense Attorney Lester addressed the jurors.

"We're all guilty of this mental breakdown. At any point we could've left the poor man alone, moved on, found answers," Defense Attorney Lester told the jury

Paula was shocked that, for the first time, Lester appeared to be almost out of this character he was in. He seemed to be awake, aware, and lucid. Perhaps Lester's little game was nearly over, and sanity could reconvene. She hoped, anyway.

"The man's entire family was infringed upon by something he didn't understand, something he couldn't grasp or comprehend, and so he became scared not only for himself but especially for his family. The very family that surrounds him now, in support," Defense Attorney Lester said with his head down, speaking from the heart, pacing back and forth in front of the jury.

"He's only scared, and rightfully so, because a horrible thing happened to a member of his family. That little furball, Samantha, died at the hands of something terrible. He was confused and angry, not actin' in a malicious way but in desperation, actin' upon those feelings of fear. A fear that somethin' worse was coming down the road that, if given enough time, he would regret not having taken care of that problem even if his loved ones might be angry at him, maybe not even forgive him. He was willing to make the ultimate sacrifice."

Lester was pacing in front of the jury, seemingly expressing his own internal thoughts aloud. It seemed less like a trial and more like Lester coming to a realization as he continued to look down, pondering.

"I think I'd like to ask all of you, the jury, to find this man innocent of all charges. He's a good man, a devoted husband, a devoted father, who was thrust into extraordinary circumstances, and reacted in equally extraordinary ways to protect those he loves. We should be thankin' this man for what he has done for every single person in this courtroom and forgive him for what he might have done. None of us are perfect and neither is he but, it's a lot to condemn a man whose intentions were nothin' but noble, honorable."

"In the end, no one was hurt. Instead, we unearthed some facts that were maybe a little too hard for some to swallow for some, and reinforced facts about the quality of others. Let's do the right thing today. Let's get this man reunited with his family and leave him in peace."

Defense Attorney Lester looked at Anthony and the entire family, smiling with a great confidence on his face.

"Your honor," he concluded.

Suddenly, something went flying across the room and hit Paula in the head.

"OW!" she yelped, rubbing her head where the object had landed.

It was a gavel.

"Oh, sorry. My bad. That one got away from me. I was sitting here, not paying attention, practicing my gavel tossing form and it kinda slipped outta my hand," Magistrate Lester replied.

"Hey, anyone see my gavel?" he asked, looking around.

Paula picked it up and threw it at him with some extra zip on it and he barely ducked the throw.

"Oh wow! I should take some tips from you," Magistrate Lester said, looking behind his bench for the gavel. He left the bench and could be heard, not seen, fumbling around for the gavel.

"Okay, it's all good. Found it. Thanks there, Zippy," referring to Paula who still looked angry from having an errant gavel bonk her on the head.

"All righty, jury, you've heard the arguments. Well, I'm not sure about some of them," motioning to a bunch of jurors who were dead asleep.

Magistrate Lester started to whisper, "Now that you… well, some of you have heard the arguments, it is time to make a decision on the case. This might take some time but, in the name of justice you must–" he was interrupted.

"Guilty!" cried out Head Juror Lester which woke the other Lesters up.

"Ummm, you guys already came to a decision?" asked Magistrate Lester.

"Oh, yeah, we came to the decision a while ago, but we were letting the defense guy babble on so we could all catch a nap. I think someone snuck out to go look for that Italian place," said Head Juror Lester, pointing to an empty seat.

"Oh, great then!" yelled Magistrate Lester who started pounding his gavel.

"Go ahead and round that fella on up then," the magistrate ordered of the other Lesters in attendance.

The Lesters all descended upon Anthony in a hurry. It was frightening how sudden it was, so fast that Paula and the kids had no time to interject between Lester and Anthony.

They grabbed Anthony, but Paula could not see in the crowd of Lesters where he had been taken off to. She held the kids close to her and kept trying to poke her head up, but it was no use. It was a blender of noise with a lot of enthusiastic yelling, some sort of activity far away from Paula and the kids. The chatter started to subside after a few minutes and as the crowd started to disperse, Paula could see something, but she could not believe her eyes.

Anthony was tied to a wooden post, standing atop piles of wood, like something she had seen in books, like the burning of witches at Salem. She was absolutely horrified.

Part of her believed Anthony would be okay. Perhaps they would be tickling his feet or slime him, something childish. This was Lester after all. The other part of Paula thought something much worse, even if farfetched, that being at the stake always ended with the accused engulfed in flames. The concern was just in the tiniest part of her brain, but it lingered because even though she always knew Lester to be merely playful, everything about his behavior, the trial specifically, had been off this night. He was more unpredictable than ever.

No matter what, Paula had had enough and started to run towards the makeshift stake. She got about halfway to the stake when she felt a powerful tug around her stomach that sent her flying back. Paula landed in a chair and saw that what grabbed her were impossibly long yellow arms that came out of the chair. Before she could get up to try and run to the stake again, she found her upper body being tightly wrapped up by the arms. She tried kicking and fussing but the arms did not budge and neither did the chair. It felt like it was nailed into the ground. Paula had been fighting the chair and did not even notice that her children were right next to her, both wrapped up with yellow arms, pinned to their own chairs.

Rodney and Robert were terrified. Paula had sensed things were off the whole time but, for the kids, it was just Lester being Lester this whole time. They knew, like Paula, that this time things were way different. The kids did not feel safe anymore, and they were in their chairs kicking to exhaustion and Robert was crying out in terror. Rodney was not crying, but the look on his face said it all. He was equally terrified, ripping at the arms that held him captive. Everything had already turned upside down in moments between the crowd and seeing their father at the stake, but these chairs were the final straw. It was obvious to all adults and children in attendance that Lester was fully out of control, and no one knew how to stop it.

"Kids! It'll be okay. All right!" Paula said, knowing that the kids probably had little confidence in what she said.

"Lester's just having a bad night and he's angry at your dad. If we just sit here and calm down, I know Lester will calm down too," she told the children, desperately coming up with anything that might relax them.

Before the kids could respond back to her, a rhythmic clapping began. All of the Lesters had created two lines they were standing in, right in front of the stake. They looked across at one another smiling, clapping in perfect harmony with one another. The whole thing was surreal, even for a Lester experience.

LESTER

A loud, booming voice came over the room like someone talking over a microphone.

"Now, coming out to perform his brand new hit single. The one! The only… LESTER!!!"

Paula looked around, trying to make sense of everything. Finally, she looked down the line, and out from behind the stake, running down the line was Lester, but he had on what looked like a wig, a mullet to be exact. He wore a flashy, shiny skintight outfit with sequins all over it, and held an equally shiny microphone in his hand. His appearance sent all of the other Lesters in a panic. They were all yelling in excitement as if The Beatles had just shown up. Some of the female Lesters were passing out, and one of the male Lesters passed out too from the mere presence of this mullet having Lester.

Paula and the kids looked on in horror and confusion, trying to wrap their heads around what they were seeing. The whole thing was like some 1980s Technicolor neon nightmare with no way out.

She looked at the kids to reassure them, but her face was white and the look of panic on her face was impossible to hide. Rodney and Robert mirrored her own terror and confusion. Paula knew that the kids could not be reassured any longer but, still, even with that she tried.

"It's going to be okay," she mouthed, nodding her head up and down, her eyebrows raised.

Returning her focus back to Lester, armed with his microphone, she could hear the overtures of 80s style keyboards, flashy electric guitar work, colliding with a steady drumbeat. There was an actual song playing. It was synth rock in all of its 80s glory, permeating the air as all of the Lesters in the line who had not passed out continued to keep pace with the rhythm of the song.

THE TRIAL OF WHATSHISFACE

Lester was moving around, shaking his shoulders, swaying his arms to the beat of the music. He smiled at everyone, winking at a few admirers, really getting into the song, waiting for his cue to sing. Now, with the spotlight focused on him, the words finally came out in a very masculine delivery.

Life can really be rough
like you're out in the cold
take to the streets every day
your dreams bought and sold
no one to fight beside you
you're all alone
then one day you're tied to a stake
crying and screaming

Lester started dousing Anthony with some sort of liquid from a canister, not missing a single dance move.

Please don't light me on fire
Let that be water
(woo-ooo-ooo-ooo!)
Please don't light me on fire
I hope that it's water

The days and nights never end
They all seem alike
Struggle to find your place in the world
Just to survive
Grab life by the hand and say
'Baby hold on tight'
The danger gets closer and closer
And now I hear you pleadin'

LESTER

Please don't light me on fire
Let that be water
(woo-ooo-ooo-ooo!)
Please don't light me on fire
I hope that it's water

Lester spun around and with his neon keytar strapped around him. He went off, doing a mean keytar solo to his adoring fans, who pawed and clawed at him with most of them still clapping. Some of the Lesters that had passed out before had started to wake up just in time to catch a glimpse of Lester before passing out all over again.

You put on such a brave face
But I can see your eyes are saying

Please don't light me on fire
Let that be water
(woo-ooo-ooo-ooo!)
Please don't light me on fire
I hope that it's water

Please don't light me on fire
Let that be water
(woo-ooo-ooo-ooo!)
Please don't light me on fire
I hope that it's water

As the music ended and the last of the guitars and keyboards rang out, Lester lit a match which made the Lesters around him really excited with heavy applause and cheering.

Anthony, Paula, and the children could only watch in horror as Lester flicked the lit match towards Anthony, who began yelling "No! No! No!" at the prospect of being burned alive. The match almost seemed to float in the air forever, taking its sweet time to land on the pile of wood that Anthony stood on. Finally, as everyone watched with great intensity, the match landed on the wood pile.

Nothing.

Lester began laughing.

"GOTCHA!"

This made all the other Lesters laugh quite a bit. It turned out to be water after all. There was a huge sigh of relief from Paula and the kids. Anthony looked as though he was ready to pass out from both relief and the exhaustion of the night's activities, but the solace could be seen all over his face.

Collectively, they knew that Lester had gone way too far, and they would have to demand him to leave once this was over. For the moment though, they were relieved that things did not go worse, that it was all one big terrible joke from Lester. Perhaps this was his anger, his way of getting back at Anthony, at the entire family, from feeling a sense of betrayal.

Paula was not sure how everyone could move forward, but she was just glad that it was all a terrible gag, and that Anthony was alive to move forward with everyone else. Paula's heart had gone from her feet back into her chest where it belonged at the sight of her husband still very much alive, even if tired and agitated.

"This, on the other hand, AIN'T water!" Lester yelled with a huge grin on his face as he pointed his keytar in Anthony's direction.

LESTER

Lester pushed down on a red painted key and flames came shooting out of the keytar and all over Anthony.

Lester laughed childishly at the top of his lungs as the flames engulfed Paula's husband. Anthony screamed in ways Paula thought no human could ever be capable of. It was so loud; it pierced her ears. Anthony quickly became buried in the flames, to the point where the hellish howling could no longer be heard and only a silhouette remained.

"NOOOO!" screamed Paula at the top of her lungs, thrashing and fighting at her restraints. The more she fought, the tighter the arms got around her. She was completely helpless. All she could do was watch as her husband, the father of her children, her everything, was burned alive. Time seemed to freeze. It completely broke her, knowing there was nothing she could do to stop it, as if it were a nightmare and any minute now, she might wake up. All she could do was cry. She had no offense, no defense. Only unbearable, unimaginable, guttural pain.

Paula was so focused on Anthony and her own pain; she had drowned the world out of her thoughts. Everything from the nerves into her body to her emotions went dead as a doornail. Short circuiting, she was still trying to get her senses back from the shock of the moment.

When she came to, when reality started to hit her again, she could hear the one thing that was worse than her own witnessing of Anthony's being burned alive - the anguished cries of her children.

"DADDY!!!"

"NO, DAD!!!"

These were the first things that met her ears when she tuned the world back in as her psyche reestablished itself.

The kids were inconsolable with grief, shock, and fear. They had just watched their own father be reduced from the most important man in their world, to nothing more than a pile of ash, like mere paper in a fireplace. Anthony's very being had been treated with no dignity or importance as Lester laughed, just feet from where their father once stood.

As the family's horror intensified, the other Lesters smiled and gathered around. As a final insult, they fastened marshmallows onto branches and extended them to roast their puffy delicacies over the open fire.

"Get away from my dad, you fuckers!" yelled Rodney who continued to kick and scream hopelessly against the restraints.

One of the girl Lesters ran up to him.

"Oh, I'm sorry. Did you want one?" she said, extending the burnt marshmallow.

There was no malevolence in her eyes, no mockery, just a big smile, offering the marshmallow up as if it were a picnic in the park.

"I'll kill you! I'LL KILL YOU!" yelled Rodney who kicked and wriggled harder than before. His rage was intense, animalistic but, as before, it made no impact on his current state. The arms had him wrapped up tight.

"Umm… I'll take that as a no," the female Lester said with a worried look on her face, looking genuinely confused as to why the boy would be so opposed to a marshmallow.

She ran back to the fire to be with her other Lesters.

Robbie had not been putting up any kind of fight at all. He sat still in his chair crying his eyes out. Between the volume of tears that came from his eyes, the snot that ran down his nose, and the drool that had come out of his mouth, his entire face was caked with a wall of fluids.

Paula wanted to tell him things would be okay, like before, but she knew it was all a lie with the evidence in front of their faces; the flames cooking her husband, filling the room with the smell of burning flesh. As the smell entered her nose, she knew she had no words for her children because she had no grasp of her own reality at the moment. It was still a terrible dream.

She only knew this much: Nothing was okay, she was not in control, and they were all at the mercy of a monster.

RATED M FOR MATURE

Paula had no idea how she had escaped. Just moments ago, she was tied to a chair, watching as someone she thought of as family roasted marshmallows and hotdogs over her dead husband's bones. The arms that held her down had, for an unknown reason, let go of her and her children.

Paula grabbed the kids as fast as she could and made haste to the house where she knew the keys to the truck were waiting. Lester was distracted, having fun with all of the other Lesters he had created. She had no time to look back or think twice about her actions, she had to go immediately; live or die. Paula thought that if she could just make it to the truck and she could get far enough away from Lester, then she could process everything that had happened. For now, it was survival. She had to be quick and decisive.

Storming into the house, she frantically grabbed the keys off of the key holder. Still holding onto her children, Paula ran out to the garage door through the house. There were no signs of life within the garage which gave her a small sense of relief, "Lester's still distracted" she thought as she got the truck doors open, ushering her children in.

The kids themselves were almost numb, acting on pure mechanics, doing whatever their mother commanded of them. They needed the most processing given the traumatic events that occurred within the barn, but they, like their mother, would have to wait. As they listlessly sat in the truck next to their mother, staring ahead, Paula fumbled with the keys and managed to get them into the ignition. She knew she was two-thirds of the way there, and it made her nervous. All she had to do was wait for the garage door to open and she could hit the accelerator and be out of this nightmare.

LESTER

"Where we goin'?!" yelled an unexpected voice to the right of the children. At the far end of the passenger seat sat Lester who had his hands on his lap, wearing his nicest driving gloves, looking forward to a leisurely drive with a big smile across his bright yellow face.

"No. No! NO!" yelled Paula who furiously started pounding on the steering wheel in pure rage, knowing she had been so close to freedom. The kids had bunched themselves up to their mother, looking for her protection, and were screaming in terror as Lester sat just inches from them.

Suddenly, Lester had transformed his appearance, looking like Anthony.

"Hey c'mon, family, why don't we all go on a trip together? It'll be like old times."

Paula and the kids said nothing, they just stared in horror, unable to move, as this perverse version of Anthony sat in front of them with a smirk on his face.

"Oh, yeah, that's right I can't go on a trip with you guys because–" suddenly he was on fire screaming at the top of his lungs, flailing his limbs around furiously.

Paula and the children all emptied out of the driver's side as fast as they could, screaming the entire time. Paula had picked up Robert to make sure she would not lose trace of him. She had no idea where to even run at this point because the truck was her only way out.

"If I can't escape, maybe I can stop him" Paula thought to herself, grabbing the kids and running to the bedroom. There were still guns in the bedroom, and Paula knew she would not need to be a good shot in these tight confines. It was her best and only option.

Running into the bedroom, she reinforced the door with anything not nailed down. She jammed the doorstop in and then summoned up enough superhuman strength to single handedly move the heavy dresser in front of the door as a reinforcement. Clearly, the adrenaline was in full effect.

"C'mon, goddamnit," she muttered to herself as she used the code to open the gun safe.

She grabbed a shotgun immediately, knowing it would provide maximum damage. Paula had never fired a shotgun before but there was no time like the present to learn. Filling the shotgun with slugs, she kept her eyes on the closed door, listening for movement, waiting for the noise of someone attempting to burst the door down. Knowing Lester's superhuman strength, the barrier would not last long and she was just hoping she could fill the shotgun before he reached the door.

"Knock! Knock!" yelled a voice behind the door.

Paula quickly pointed the loaded gun at the door, trying to aim as her body shook so violently it felt as though her skeleton might jump out of her skin. No one could answer or would answer Lester's attempt at a joke.

"I said KNOCK! KNOCK!" Lester repeated even louder than before. It was not threatening or intimidating but still playful and cheerful in delivery.

"FUCK YOU, MOTHERFUCKER!" Paula savagely screamed at the top of her lungs.

She was breathing heavily, still trying to keep her aim under control as she pointed the gun towards the door. There was a brief moment of silence.

"Umm… fuck you, motherfucker who?" he responded to Paula, still stuck on whatever knock-knock joke he was working with.

"Oh! wait! That's not how knock-knock works. I think I done messed up the joke," Lester said to himself outside of the doorway, clearly confused.

"Oh well, when life gives ya lemons–" he paused.

LESTER

With a mighty boom, the door exploded into chunks of wood as Lester's hand came punching through it. Paula and the children were freaking out and, for some reason, Paula could not bring herself to pull the trigger. She froze up looking for the right shot, still not having a clear, definite shot on him.

"That's all folks… that's all… folks," Lester kept saying, attempting to get his head through the hole he created but the hole was much too small for his head.

"Oh man, I don't think I'm doing this right, either. It looks way easier when Porky Pig does it."

He took his head away from the door for a moment and then a second later the entire door exploded, bits of wood flying all over the room. Lester had completely smashed the door open which caused the dresser to go flying a few feet back.

"FOUND YA!!" Lester said exuberantly, looking at Paula and the two kids.

"Stay back, goddamn you!" Paula yelled, steadying her gun on Lester as Robert and Rodney stood behind her, hiding themselves, shaking uncontrollably.

"You know, with all these people pulling guns on me tonight my feelings are starting to get awful hurt," Lester said back to Paula with his hands on his hips.

"I fucking mean it!" asserted Paula, putting some tension on the trigger, ready to shoot at any moment. Without any warning and fast as light itself, Lester moved forward.

"Woop!" he said as he plunged his finger into the barrel of the gun.

Paula was completely shocked and had no idea what to do. Lester sat in front of her with his finger in the gun, chuckling away at his stroke of mischievous genius. She could not fire the gun. Even if it did manage to kill or harm Lester, it would likely explode, harming herself and, even worse, the kids. She knew she was trapped. There was one last move up her sleeve. With the rifle in hand, and with Lester's finger in the barrel, she quickly bent the entire rifle upward in a move that surely would break his finger. Paula knew it could buy her some time to at least get out of the corner that her and the kids were now in.

"Ow! Ow! Ow! Uncle! Uncle I seyz!" shouted Lester loudly as his finger bent all the way back in an extremely unnatural fashion.

As it did, Paula shouted for the kids to run away. Without hesitation the kids ran for their lives around Lester and the door. Lester was on his knees with his finger bent up, still pleading in pain. Paula knew there was only one option. She pointed the finger plugged barrel at Lester's face, closed her eyes, and pulled the trigger.

The explosion was loud and staggering. It knocked Paula onto her ass. The ringing in her ears was overwhelming and painful; she felt as though she may never hear again. In her disorientation, she opened her eyes to start looking around the room. She clumsily hit at her ears with her hands to somehow recalibrate her hearing which, of course, did nothing.

Turning her attention to Lester, she could see that he was on the floor too, she could see him flat on his back with his shoes propped straight up. Upon seeing Lester, presumably injured or dead, Paula took a moment to regain her surroundings and rest. She knew there had to be damage, but the shock of the blast disabled her from feeling where the damage was.

In her left ear, the ringing had started to subside a bit. This ear was on the other side of the blast she remembered, as the muddiness around her became a little clearer with a smidge of treble making its way back into the ear. Just as she had thought about making her way to the bathroom mirror to find out what injuries she had received, Lester shot straight up into a sitting position, still on his butt. His face was all black with his hair blown back, like something out of a cartoon, and he began coughing out smoke from his mouth.

"Mama Mia! That's a spicy-a meat-a-ball-a!" he exclaimed, coughing out a few extra puffs of smoke.

In her discombobulation, Paula was trying to yell "No!".

Her words were mere inner dialogue that could not escape her mouth. She was too weak, too concussed, and just kept mumbling the words, helplessly pawing at Lester in some feeble attempt to attack him but she merely fell onto her face.

"Now why'd you go an' do that for?" Lester asked Paula.

She seemed to be able to hear him out of her good ear while she was on the floor, which was a temporary relief. As she tried to get up, trying to regain her balance seemed impossible with her right hand, her dominant hand. Her hand had been broken, she just knew it, and she attempted to use her left hand to help get back up. Though she was panicking inside, there was nothing her body could do to match her ambitions of running away. Instead, she just stood up.

"You went and messed up ol' Lester's face and, look at you, you're spillin' ketchup all over the place," he laughed.

It dawned on Paula what that meant. She did not have the power to get to the mirror, she finally looked down at her body, now that she was more aware, and the shock of the explosion was wearing off. In horror, her eyes got wider as she saw blood all over herself and she scrambled to see where the blood had come from.

It was when she went to feel her face with her right hand that things became obvious. There were no fingers touching her face. Paula looked down to her hand and screamed as she saw all of her fingers missing and most of her hand gone as well. It became clear that her strength was draining, not just from the explosion, but mostly due to losing so much blood from where there used to be a hand.

"Oh noooo!" laughed Lester, who treated the situation as if Paula had slipped on a banana peel.

"Oh, you should see your face, I tell ya," he continued, still laughing and holding his stomach as if it were hurting from all of his laughter.

Still shaken and in shock, there was nothing more she could do but break down and start to cry. In this moment she knew that she was totally defeated. Blood and flesh hung from a nub near her wrist. The thing she tried to kill was totally unaffected, mocking her, and everything was completely hopeless.

"Oh, shucks. I didn't mean to make you start leakin'. Here let me go ahead 'n' fix that for ya," Lester said as he stopped his laughter, replacing it with a more caring tone.

He grabbed Paula's right arm and Paula tried protesting by mumbling at him and swatting at him to no avail.

"Come on, now. Ol' Lester's gonna make it all better," he said with a big grin.

As Paula continued to swat at Lester and shuffle around, that's when she noticed in his other hand a steam iron. Now she protested even more, knowing what the iron meant. She struggled but seemed to gain newfound strength with the surge of adrenaline that shot through her body. Paula was like a wild animal, thrashing, doing anything to put as much distance between herself and that red hot iron. The iron itself was cartoonish in nature; bright yellow with an adorable little, shiny happy face on the bottom of it that started talking in a cutesy voice.

"Oh, is this our little patient?" it asked, smiling the whole time.

The iron's eyes were big and obnoxiously cute. In her weakened state, all Paula could do was shake her head at the iron and pray it would show her mercy. As she shook her head and kept trying to say no, the iron let out a whole bunch of steam.

"HERE WE GOOOO!" the iron happily shouted out with the biggest smile, as if it were about to take off on some magical adventure.

Paula, who just moments ago blew off her own hand, had never felt such searing pain in her entire life as the molten hot iron pressed against the nub of her wrist. Every single nerve, every ounce of her being was on fire and, as much as she fought it, she could not escape Lester's superhuman grip. She was stuck in the throes of a pain and suffering that truly defied all comprehension. It was an agony that Paula believed impossible to exist, and yet there she was, enduring every second of what felt like an eternity.

As the iron pressed hard against the nub, she screamed a howl that could have easily been heard in another state. It was nearly inhuman as she bellowed out every ounce of pain from her gut. Finally overloaded, Paula succumbed to the extreme amount of shock, and passed out.

It seemed like hours had passed and, as she came to, Paula had thought the events of the last few hours were all a bad dream. Dreary and feeling rested, she started to open her eyes and gradually bring herself back to reality. Slowly, it hit her that this was, in fact, not just a bad dream. Though she was afraid to look, Paula peeked over at her right hand and, sure enough, there was a cauterized stump at the end of her wrist.

As she saw the missing hand, the cauterization, she began to cry. It was the kind of crying reminiscent of childhood, where it comes from your stomach. The tears welled uncontrollably as the truth of the situation hit her like a truck. Her husband was dead. Her hand was gone. She had no idea what to do at all. There were no next steps. There was no escape, and no one would be able to help her. All possibilities were now exhausted and futile.

"Where are my kids?" she asked aloud to an empty room.

Paula looked around for signs of Lester, but he was nowhere to be found. Her moment of self-pity turned to panic as she realized she had been out for what seemed like an entire day and who knows what Lester could have done in that time. She attempted with all of her strength to get to her feet to go search for her children.

Her heart was racing a million miles an hour and she mustered up just enough strength to call for the kids as she stumbled through the room and down the hallway.

"ROBEEEERT!? RODNEEEEY?!" she screamed out.

There was no answer, which only made her worry even more. As she continued her search, she found herself occasionally tripping when trying to balance herself on objects with her now missing right hand. At one point she fell forward onto her face, and it took her some time to get back up. She felt alone and helpless in every way possible. At this point, she just wanted to see the kids, to know if they were okay.

"Kids! Where are you!?" she yelled out.

"Lester! Give me back my kids. I want my kids!" again she yelled out, hobbling around covered in blood, sweat, and tears.

"ANYONE!?" Paula cried out as loud as she could, still looking for any signs of life.

With the clear absence of anyone within the house, she could only assume that everyone was in the barn, Lester's home.

Walking outside, she could hear random noises coming from the barn. She could hear multiple voices, which gave her hope that the children were at least still alive. It was enough. Paula picked up her pace and half jogged to the barn. As she opened the door with her good hand, she could see her kids huddled up with each other in a corner of the barn as Lester stood in front of them laughing.

"Oh, there she is!"

Lester turned to see Paula.

"Well, I've got good news, and I got some bad news," Lester said to Paula as she looked at him, wondering what news could possibly be good.

"The good news is that I found your hand. Bad news is, well, it's in, like, a hundred pieces or so," he said, showing her a dustbin full of her own hand or at least the bloody, blackened bits of what was once her hand.

"Could always glue it back together, right?" Lester chuckled.

Paula stared in disbelief. The whole thing was a goddamn joke to him. It was sick and demented. The perversion of his sadism jolted her brain and gave her chills up and down her entire body.

Paula knew that she had no way to win this battle so, for the sake of her kids, she knew she would have to play along with Lester. Perhaps getting on his good side would be the best approach. If she could gain Lester's trust then she could find some way to buy enough time to enact a strategy, some way to let the kids free. She accepted that she would not make it out of this alive. It would have to be a sacrifice to ensure her kids' safety.

"I'm okay, Lester. And" -she closed her eyes, sickened to say the next words- "thank you for stopping the bleeding," Paula timidly said to Lester.

"Well, shucks, it ain't no thang but a chicken wang!" Lester said with a laugh as he tossed the dustbin full of her bits of hand off to the side.

"See, what I'm trying to do out here is get a little party started. I'm really feeling up to some party time. I heard some music a few weeks back that really peppered my steak, you know."

Paula, trying to use her new strategy, wanted to be ever so helpful to Lester.

"Oh, what kinda music was it?" she asked.

"Well, it had a steady beat and was talking about being a Barbie girl or something rather, I think," he pondered aloud.

"Oh, that's my old 90's house music stuff. I could probably find that for you, I've got the CD mix in the house," Paula said, hoping to continue their rapport.

"Well, slap my knickers and shine my shoes! You go right on ahead and git that CD. It'd be perfect for our party!" Lester replied, jumping up and down, doing an Irish jig in the process.

Paula looked at her kids, who were still scared and huddled up together.

"Hey, Lester, maybe I can take the kids with me because I might need some help finding the CD," she nervously said, using the statement as a way to get her kids away from Lester and the barn.

"Oh no, they're good here, enjoying my party planning. They're gonna be my little helpers. Right, guys!?" Lester looked at the two, looking for their confirmation.

They both nodded their heads up and down, grimacing the whole time. The two would not dare contradict Lester, given what they had seen tonight.

Knowing that Lester might get suspicious, Paula would not test her luck and repeat the request. It was enough to go search for the house mix CD inside of her home. She knew that it could buy her even more time to come up with any kind of plan. There was no knockout punch in her strategy. This was going to take time and careful footing. Lester might have superior strength and magic at his side, but Paula knew that he could at least be outwitted. Perhaps, she thought, she could win the game with this strategy.

Paula ran into the house to go retrieve the CD. She knew where it was, but it bought her some time to breathe for the first time in what felt like days, even though it had been only hours. Grabbing herself some water and something to eat, she thought of how she could get the kids away from Lester.

One thing she knew she could do was eliminate what seemed to be his source of power - candy. She had kept it all in one place so finding it was the easy part, but how to dispose of it?

If she lit a fire, then Lester might become suspicious of her activity. If she buried it, he would still be able to find it. She finally thought of something that could work. Paula decided to put it down the garbage disposal unit.

As she ran the disposal, she kept checking outside to make sure nothing came out of the barn. Bit by bit, she disposed of them in increments. That was the strategy: taking away his magic with every bit of candy she destroyed.

"There you go, you son of a bitch. There goes your power pellets."

She smiled as the disposal did its work. Before she knew it, the candy was completely gone. Now, he would be powerless. His strength made him dangerous, but his magic made him nearly impossible to escape, especially since he seemed to be able to teleport at will. With the candy ground up and down the drain, Paula knew she had better get the CD, and fast, as Lester was bound to get curious.

She picked up the CD and ran out the door, heading to the barn. As she entered the barn the kids were still huddled, keeping to themselves as Lester kept switching around the radio dial on his stereo.

"Darn tootsies! I can't find a dang thing on this ol' hunk-a-junk," he complained, still turning the dial.

RATED M FOR MATURE

Paula flashed the CD up in the air much to Lester's delight.

"You found it!" he said, jumping up and down.

"I never thought you were going to make it back. Thought you took off or something. Was just about to send the search party after you," he said, laughing.

Paula wondered if this was a veiled threat or a legitimate joke, but she chuckled either way to stay in his good graces. Lester plucked the CD right out of her hand and popped it in.

The beat started up, and without hesitation, Lester started dancing to the infectious dance music which could have been straight out of a club in the 1990's. His dancing was not even remotely good as he juked and jived around performing in sort of a flail, randomly jutting out various body parts, but he was definitely lost in the music. As Lester got more into the music, random lights seemed to start flickering all over the barn just like those in a dance club with strobes, flashing, and even lasers.

"All righty everyone, git in on this. Git doooown!" he yelled, losing control of himself to the music, dancing up a storm; a bad storm, like a hurricane. Naturally, no one got near him, but it gave Paula an opportunity to dance off to the side with the kids and talk to them for the first time since before she passed out.

"Oh my god, kids, are you okay? Are you hurt?" Paula asked the both of them looking up and down their bodies for any signs of distress.

As she did this, the kids finally got a look at her missing hand up close. Rodney froze up, staring at the nub and Robert was unable to help himself, he started to sob at the sight of his mom's charcoaled nub.

"Shhh. Shhh, honey, it's okay. It's all right. What matters is that I'm here," she said tearfully, trying to stroke his head and calm him down.

"He stole your hand, mommy!" he was yelling as tears slid down his face, inconsolable. The kids were both distraught and rattled from a lack of sleep. All within one night, their dog had been killed, their father murdered, and now their mother stood before them mutilated by the dancing monster that stood a few feet away from them.

"Mom. What are we gonna do?" asked Rodney who tried to change the subject of her missing hand, knowing that there were more pressing issues.

"I don't totally know yet, sweetie, but it's important that you know that you're in charge of your brother, okay?" she said, tearing up a bit, realizing the severity that she likely would not make it through this alive.

Rodney, too, uncharacteristically teared up because, deep down, he knew the same exact thing, that his mom might not live through whatever this horrible ordeal was. He nodded his head, showing her, he understood completely what had to be done.

"I can't get into things too much here since he's close by, but we'll talk about a plan later, okay?"

They both nodded their heads in agreement.

"For now, I just need you to play along with Lester. I know that's really hard with everything that's happened but, if we're going to make it out alive, then we need to bide our time, wait for our moment. We'll get through this," Paula said as she put her good hand on Rodney's head and then stroked Robert's head in a comforting fashion.

They all collectively noticed that Lester was not paying any mind to them at all. The lure of the music seemed to have him in a hypnotic trance that he could not seem to pull himself away from. Lester had been dancing and strutting around to the house music. It was a one man party, and he had no care in the world.

Paula saw this as an opportunity. She got the kids to follow her lead and she slowly inched her way to the barn door with the kids in tow. Once they reached the door, they noticed that Lester was still in a dance trance, going even harder than before, shuffling his feet around and shaking his hips. He was totally in a world of his own. With such a distraction, Paula took her chances and made her way out of the door with the children.

She remembered that she had left the keys in the ignition of the truck. Running through what was now daylight, Paula was skeptical this plan would work but she had to try. Rolling up to the side of the driver side window, she could see that the key was still there, just waiting to be turned. The kids shuffled into the truck on the passenger side, and, with no signs of Lester, she went to turn the key, hoping they might just make it out. As she turned the key, there was no sound at all.

"Come on goddamnit!" she yelled, trying to will the car to start up, but it was as if the truck had nothing under the hood.

Sure enough, Paula popped the hood, and the engine was missing, torn out completely. She knew that Lester was strong but, this power was beyond Herculean, it bordered on Superman-like strength.

"All right, kids, we don't have a choice. It's a long way into town, but we gotta walk. I know it seems impossibly long, but we have to get some distance between us and Lester. Do you understand?"

Both kids nodded, understanding exactly what needed to be done.

Rodney, curious, asked Paula the simplest question.

"Mom, can't we just call the cops?"

LESTER

She had been in such a flurry since the madness began hours ago with Mr. Squiggles, it had not occurred to her that there was an outside world, much less police. When she finally thought of Rodney's question, she knew this was not an option.

"Rodney, we're on our own," Paula stated, realizing the isolation of their situation.

"If we call the cops here, we'd have to wait. Then they would show up and be killed for it. They'd never stand a chance, not even with the guns. It's up to us, guys. I'm so sorry," she stated with her shoulders slumped, face pointed at the ground, feeling almost sick.

"Now, come on, guys. We have a lot of walking to do," Paula glumly said as she started walking out of the garage and towards the main road. She hoped literally anyone would come down the road and give them a lift because it was a good 10 miles towards any kind of civilization.

"Mom, what about water 'n' stuff? It's going to get hotter, we'll die of thirst out there," Rodney asked of his mom.

It had not dawned on her to take food or water, just to get away from Lester but she knew that if they did not get supplies, Rodney was right, they would probably be lucky to even make it five miles, especially in their current shape. They had to get back inside the house and fill up.

"Okay, guys, we're gonna head back in and grab as much as we can and put it in a backpack, and then we leave. Got it?"

The children nodded their heads once again as if they were on autopilot.

Inside, they began grabbing whatever snacks they could, with the kids eating many of the snacks as they gathered supplies.

"Kids, save some for the trip," she reminded them.

"Sorry, mom, but we're starving," said Robert which in turn made Paula feel a little guilty.

They were right to eat all of the food, not having eaten anything since their early dinner. That pizza seemed like it was so long ago that it may have well been another lifetime.

"All right, kids, I think we're all loaded up with as much as we can handle. Now let's go do this thing. It should be a cakewalk. I know that the both of you are strong enough to do this."

This made the children smile, even if the smiles were weak and exhausted.

And with that, they were ready to start their hike. Now outside, they were careful to walk quietly, with both children tiptoeing. Suddenly, they jumped as a sound broke the silence.

"Where we goin'?" said a high-pitched voice from the side of the house.

To no one's surprise, it was Lester, waving at Paula and the kids.

Paula wanted nothing more than to cry. She wanted to break down, cry, and then lie down and die. This whole situation was impossible. Their chance gone. Still, she had to play the long game.

"Lester, done with your music? Maybe we should start a new dance party? Wouldn't that be fun?" Paula smiled at Lester, clasping her backpack.

"No, I'm okay for now. I got my big bad boogie on and now I'm looking to adventure, so it's plung dang awesome I found y'all ready to go on an adventure too," Lester said, approaching them with the happiest look on his face.

"So. Where are we all going?" Lester asked again.

Paula tried thinking of a lie but was at a loss of thought, much less words.

LESTER

"Umm… we were actually just getting ready for a later trip."

Paula knew the best thing to do in the moment was get her kids some rest so they could make a break for it some other time, when Lester was in another dance trance.

"Yeah, we were going to adventure but I realized the kids were dead tired and so I'm putting it off for now but maybe you can join us later?" Lester looked at her for a moment.

"Fooey! That's just nonsense. It's a beautiful day out and I'll be darned if we don't enjoy it," Lester insisted.

"But the kids are tired. They're hungry, Lester," Paula pleaded with him, confused at his insistence.

"Don't worry, I'll make sure they're well taken care of. Gonna make mighty warriors out of these young lads just yet."

Paula was quite incensed by Lester's attitude.

"Listen, Lester. I don't mean to be rude, but they have to sleep, and that is just what they'll be doing," she said, grabbing her kids and turning around towards the house.

Lester followed them in without saying a word. Paula took some comfort that perhaps he could still take a command or respect it. Perhaps the kids could get some much welcomed sleep, maybe she could. If they could all rest, then their plans would come to greater fruition.

"WE'RE GONNA GO ON AN ADVENTURE! WE'RE GONNA GO ON AN ADVENTURE!" Lester started singing at the top of his lungs, jumping around the house.

"Lester, please. We just need a little peace and quiet," Paula tried to reason with Lester in a very calm demeanor, still trying to game Lester.

"WE'RE GONNA GO ON AN ADVENTURE! WE'RE GONNA GO ON AN ADVENTURE!" Lester sang louder, still jumping up and down. He yelled his song so loudly, it hurt everyone's ears.

RATED M FOR MATURE

"LESTER! Just stop. We need rest," Paula said, getting increasingly agitated.

Lester pulled a little Lester action figure out of his back pocket and started waving it in front of the kids' faces.

"HEY KIDS! DON'T YOU WANNA GO ON AN ADVENTUUUUURE?! DON'T YOU WANNA GO ON AN ADVENTURE!?" Lester said even louder than before. His jumping was so aggressive that it shook the house.

"NO! We don't want to go on an adventure! Not with you, not ever! I WANT YOU TO DIE!" yelled Rodney as he tore the head off of the action figure and threw it to the ground.

"I hate you! You killed my dad, you killed Samantha, you hurt my mom!"

Paula interjected as he ranted, knowing how dangerous Rodney's words could be.

"Sweetie, you just need some rest, okay? Let's bring you to your room."

Rodney actually pushed Paula away a bit, resisting her attempt to usher him to the room.

"No! I need this yellow piece of shit to die! I! HATE! YOOOU!" Rodney let out a primal yell as he cried tears of rage.

Lester sat still for a minute, taking in everything that just happened. For a moment it looked as though he was sobering up, coming out of an almost drunken state. He reached down to pick up the dismembered action figure and stared at it for a moment quizzically. After looking at it for a minute, trying to piece its head back together he looked at Rodney.

"Well, shucks! You know, you're right," Lester said as he threw the broken up action figure over his head.

"Why go outside in all that heat when we can just have ourselves all kindsa fun in here!"

LESTER

Paula knew this was bad. Lester seemed to have an idea, and with his horrific imagination, she knew anything was possible. It put her on edge.

"Lester, sweetie, what are you doing?" Paula cautiously asked, still being overly sweet to keep up her ruse.

"Well, by golly! I'm glad you asked!"

Just as Lester finished his sentence, Rodney disappeared into thin air.

"Rodney?!" Paula instinctually yelled out.

"Oh, don't you worry none. That little hot tamale is in the bedroom,"

Before Lester could continue, Paula grabbed Robert and she ran into the bedroom to check on her son. She had no idea what to expect and it made her mind race a million miles per hour. When she got into the room, she was surprised to find no one was there.

Still thinking in diplomatic terms, Paula kindly asked, "Lester. Where is Rodney? I don't see him in here."

"Oh, of course you can't see ol' Hot Rod, silly. I ain't turned on the ol' video game doohickey," Lester explained as he reached for a game controller.

"Video game? Lester, what is going on?" she nervously asked, thinking the worst.

"Oh, me and my li'l buddy are gonna have some gametime. He don't wanna go outside and he seems awful sore about a few things, so I'm thinkin' it's time to have some ol' Lester 'n' Rodney time."

Paula did not like this one bit. She lacked the imagination required to understand where Lester might be going with this impromptu activity. Robert stood close to her, hugging her leg, looking up with worry written all over his face.

As the console turned on, a CGI version of Rodney appeared on the screen.

"Mom!? Robbie!? Anyone!?" he yelled while weightlessly floating upside down in confusion.

"RODNEY!" she yelled out to him.

"Lester. Please. Let my son out of there," she tried to reason as she shook.

"No can do, ma' good lady. We're just getting started," Lester replied enthusiastically as he put on a headset that appeared to be of his own creation. The writing on the side it in neon green, proclaiming "L3ZT3R IZ 1337"

"Now, why don't you two kick up a seat and enjoy the show, I've got a noob to own," Lester said as he snapped his finger.

Two chairs popped up quickly. Before either Paula or Robert could move, Lester-like arms came out of the chairs and pulled them into the cozy bright yellow seats.

"Don't worry, I gotcha covered. There's drink 'n' snacks, all kindsa goodies for all yer face holes," Lester said as he gestured at the chairs that held them captive.

As promised, the chairs had drink holders and little snacks for their viewing displeasure.

"Lester! Let me out!" Rodney yelled out as he continued to float around the space of the TV screen.

Ignoring his pleas, Lester flipped through the various video game titles.

"Oh, we love playing this one Rodney!" he exclaimed as he chose *Bound by Blood*, a military first-person shooter that was popular among the gang.

"All righty, a little player versus player me thinks."

Lester chose the option for Player versus Player Death Match that led to a loading screen. As the countdown showed up, Lester looked back at Robert.

"Hey, maybe you can get in on this. You play the winner."

LESTER

Robert just shook his head side to side nervously.

For Paula, she was unsure what Lester's intentions were. At this point, even when things seemed to be back to normal, it was anything but. She said nothing, but the whole thing unnerved her. The calmer they remained, perhaps the more Lester might calm down. This was her thought, anyway, as the combatants took the field.

"Rodneeeey. I'm findiiiing yoooou," Lester teased as he stalked the landscape searching for his opponent.

Lester had only walked a few feet and his controller rattled from the explosives damage he received from behind him.

"AH! YOU RASCAL!" Lester yelled out.

As he turned around, he faced an avatar of Rodney spraying machine fire at him which caused mortal injuries to his character.

"What!? You must be using some kind of cheat code, ya little scamp!" Lester angrily protested as his character began to respawn.

"There's no cheat code. You just suck, you fucking noob!" Rodney taunted Lester, running across the screen to find his next hiding spot.

As Lester respawned, he hunkered down looking a little more serious, likely annoyed from having died so quickly.

Paula watched as Lester charged through various buildings. She was hoping that Rodney would repeat his previous success in besting Lester, though it occurred to her that it might actually make the situation worse.

Lester opened a door and Rodney was waiting for him on the other side, unloading a hail of bullets into his unsuspecting avatar.

"GIB GOBBITY DOO DAD STUPID CONTROLLER!" Lester yelled in frustration.

He stood up.

"If you want something done, ya gotta do it yourself!" he angrily blurted out as he jumped into the TV turning into a Lester avatar.

"Oh, all right, now that feels a lot better," he said, looking around while holding his assault rifle with a big smile on his camo painted face.

"It's noob killin' time," he continued as he set out to find Rodney.

Paula and Robert could only see the action from Lester's point of view as he ran around from cover to cover humming show tunes to himself. Paula knew that Lester showing up into the game was not a good thing. He was angrier and more agitated than before and, given his current state, this did not bode well for Rodney.

"Lester. Just play another game. Something you're really good at, like that little cartoony game you love," Paula shouted, hoping that the change of scenery might do some good. She was trying her best to manipulate the situation.

"No way! This is war! It's about pride, honor, 'Merica, bald eagles, Hulk Hogan 'n' stuff," Lester shouted out of the TV.

"Oh, darn it. Now you made me lose ma' hiding spot," Lester huffed as he ran for another place to hide.

As Lester ran into an abandoned plane, he surprisingly caught Rodney from behind.

"Eat lead, mama's boy!" screamed at Rodney as he pulled his trigger and let loose a barrage of bullets.

Rodney got around the corner but was struck by a few bullets on the way out. Lester had played this game with the boys before but this time, something was very different as Rodney let out an audible yell that overrode any compression the TV set had.

"MY ARM! MY ARM! I'M BLEEDING! I'M ACTUALLY BLEEDING!" Rodney yelled out in panicked terror.

LESTER

"And this li'l doggy's on the hunt," Lester mocked as he continued his pursuit on Rodney.

Paula and Robert could only helplessly watch as Lester dashed around, looking for his prey.

"LESTER! STOP!" Paula pleaded with Lester, her eyes creased, and her face pained.

He ignored Paula's pleas and continued his relentless hunt. The hunt that was marked by a trail of blood that poured out of the arm of the young, terrified child who was now running for his life.

At this point all Paula could do was try to help out Rodney, now that Lester had tuned her out. There was a bigger picture but, in the here and now, all that mattered to Paula was keeping Rodney alive.

"Rodney! He can see your blood. Cover up your wound and hide. He's right on you."

"Rodney don't forget your specials," Robert added to the conversation, referring to his player's special abilities of planting explosive traps.

Suddenly, yellow hands came up over the mouths of Paula and Robert.

"That'll be enough from the peanut gallery," Lester muttered as he continued his mission.

Watching Lester, Paula noticed that the blood trail started to decrease. He had heard Paula which instantly made her feel better. Though not much, in a time like this, even the small things were a feeling of elation.

"Nowhere for you to run, Rodney, my man. Come 'n' git your bullet sammich," Lester mocked Rodney as he slowed his pace, becoming more defensive.

Lester looked around a bit. He said nothing but everyone could tell he was considering his next strategy. Slowly, he entered a building. It was dark with plenty of boxes. He peeked around each one, gun barrel drawn, hoping to get the drop on his victim.

Paula and Robert tried shaking their mouth restraints, even tried biting. No matter how much they did, there was no give. Their attempts at speaking or shouting were just a series of muffled sounds.

"GOTCHA!" Lester exclaimed.

He charged forward to a mishmash of boxes on the far end of the building. Paula had no clue what had tipped Lester off, she just hoped Rodney would be able to run as fast as he could.

Before Lester could make it to the boxes, Rodney went running out the other side of the boxes as fast as he could to another stack of boxes, using them as cover. Then, before Lester could figure out what happened, Rodney held up a remote in his hand.

Lester slumped his shoulders down and a grimace poured over his face.

"Dookie."

Rodney hit the trigger on the remote, causing a decent sized explosion.

Lester yelled as his avatar went flying through the air and hit the ceiling. Rodney's avatar could be seen getting knocked back a few feet. The impact knocked the air out of the young child, and he could be heard groaning.

As Lester started to respawn, his avatar could be seen throwing his weapons down in frustration as he started jumping up and down on them.

"DING! DANG! CHEATING BUTTED NO GOOD RACKIN' FRACKIN' SON OF A ROASTED MARSHMALLOW!"

"I won, Lester. Now let me out of here. You can't beat me," Rodney responded off in the distance, likely from a new hiding spot.

Lester sat still for a moment, rubbing his chin.

"You know what? You're right. I can't beat you - at THIS game."

Everyone sat anxiously silent, waiting for Lester to follow up this reply.

"I say we play another game. I think it's time for a little ol' *Blood Storm*!" he said with great glee, smirking.

"NO! KNOCK THIS OFF!" Rodney yelled at Lester, just wanting all of this to be over. Paula knew how exhausted her son was and it weighed on her as she sat restrained, unable to even mouth her dismay. She squirmed in frustration, her screams muffled by the yellow hands that seemed to apply even more pressure.

The screen went black. Then came up the logo for the street fighting game, *Blood Storm*. This was the last thing Paula wanted. She knew very little about the video games her children played but this one she knew about from the media. It was a fighting game where the characters mutilated and killed each other in horrible ways.

The recurring thought Paula had was, "If Rodney is taking real damage, then does that mean he'll die in the game?"

Before she could think of anything else, the game started and a menu to select characters started up. All the normal characters appeared for selection but among them were two new additions: Lester and Rodney.

Rodney was the same scrawny little kid that he had been in real life. He looked around, confused at his new surroundings. He continually rubbed his arm, even though the wound from the bullet of the previous game had disappeared.

For Paula, this gave her just a tiny ounce of hope.

Across the screen, there stood Lester. This version of Lester was just like the real world one, but the noticeable difference was that he had a Herculean physique. He strutted around with giant muscles, arms out as if he were carrying two barrels, showing off his lats. This did not look promising for Rodney. He would have nowhere to run in this game.

"All right. This is between ME and the boy. The rest of you gotta skedaddle," Lester informed the other game characters. As he did, most of them shrugged and slowly walked away offscreen, mumbling to each other on the way out.

"So ya' little donut hole. You ready to eat defeat?" Lester asked Rodney.

"Hey, this is no fair. You're way bigger than me. What the hell am I supposed to do?!"

"You've been playing this game a long time now so you must know plenty of kung-fu, karate, whosyamama and whatever else by now. Not my problem," Lester said as he did a series of stretches.

"At least give me a weapon or something. You're like ten feet taller than me and super buff, you damn cheat."

Lester pondered the request for a moment.

"I guess you can't deny a dead man his last request. Okay, I'll give you some weapons that won't do ya' a lot of good. What kind did you want?"

It was an important question, but Rodney instantly blurted out, "Katanas!"

"Oh, you want them fancy ol' ninja swords, eh? Well, then here ya' go," Lester said, as two sheathed katana blades appeared, strapped to his back.

Rodney looked happy about his choice and Paula let out a temporary sigh of relief.

"You should've gone with a rocket launcher. I mean, that would've been waaaay better than them silly little toothpicks you got on your back now," Lester said as he shook his head.

"Rocket launcher?! I didn't know that was even an option!" Rodney yelled back at Lester with a look of annoyance.

"Well, you know now," Lester replied, shrugging his shoulders.

"Then I want the rocket launcher!" Rodney demanded.

"Nope. Too late now. Good luck with your little stabby bits though."

Rodney stared with his jaw open. He had been so impatient that he stepped into a Lester trap by not asking enough questions. Now, he had to live with his choice and make the most of it.

"All righty, everyone. HERE WE GOOOOO!" Lester giddily said aloud as the fight screen came up.

In the background was a dark dungeon with only a few candles offering up any source of light in the entire arena. Chains swayed above, and off to the sides there were ditches with sharp spikes in them.

"Better watch your step because each one is a heck of a doozy," Lester warned his opponent.

Rodney looked behind him and saw the spikes. The reaction on his face was that of total fear as his body matched by visibly shaking. His breathing was arrhythmic as he moved up a few inches and planted his feet.

Paula started to squirm again as the restraints squeezed her tighter. She could do nothing but sob. Her cries were muffled as she closed her eyes, trying to think of something, anything she could do to avoid what she knew was going to happen.

"FIGHT!" the announcer on the video announced as the word was spelled out in a bloody red font.

Lester slowly and confidently moved forward without missing a beat. Rodney was thrown off by how quickly Lester approached him and, as a result, started to move around the arena to get any kind of distance between himself and Lester.

"Oh, it's no fun if you keep moving around like a little angry chicken," Lester chuckled.

Rodney was completely caught off guard as Lester charged at him. Instinctually, Rodney moved to avoid Lester, and as Lester got closer, Rodney narrowly avoided him and swiped his sword at his attacker.

"Oh, man, you got me good on that one," Lester said as he raised his left hand up to reveal a missing finger. He put on a big smile.

Rodney stood his ground on the opposite side of the arena, shaking even more than before, holding both swords. Terrified and high on adrenaline, his eyes were as big as plates as he waited for the yellow monster's next move.

This time, Lester slowly moved with purpose. As he moved forward, he walked in whatever direction Rodney moved in, attempting to corner Rodney. Lester's footwork was oddly impressive as he seemed to keep Rodney from gaining any advantage.

Lester was finally within striking distance. He kept poking his hands in, attempting to grab Rodney. Every time he did, one of the swords would wildly swing and narrowly miss Lester's outreached hand. The whole time, Lester giggled, as if he were toying with Rodney.

Without warning, and with impressive speed, Rodney ran to Lester's right side and as he did, Lester put his left arm out to grab the little bolt of lightning. As he tried to do so, Rodney swung his sword with as much power as he could and off came Lester's left hand.

"YES!" Paula muffled through her captor's hands. Looking over she could see that Robert was equally excited and his eyes were big. It seemed impossible but at the same time they both had a look in their eyes as if to say, "There's a chance!"

Now, Rodney was jumping around like he was Bruce Lee. His prior lack of confidence was gone and replaced with a cockiness. Paula wanted to yell at him not to get ahead of himself, not to get arrogant, but the restraints let out nothing more than frustrated grunts.

As he danced around the arena, Lester held up his new nub.

"Now look what ya gone and done."

He picked up his left hand.

"Aw man, I really liked that hand," he said as he looked down sadly at his lobbed off appendage.

Suddenly, Lester moved faster than Rodney could react.

"CATCH!"

Lester threw his hand right at Rodney's unsuspecting face. The combination of speed and weight of Lester's beefy hand gave Lester just enough time to close the distance as he made his way over to kick Rodney in the side.

The muscularity of Lester's leg was dense. It felt as if it weighed one hundred pounds, and it sent Rodney flying across the arena. He hit the ground with an audible thud, and he let out a pained scream. His body continued to slide across the arena and edge toward the ditches where the sharp spikes awaited him. Luckily, his body lost momentum and he stopped just inches from falling off.

Dazed from the impact, Rodney got up on adrenaline alone. Standing up on his feet he quickly looked for his katana blades.

"Looking for these, buddy?"

Looking over, Rodney saw one of his katana blades. Standing over it was a giant, 'roided up Lester waving at Rodney with a big smile on his face.

Rodney could only stare in disbelief.

"Shit."

"Oh boy, talk about your dumb luck. The other one fell in one of them little ol' spikey bits. Guess the only way to get a sword now is coming on over here to get it," Lester said as he continued to smile.

Rodney stood still. It was obvious from everyone's point of view that he was considering his options as he just stared at the blade.

"Think fast!" Lester yelled as he threw his hand again.

This time Rodney ducked, and the hand missed him. Lester stayed in his spot this time, not wanting to give up his leverage on the sword.

Lester laughed, "HA! Almost got ya'"
Rodney was shaking again, being thrown off balance from the hand. At least he knew Lester had nothing else he could throw at him.

Paula was trying her best to scream at Rodney. She would tell him not to fall for it, to test Lester's patience and have him come to you. Due to the restraints, she could say nothing as Rodney made a major tactical error.

He was going to go for the sword. She could see it in his eyes.

"Here goes nuthin'," he said to himself.

Running towards Lester, Rodney appeared to be aiming for Lester's left side, knowing his hand was gone and it was his best chance to get his only means of protection back. At the last second, as he got closer, he noticed how big and wide Lester's stance was, so he went and slid between his legs.

The move genuinely caught Lester off guard.

"SON OF DOG BOOGER!" he yelped as the brave; young child strode across the dungeon floor.

As he got behind Lester, he reached for the katana blade and managed to get his hand on the handle.

LESTER

"YES!" Paula yelled under her muzzles.

Rodney looked as surprised as anyone that it worked. The surprise was only as big as his smile as he started to pull the katana towards him. As he did, he suddenly felt it lose its give.

Lester had planted his foot on the sword.

It gave Lester just the moment he needed. As Rodney jerked back, he lost his balance and went tumbling towards the ditches. Falling toward the spikes, Rodney screamed and closed his eyes.

Paula closed her eyes too. There was no way she could look. It was too painful.

To everyone's surprise there was silence, and to Rodney's surprise, he was not dead. In fact, someone was holding the front of his shirt. It was Lester.

Rodney turned his face to Lester, his eyes wide open.

"What? Why did you do that?"

Hearing the sound of her child, Paula opened her eyes. Robert and her both looked at each other, shocked. It made no sense.

"Why?" Lester asked back to Rodney.

"Well, because I ain't lettin' you off that easy, hombre," he said as he giggled.

With brute force, Lester quickly yanked Rodney by his shirt which sent him flying over Lester's head and hard onto the opposite side. It was like a hammer coming down on a nail. The impact knocked all of the air out of Rodney.

The look of shock that adorned Paula and Robert's faces earlier now were pale white and full of terror.

"Oh, darn it. You played a heckuva game and you lost. You know what that means," Lester said as he slowly lumbered over Rodney.

Completely dazed and staggered, Rodney tried talking and batted at Lester in a weak attempt at fighting him off.

RATED M FOR MATURE

Paula screamed loud enough to be heard through the hands that blocked her mouth. Robert too was now squirming and screaming loud enough to be heard, adjoined with tears. He had played this game enough times to know what happens when you lose at *Blood Storm*.

"Now, let's go ahead 'n' pop that ol' melon off," he gleefully said as grabbed down at the back of Rodney's small neck with his giant right hand.

"No… No… Mom? I– I don't wanna die…" a stunned Rodney said, still concussed from being thrown to the ground.

"HERE WE GOOOO!" Lester said with a big smile on his face forcefully tugging at Rodney's head as he used his foot on Rodney's shoulder to tug as hard as he could. Rodney was convulsing, still pleading and crying as in his final moments as Lester slowly used his strength to completely tear the head from the torso. It looked like someone pulling taffy apart as the slow tension did its work with most of the spine attached to Rodney's head. Blood was everywhere, mostly on Lester who was gleefully cheering at his accomplishment.

Paula had seen unimaginable horrors throughout the course of this day. Things she never imagined possible, even in hell, but this was something she could not prepare for, not physically or mentally. She profusely threw up. The hands that held her captive moved away from her all at once. The hands with puke on them, wiped the hot vomit back onto her. Her brain was overloaded with the sheer shock and violence in front of her. This could not possibly be real.

Free from the chair, she fell to her knees. Paula was numb, staring off beyond the TV that Lester inhabited, trapped in her thoughts, far away from the reality she was currently captive to. With her ears ringing, she could not hear Lester or Robert, who sat confined to his chair, screaming, and crying; his face contorted in both pain and fear.

LESTER

Paula's brain could not process the horrific images of her firstborn having his head forcibly removed and his killer standing there, inches away, celebrating, seemingly taking pleasure in every ounce of her pain. They were just toys to him and nothing more.

Sitting on the floor, she looked back up listlessly to the TV.

"Oh hey, I didn't forget about you. Here's a li'l ol' souvenir," Lester said directly to Paula.

Something came flying out and hit her in the stomach. She looked down and staring back at her was the severed head of her oldest son, Rodney Bowline. Still shell shocked she observed her shirt and pants which were covered in blood. As she continued to stare and observe, reality started to come back to her.

"This has to be a dream… a nightmare…" she muttered to herself.

She closed her eyes for a few moments.

With her eyes still closed, she looked back down, and slowly opened her eyes back up expecting to see this horrible hallucination gone. Instead, her son's dismembered head sat on the ground with his eyes rolled back, and blood pouring out of his neck.

She blankly stared another minute, breathing rapidly.

"NOOOOOOOO!!!!" she screamed out in a way that could only be described as primal. It was so long and hard that it took the wind out of her, and it made her collapse into a hunched over position where she profusely cried. Every single gasp and tear took the full of her breath, making her body heave up and down.

Coming to her senses, Paula could hear the world again. As Robert was released from his seat, Paula quickly rushed over to sweep him up in her arms. She hugged him tightly, letting him wrench out all of his emotions. It was unbearable knowing that there was nothing she could do to possibly comfort him at all as she was barely even functional at the moment.

She would not promise him that things would be okay. She lost three family members already, having no say in their living or dying, and she knew that she was helpless: beyond bargaining, escaping, or defending. Comfort and promises were no longer an option, only death. She just hoped it would be swift.

WHEN LIFE HANDS YOU LEMONS

Paula clutched her son with no intention of letting him go. She thought of nothing else in the moment but giving him all of the love and peace she could offer, even if only for a moment. With no options left, she decided she was going to pick him up and simply leave. Paula could hear Lester shuffling around inside the TV still, doing something but she chose not to look, acting on her decision instead.

"What's the worst thing that Lester could do? Kill us?" she thought, as she swooped up her remaining son and began to walk towards the front door.

"MOM!" she heard a voice call out to her.

She turned around.

Paula stared down the hallway. Just around the corner she could see her son, Rodney, peeking his face around the corner. This was impossible. She watched him die.

"Hey, mom. I'm sorry about what happened," he said.

His voice was a perfect match, he had the right facial expressions. The desperation of want and need stopped her dead in her tracks. In her mind, she knew it was a cruel trick, but she found it impossible to move, hanging onto an impossible hope that this was her son.

"Lester and I were playing a trick on you. We stopped it because it went too far. We're sorry to you, too, Robbie," Rodney continued, apologizing to the both of them, looking guilty.

"Rodney… I don't think I understand. Where's Lester?" she asked, bewildered, and confused, trying to figure out what was happening.

Then she heard laughter.

"GOTCHA!" Lester continued to laugh as he came around the corner showing that he had been playing with Rodney's head, almost like a puppet.

Rodney's head started singing, "I'm still dead dead dead, yeah, I'm totally dead! Cha cha chaaaa!"

As he sang, Lester did a little dance, bouncing around to the perverse ditty.

"All right, say goodbye, Rodney boy," Lester said to the head.

"Goodbye, Rodney boy," the head said back with a wink and smile to Paula.

"Oh boy, now that was a messy trick but worth the look on y'alls faces," Lester said as he pulled his hand out from the meat of Rodney's neck, dropping the head on the ground.

"Oops! Didn't mean to drop him," he said apologetically, wiping the blood from his hands on some of Paula's clothes hanging in the hallway closet. Paula shot him a look, the kind of look that wished the most unpleasant of things. There was pure murder in her eyes.

"Tough crowd. Tough crowd," Lester said, jerking at his collar.

"All righty, well I got a doozy for ya. Ahem. What did the mother say to her son?" he looked around the room for an answer, not just Paula and Robert, but beyond them as if there were a crowd.

"No guesses?!" he asked with a big smile.

"She said, 'don't lose your head!'" which made Lester laugh furiously.

"Get it because–" as he slapped his knees, Lester noticed Paula looking at him furiously with tears in her eyes.

"Oh boy, here we go with the ol' PC police," rolling his eyes.

LESTER

"I done made your mom angry, kid," he said, talking to Robert who sat still, scared, looking directly at Lester.

"You know, I've got to say that I've been to a million places all over the world and this crowd is tougher than my mama's cooking," Lester threw his hands out sideways looking for applause from his cheap joke.

Sensing that his audience was in no laughing mood, Lester switched gears.

"It's the darndest thing. I guess I've been having so much fun that I done forgot to eat my tasty sweet bits. Why don't we mosey on over to my dojo and go see about getting some teeth trimmins'," Lester said with a big smile on his face.

Suddenly, to even her own surprise, Paula started laughing uncontrollably.

"Well, shucks I knew I was bound to tickle your ol' funny bone!" Lester exclaimed.

"No, no, no," Paula interjected, coming down from her laughing with a face that read victory all over it.

"You won't find that precious candy anywhere, you yellow goofy bastard," Paula said with a celebrative smirk on her face as if she scored a point in some game.

"It's allllll gone, your stupid magic. I dumped all the candy. Every. Last. Bit."

The statement gave her a smile that reached ear to ear. It dawned on her that she had given too much away, clearly a result of exhaustion.

"You… you took my candy?" Lester said, with his brows perked up, looking sad.

"That's right you son of a bitch. Now, you've got nothing." she said, putting her face closer to Lester's. That cat was out of the bag, and she wanted to rub this win in his stupid, yellow face. It was all she had left.

"What do you think about that?" she said now nearly nose to nose with Lester.

WHEN LIFE HANDS YOU LEMONS

"Well, I think that's no problem. There's always sunshine behind the clouds," he said now with a big smile on his face.

"I've got all the candy I need jiggling around in that skull over there," he pointed at Robert.

Paula quickly put the words together and now her prior confidence was met with instant terror.

"No, no, no. It's candy that fuels your magic!" she muttered in disbelief, while wrapping Robert up in her arms.

Lester laughed.

"Shucks, no. I'm just a real picky eater is all, and candy is my personal favorite, but since I'm all out I'm gonna have to replenish the ol' Lester magic with something else."

Paula tried to run as fast as she could to the front door, but he stuck his big foot out which cartoonishly reached down the hallway and around her foot.

"Ooops!" he exclaimed as the extended leg tripped Paula, and she fell on her face.

She could feel the weight of Robert slipping out from her arms.

"Well, look at that. There's still a tiny bit of magic in the ol' tank!" Lester happily remarked.

"Noooo! Mom! Don't let him get me too!" yelled Robert as he cried tears of terror, being pulled back down the hallway by Lester.

Paula latched on to Robert's upper half, trying to regain custody of her son.

"Let him go! Goddamn you! You let my son go! Haven't you already done enough?!" Paula yelled at the top of her lungs as she pulled with all of her strength.

Unfortunately for Paula, she could feel the immense strength of Lester, as if Robert was being pulled by a truck, and it dragged her down the hallway towards the bedroom with Robert as she attempted to hold on.

"I DON'T WANNA DIE!" Robert yelled even louder, now crying to the point of hyperventilation, frantically yelling for his mother.

With one yank, Paula's grip was loosened, and Robert was now out of her possession.

"NO!" she furiously yelled in desperation as she watched her son end up in Lester's clutches.

Before she knew it, Lester started knocking on Robert's head in a hard fashion. Robert screamed in unbearable pain as the top of his skull started to cave in from the superhuman knocks on his head. His scalp crumbled inward like an eggshell. Paula, now unhinged, jumped at Lester and started attacking him, trying to pry Robert from Lester's clutches.

"Don't worry, Paula. I'll share but you gotta wait your turn," Lester said, giggling as he gently pushed her away, which knocked her on her ass.

Lester stood in front of her, removing layers of Robert's scalp. Hair, skin, muscle, Lester picked it all off one by one before finding the opening of the skull he had created. Robert's eyes rolled into the back of his head. His various limbs twitched furiously, making disturbing grunts with whatever life he still had in his young body. The young boy's body stiffened up as Lester dug his hand into Robert's skull and dug out his brain.

"Now that's what I call the catch of the day!" Lester exclaimed, chuckling warmly, as he ate chunks of Robert's brain like a small child eating their spaghetti. He did it with glee, eating away while covered in Robert's blood and fragments of his skull, with the biggest smile on his bright face.

"My baby, you took my baby–" Paula said as she stared off in a complete daze, bearing witness to this gruesomely disturbing moment.

WHEN LIFE HANDS YOU LEMONS

"I can't believe–" she mumbled incoherently to herself, looking around aimlessly, pulling at her hair. She growled in anger and frustration, punching her hand into the floor multiple times.

Paula was in a rage, beyond grief or sadness. She wanted to murder Lester and wipe that evil, obnoxious grin off of his bright yellow face. With Lester distracted, she leapt over him to get to her room and grab a gun. This might be her one chance. She had no ambitions to escape now, the only thing she wanted was revenge, even if it was the last thing she ever did. Lester paid no mind to her movements, and she was able to get her good hand on the gun. She picked it up, pointed it point blank at the back of his head, and furiously blasted away at the evil son of a bitch that just killed the final member of her family.

"DIE!!!" she screamed at the top of her lungs as the succession of small explosions gave way to a repetitive clicking of the trigger. The chamber empty, Paula looked up at the damage. The bullets had made their way in through the hard flesh.

For a moment, she thought she had succeeded in killing him, but she knew it would not be that easy, if even possible. Sure enough, Lester's wounds slowly closed up. She stood still, anticipating his next move. Slowly, his head turned all the way around, opposite of his body. Now completely backwards, still smiling at her, Lester spit all of the bullets at Paula's feet.

"You lost theeeese," he said playfully.

"Like gettin' a mouthful of seeds up in yer beak," he continued as he turned his head back in the right direction before finishing up his sickening meal.

Paula collapsed. She was exhausted, beaten, hopeless. Everything she loved was dead, destroyed in the worst possible ways. One by one, she sat by unable to do anything as her family suffered horrific deaths, scarring her mind, staining her soul.

LESTER

As she laid on the floor, devoid of all tears now, she wondered what she could have done to reverse the actions that played out. Every path always led to the same answer; that she should have never accepted Lester into her life to begin with. Everything from that moment forward always ends this way. It was all her fault.

There was only one thing left to do. She looked at the gun and knew that the bullets were all spent, but there was broken glass littered throughout. If only she could get to it and release herself from this pain and misery, she could finally be free. Death was a far greater comfort than what she was feeling. Even if Lester were to leave right then and there, she could never move forward. She was completely obliterated. Killing herself was the only true way out of the situation.

She crawled over to a massive shard of glass from a broken frame, as Lester continued to pay her no mind. Slowly, she made her way to the shiny object and sat down beside it. Picking up the long, jagged piece of glass, she stared at it, considering what she was about to do. There was just the slightest bit of hesitation because she realized that this was it, no turning back.

Every bit of joy or happiness was gone from the world and, no matter how much she tried to rationalize things, this was the only way out. She just had to be brave enough to jam the shard into her neck. Slowly she raised the glass in her hand. She thought one last time of Anthony, Rodney, and Robert, and closed her eyes, ready to plunge the chunk of glass into her neck. With certainty and determination, she felt her muscles tense up and, with all the force she could muster, thrust the sharp fragment toward her neck.

“Whoops! We can’t have that,” said Lester.

Paula felt the glass stop just inches from her neck.

“What the hell?!” she thought.

WHEN LIFE HANDS YOU LEMONS

She opened her eyes. Lester's iron grip held her hand in place without any budge. Quickly she attempted to use leverage and jam her neck into the glass as it stood still. Lester was one step ahead of her and pulled her arm away. The force hurt her arm, forcing her to drop the glass.

"You can't leave the show now! The magic is one hundred and twenty percent back! Playtime's just begun!" Lester shouted in glee as Robert's blood drooled out of his mouth.

"Oops! Cleanup on aisle: My Face" he said, laughing at his own joke.

Having eaten what was left of Robert's brain matter, he cocked back Robert's skull like a cup, getting out every last drop of blood within the skull.

"Now, that hit the spot!" he said, wiping his lips off with his own sleeve.

"Why can't you just let me die!?" Paula yelled at the top of her lungs.

She broke down in tears at the end of her sentence, going limp to the ground. Crying on the floor, all she wanted was the release of death and it had been mere inches away. It was beyond cruel that, after everything he had done, Lester would not allow her this one thing.

"What do you want from me?" she growled.

"What do I want from you?" repeated Lester.

"Well, shucks, I just wanna have some fun. Don't you?" he asked Paula.

She shot up, "How in the hell is any of this fun? You killed my children, you killed my husband, you took away everything from me!" yelling so hard, her voice was becoming hoarse.

Paula was practically out of her mind. she shot straight up and got into Lester's face.

"I want back everything you took from me. That would be fun. This is the opposite of fun, you murdering psychopath!"

"Umm… you are really close to my mug. Awkwaaaaard," he said as he released Paula and walked backwards away from her.

"Well, listen if it's your family you want then, well, let's do it. Let's get them back!" he said with a big smile on his face, drawing his arms close to his body, balling his fists in excitement.

"Oh boy, this is gonna be a good one. I've never done this one before!" he said, dancing around.

"Do what, exactly?" Paula responded, genuinely confused.

"We're gonna bring em' back, silly. It's like when you break something, you just mend it on back together, right?"

The wall opposite the window started to break down and within it a stage could be seen, like that of a play theater.

"Oh, wowzah! We're gonna take care of that li'l ol' nub of yours too." Lester said as he scrambled around, going behind the curtain, backstage of this new theater.

"I'll be back in a jiffy!" he said from backstage.

Paula's need to kill herself was overridden by her curiosity and she simply stared at the stage.

"I did it! I think I actually did it!" yelled Lester from backstage. He poked his head out from behind the curtain.

"Paula, you'll never believe it! Just sit right there, they're coming," he said as he pulled his face behind the curtain once more.

Paula could feel her heartbeat increasing as her stomach soon began to dance around. She attempted to take deep breaths, but it seemed as though the more she did, the faster her heart rate was. It actually made her more nervous.

"Where is this going and why can't I look away?" she thought to herself.

WHEN LIFE HANDS YOU LEMONS

The lights dimmed around her. Over a loudspeaker that was invisible to Paula's eyes, Lester's voice announced, "And now presenting to you from, uh, wherever this is, it's the Fabulous Bowline Boooooooys!"

Music started to play. It was an upbeat, loungey song that permeated through the air. There were random spotlights, but they seemed to come from nowhere, off in the distance beyond her scope. She could hear tap dancing from off the stage and it got closer by the second. Paula knew that this was odd, and she steadied herself for whatever was coming out.

From behind both curtains she could see tap dancing feet emerging which revealed the familiar looking clothing of her children. As more clothes met the spotlight, she could see stained, dried blood on the clothing. Finally, the whole of their bodies were out for display. Two children both with their heads missing were tap dancing on the stage. It was only now that Paula had noticed the limbs being manipulated by bloody strings that went into the ceiling, being controlled by yellow hands.

They continued to do their horrible dance as Paula watched on. She was too numb for shock or anger. Instead, she just watched in a trance-like state as blood came gushing from their necks every so often during the dance, splattering anything around them.

"Fine dance, don't you think?" said a furious voice.

Paula heard it, but she did not know from where.

"They're doing this because of you, you know?" the voice said again.

Paula looked around again, the voice was coming from below her ears. When she finally looked down, she jumped onto her feet and screamed.

On her nub, where her hand used to be, was her husband's head.

LESTER

"Why did you let him into our lives, Paula? He burned me alive and then he murdered our children!" Anthony said, wincing in pain.

"Why did you do it!?" he asked angrily.

"I… I don't know… I–" she stumbled over her words, attempting to cry, but she was so weak and exhausted, she could not form tears anymore. All she had was a pained face looking for words.

"I didn't know this would happen. I mean, no one could've," Paula said, trying to offer some answer to Anthony.

"Some strange being comes walking into our lives and instead of thinking of your family first, you move on to the next big thing. TYPICAL!" Anthony yelled.

"Now, we all get to suffer because of YOU!"

Paula had her head down hoping to wake up from the nightmare.

"Look at our kids. LOOK AT THEM!" he yelled again.

Paula looked up and saw the bodies of her children dancing around in a synchronized fashion, kicking their feet, swinging the dancing canes, twirling. Blood that had been pouring out of their necks drenched the stage and decorated the curtains. As she stared, some of the blood sputtered out and landed on her.

"I hope you like the show, Paula. You're the one that created it," Anthony angrily said to Paula.

Without warning he spat on her face.

Paula screamed at the top of her lungs as her senses were overloaded. All she wanted was a few seconds to think, but the chaos was all around her and every fiber of her being was on fire. She could not think, she could not pass out, she could not die. The only thing she had control of was this ability to scream. It was the only thing she could think to do.

WHEN LIFE HANDS YOU LEMONS

As she did, Anthony started screaming, mocking her. The more she screamed, the face, where her hand used to be, started screaming louder.

Now completely unhinged, she hastily ran into her bedroom, jumped on top of the bed and flung herself out of the bedroom window. She hit the ground only temporarily as she got back up right away and began running.

Behind her, through the broken window she heard Lester, "Whoa! That was awesome!"

Amped up on adrenaline and totally delirious, Paula did not feel the pain of the crash or any of the shards of glass that had punctured her body. The only thing she felt was an instinct to run. She had no idea where she was running, but she had to get away from this house, this land, anywhere from here, and began running down the road at full speed.

It was oppressively hot, and the sun was beating down on her, but Paula had no care at all because, if anything, the sun could only help her die. She just knew she had to keep running until she passed out. There was no plan in place, but anything was better than being back in Lester's clutches.

After what seemed like at least two miles, Paula finally started to gas out and came to a jog. It was still quite a trek to town, but Paula was determined to get there or die trying.

"You can do this, Paula. C'mon, you can make it. You've literally got nothing to lose here. Keep going!" she told herself, picking up her pace once again.

As she ran, she began to worry when she might run into Lester again, when he might catch up to her, mocking her attempts at escaping with his exaggerated smile and hearty high-pitched laugh. She was undeterred though, knowing that she had escaped, and action was better than nothing.

"If I can just make it to town, that's all I have to do. Even with his magic, he can't possibly know where I am. He's never been outside of the property," she said to herself aloud, keeping herself company.

Paula had been jogging and running on and off for hours. She had no idea of just how many hours it was; it felt like days. Her skin was red from the sun, she had very little left in the way of saliva, and she was having trouble seeing straight but, finally, there it was - the town.

As the sun was going down, she stumbled into town, hobbling the entire time with her feet totally worn out from the endless running. The soles of her feet were completely shredded up and bleeding. This did not even occur to her until the peace of finding civilization grounded her back to reality. The pain that previously benefited from adrenaline, came back to her all at once. Still, she marched forward toward the finish line.

"Heeeeelp! Anyone! HEEEEELP!" Paula yelled at the top of her lungs as she got into town.

It was dark now, but she could see many businesses still open. Paula was surprised that no one could hear her pleas. She picked up a rock and threw it as hard as she could through a window. As soon as she did, she fell to her knees. Everything had caught up to her. Her vision started to go, and her head was beginning to feel very light as she began to lose consciousness.

Paula had one fleeting thought as she began slipping into the black. It was a calming thought that brought a smile to her face.

"Finally. It's over."

Her body, now in full shock from the inhuman amount of abuse she had absorbed, shut down. On the sidewalk she laid; nothing but a pile of bloody rags, sunburns, bruises, cuts. Anyone that stumbled across her would rightfully assume she was dead.

Despite it all, still, she breathed.

MOVIN' ON UP

Slowly, Paula came out of a long peaceful sleep. She felt the most rested she had felt, maybe ever. There was peace and quiet as she came to.

"Had it all been a bad dream?" she thought, as she continued to emerge from dreamland.

The room was dark, almost too dark and she found it difficult to make anything out. As she attempted to get up, there was resistance. It was obvious to her that she was restrained which made her quickly struggle and fight to get loose.

"Hello? Anyone! Let me out! Let me out of here!" she screamed into the blackness of the room.

Suddenly, a bright, blinding light came down on her from above. It pained her eyes. She recoiled back, clenching her eyes shut.

"Please, can someone tell me what's happening?!" she yelled out.

There was no response.

Her heart raced a thousand miles an hour, knowing that something was wrong.

"Let me oooooout!" she screamed one more time, fighting the restraints.

"All right, class, can everyone see me?" asked a high-pitched voice.

Cracking her eyes open, adjusting to the extreme brightness, Paula could see Lester, dressed in surgeon scrubs, his head hovering over her. As she turned her head around, she could see other Lesters sitting above and around her as observers, as if she was part of a surgical presentation.

Paula knew exactly what was going on, and the knot in her gut tightened up so much that it was nearly excruciating.

LESTER

"No! No! No! I got away! I got away from you, this isn't fair. IT'S NOT FAIR!" she screamed as tears leaked from the sides of her eyes while she thrashed around.

"Hey, quiet down there, you're gonna make me look bad around my students," Lester whispered to her.

Paula could not begin to fathom just what Lester had in store for her, the very thought drove her to a desperate madness, hoping that she might pass out again in shock.

"So, we've got all kinds of tools here to do… stuff with on people," he said, curiously looking at the surgical instruments that laid before him.

"Well, this thingamajig looks all important like. All right let's see what it does, class," Lester said as he picked up a scalpel.

"Okay, so everyone observe the pointy thingy," to which the class started writing notes.

Looking at it in his hand, Paula instantly started to clench her body, trying to do anything to cover her stomach, assuming that is where the scalpel would go. Kicking and screaming, she tried contorting her body to fight what was coming.

"Okay, class, let's cut this turkey open and see what's inside," Lester said as he put the cold scalpel to her stomach.

Paula fought back more and more, but it was no use. From the point of her sternum, she could feel the blade enter her skin. The pain was hellishly unbearable, even compared to everything else she had already suffered. She screamed so loud that it hurt her own ears. Slowly, the instrument made its way down her stomach as she continued to writhe in pain. The blade's journey ended at the furthest point of her lower abdomen.

"Oh, boy, it looks like there's all kindsa important stuff in here. I wonder what this is. Looks like sausage links!" he said as he grabbed a part of her intestines and casually pulled them up.

If the pain Paula felt from the scalpel cutting into her was unbearable, then this was in a realm that defied human comprehension. She let out a guttural scream that could have been heard in outer space.

As she laid on the operating table crying, the adrenaline kicked in and it made her dizzy. She only hoped she could pass out as Lester continued pulling more of her intestines out.

"Ummm, I have no idea what any of this is, so I'm just gonna stuff it back in," Lester said as he grabbed her intestines and stuffed them back into the hole in her body. How she was even still alive was beyond her.

"Why can't I just die?" she thought to herself, hoping the end would come soon.

"Oh, I just came up with a great idea!" Lester said, reaching for what looked like surgical pliers.

"I'm super-duper interested in seeing how these work."

Paula was unsure what he meant but she tensed up again. Still reeling in pain from her exposed abdomen, she was unable to fight back or struggle anymore. All she could do was stare at Lester as he slowly brought the surgical pliers toward her eye. Paula still had control of her head and shook it side to side, fighting what she knew was going to make her last violation pale in comparison. Lester grabbed her head to stop the shaking.

"Git on over here, ya little bugger," Lester playfully said as the pliers got closer.

Paula could not fight it any longer. He was about to do his worst, and there was not a single thing she could do to stop it. She screamed as loud as she could, but the screaming stopped as her insides jiggled around causing immense pain. Her eyes were clamped tight, but she could feel the pliers touching her eyelids. Lester slowly opened her eyelid with his free finger, and in came the pliers.

Paula flailed around screaming at the top of her lungs, she was fighting at the air. Somehow, she was free of her restraints but now she could not see Lester anywhere in sight. Even more peculiar was that she looked down at her body to see there was no blood, no guts, no opening at all, just blankets. It dawned on her as she looked around that there was no audience and no Lester, it was just a boring hospital room. Her confusion grew as nurses came running into the room.

"Mrs. Bowline, you're okay. You're at the hospital and you've been asleep for over a day, your body needed the rest," said one of the nurses, trying to calm her down.

"We've had you under observation the whole time. You're safe," the nurse tried to reassure Paula.

"No, I'm not safe. I'll never be safe," Paula said as she shook and started to cry in sheer terror.

"You have to let me out. You all need to leave or he's going to get you too," she continued, looking at both of the nurses with pleading eyes.

"Who will get us, Mrs. Bowline?" the other nurse asked, looking confused and worried.

"Lester. I can't explain but he killed my family, he tortured all of us, and he killed them," she said frantically.

Even in her fragile state of shock, Paula knew the nurses were confused as she babbled on. She probably looked mad.

"Look, he did this too," she said, putting her arm out, showing off where her hand used to be.

"Jesus Christ!" the second nurse accidentally said aloud.

The first nurse gave the other nurse a glare of annoyance for her lack of professionalism, but even the first nurse could not hide her own visible shock.

MOVIN' ON UP

"This man chopped off your hand?" asked the first nurse.

Paula nodded her head up and down.

"You say that he also killed your family?".

Again, Paula nodded her head up and down as she continued to uncontrollably shake and cry.

Paula was starting to ground herself, but the shock of the nightmare had her on edge. At any moment she expected Lester to come popping out of somewhere to surprise her. His playful cruelty knew no bounds and she believed deep down in her heart that she had not truly escaped him. The thought made her physically ill, anticipating Lester's presence. There was little she could do to calm down. Hyperaware, she kept rapidly looking around the room. Paula knew she must have looked like she was on drugs.

"Mrs. Bowline. I know a lot has happened, but it is best if you stay here. You've clearly been through something extremely traumatic, dear. You were dehydrated beyond belief. Honestly, you were lucky to have made it into this bed alive, I won't even get into all of the sunburn and cuts on your body. Please believe me when I tell you that this is the best place for you. Also, no one's gonna hurt you because we've got security around here. They're a great bunch."

Paula thought about what the nurse said, slowly processing the information. Staying at the hospital made the most sense. She had nowhere to go except to her sister's place, but she dared not make that phone call and risk endangering her sister's family. If Lester showed up, who knows what horrors he would inflict on each of them. No. This was her only option.

"Just lay down and rest, dear. I'm going to go and get you something to calm down. It won't put you to sleep but it will help you relax. You definitely need that right now," said the first nurse as Paula nodded in agreement.

LESTER

She was stuck here and needed to sort her head and calm down, but she was incapable of doing it on her own.

After the nurse gave her the pills that calmed her down, Paula spent most of the day drifting in and out of sleep. Having gone through hell, the intermittent moments of sleep were nice and relaxing, but she jolted awake every so often. She was fighting sleep, attempting not to dream. She knew if she dreamt, they would be horrific nightmares. As the days went on, Paula gradually slept more on her own, having only the occasional nightmare. In some ways, the events that took place less than a week ago felt like a lifetime ago.

In times of being awake during her stay, buried deep beneath it all, was the realization of losing everything. She stuffed it down, attempting to enjoy her newfound peace. It felt good to rest, to eat, use a bathroom, and talk to the occasional member of staff. It was all mundane, but so normal, and, above all, safe. The further she got away from the time she ran away from the house, the further away she felt from it.

Among the ins and outs of staff, Paula had also been visited by the town's sheriff. The nurses had called him immediately the night Paula came in. Between her condition and hearing her story about torture, mutilation, and murder, the nurses wasted no time, and neither did the sheriff. He came in the following day to ask Paula questions, but she was in no shape. It was not until the third day that he had his chance.

"Hi there, Mrs. Bowline. I'm Sheriff Fairfield, and I've got a few questions for you. I know this is tough, but do you think you're up for answering a few?" he asked Paula with a kindly, sympathetic voice.

She did not speak but instead nodded her head up and down, feeling a knot in her stomach. She knew she was going to have to relive what happened. Something she had avoided since the moment she escaped that house.

MOVIN' ON UP

"Now. We've been out there, and the house is in complete shambles. I've got a guy out here, used to work in Houston and has seen just about everything. Can you in your own words tell me exactly what happened in that house?" Sheriff Fairfield asked, looking concerned.

Realizing that the Sheriff would think her crazy if she started babbling on about a yellow skinned superhuman, she attempted to tell the story in a more grounded fashion. She could not risk looking crazy.

"Well. There was this… guy," she struggled.

"My family took this guy in who was hitchhiking," Paula said, looking down, trying to manage her words.

"He seemed really friendly, real helpful, you know, wouldn't hurt a flea," she continued, now looking out the window, rocking herself.

"One night, after helping me and my husband out with some stuff, he went crazy."

Paula looked back down at her feet, and she started to cry.

"First, he killed our dog, Samantha. My husband tried to stop him from causing any more harm, so Lester lit him on fire and burned him to death."

The tears became more prevalent.

"He killed my oldest, Rodney by tearing off his head and he bashed my Robert's head in and–" she stopped, catching that she was about to tell the Sheriff, this man grounded in reality, that the person of interest ate her youngest son's brains right out of his skull, in front of her.

"And, what, Mrs. Bowline?"

Now sucked into the content of her story, Sheriff Fairfield had to know what happened next. It was part job and part morbid curiosity.

"...nothing. He died," she continued, crying even harder than before.

"And after I had to watch them all die one by one... I jumped through the goddamn window and ran for my life as fast and hard as I could," looking up at the ceiling clutching her hands.

"If only I had that much in me when he was murdering my fucking kids."

"Now, now, Mrs. Bowline. From what we'd seen out there, you were dealing with some insane S.O.B. Whoever he was, well, we don't think this was his first time. Pardon my French, but the evil son of bitch didn't leave a single fingerprint anywhere. I've still got my guy scouring that place for them," he said in genuine frustration.

Paula could tell he was truly bothered by the events that took place, and the prospect that this Lester guy might get away with it.

"I'm sure you did everything you could for your children and your husband. I mean, if your own husband, armed with a gun, couldn't stand a chance, then what chance did anyone have?" he said, looking at her.

"Oh, um, I hope that didn't come off as sexist. I'm... I'm just saying–"

Paula chuckled, "Oh, sexism is the least of my concerns, Sheriff. I appreciate the kind words and I'm sorry if I'm out of sorts right now but, I don't think you'll find anything at my place."

"What makes you say that?" Fairfield asked with his head cocked sideways, confused.

"Truth is. He's not human."

"Yeah, you can say that again," Fairfield chimed in.

MOVIN' ON UP

"No, Sheriff, like literally not human at all. He's magic. You'll never find him. If he wants to be found, well, he'll simply come find you."

The sheriff had both a look of shock and bewilderment.

The rest of the conversation was about the identity of the killer. Roughly six feet, big blue eyes, slender, a little brown tuft of hair on his head, Caucasian with yellowish skin, and an everlasting smile from ear to ear. It was the best she could come up with given that she did not wish to end up putting an innocent man in jail. Though they pried, she also could not offer them any last name as he was simply Lester.

Through the questioning, Paula could only think of one thing, and it was that she hoped that they did not find Lester. She knew that if they did, it would be a bloodbath on whomever came across him. There would be no justice in the matter, much like dealing with a natural disaster, like an earthquake or a hurricane. These forces of nature come ripping into your life and kill things indiscriminately, as did Lester. It would simply be best if everyone ignored him. Her only true wish was that no one else would suffer as she did.

Days went on in the hospital, and she got physically better each time the sun rose. Mentally, that was an entirely different thing. Paula wanted nothing to do with any kind of therapy. She was pushing down the things that happened in the house and she knew she could never truthfully open up about what happened. No matter how understanding a therapist might be, no one would ever believe some cartoonish otherworldly humanoid was responsible for murdering her loved ones.

The most surprising part was the cooperation and sympathy she got from the Sheriff and local law enforcement. With how outlandish her story was, and the total lack of evidence at the scene, she figured she was sure to be the main suspect. It stood to reason that, as she got better, the interrogations would begin.

After dealing with Lester, that seemed like a walk in the park. It never came though. Instead, the local authorities and beyond started up a manhunt for an individual named Lester and her story became national news. Paula refused interviews but anytime she turned on the news, her life was smack dab in the middle of the spotlight. She was amazed how quickly the story spread.

In the mess of everything that happened, Paula had no idea what she would do going forward. She had nowhere to stay and did not have any friends locally. For the sake of everyone's lives, she kept her distance, but it never occurred to her that, thanks to the media, her plan of keeping her distance would not last very long. It was toward the end of the week when she got the phone call.

"Jesus Christ almighty, Paula!" was the first thing that Denise said on the other end of the phone to Paula.

On one hand, Paula felt terrible that she could not tell her sister what happened, that she did not call her when she was admitted to the hospital. On the other hand, Paula knew it was for the best because she could not stand the idea of Denise and her family being subjected to a fate worse than death if Lester ever found her again.

"I'm seeing on the news that everyone is dead and you're the only one that made it out alive? Are you okay? Why did you not get a hold of us?" Denise hastily inquired.

They were all valid questions. Paula was going to have to spin some half-truths.

"I'm so sorry, sis. I've just been out of it for days and I needed to process what happened, you know. I barely knew my own name for the first two days or so," Paula responded, making the best excuse she could.

"Well, I know things are crazy down there with reporters but when are you supposed to get out of there?"

"They want to keep me until Monday for further observation. Physically, I guess I'm okay, lots of scars 'n' such but I think they're keeping me in because of, you know, mental stuff. Wanna make sure I can get out of here without freaking out."

"Freaking out." She pondered the term for a moment. Paula had wondered if she could actually leave the confines of the hospital as anything outside of this comfort felt alien and scary to her.

"Okay. Well, I will be there to pick you up on Monday and bring you here. We have an extra room, and the family knows what is going on. You have a safe place, sweetie," Denise warmly affirmed.

"No. I don't think that's such a good idea, sis," Paula said with hesitation.

"It is, Paula. You have nowhere else to go and you need to be with family. I am sorry, Paula, but I am not asking."

"Denise, you understand that if Lester finds me again, he will kill all of you," Paula quickly interjected.

"Honey, let him try. We have got dogs and we are armed with guns. This place is practically a fortress," Denise replied in a manner that made her sound hundred percent confident, bordering on cocky.

"No. You don't get it. None of that stuff will stop him. We had guns, we had Anthony," Paula paused to cry and finish her thought.

"He will literally kill your entire family while you watch, and there will be nothing you can do to stop it. If you're lucky, he might actually kill you," she continued, clutching the phone, shaking.

All of the memories started to flood back as Paula fought back more tears as the silence on the other end of the phone lingered.

Denise finally spoke again after allowing Paula a moment to cry. Clearly, she was trying to find the right words to respond to the shocking outburst from Paula.

"My word, Paula. I am so sorry."

That was all she could say. Paula knew her sister was dumbstruck. Rarely was Denise speechless.

"Don't come here, Denise," Paula said firmly.

She knew that there was enough money in her account to get her some shelter. Risking her sister's family was not an option. Paula would do anything she could to dissuade Denise from coming to the hospital and picking her up.

"I'm probably a liability right now, myself. I'm a nervous wreck. I scream in the night. I've got suicidal thoughts. I'm probably more liable to hurt others than I am myself right now."

This was a lie of course but anything to stop Denise from coming to get her.

"Paula, I do not care. You are my sister. We are family, there is no way I am gonna let you down and–"

"Family! Family! Family!" Paula cut her off.

"I don't need your family. I don't need you. I don't fucking need looking after. What part of this don't you get!? I want to be left alone! Does that register through your thick skull into your tiny brain? I don't need your saving."

Having already said enough, Paula wanted to make sure to drive the dagger.

"If I want anyone to come walking through those doors, it sure as hell wouldn't be you."

"Paula, I know you are angry but–"

MOVIN' ON UP

Paula hung up on Denise without batting an eyelash. As she did, she bawled her eyes out in a pain that she had not felt since she was back at the house.

She told herself this was necessary, but it did not make it any less painful. Knowing she would have to cut her sister off to protect her was the hardest thing she could ever remember having to do. Paula felt sick. She could feel it in her gut, like someone had grabbed her insides and twisted them tight.

Rocking herself back and forth with her face buried in her palms, Paula knew that, even with her harsh phone call, Denise would still come by. She would have to check out early if she could and get a jump on things. It was dire that her sister not physically be anywhere near her. Paula knew that it would be likely that she would not be able to see Denise again for a very long time, if ever. She felt Lester around every single corner and in her eyelids when she closed them to sleep. It would not be a stretch to say she felt diseased or cursed.

Her sister did try to call again once more that day, but Paula refused to take Denise's call. She wanted Denise to be angry at her, she wanted her to hate her even, because it would make this next part much easier.

On Sunday night, the day before she was supposed to be checking out, Paula knew her sister would be there no matter what, waiting for her. Paula insisted with her care team that she be let out that day so she could get a jump on her sister and make sure the two of them never would meet. The doctor could not keep her there as, technically, she was sound of mind.

After releasing herself from the hospital, Paula went to her bank to withdraw everything she had. Cash in hand, she had no idea what to do, but right now everything was impromptu for her. She at least knew she had enough to live on for a while, at least in terms of shelter and food.

With that pool of cash, she found herself in a cheap motel room not too far from the hospital. Empty of people and noise, Paula felt terror once again. She imagined this would be the perfect place for the yellow bastard to get her. However, there was nothing she could do because there was a bigger picture here. It was decided that she would hop onto a bus and get as far away from her sibling as she could.

Every decision was about stuffing her feelings and emotions down, trudging ahead. Paula knew it was all necessary to protect her sister. The knot in her stomach continued to grow as she realized that this overnight stay in this motel room would be the last time she would ever be Paula. She had been a mother, a sister, a wife. All of those titles would officially be gone and dead tomorrow.

As she woke in the morning and packed her things up, Paula could not shake her curiosity. She had to know if her sister came by the hospital. She was in no hurry, so she spent a better part of the day sitting across the street out of view, eyeballing the parking lot. It was not long before she saw her sister's car pulling into the parking lot. It was just her, alone.

Denise walked into the hospital and about a half hour later, she walked out crying. Paula could not remember the last time she had ever seen her sister cry, if ever. This, in turn, caused Paula to cry. She sobbed so hard; she began to shake uncontrollably. It was the realization that this was all real, not just some bad dream. Everyone was really dead. They had all suffered horrific deaths, and they were not coming back.

For her survival, Paula would now have to disown her sister to keep her from Lester. The entire ordeal was so extremely unjust and unfair. She wished that she had died. A fleeting thought nearly compelled her; that it was not too late to make that happen, to release herself from all of this pain. Still, she decided she would see what tomorrow would bring.

MOVIN' ON UP

Tomorrow would have to wait, though. The cab she had called for arrived, and she slowly made her way inside. Paula had the courage to get into the cab which would bring her to the bus station a few miles outside of town. She wondered if she would have the courage to get on that bus and leave for good. Each step on this path was painful, including figuring out where she would go.

Not wanting to risk being found, she decided for a bigger city where she could get lost and blend into the crowd. This was not only to ensure she would not put Denise in harm's way, but mainly so that she would never come face to face with that yellow murdering ghoul ever again. She knew that Lester did not want a crowd, and this would be the best way to get him off her scent if he decided to finish what he started.

As she left town in the cab, she could see the town and all of its buildings fade into the distance one last time. It began to feel like a dream once again as she came to a crossroads. In her mind, she wanted to disassociate herself from what had happened, but she also wanted to feel, she wanted to mourn. The way she figured it, she would have time to dwell on it later or maybe she would simply move on, like it never happened. That last thought nearly made her sick to her stomach.

Off into uncharted seas she went. She was scared, lonely, heartbroken, and confused. Paula turned her head forward. She knew there was nothing she could do and looking back was only hurting the more she did so and, worse yet, she might change her mind.

"Everything okay back there, ma'am?" asked the cab driver.

"Oh, yes. I was just saying goodbye to some family earlier is all."

"Sounds like fun," he replied.

"Unfortunately, it was to pay my respects to the departed," Paula said as she looked out the window at the sun.

"Oh, I'm awful sorry, ma'am. Didn't mean to pry or nuthin'"

"No, that's okay. Reminds us how lucky we, the living, are and what we have to look forward to," Paula said with a smile on her face.

She did not fully believe this, but it was a good cover and she thought if she said it aloud, that somehow maybe even she could believe it.

A HAPPY ENDING

Years had gone by, and Paula settled into her new life. She had a decent job, working in accounting for a local car dealership. There was also a nice apartment, fully furnished with all of the modern comforts one could ask for. This new life also included a new name on top of everything else, transforming her identity forever, leaving no hint of the one she left behind.

Her name was legally changed to make sure that she would be incredibly hard to find, if not impossible. Her brand new name, Diana Bailey, was an ode to one of her favorite people, Diana, Princess of Wales. Bailey was just a name she liked and thought it complimented Diana well. Truth was, she was not too picky. Anything other than Paula Bowline. Also, it was a symbolic way of putting her past behind her. One that, even months into her new life, she put in the back of her mind. Perhaps not intentionally. All the memories of the past would be locked away in her waking hours, never daring to open them again.

Fortunately for Diana, time had blown by. In that time, she established a life that included new routines and new friends. Though she was never quite the same as before, she had adapted. Still feeling weary, skittish, and paranoid due to her encounter with Lester, Diana took everyday step by step. It was a healing process, and she was constantly finding new ways to adjust and thrive in her new surroundings.

Diana had finally reached a place in her life where the nightmares dwindled down to a rarity, she stopped looking around every corner, and she did not jump at every noise. Life had become something close to normal. Though she could never replace her old life, she decided to start a new one by eventually dating.

LESTER

In the dating world, Diana had her ups and downs, but after about seven years into her new life, she finally met a very kind man named Tim. He was a man of good humor who was extremely patient and had a way of making Paula always feel better, at peace. He had a way about him that made his personality overshadow his physical appearance.

The first thing that stood out to her was that he looked like Wimpy from the Popeye cartoons with his portly body and bushy mustache. Ironically, he was not obsessed with hamburgers like the character was. This was actually how they first met, when she made the comparison out loud while at a noisy bar. Unfortunately, this was one of those instances where the room got silent just as she said it to her friend. Diana all but died of embarrassment as the man turned and stared directly at her. Her mouth ajar, unaware of what to say, Tim quickly countered by saying, "I'll gladly pay you Tuesday for a date today," which drew the laughter of the surrounding customers.

Diana took Tim up on his offer, and spent hours that night talking to Tim. The conversation was natural, like talking to an old friend. She knew by the end of that night that she would not be single for long. The moment she got home, she thought about nothing else other than seeing him again. They quickly began a courtship, seeing each other every day. If Diana missed out on Tim time for even a day, she would get withdrawals. No one made her laugh or think quite as much as Tim had. She almost felt guilty for being this smitten with someone else again.

The months did their dance, and Diana was fully in love. Tim and Diana never fought, and it was rare they were apart. The only condition she had moving forward was that she did not want to have children. Though she never gave the real reason for this, making up a story about multiple miscarriages, Tim was totally fine with it. He liked kids but it was Diana he was in love with, not the idea of some phantom child.

A HAPPY ENDING

One thing she was open to, was the idea of marriage again. She explained that she had been married before and that he had died, but she had not gone into specifics. Just like the children, she fabricated a story explaining that there was an accident on the job and her husband, Anthony, had passed away. Diana absolutely hated telling these lies because it felt deceptive, and not just that they were little white lies. Like everything else she did to get to this moment, she realized it was for the greater good. Besides, her truth is one no one would ever believe, and not worth repeating.

When the big day finally arrived, no one was happier than Diana. Her life was truly at peace now and she knew Lester was in the past. She would always miss her children; she would always miss Anthony. At times she did feel as though she had betrayed them because she survived and got to move on. In some ways, it felt like she was spitting on their graves. As much as the occasional feeling hurt, she knew she could not live in the past, and they would not want her to either.

Inside their quaint apartment, Diana and Tim shared a small breakfast with one another before heading out to the chapel, enjoying the serenity of the crisp summer day outside their window. The aroma of coffee, bacon, and toast filled the air. Diana closed her eyes and sniffed the air, enjoying the fragrant smells. The ambiance was perfect for such a fine day.

"Honey, everything is going to change after today, you know," Tim said with a nervous smile. "I mean, it will be great but different."

"Oh, Timbo, it's going to be exactly the same, but instead we'll have this little title telling us that we're bound by paper to another. Don't worry, you won't wake up to some demonic she-bitch. I promise… ish," she chuckled.

LESTER

Still chuckling himself, Tim looked up at her, "I just want you to know that I consider myself the luckiest guy around," he kindly said.

"I know there's things you can't tell me about your past because they're painful, but I just want you to know that every day, moving forward, you'll never feel that way again. Not if I have a say in it."

He patted her hand, smiling at her.

It warmed her heart to hear his calm, relaxing voice assure her that the best was still to come.

"Oh, also, those were NOT my vows. For that, you have to wait for the wedding and whatnot," he laughed.

Getting ready to head out the door, there were a flurry of things they seemed to keep forgetting, running up and down the stairs to the apartment. Finally, Tim was ready to take off but, of course, one more thing. Diana had forgotten her mother's pendant. She was not going to get married without a piece of her mother there with her. So, of course, she had to go run up the stairs for what felt like the millionth time today. Getting married was exhausting.

Diana looked around the apartment, taking in the future. It made her giddy. In her giddiness, she ran to the bedroom to retrieve her mother's pendant. She put it on, looked into the closet mirror and stared at her own reflection.

"Mom, I wish you could be here," Diana said, staring at herself with a truly heartfelt smile.

With that, she walked out of the closet and heard doors slam behind her and off to the side. She looked around in confusion. This was not her room. This was not even the apartment.

"SURPRISE!!!" a high-pitched voice yelled. From behind a bed, to her absolute horror, Lester jumped up wearing a party hat and had a party blower in his mouth, blowing into it as hard as he could.

Diana looked around the room to see smashed glass, a torn up bed, a disheveled dresser, and the corpse of a young boy with his skull emptied out. It dawned on her that it was the very same room she had jumped out of and ran from so very many years ago. She quickly turned to the cracked mirror. It twisted her mind because she was still older, wearing the same dress she had with Tim for breakfast, sporting the gray hairs she had developed over the years.

The sheer magnitude hit her in a way she had not felt in close to a decade. She had almost convinced herself that all of this had been one bad nightmare, that it was a lifetime ago, maybe someone else's lifetime. Here she was though, back with Lester, back in the house. The brevity cracked her psyche and made her feel ill, lightheaded. She fell to her knee in shock, trying not to pass out. Raising her head, she looked up furiously at Lester, shedding tears from her eyes.

There was no new life, no Tim, no Diana, no peace. She was always going to end up back in that room with him.

"How?! This is not possible. I got away from you! I was gone for years! This is not fucking possible!!!" she yelled at the top of her lungs, looking for an explanation amidst her anger and despair.

"Years?"–he laughed– "You were gone for maybe about five minutes and then you came wanderin' right into here through that little ol' door there," pointing at the door behind her.

"Five minutes?! No. NO! I led a whole goddamn life out there! I was gone for years! I had a job! A husband!" she furiously yelled, spitting as she did.

LESTER

"Husband? Well, shucks, the only one I know about is that Cajun fried fella out there in the barn. Or, you know, what's left of him, I suppose," Lester said as he shrugged.

"But, yeah, it's been about maybe five minutes, ten at most, at least according to the ol' clockaroo and the calendar."

Paula had to validate Lester's claims by looking and, sure enough, the calendar was the same as the day she had left. She also noticed that the window she jumped through had been smashed, she had jumped through it. That part really happened. The more she thought about it, the less sense it made, even by Lester standards.

"How did you find me?" she growled at him with daggers in her eyes.

"Well now, you know there's nowhere you can go where ol' Lester won't find ya," he said with a giant smile on his face, hands placed at the sides of his hips in an almost superhero-like pose.

"Oh, and I almost forgot. That guy missed you," he pointed at her bad hand.

Diana heard a familiar voice from a time long ago.

"Married to someone?! What was I to you?! Was I nothing?! Were the kids nothing?!" yelled the voice.

It was Anthony's face again, still attached to her wrist where her hand used to be, just like before, but this time it had maggots on it, looking slightly decayed. She screamed and slapped at the maggots that crawled up her arm.

"That is IT!" yelled Paula.

She marched right up to Lester, who looked around like someone in trouble.

"Oh, boy, I'm a hot tamale right now," Lester said nervously.

Paula got into his face, "I am NOT afraid of you anymore. My time away taught me who I am, and just how strong I really am. It's what you feed on. You're just a lowly parasite who latches onto people's fears, none of this is actually real."

Lester looked around awkwardly as if he were being confronted by a crazy person.

Paula closed her eyes, "I take back every single ounce of fear or power I ever gave you, Lester. I will leave you without purpose, without a name. I am in control here, not you!" Paula said as she kept her eyes closed.

True to her words, Paula could feel power well up inside of her. It was all an illusion and clearly Lester thrived on her inner insecurities. She had figured out over the years that she was the power behind his magic, not candy or food, but Lester was leeching off all of the bad things within her, feeding him and making him stronger with each passing moment.

"Lester! I release you. This is my life, and you are banished from it!" she said, still with her eyes closed.

She could feel wind whipping through the room.

"What's this?" Lester said aloud in confusion.

The winds circled faster and faster.

"Oh no, we ain't in Kansas no more, Toto!" yelled Lester.

Paula could hear him struggling. This whole time she was right - he was a parasite. The thought brought her great joy which seemed to make the wind around her more powerful and made Lester verbally struggle.

"You sure we can't talk about this? Maybe hug it out?" he yelled.

"You can go to hell, where you belong!" Paula yelled out, summoning even more power.

"I'm awful sorry about everything. What if– what if I bring everyone back? Does that sound swell?" Lester cried out.

LESTER

Paula knew that he would never give her back her family, she would never have her peace as long as he was alive. There were no more compromises or negotiations, he was done. Instead, she looked deep within and thrust her arms out to release an energy from within that she did not know existed.

"Noooooo!" yelled the high-pitched voice as it faded off into nothingness.

The room instantly fell silent. The wind died out as quickly as it came. Paula dared not open her eyes. For as much as she felt triumphant, she had also been wrong before. This time, she felt a different energy in the air. The difference seemed to fill her very being.

She stood still in the quiet of the room, breathing in and out, attempting to slow her heartbeat down. With everything she had been through, she needed some time, even just a moment, to get her bearings. The wind gently coming through the window was oddly comforting, like everything would be okay when she opened her eyes. The sound of wind was accompanied with another sound.

"Mom?" said a familiar voice.

The voice, thankfully, was not a high-pitched one, it was a scraggly little voice instead. It was the voice of her son, Robert. There are not many sounds in the world that could have possibly made her so happy that, for the first time in what felt like forever, could make her cry tears of true happiness. She smiled and opened her eyes.

"Rob–"

"Zoinks!" was all Paula heard as she opened her eyes, and two fingers poked them.

The pain made her eyes throb as if they had been pushed into the back of her head. As she reeled back in pain, she tried opening her eyes, and as one of them gained a little clarity she could see that the room was exactly the same but only messier from all of the wind.

A HAPPY ENDING

"GOTCHA!" yelled Lester as he danced around in giddy fashion, having played yet another cruel, elaborate joke on this poor unfortunate soul.

"You should see the look on your face," he laughed uncontrollably.

"I mean" –he laughed hysterically– "honestly" –he was bent over laughing harder– "how many times are you gonna fall for the ol' dead kid joke?" he asked, slapping his knees as tears streamed down his face.

Paula could only look at Lester as he mocked her and danced around. She was completely and totally defeated. There was nothing she could do to stop what Lester willed to happen. She was positive that his being was parasitic in nature and that she would be free of him by refusing him. She would have betted her life on it. There he stood though, unfazed by her anger, her pleas, her tears. There was no way out.

"Why?" she cried.

"Why are you doing this to me?"

Lester took a moment to think.

"Doing this to you? Why are you doing this to me, ya ol' charmer you?" he said playfully.

She stared in befuddlement.

The only thing she had left was desperation and rage. In one last fit of anger, she ran up to Lester and beat on him with her one good hand.

"Get out! Get out of here, Lester! Get out of my LIIIIIFE!" she yelled as loud as she possibly could.

"Get out?" Lester asked, looking genuinely offended.

"I said GET OUT!" she yelled again, knowing how useless it was.

LESTER

"Oh, shucks. Looks like Lester done overstayed his welcome."

Lester walked around the house, looking for something. Paula followed him in her weakened, drunk-like state.

As she made her way out to the living room, she saw Lester with his hobo stick slung over his shoulder.

"Well, I know when I'm not wanted," he said, putting his chin into the air.

"I can see that the ol' honeymoon is over," he added as he started walking to the door.

"That's it?" Paula asked, confused.

"Yeah, if you ask ol' Lester to leave then he has to leave. It's in the rules," Lester said with his head slouched, looking sad.

She stared in disbelief.

"...what?" asked Paula, looking for clarification.

"Well, cheeseburgers! You see, if you ask me to leave I gotta go. It's bad manners otherwise, and it's against my own little set of rules I got. See!"

Lester proceeded to whip out a crudely drawn piece of paper that was mostly written in different pens, crayons, markers, and one of them looked like it was written in blood. It read:

1. Don't eat no pineapple pizza
2. Make sure to hydrate plenty
3. Make lots and lots a friends
4. Always do your compostin'
5. If someone tells you to leave, you gotta leave

"It's an always growing list, but you get the idea," Lester said, taking back his list.

"Thanks for letting me stay and putting me up 'n' all. I had a great time!" he said jubilantly.

As he walked out, he grabbed the door and just as he did, it fell off the hinges.

"Oh boy! Lemme go ahead and fix that."

Paula continued to stare as Lester kept trying to prop the door back on the hinges, doing it wrong at every turn.

"You know, I'll just uh… leave it. Probably making things worse with this little devil over here."

Paula watched as Lester propped the door up against the wall.

"Aw, boy. Geez. Um, sorry about breaking your door and, you know, killing your whole family and everything. You have a good one, Mrs. B!"

Paula looked outside the window as Lester happily skipped down the street singing "Zip-a-Dee-Doo-Dah" with his hobo stick in tow. The sun cast down on him as his long shadow painted the landscape.

The door, for all the effort given, fell over, startling Paula.

Alone, Paula looked around the empty house. Every single thing was broken, dirty, mangled, and disheveled. The entire house looked like someone had set a bomb off and she was not lucky enough to be in the middle of it when it went off.

She sat on the one place on the floor that did not have debris. Sitting there, by herself, she thought of nothing, holding herself in some weak attempt at consolation. The house was dead quiet. It seemed like even the wind had stopped moving. All life had left every square inch of this home. Anthony, Rodney, Robert, and now, Tim, were all gone. It was as if they had never existed at all.

Death. Death was the only release. Moving on with Tim she found a second life but now even that was robbed, and she knew that further attempts would meet the same fate. Her life would be a boomerang, always returning to the sadistic hands of Lester. Yes, the only answer was to finally end it all.

As she slowly got herself back up, she looked around the room to see all the chaos around her. It all felt so eerie, the silence. It was as if she was the last person on Earth. Slowly, walking around glass and destroyed furnishings, she made her way to the bedroom. A bullet. That was her ticket out of all of this. All she would have to do is put the gun to her head and pull the trigger, and it all ended. Sweet relief.

Still, she was skeptical. Lester had prevented her before and every single one of her actions usually turned into some cruel, sadistic joke at the hands of her monstrous houseguest. Paula picked up the gun with her hand and a tear streamed down her cheek. It was not because she was sad, no, it was because she knew she was close to being reunited with her family. Paula believed in the afterlife and was at peace with her decision.

As she raised the gun to her head, she expected to see a yellow hand prevent her from finishing the deed. Instead, there was nothing. Just Paula and the gun she held to her temple.

"This is it," she told herself as she shook, closing her eyes.

It felt so wrong and unjust to die like this, so alone and unsung. Denise would never know what happened to her, Anthony, and the kids. The peace she thought she had, drained away. These realizations stalled her from pulling the trigger.

"Pull the fucking trigger you coward!" she yelled out loud to herself.

There was a brief moment of clarity when she yelled at herself. It was that this might be her only chance and she would face something far worse if she failed to take her life.

Thinking about her loved ones both dead and alive, she closed her eyes again and pressed the gun tight to her head.

A HAPPY ENDING

"I LOVE YOU!" she yelled out to her phantom family that could not be there to witness her exit from this world.

BANG!

Her body went limp. Lying on the ground, a pool of blood began to form around her head. The eyes were still closed and, finally, she looked at peace as her outstretched hand held the pistol. The house stood still, a mere construct that gave no hint that love, or laughter had ever graced its structure. It was as dead as the bodies that would soon rot within.

Outside, the various bushes and trees seemed to weep as they swayed to the gentle breezes that passed through them. There were no cars on the road, no noises nearby or in the distance. All things living seemed to stay away from this domain. It was a place of death, giving off a pungent stench that repelled all creatures for miles around.

All but one creature that is.

Paula.

She opened her eyes, disoriented. Looking around, there was no gun, broken glass, or shabby house within eyesight. Instead, she was now outside on the side of a road. For some reason she felt very low to the Earth, more so than usual. Before she could gain her bearings, Paula heard a sound quickly coming up from behind her.

It was a sports car going extremely fast, barreling down the road. Unable to react, Paula stood still as the car lost control and with a ground shaking amount of force, the car crashed into a tree just off the side of the road, near Paula. The sound of the crash was so loud and violent, she found herself turned away for a long period of time, afraid to see the results.

The car was completely totaled. She attempted to look around the front of the car, but she struggled to gain any height, still confined to the floor. It took some time but as she finally managed to get to the front, she noticed two bodies. One was missing a head and the other had their entire head smashed in. Both young boys. Paula had the air knocked out of her. It was Rodney and Robert.

Unexpectedly, a voice came crying out from the passenger side. The individual was clearly suffering from a head injury as their voice slurred and bumbled random words. Among the gibberish, some distinct words came out.

"Someone… help…"

Paula did her best to run to the car to help out but, again, her movement was hindered, and she could not fully stand. As she tried to move towards the car, it went ablaze.

The voice got louder.

"Please help me. Anyone? I'm stuck," the voice said, becoming more lucid.

Paula was taken aback by how quickly the flames did their job and frustrated by how little she could move. She tried screaming out to let the voice know she was there and that she wanted to help. The only thing that came out was what sounded to her like yelling. She was incapable of forming words.

"Is someone there? Hello?!" the voice got even louder and more distinct.

Paula realized that it was Anthony.

She yelled out and struggled even more but nothing happened. As she did, it was nothing more than a hoarse barking and more crawling.

A HAPPY ENDING

"Oh my god! I'm going to die! No. Please, anyone!? HELP!!!" he screamed out as the flames lit up the inside part of the car where Anthony sat.

In all of her frustration, Paula could do nothing but watch and listen as she felt the heat of the flames get warmer by the second. Not again. This was unbearable to her, maybe even worse than the first time.

Finally, she heard her husband cry out in pain as the flames engulfed his body once more. It was slower this time, and his cries of anguish were much more prolonged. Each moment was pure agony as she had no way to muffle his pain. His yelling was intermittently cut off by his cries, like that of a small child, something she had never heard Anthony do in all of the years she knew him.

Suddenly, the suffering was over. There was no more crying or screaming as the flames covered the entire inside portion of the car. Slowly, she scrambled away to avoid the unpredictable flames. As she observed the car in disbelief, she began to cry which came out like whimpers. Looking at the mutilated bodies of her sons, she watched them catch on fire as well.

Everything had happened so fast that Paula had no time to consider why she was still alive and how she got here. The thought crept in, and it froze her in place, making her more terrified than ever before.

"Oh, don't worry," a high-pitched voice rang out behind her.

"NO!" she thought.

She quickly turned around to look up and see her living nightmare staring down at her. Without thinking about it, Paula backed up, whimpering as she did.

"Yep. Those little ol' angels went right up to heaven. Big guy did too!" Lester exclaimed with a big smile on his neon yellow mug.

The revelation stunned her.

"Heaven?" she thought, as she stared back at the burning car.

"They went up, up, and away, and then you ended up here with me," Lester jubilantly stated to Paula.

In frustration she yelled at Lester.

"What do you mean heaven, you son of a bitch?!"

Once again, she noticed that what came out was a lot of yelling which still came out like a hoarse barking.

"Oh boy!" –Lester laughed– "You still ain't figured it out yet, Paula? Or should I say - Samantha,"

If the revelation of heaven had stunned Paula, then this sudden comment had completely knocked her off of her rocker. It tore up any last ounce of sanity she may have had left. Finally, she looked down and noticed where her hands once were, paws stood in their place.

She wanted to reject the idea, but it was of no use. She was a dog. The family pet that she previously had a hard time remembering. It made sense while at the same time, it made no sense at all.

"What the hell was this?!" she fearfully pondered as she whimpered harshly.

Instantly, she turned on Lester and started to yell at him, but every single word disintegrated into barking. Mocking her, Lester just barked back at her, right in her face, smiling the entire time with his eyes closed. Her defeat was sudden and swift. There was absolutely nothing she could do.

"Oh yeah, li'l doggy! We're going to have a good ol' time. Just you and Lester. Friends forever!"

He began to dance around like he had just won the lottery. His giddiness made Paula sick to her stomach. She knew

356

exactly where she was and that there would never be a way out of this. It was beyond comprehension.

Suddenly, she heard a noise. It was a truck coming down the road. Gaining more mobility, Paula wandered to the side of the road again. She could see in the truck that it was herself and Anthony pulling into their home. There was the barn, the front yard, the house. It was all fixed up as if nothing had ever happened.

The truck came to a stop at the end of the driveway and the other Paula got out of the car, shuffling around with Anthony's assistance, as if she had just come home from the hospital.

"IMPOSSIBLE!" Paula thought to herself in total shock.

"Well, it's about time for me to go shovin' off to the barn. About time to do it all over again, and boy oh boy do I have some great ideas this time!" Lester said as he kicked his heels in the air and ran off to the barn.

Contemplating everything that unfolded since awakening, Paula could not bring herself to move, standing still on the road. Off in the distance she heard the sounds of a homecoming with love and laughter. She knew exactly what was coming and how powerless she would be to stop it. After everything she endured, she sat alone hopelessly on that road, surrounded by what seemed like ghosts. She was obliterated.

As Paula stared off contemplating her situation, she had the same recurring thoughts that plagued her mind.

This is not temporary.

This is not a nightmare.

This suffering will be eternal.

LESTER

A lone road. A lone house. An ordinary family welcomes their mom home. Just feet away lies the wreckage of a sports car, wrapped around a tree. It is a scene immaculately created by an engineer of pain and misery, down to the smallest detail. The tires, the license plate, every drop of blood.

Scaling a nearby billboard there is a distracting advertisement that could catch the eye of any person: A bright neon yellow cartoon character with a bowtie and suspenders, and the jolliest of smiles. Just above his head, a dialogue bubble in all capital letters floats.

"HERE WE GOOOOO!" the vivid, yellow mascot happily yells out.

It's a nice, colorful ad for a place called Lester's Burger Shack where the motto says, "Bring your appetite, bring your friends!"

THE END